THEIR FIRST
FAMILY CHRISTMAS

BY
ALISON ROBERTS

Published in Great Britain 2016
By Mills & Boon, an imprint of HarperCollins*Publishers*
1 London Bridge Street, London, SE1 9GF

© 2016 Alison Roberts

ISBN: 978-0-263-91522-8

THEIR FIRST FAMILY CHRISTMAS

BY
ALISON ROBERTS

THE NIGHTSHIFT BEFORE CHRISTMAS

BY
ANNIE O'NEIL

Christmas Eve Magic

Reunited on the night before Christmas!

The hospitals are bustling, the snow is falling
and Christmas is fast approaching.
Dr Emma Matthews and Dr Katie McGann
have just one more nightshift to go, and for
both the magic of Christmas is all around,
because happy-ever-afters are about to
land under their Christmas trees.

Let authors Annie O'Neil and Alison Roberts
sweep you away on an unforgettable
festive ride you won't forget in:

Their First Family Christmas
by Alison Roberts

and

The Nightshift Before Christmas
by Annie O'Neil

Available now!

Alison Roberts is a New Zealander, currently lucky enough to live near a beautiful beach in Auckland. She is also lucky enough to write for both the Mills & Boon Cherish and Medical Romance lines. A primary school teacher in a former life, she is also a qualified paramedic. She loves to travel and dance, drink champagne and spend time with her daughter and her friends.

Visit the Author Profile page at
millsandboon.co.uk for more titles.

CHAPTER ONE

'ALMOST HOME TIME, EMMA.'

'I know.' Emma Matthews beamed at the triage nurse behind the central desk of Glasgow's Eastern Infirmary. 'I'm so excited. What is it about Christmas Eve that can make you feel so much like a kid again?'

She hadn't felt like this in *so* long. In all honesty, she hadn't ever expected to be able to feel like this again, let alone today of all days. These moments of joy that had surprised her in the odd quiet moments of this long shift were something to be treasured—rare jewels in a landscape that, by rights, should have been the bleakest ever.

'Presents,' Caroline offered. 'And being able to go out for drinks knowing that you've got a day off to recover. Are you coming to the pub with us after work?'

'No.' Emma shook her head. 'I've got a date.'

'No way…' A registrar paused as he reached for a set of case notes on the desk. 'Did I hear you say you had a *date*?'

'With my *daughter*, Alistair,' Emma said. 'Don't you go spreading ridiculous rumours.'

As if she had time to go on any other kind of date.

Or the inclination, for that matter.

'It's a date to decorate the tree and hang up our stockings,' she added. 'And put carrots out for the reindeer.

And some of the shortbread Mum will have been baking has to go out for Santa. You know…the really exciting stuff…'

Alistair rolled his eyes, tucked the notes under his arm as he glanced up at the board and then headed for one of the curtained cubicles that lined the side walls of this area.

Caroline was far more impressed with the date Emma had lined up. 'Aww…cute,' she sighed. 'Lily's, what… eighteen months old now? Old enough to get excited.'

'She calls it Kissmas.' Emma smiled. 'And yeah…it's the cutest thing ever.' A new family tradition had been born—kisses for Kissmas—and Lily was only too happy to oblige. She couldn't wait to get home and have those small arms wound around her neck as Lily plastered her face with more of the festive affection.

She reached up to erase the name in the space for Curtain Seven. 'Guess what three-year-old Colin had jammed up his nose?'

Caroline shuddered as she reached for one of the phones on the desk that had started ringing. 'Do I want to know?'

'It was a little ball from the top of a Christmas decoration. Like one of those…' Emma waved at the brightly coloured miniature tree on the end of the desk where some tiny Santas dangled with white bobbles on the top of their hats.

Not that Caroline was listening anymore. 'But I told you we need a bed urgently,' she was saying. 'Now. We're short-staffed in ED as it is, with this flu going around, and we're filling up. We don't have room to hang on to patients who need admission. I don't care how you do it—just find us some space—'

She ended the call as the radio behind her crackled into life.

'Rescue Three to Eastern Infirmary. How do you read, over?'

Caroline grabbed the microphone. 'Go ahead, Rescue Three.'

'We're coming to you with a six-year-old, status epilepticus… Vital signs as follows…'

Emma was only half listening to the transmission, her gaze sweeping the department. Thanks to the flu that had been felling staff in the last few days, she had been the only consultant on today. She had two registrars and three junior doctors along with the nursing staff and technicians but many of them were due to finish their shifts when she was—in thirty minutes—at six o'clock. She needed to check how many medics would be here to work with Stuart Cameron, the head of this ED, when he came in to relieve her. As usual, he'd put up his hand to work the Christmas Eve night shift so that as many of his staff as possible could be at home with their families.

Emma's heart squeezed with another moment of warmth that gave her a lump in her throat. Stuart was not only the best ED specialist she knew, he was also the kindest man in the world. She wouldn't have got through this last year without him, that was for sure…

And she needed to make sure she was on top of everything going on in here at the moment so she could give him a competent handover. Oh, and she needed to remember to fetch his gift from her locker—that very expensive bottle of aged Scotch whisky that she knew he would love. She'd wrapped it last night and given it a gorgeous, tartan bow.

'What's the ambulance ETA?' she asked Caroline.

'Ten minutes. And you should know that they haven't been able to get IV access.'

'Okay. Thanks.'

Would the child with the uncontrollable seizures arrive before Stuart did? If so, Emma would have to handle this case. At least both the resus rooms were empty at the moment. She walked towards one of them, catching Alistair's eye as he emerged from behind a curtain.

'Might need you in a few minutes,' she warned. 'Six-year-old incoming with status epilepticus. No IV in. I'll get an intraosseous kit out in case we have problems, too. He'll need IV meds asap.'

She glanced over her shoulder as she heard the distinctive whoosh of the automatic doors that led to the ambulance bay. Was the paediatric emergency arriving early?

No. Emma breathed a sigh of relief. It was Stuart Cameron, who would have parked in the 'Consultant On Call' space beside hers at one side of the ambulance bay. He was bundled up in a thick coat, scarf and hat, looking like he'd come in from Arctic temperatures, and Emma felt another beat of excitement. Was it possible they'd actually get some snow for Christmas?

Not in the city, of course—that never happened these days. But out in the countryside a bit, where she lived with her mother in her tiny whitewashed cottage—well... they might just get lucky...

Stuart was unwinding his scarf and then unbuttoning his coat as he came further into the department. As he got closer, and took off his hat, alarm bells began ringing for Emma.

'You don't look so good, Stuart.'

'I'm fine.'

'Come with me,' Emma ordered. She led him into the resus room and pointed to a chair. 'Sit.'

Stuart shook his head, peeling off his coat. 'I don't need to sit. I need you to give me a handover so you can get home to Lily and—'

He stopped talking abruptly and Emma could see the way his features froze as he closed his eyes.

Her tone was gentle now, almost a whisper. 'What's hurting, Stu?'

He raised his right hand as if to fend her off. 'It's nothing. A touch of the flu coming on, maybe.'

But then his hand went to his other arm and gripped it.

'You've got pain in your left arm? Any in your chest?'

Stuart didn't respond. Emma stared at him, a knot of fear taking root in her belly as she took in the way the colour was fading from his face to leave it looking grey and the beads of perspiration appearing on his forehead.

'On the bed,' she said. 'You're not going anywhere until I've done a twelve lead ECG.'

'There's no need to fuss… I'll just sit for a moment.' He perched on the side of the bed. Was it her imagination or was Stuart sounding slightly out of breath? 'There was an ambulance pulling up as I came in…you'll be needed…'

'I'm needed here.' Emma took a step towards the door and leaned out. 'Alistair?'

His head appeared through a gap in a nearby curtain. Behind him, Emma could see the doors sliding open again as paramedics wheeled in a stretcher.

'You take the lead on the boy in status epilepticus. I'm going to be busy in here for a few minutes. Call if you need me.'

Turning back, she was relieved to see that Stuart was now properly on the bed, lying back on the pillows.

'Sorry about this, lass,' he murmured. 'It's the last thing you need when you're due to go off shift.'

'The last thing I need,' Emma said quietly, 'is for you to be unwell. I'm not leaving until we find out what's going on.' She reached for a plastic mask and tubing that she attached to the overhead port. 'Here…let's give you some oxygen.'

A nurse came into the room, clearly on a mission to find something, and stopped in her tracks. 'Oh, no… what's happened to Dr Cameron?'

'Help him off with his shirt,' Emma said calmly. 'I want to get some monitoring dots on. And then get me the twelve lead ECG machine.'

The nurse's eyes widened. 'Okay.'

'What did you come in for?'

'An intraosseous needle. It looks like it's going to be a mission to get a line into the little boy that's just come in.'

'You get that, then. I'll do this.' Emma took over un-buttoning Stuart's shirt. He had his eyes closed but she could tell by the look on his face how much he was hating this. 'It's in the top drawer of the IV cupboard,' she added. 'And don't go telling everybody that Dr Cameron's in here. Until I say otherwise, this is private.'

'It's probably a fuss about nothing,' Stuart muttered. 'Bit of indigestion, that's all…'

Emma had sticky dots on his shoulders and just above his hips. She waited for the interference to clear on the overhead monitor. And then her heart sank.

Stuart opened his eyes. And then shut them again.

'Guess it's not indigestion, then…'

'No.' Emma swallowed hard. 'You've got significant

ST elevation in leads two and three. We'll know more when I do a twelve lead but this looks like an inferior infarct. Have you had any aspirin today?'

Stuart shook his head.

'And you probably need some morphine, don't you?' This time it was a slow nod.

'We'll do that first, then. And bloods. And I'll get someone to page Cardiology and make sure the catheter laboratory is available.'

Angioplasty was the definitive treatment to unblock the coronary arteries causing this heart attack. It could prevent Stuart being left with any lasting damage. It could also save his life. Emma didn't want to leave his side. What if he went into cardiac arrest?

But there was a whole raft of things that needed to be done immediately and Emma wasn't about to let someone else take the lead role in caring for this man.

Stuart Cameron probably should have retired years ago—before Emma had arrived to follow her passion in emergency medicine—but she would be grateful forever that he'd loved his work too much to leave. He was the closest thing she'd had to a father since she'd lost her own when she'd been only sixteen. A father figure, mentor and close friend all rolled into one. He was one of the most important people in her life—the people she truly loved— and that was a group small enough to be counted on the fingers of one hand. Lily, her mum, Jack...and Sarah...

Maybe it was that fleeting thought of Sarah that made the fear kick up a notch. Was history repeating itself? Was she going to lose someone so special that it would feel like the end of the world—on the eve of the day that was all about celebrating exactly those people?

Like she had last year?

No...she couldn't let that happen.

Maybe it was a blessing that Stuart had ignored any warning signs and come into work. He was in the best place possible to deal with this and she was going to make sure that nothing got in the way of his treatment.

There was no point in trying to keep the news of this crisis away from the staff here now and Emma knew that she was far from the only person who would be desperately worried about Stuart. Within minutes, she had people falling over themselves wanting to help. A nurse was rushing blood samples away to be tested and a technician was capturing a twelve lead ECG trace. She had given Stuart pain relief herself and had also made the call to the cardiology department. It was no surprise that a cardiology consultant came down to the department herself, instead of sending her registrar.

'Goodness me, Stuart. What kind of Christmas surprise is this?'

'Not the best kind.' Stuart's smile was apologetic and his gaze included Emma. 'You'll have to call someone in, lass. Doesn't look like I'll be taking over this shift.'

'Don't even think about it,' Emma told him. 'It's all under control.'

It was a white lie. The senior staffing issue for the night was far from under control. Knowing that they were off, most of the doctors had headed out of town for family gatherings. Caroline had been making call after call with no success.

'Here's the latest twelve lead.' She handed a series of graphs to the cardiology consultant. 'Looks like it's evolving to include a lateral extension.'

'Enzymes back yet?'

Emma nodded. She handed over the result sheet, reluctant to voice the figures that would tell Stuart just how serious this heart attack was looking.

'We're all ready for you upstairs,' the consultant told Stuart. 'And I'm going to do your angioplasty myself.'

'I'll bet you were supposed to be heading home by now, too.'

She just smiled at her colleague. 'Consider this my Christmas gift to you, my friend. I've never forgotten how kind you were to my father when he came in here with his stroke all those years ago.'

Emma took hold of Stuart's hand and squeezed it for a moment as the orderly unlocked the brakes on the bed and prepared to start moving him.

'It'll be okay,' she told him. 'I'll come up and see you as soon as you're in CCU.'

'No you won't. You'll be home with your Lily by then.' He gave her fingers a return squeeze. 'You need to be away from this place tonight, love. I know how hard it must be…'

Emma had to blink against the sudden sting of tears.

'I'm doing fine,' she whispered. 'Thanks to you…'

There was so much more she could have said. So much she would want to say—just in case this was the last chance she would ever have—but the bed was moving already.

'I'll call you when we're through,' the consultant said as she left. 'Try not to worry—he's going to get our platinum service.'

Emma was left standing in the empty space where the bed had been. Littered around her were the plastic wrappers from syringes and IV supplies. The top of a glass drug ampoule was still spinning after being knocked and an ECG electrode was stuck to the floor where it had been dropped. There were no Christmas decorations in here because it had been deemed inappropriate for patients—and their families—who might be facing an unsuccessful conclusion to a life-threatening crisis.

She could hear the sounds of a busy—and very well decorated—department just through the doors. Clearly, the first of the alcohol-related injuries were arriving, judging by the raised voices and the loud, tuneless singing of a Christmas carol that was happening out there.

It was only then that she realised she was standing in the same resus area that she'd been in last Christmas Eve. Where she'd had to sit and hold the hand of her best friend as Sarah had taken her last breaths.

She couldn't hold back the tears by blinking now. Turning, she ripped some paper towels from the dispenser by the sink and pressed them to her face.

Only a few minutes ago, she'd been blessed by one of those jewels of excitement but now she was teetering on the edge of that dark space she never wanted to enter again.

It was all going wrong.

There would be no decorating the Christmas tree tonight and attaching those very special ornaments to the top. How many tears had been quietly shed as she'd crafted those two little felt angels—a mummy one and a daddy one—in memory of Lily's parents? Putting them in pride of place at the top of the tree and sharing a moment of remembrance was going to be a new, private Christmas tradition just for her special little family.

Like kisses for Kissmas.

She wouldn't be hanging up the stocking that she had embroidered Lily's name on, either. No putting carrots out for the reindeer. No squeezy cuddles or sticky kisses to make everything seem worthwhile.

And no Jack, either.

Had she really thought that this anniversary might be the one thing that would persuade him to come back?

To see Lily, at least?

She'd been hoping for far too much. But right now, it didn't seem to matter. She needed to refocus those hopes and give them all to Stuart for the next few hours. Knowing that he was going to be all right was the only Christmas magic she needed now.

'You okay, Emma?'

'Mmm.' A quick swipe with the paper towels and Emma was ready to turn around. 'How's it going, Caroline?'

'Not good, I'm sorry. I can't find anyone to come in. Alistair's going to stay on, though, and I can probably find an extra registrar from somewhere. We've cancelled our drinks. Nobody's really in the mood anymore…'

'I'll stay,' Emma told her.

'But—'

'There's no way I'm going home until I hear how Stuart's doing and by then Lily will be fast asleep, so I may as well stay until the morning crew gets here.'

'Are you sure?'

'I'm sure. I just need to ring Mum and let her know what's happening.'

She was getting good at these white lies, wasn't she? Emma wasn't at all sure about this. It would mean she would still be in the department late this evening and how hard was it going to be not to remember every agonising detail about last year?

But she didn't have a choice.

Any more than she had had a year ago, when she'd given that solemn promise to Sarah.

She'd coped since then. And she would cope now.

Because that was how things had to be.

* * *

Man, it was cold…

Despite the full leather gear and a state-of-the-art helmet, Jack Reynolds was beginning to feel like he was frozen to the seat of the powerful motorbike beneath him.

It was time he took a break but he was so close now. In less than an hour he'd be hitting the outskirts of Glasgow and then he could find his motel and thaw out with a long, hot shower.

And tomorrow, he'd do something he'd sworn he'd never do.

He would celebrate Christmas.

Well…maybe *celebrate* wasn't exactly the right word. This journey was more like the world's biggest apology.

He just happened to have a brightly wrapped gift in the pannier of his bike that the sales assistant in Hamleys—London's best toy shop—had assured him would be perfect for an eighteen-month-old child. The little girl he hadn't seen in nearly a year.

His goddaughter.

And his niece…

A wave of the sensation that had grown from a flicker, that had been all too easy to bury months ago, to its current unpleasant burn generated a warmth that Jack would rather not be feeling right now, despite the chill of the wind seeping into his bones.

An unfamiliar feeling that he could only identify as shame.

Who knew that grief could mess with your head enough to turn you into someone you couldn't even recognise?

How painful was it to start realising how much that could have hurt others?

At least Lily was too young to have been affected by

it, but what on earth was he going to say to Emma to try and start mending bridges?

He'd been unbelievably selfish, hadn't he?

It had been all about him. He'd lost his twin brother, Ben, in that dreadful accident and it had felt as if more than half of himself had died that night.

But Emma had lost Sarah, who'd been her best friend forever, and they'd been as close as sisters. Closer than most sisters, probably. What had given him the right to think his loss had been greater?

The traffic was building up as the M74 into Glasgow bypassed the township of Uddingston. Somewhere in the darkness to the left the river Clyde was shadowing his route into the city he'd never really expected to see again. He'd turned his back on everything there—and every*one*—when he'd walked out all those months ago.

The rain spattering his visor felt different now. There was a sludgy edge to it that was making visibility worse than it had been and the lights of the vehicles around him were blurred and fragmented. Signposts warned of the major road changes ahead where the M73 joined the M74.

That was where it had happened, wasn't it?

Where Ben and Sarah had had the accident that had claimed their lives exactly a year ago today?

Almost to the minute…

There was a new burning sensation now, behind his eyes this time, and he recognised that feeling.

It had been only a couple of weeks ago. In the burning heat of an African summer, when one of his colleagues had started reminiscing about English winters. About Christmas…

He could have sworn that Ben was right beside him, giving him one of those none-too-gentle elbow nudges in his ribs. Saying the words that had been the last thing his brother had ever said to him.

'See you tomorrow, bro. For once, you're going to enjoy Christmas. Me and Sarah and Lily...we're going to show you what Christmas is all about. Family...'

It hadn't been the first time he'd found a private spot with the view of nothing but desert but it had been the first time in forever that he'd cried. Gut-wrenching sobs that had been torn from his soul. And that was why he recognised this painful stinging sensation at the back of his eyes.

It couldn't happen now. Not in heavy traffic and with what looked like sleet getting thicker by the second. There was an exit lane ahead and he needed to change lanes and make sure he was well clear of any idiot who might decide to take the exit unexpectedly.

Like that dodgy-looking small truck that was crossing the line directly in front of him.

Tilting his body weight, after checking there was a gap in the lane beside him, Jack flipped on his indicator and glanced over his shoulder again to check the lane was still clear.

Where the hell had that car come from? And what did it think it was doing?

No-o-o...

Text messages had been frequent over the last hour, including one that accompanied an adorable photo of Lily, bundled up like a little Eskimo in her puffy, pink jacket, with tinsel in her dark curls, crouching down to put an enormous carrot beside a bucket of water. Emma could see the ropes of the swing hanging from the branch of the old oak tree in the garden in the background so she knew exactly where the bucket had been placed.

Exactly where she should have been, too.

Just as well she was too busy to dwell on the unexpected turn her evening had taken.

The waiting room was crowded but the curtained cubicles were all full right now. Every doctor had several patients to cover and Emma was trying to keep herself mobile so she could help wherever she was needed. She just had to decide on the priority as she looked at the list on the glass board.

It wouldn't be the drunk in Curtain Eight who'd been punched in the nose and had a septal haematoma that needed draining. Or the teenager that had downed enough alcohol at a work Christmas party to collapse. Someone else could supervise the administration of activated charcoal there. Was it the young woman with epigastric pain in Curtain Four? The dislocated shoulder in Curtain Two that needed sedation and relocation? That was a task that needed quite a lot of physical strength sometimes so she might need to wait until Alistair had a free moment, and he was busy sorting pain relief for that nasty foot fracture that had come in a little while ago when an elderly man had fallen from the ladder he was using to hang twinkly lights in a garden tree.

The X-rays were up on the screen beside her and Emma couldn't help leaning in for a closer look. A Lisfranc fracture and a fracture/dislocation of at least two other joints. This patient was going to need some urgent orthopaedic management as soon as pain relief was on board and a plaster back-slab applied. He'd need to be kept nil by mouth, too, in case a theatre slot became available.

The baby, Emma decided. The one with the rash that looked like a bad reaction to antibiotics. She'd just pop her head into the side room and check that something had been given to settle the miserable infant and calm its mother.

And she wouldn't look at the clock on the way.

It was getting too close to that time.

The moment her world had started to fall apart this time last year. When those sliding doors had opened for two stretchers to be rolled in amongst a team of paramedics that all had the grim faces that advertised how bad this accident had been. With the policeman behind them carrying a baby in its car seat.

Not that she had had any idea of how bad this really was. Neither had Jack, who was standing in one of the resus rooms, having been summoned as the orthopaedic component of the major trauma team that had gathered to receive the victims of the MVA out on the M74.

The injuries had been so bad, he hadn't even recognised his twin brother in those first minutes. It had been Emma who recognised Sarah on the second stretcher. Still conscious. Asking over and over whether Lily was all right and where was Ben?

She'd had to go into Resus One. Just as Stuart was shaking his head before he glanced up at the clock.

'Time of death, twenty-two thirty-five...'

'Jack?' It had been so hard to get the words out. *'Jack...? I think... I think this might be Ben... I'm so, so sorry...'*

Later, she'd wondered if he'd already guessed but had been too shocked to process the information. You'd think that the kind of connection between twins would make it plausible but Jack and Ben had been opposite sides of the same coin, hadn't they? Ben was the quiet one. The responsible one. The perfect husband and father material that Sarah couldn't believe how lucky she'd been to find.

Jack might have mirrored his brother's career in medicine and achieved even greater popularity and success but he was the wild one of the pair.

She'd been warned by Sarah to stay away from him.

Jack had been warned by Ben to stay away from *her*.

Not that their disobedience had mattered in the end, because any connection as far as Jack was concerned had evaporated in the instant she'd passed on that devastating news.

It was another thing she'd lost that night...

Emma sucked in a deep breath. The noises around her seem to be amplified for a moment as she dragged herself back to the present. People shouting. Babies crying. A shriek of pain. Phones ringing. An ambulance call coming through on the radio. Caroline should have gone home ages ago but she was still there, fielding the calls.

'Go ahead, Rescue Seven. Reading you loud and clear. Over...'

'We're coming to you with a thirty-six-year-old male, result of a motorbike accident on the M74. Query chest injury. Multiple contusions. Query fracture left tib/fib. Vital signs as follows: GCS fifteen, heart rate one-twenty...'

Breathe, Emma told herself. Without thinking, she reached up to touch her hair, finding the inevitable tight curl that had sprung free from its clip and making sure it was trapped again. It was an action that always made her feel that little bit more in control.

This was just another accident. Not even a particularly serious one, by the sound of things, but she wasn't going to take anything for granted.

'I'll be in Resus One,' she told Caroline.

'Want me to activate the trauma team?'

A GCS of fifteen meant that the victim was conscious and alert. Okay, he might have a chest injury but he was breathing well enough for the moment. Part of her job in charge of this department was to make sure she used potentially limited extra resources as wisely as possible.

'Not yet. I'll take a look at him first. How far away are they?'

'About five minutes.'

Emma couldn't help glancing up at the clock as she walked into Resus One and pulled on a disposable gown and some gloves.

Twenty-two thirty. It would probably be twenty-two thirty-five as they rolled the stretcher in.

Breathe, she reminded herself again, as she heard the whoosh of the ambulance bay doors.

Alistair came in and grabbed a gown, closely followed by a nurse. And then the stretcher arrived. Nothing could have prompted Emma to take a breath when she saw who was on the stretcher. The opposite happened as her body and brain both froze. There was just enough breath left to utter a single, horrified word.

'Jack...?'

CHAPTER TWO

THE JOY CAME from nowhere.

It caught her in that moment when Jack opened his eyes and his startled gaze met her own. When she saw the flare of recognition and something more... Relief that he was in a place he knew he'd be cared for? Or was it because he wanted to see *her*? Was it the reason he'd finally come back?

It only lasted a heartbeat, that joy, but in that instant, every cell in Emma's body was singing.

He's come back...

Jack's here...

But following so closely on the heels of joy that it morphed with it and then took over was fear.

He's hurt...

Maybe badly hurt...

She could see the lines of pain etched on his face and in the way he was pressing his lips together as he closed his eyes again.

This might be the biggest challenge of her career so far in not allowing emotional involvement to interfere with delivering clinical excellence but, to her surprise, Emma found she was up for it.

It was a relief, even, to turn away from such overpowering feelings to something she knew she could handle.

The paramedic who was giving a rapid but thorough handover had her full attention.

'High-speed collision. Mr Reynolds got cut off by someone coming into his lane. He swerved, apparently, but lost control of the bike. GCS is fifteen but he may have been KO'd briefly. I suspect the bike landed on his left leg. We've splinted the possible tib/fib fracture there. The chest injury may have come from contact with the handlebars. One sleeve of his jacket got ripped so there's road rash and a potential fracture on his left forearm.'

'Got his helmet?'

'Yes. Superficial damage but it's not broken.'

Emma nodded. She listened to the quick summary of the most recent vital signs and glanced at the monitor, which was showing a rapid but normal heart rhythm. His oxygen saturation level was also good.

'Let's get him on the bed.'

As lead physician, it was Emma's job to be at the head end of their patient. The ambulance crew had put a neck collar on Jack, quite correctly assuming that the mechanism of injury could mean he had a spinal injury, so she had to ensure that the transfer from stretcher to bed did not do anything to risk making it worse. Having the paramedics here was helpful in having enough people to do the job well.

'Three on each side, please. On my count…' Emma put her hands on either side of Jack's head. Mostly, all she could feel was the plastic collar but at the base of her hands she could feel the warmth of his scalp. The softness of that shaggy black hair…

'One…two…*three*…'

A smooth transfer. Emma had a moment to scan her patient and assess his airway as her colleagues went into a well-rehearsed routine.

Alistair was unhooking the leads of the ambulance monitor to replace them with their own. A nurse had a pair of shears in her hands.

'I'm sorry, sir, but I'm going to have to cut the rest of your leathers...'

Jack nodded, but didn't say anything. His eyes were still shut.

'Keep your head still,' Emma reminded him. 'We haven't cleared your neck, yet. Your sats are good but are you having any trouble breathing?'

'No.'

She hadn't expected the effect that hearing his voice again would have. She had to swallow past the lump that appeared suddenly in her throat and felt like a rock.

'Sinus tachycardia,' Alistair said. 'Blood pressure's one-thirty on eighty.'

Probably higher than normal for Jack.

'What's your pain score?' she queried. The paramedics had already given him some morphine but maybe it hadn't been enough. She didn't need to give Jack the usual range of zero to ten to pick from, with zero being no pain and ten the worst ever. He knew.

'About five, I guess. Maybe six.'

'Let's top up the morphine,' she directed Alistair, as she hooked her stethoscope into her ears. 'I'm going to have a listen to your chest,' she told Jack.

His chest was bare. The leather jacket had been unzipped and the black T-shirt beneath had been cut. His skin was far more tanned than Emma had ever seen but that whorl of dark hair was exactly the same. And she knew exactly what it would feel like against the silk of his skin, if it had been her fingers rather than the disc of her stethoscope she was pressing against it.

Oh, help... Maybe she should stand back and let

Alistair take over here? Or call in part of the trauma team? They were probably going to need at least an orthopaedic consult but that should probably wait until the necessary X-rays and other tests had been done.

Alistair was drawing up the morphine. He held the ampoule so that Emma could do the drug check. Her nod was brisk. Happy with Jack's breath sounds, she wanted to start a neurological check. The potential head injury was high on her list of concerns.

'You know where you are, Jack?'

One side of his mouth curled into that ironic smile she remembered so well.

'Oh, yeah... Unless the Eastern got shifted recently?'

'And can you tell me what date it is today?'

The smile vanished and Emma knew, with what felt like a kick in her gut, that the pain in his eyes had nothing to do with his injuries. It was a standard question but how insensitive was it, given these particular circumstances?

'It's Christmas Eve,' Jack said softly. 'I'm... I'm sorry, Red.'

The old nickname, bestowed in honour of her wild, auburn hair, was almost her undoing.

Nobody else called her 'Red'. Never had, never would...

Not even Sarah. She used to make Emma laugh when they were kids by calling her the 'Ginger Ninja' and there was nobody else in her life that would dream of doing that.

This time, the lump had jagged edges and there was no way of stopping the sting that got to the back of her eyes.

'I'm sure you didn't do this on purpose.' Her voice sounded odd, coming from around the edges of that lump. 'I'm sorry, too.' She gathered some strength she didn't know she had. 'But don't worry—we're going to look after you.'

The nurse had finished cutting the leather of his bike pants and was working on the sleeves of his jacket. She had to pause while Alistair flushed the IV line, after injecting the painkiller.

'I'll draw some bloods,' Alistair said. 'Including an ETOH level?'

'I haven't been drinking.' Jack's words sounded a little slurred but his face had relaxed a bit, suggesting that his pain level—which Emma suspected he had under-reported—was dropping, so it was quite likely the morphine was making him sleepy.

Alistair's look said it all. The slurred words were no surprise. This was Jack Reynolds, wasn't it?

A flash of anger caught Emma unawares. Okay, Jack had left here under a huge cloud but there'd been a reason for that, hadn't there? A reason big enough to make it, if not forgivable, at least enough to offer the benefit of doubt now.

The nurse cutting away clothing had caught the look and her eyebrows rose.

'This is Mr Reynolds,' Alistair told her. 'He used to work here. He was one of our orthopaedic surgeons.'

'Oh…' The young nurse looked impressed. 'I'm so sorry, Mr Reynolds…about having to cut your leathers. I know how expensive they are.'

'It really doesn't matter,' Jack muttered. 'And call me Jack. I'm not at work at the moment.'

Emma caught her breath. Was he planning to be at work in the near future? Was *that* why he'd come back? But why would he choose today, of all days, to come back to Glasgow?

But then again…why wouldn't he?

One of the junior doctors who had joined the team had taken off the dressing that covered Jack's arm injury.

'Can you wiggle your fingers for me, Jack?'

Emma was still holding her breath. The scraped skin looked raw and painful but if he'd broken bones it could affect his future as a surgeon and that might destroy what had always been the most important thing in his life. Jack Reynolds might still be seen as a badly behaved maverick by some—Alistair, for instance—but nobody had ever had anything other than praise to offer about his work as the rising star of the orthopaedic surgical department. Ironically, he'd been heading towards specialist trauma work and had been the best available for injuries that had the potential to seriously affect someone's quality of life. Like neck fractures or mangled hands.

She released the breath in a sigh of relief as she saw the way Jack was able to move his hand. And he could make a fist and resist pressure without it causing undue pain in his arm so it was unlikely that any bones had been broken.

He might not be so lucky with that lower leg injury that Alistair was assessing. The nasty haematoma on his calf could well be the result of an underlying fracture and it was causing some pain to try and move his foot.

Neither of those injuries was in any way life-threatening, however. Emma was more concerned about the bruising on Jack's ribs and whether he had a head injury. Despite the protection of a helmet, if he'd hit his head hard enough to lose consciousness, even briefly, he was very likely to have a concussion and possibly something worse, like a bleed, going on.

'Take a deep breath for me, Jack. Is it painful?' Emma put her hand over skin that was mottled with early bruising.

'A bit.'

'We'll get some X-rays done soon. You might have broken a few ribs. Let me know if you get short of breath at all.'

'I'm fine.' Jack had closed his eyes again. 'The department looked busy out there. You must have patients who are worse off than me.'

Emma ignored the comment. And the look that Alistair flicked in her direction. He knew. Not about how close she'd been to Jack, of course—keeping that a secret had been part of the excitement—and he hadn't actually been in the department this time last year but there would be very few people in this hospital who hadn't heard every single detail about the heartbreaking tragedy she and Jack had been so much a part of. The aftermath had been the hot topic for gossip for weeks as well. And everybody knew how much Emma's life had changed when she'd finally taken responsibility for Lily.

Maybe Alistair thought she should step out. That she would prefer not to be caring for Jack after those traumatic weeks that had ended in a battle that everyone believed Jack had deserved to lose.

She couldn't let him—or anyone else—know just how far from the truth that was. Her next words came out a little more sternly than was probably warranted.

'Don't move your head. I'm undoing the collar so I can have a feel of your neck.'

Jack couldn't see Emma because she was standing behind his head.

But he could *feel* her.

Not just the obvious touch of her fingers on his neck as she pressed her thumbs on each side of his spine, putting systematic, gentle pressure down the midline to check for the presence of tenderness before moving further from the midline to repeat the process.

No. He could feel her in a much more ethereal sense. He hadn't known which hospital he was being transported to after the accident and he hadn't been feeling that great when he'd arrived, but even with his eyes shut, he'd known that Emma was in the room.

He had felt something of that aura of determination and genuine caring that made Emma Matthews stand out in any crowd of equally intelligent and successful medics.

And then he'd opened his eyes and she looked *exactly* the same. Those bright hazel eyes. The matching freckles sprinkled over a button of a nose. Jack could even see the usual coils of that astonishing hair that had wormed their way out from beneath the prisons of their clips.

It hit him like a brick. All that time he'd been away, he'd been so convinced that he didn't miss her. That she was just another one of the stream of women that had shared his life—and his bed—for a limited time.

But he *had* been missing her, hadn't he? Every minute of every day. And all that accumulated emotion coalesced into one king punch that was far more painful than anything going on in his battered body at that moment. He'd had to press his lips together against the pain. Screw his eyes tightly shut so that he didn't keep staring at her and making the pain worse.

And now she was touching him and it made him remember how clever those small hands were. How gentle Emma was.

How the touch on his skin made it feel like he was being caressed by a whisper of a delicious, cool breeze on the hottest day ever. That coolness had been an illusion, though, hadn't it? It could flick in a heartbeat to a heat that no other woman had ever evoked.

Jack had to stifle a groan. The morphine was clearly scrambling his brain. He shouldn't be thinking of something like that. It was over. Dead and buried. And he'd been the one to kill it.

Emma must have heard the small sound. 'What's hurting?' she asked. 'What's bothering you?'

Oh…that was a question and a half. Would she actually want to know about the guilt over abandoning his brother's child that had been hanging around his neck like an ever-increasing weight?

The shame of the way he'd behaved in those dark days? The way he'd treated *her*?

Even if she was prepared to listen to him, it would have to be a very private conversation and there were others around. He could feel the sting of the damaged skin on his arm being cleaned and redressed. Of his lower leg being unwrapped from its temporary splint. And he could hear the voices of new arrivals—the radiographers, probably— who would be preparing to operate the overhead X-ray machines.

'Is it your neck? Was it here?' Her fingers were pressing again on the last spot she'd touched at the bottom of his cervical spine.

'No…my neck feels fine.'

'Really?' Emma's face appeared as she moved to one side of the bed. So close to his own he could see those unusual golden flecks in the soft brown of her irises. 'And you really haven't been drinking?'

That hurt. He might have been a complete bastard in those last weeks but he'd never been less than honest with her. With anyone, for that matter.

He saw the flicker in her eyes. 'Sorry… I just needed to be sure.'

'Yeah…you always were very thorough, Dr Matthews. It's a commendable attribute.'

That earned a tilt of her lips that was almost a smile. 'There's a checklist for determining whether a cervical spine is stable, as you well know. You don't seem to have any midline tenderness and there's no evidence of intoxication. You seem to be reasonably alert and oriented to time and place.'

Jack could feel his own lips curve. 'Cheers. Under the circumstances, I'll take reasonably alert as a good thing.'

Emma unclipped her small pen torch from the top pocket of her scrubs tunic and flicked the light on. Jack kept his eyes open and stared straight ahead as she moved the beam to check his pupil sizes and reactions.

'Equal and reactive,' she said. 'There's only one other thing on the checklist. Do you remember what it is?'

Clever. She was throwing in something completely different as another check on his neurological status.

'Whether there are any painful, distracting injuries, like a long bone fracture.'

'And is anything painful enough to qualify as a distraction?'

'No.'

'Mmm… Okay, then, I reckon you pass.' She looked away from him to someone he couldn't see. 'I'm happy to leave the collar off but I'd still like a cervical X-ray series, please. Along with chest, pelvis, left tib/fib and the left forearm.'

'Do you want a lead apron?' someone queried.

Emma shook her head, looking down at Jack again. 'I'm happy that your condition hasn't deteriorated in any way. I'm going to duck out and get up to speed with what's happening in the rest of the department until I get your X-rays up on the computer. I won't be far away and someone will come and get me if I'm needed.'

Jack nodded. He closed his eyes as he did so because he didn't want Emma to see how much he would have preferred for her to stay here.

He had no right to put any kind of pressure on her.

About anything.

Alistair had beaten her to the patient board and he was frowning as he scanned the changes that the last ten minutes or so had produced.

'We've got to clear some space,' he said. 'Waiting times are getting to an unacceptable level.'

'I'll see if we can get another registrar or two on board.'

'We've got an ambulance arriving in the next few minutes,' Caroline warned them. 'And the police. Sounds like a turf war broke out between a couple of Santas selling hats or something.' She tried to suppress a grin. 'Could be serious. One of them got stabbed, by the sound of things.'

'I'll take it,' Alistair said. 'But do you want me to help with that dislocated shoulder in Curtain Two first? He's been waiting a while.'

'I'll get one of the housemen. It's only brute strength required.' One of the junior doctors—a young Australian called Pete—was heading towards her, in fact, but Emma didn't get the chance to speak first.

'Can I get you to have a look at my patient when you've got a minute? Twenty-nine-year-old with epigastric pain but I don't know if it warrants a scan.' Pete was frowning. 'There's something about her I just can't put my finger on.'

It didn't sound too urgent. 'Can she wait for a bit? I need you to help me get a shoulder back in. Set up a sedation trolley in Curtain Two and I'll be with you shortly.' She paused beside one of the bank of computer screens available to call up patient records, check test results and review X-rays. The first digital image from the resuscitation room Jack was in had come through. A chest X-ray.

Emma peered at the screen as she zoomed in and hovered over the area that was so bruised. There didn't seem to be any broken ribs. This was good. Maybe she could stop worrying about the possibility of a pneumothorax and a sudden deterioration in Jack's ability to breathe.

Another worry resurfaced in the wake of that relief. Picking up the desk phone, she punched in an internal number.

'CCU, Charge Nurse speaking.'

'Hi, Steve. It's Emma Matthews here, from ED. Any word on Stuart Cameron yet?'

'They're just finishing up in the cath lab. He's had three stents put in. Apparently there was a hundred percent occlusion of his left main stem. ECG changes are resolving already, though, so he's been incredibly lucky.'

'Oh…thank goodness…' The wave of relief was enough to make Emma's legs feel wobbly.

'We're expecting him in here shortly. We've got the private suite ready.'

Emma smiled. 'Tell him I'll be up to visit the moment I get a break.'

'How's it looking down there?'

'Usual festive season chaos. A surprise around every corner.'

Ending the call, Emma went to find Pete, who was waiting for her outside Curtain Two, alongside a pretty young nurse.

'Really?' Emma heard him say. 'He turned up at work *drunk*? When he had a theatre list waiting?'

'That's not the worst of it,' the nurse responded. 'He was the legal guardian of his baby niece—her only living relative—and he just walked away…'

'No way…'

They had their backs to her so they hadn't noticed Emma approaching. Maybe the nurse was carried away by having something that had captured an attractive new doctor's attention so completely. She leaned in closer.

'Nobody's heard a peep from him since and that was nearly a year ago.'

'So why has he come back now?'

'Who knows? Maybe he's come back to claim her finally.'

Emma stopped in her tracks. She could feel the blood draining out of her head, leaving a nasty spinning sensation.

She'd thought he might have come back to see Lily.

To see *her*, even.

Or even that he might have been planning to work here again.

But to have come back to claim guardianship of the only living member of his family?

It made sense.

Sickening, terrifying sense, because it wouldn't be the first time…

She could actually hear those furious words. *'She's my brother's child. Now she's mine.'*

It also made her angry.

'I hate to break up the party,' she snapped, 'but I'm sure you've both noticed how busy this department is at the moment. Let's get on with doing the jobs we're being paid to do, shall we?'

The pair jumped apart, the nurse's face reddening as she fled. Emma ignored Pete's muttered apology. The anger was still there. They wouldn't be the only people gossiping in corners tonight after the dramatic reappearance of Jack Reynolds and no doubt they'd be picking over her own part as one of the major players in what had been a series of events worthy of a soap opera's plotline.

Most of the anger was directed elsewhere, however, and it came from a place of fear.

Everybody knew she was Lily's mother in every way it was possible to be a mother, other than having given birth to her precious little girl. But legally she was no more than a godparent. No formal adoption process had ever been initiated. How could it have been when her legal guardian had simply vanished?

Would she have enough grounds to fight if Jack really had come back to claim Lily?

Relocating a shoulder was the perfect task for Emma right now. With her patient well sedated, it needed careful positioning and then an intense physical effort to pull the arm hard enough to create the space for the ball of the joint to slip back into its socket. She had been going to ask Pete to do it but instead she had him stabilise the patient's body while she did it.

There was always satisfaction in hearing the joint click back into place but this time what was even better was the release of that angry tension that had settled in Emma's belly like a stone. By the time she headed back to the computer to check the rest of Jack's images, she was feeling a great deal calmer.

For a moment, though, the images on the screen were blurry.

She was back in time again. Sitting beside the bed of someone she loved so dearly and they had both known that they had very little time.

'Promise me, Em. Promise me that you'll take care of her.'

Sarah's breathing had been becoming rapidly more laboured and there had been nothing they could do.

'Jack would be a disaster. He's irresponsible... He's never even wanted a family...'

'I promise...'

How hard had it been to hold back her tears?

'Cross your heart and hope to die?'

The old childhood vow. The one that could never be broken.

Not that Emma had been able to repeat the words. She had only been able to nod. And smile. And squeeze Sarah's hand so hard it would have hurt if she hadn't already been beyond feeling pain...

It took a huge effort to shake off the distressing flashback. To focus on the images in front of her. Amazingly, Jack hadn't broken any bones, probably thanks to the well-padded leather gear with its built-in body armour. All that was needed was treatment of the soft-tissue injuries and observation for long enough to be sure that there was no head injury being missed.

Taking a deep breath, Emma went back to Jack's room. The radiographers had gone and the nurse who had stayed with Jack was peering wide-eyed around the door as stretchers surrounded by police officers as well as paramedics came through the ambulance bay doors. That the patients on the stretchers were in red and white Santa suits only made the spectacle even more riveting. Alistair and the small team he had gathered were waiting in front of the other resuscitation area.

'You go,' Emma told the nurse. 'They'll need extra hands. And call me if I'm needed.'

'What's going on out there?' Jack had a pillow under

his head now but he was trying to prop himself further up on the elbow of his uninjured arm. 'Sounds like something major.'

Emma stepped closer. The fear—and the anger—had resurfaced on seeing Jack's face. It made no difference how much she loved this man. She would fight to the death if she had to, to protect what was most important.

'I won't let you do it,' she said quietly. 'Not this time.'

Jack looked bewildered. 'Do what?'

Emma swallowed hard. 'I won't let you take Lily away from me.'

CHAPTER THREE

YOU'D HAVE TO know Emma well to see the fear beneath the fury of the words she had just bitten out.

Jack knew Emma very well.

He could see the fear and he hated himself for having been the person who'd caused it. He had to put this right. Fast.

'I wouldn't do that,' he said quietly. 'Do you really think that's why I've come back?'

The shake of her head was sharp enough for another curl to escape its clip. Emma took a step closer to the bed. Because the wide door of this area was ajar, the noises of the department were still there, but they were no more than a background buzz. It wouldn't matter how quietly Emma spoke, he would still be able to hear every word because that was all that mattered in this moment.

'How would I know?'

Jack could hear the edge of tears roughening her words and could see the way she was fighting for control by the ragged breath she sucked in. He could also see that she had something else to say, so he remained silent.

He watched the way Emma composed herself. A long, hard blink and a swallow that looked painful by the jerky movement of the muscles in her neck. When she opened her eyes again, she was staring down at her hands—as if it was too hard to meet his gaze.

'I've been waiting, Jack,' she said softly. 'For nearly a year, I've been waiting for you to come back. I've shut my ears to everything people have said and held on to the belief that one day, it would happen.' Her head shake was slower this time and she must have felt the tickle of the errant curl because her hand went up to smooth it away from her face. 'I've been hoping—every day—that *this* might be the day I'd hear something...'

Making Emma scared had made Jack feel like a bastard but this was worse. Much worse.

She'd been thinking of him every *day*? Hoping he would do the right thing and come back?

What had other people been saying? That he was gone for good and maybe that was for the best?

Maybe it *would* have been better if he hadn't come back...

'And today, of all days...' Emma's voice was little more than a whisper. 'When the memories were ambushing me around every corner. You come back with no warning and...and you come back looking like you might be nearly dead?'

Her bottom lip wobbled and it was too much.

She cared about him, didn't she?

Really cared...

Apart from the memory of his mother that had no more than a dreamlike quality now, there had only ever been one other person that had felt like that about him and, in a way, Ben's death had given him freedom. There was nobody to worry about him. If he kept it that way, it would work both ways and he wouldn't have to worry about anyone else. Or face the agony of having them torn from his life.

But, for some unfathomable reason, Emma cared…

And, like it or not, he cared about her, didn't he? He wouldn't be feeling this wretched if he didn't.

Jack stretched out his hand but he couldn't quite reach hers. He left it there, hanging, in midair. For a moment, he was aware of an increased urgency in the sounds coming from outside the door—from the resuscitation area right next door to this one—but then he shut it out again. This was more important.

'I'm sorry,' he said. 'I'm really sorry, Red.'

There was a long, long moment of utter stillness then. He knew Emma was looking at his hand—trying to decide whether she wanted to touch him in a capacity that had nothing to do with his medical care?

He wanted that touch. It might be the only thing that could give him any hope that he could put any of this right. He leaned into his arm, stretching it a little bit further, and he turned his hand over, to offer his palm.

'Careful…you'll pull out your IV line.'

But Emma had caught his hand and, after she'd stepped closer to take the tension off the narrow plastic tube, she didn't let it go. Jack curled his fingers around hers, willing her to look up and meet his gaze.

When she did, he almost wished she hadn't. He was enveloped in something that felt like anguish.

'Why did you come back *today*, Jack?'

'Because…because it's Christmas,' he said, his voice catching on the last word.

'But you *hate* Christmas…we all knew how much you hate it… That was why Sarah and Ben were bringing Lily to Glasgow. They knew you'd never go to see them in London.' Emma's words were tumbling out. And her eyes were widening, as if she was realising something horrific for the first time.

'You blame yourself, don't you? For the accident…'

Jack had to close his eyes for a heartbeat. To squeeze her hand sharply as a warning it was too soon to talk about that. He wasn't ready. Maybe he would never be as ready as he'd thought he was.

'It seemed like a good time to try and make peace,' he managed.

Peace with the colleagues he'd let down?

Peace with Emma?

Peace with Lily for when she was old enough to understand?

Yes, on all counts, but if Jack was really honest, he needed to make peace with others in order to make peace with himself. That was why he'd come back.

Christmas, and the dreadful anniversary it represented, had been the catalyst. How could he have been so selfish not to realise how hard this anniversary was going to be for the only other person who'd been so devastated by it? Okay, he hadn't intended to turn up on a stretcher in the Eastern's emergency department but he'd made things so much worse.

For Emma—and for himself. He would never have chosen to be in here tonight. And he'd had no idea that Emma had been waiting for him to come back.

Hoping every day that *this* would be the day?

He didn't know quite how to even start processing that yet because…

Because there'd never been a promise of what they'd had being anything more than what it was—a bit of fun. Forbidden fun, at that…

And because he had no intention of staying?

He couldn't let Emma know that. Not yet. Not until they'd had a chance to really talk—if he could bring himself to go so far back into that dark space.

For now, the only thing that was important was to let Emma know just how sorry he was and there were no words that were available.

So he tried to put his apology into the way he was holding her hand. To send a telepathic message through his fingertips, and in the slow stroke of his thumb across the back of her hand.

And it seemed to be working. His gaze held hers and he could see the anguish fading, along with the horror that was tinged with an empathy he couldn't accept yet. But he *could* accept the strength of a connection he could never have with any other living person. And he could feel something else in that turbulent mix of emotion.

Hope, maybe? That not only peace might be possible but that he could find something solid in his life again? Something that could shape a future that he couldn't yet define?

'Emma...'

She dropped his hand as if she'd been caught doing something inappropriate with a patient, her gaze snapping to the door where someone was calling her.

'We need you. Tension pneumothorax next door and he's crashing.'

There were two patients in the adjoining resuscitation area, a crowd of medical staff, two police officers and three hospital security guards. A crumpled red jacket with white borders lay close to a large puddle of blood. Alistair had bloodstains on his scrubs.

'I've got an arterial bleed here that I can't let go of...'

Emma looked at the man on the other bed. His skin had a bluish tinge and he was gasping for breath, his level of consciousness clearly dropping.

'Sats are dropping fast,' Pete told her. 'And blood

pressure's crashed. No breath sounds on the left side. I've tried a needle decompression with no improvement. We're setting up for a chest tube.'

'That can wait.' Emma pulled on a pair of sterile gloves. 'A simple thoracostomy is going to be faster. Have you done one before?'

'No.' Pete looked anxious. 'I've never even seen one.'

'Okay, watch this time.'

While it would have been a good teaching opportunity for a junior doctor, this patient's condition had deteriorated too far to make a slow procedure acceptable. Emma grabbed the swab sitting in a bowl of disinfectant solution on the top of the chest drain trolley and painted the side of the man's chest.

'See the jugular vein distension?' she asked Pete, pointing at the man's neck. 'We haven't got much time.' The air and probably blood accumulating in the patient's chest had made the lung collapse and would prevent the heart beating in a short space of time.

Emma felt for landmarks with one hand, a scalpel in the other. 'I'm looking for the fourth or fifth intercostal space in the mid-axillary line,' she told Pete. 'And now I'm going to make a five-centimetre incision—just through the skin.'

The man was conscious enough to be groaning with pain.

'Sorry, mate,' Emma said. 'It won't be for much longer.' This was a necessary evil to save his life and Emma had trained herself to get past how bad it made her feel to inflict pain in situations like this.

She crouched to put herself at eye level with the incision. 'I'm going to use the forceps to do a blunt dissection now. It's safer to be looking at the same level.'

Dropping the forceps back onto the trolley, Emma

put her finger in the hole she'd made in their patient's chest and worked it further in.

'Be careful when you're doing this,' she told Pete. 'You might come across fractured ribs that will be sharp. Look, you can see the blood and air that's being released…'

'Oxygen saturation is coming up,' a nurse reported. 'I'll get another blood pressure.'

'I can feel the lung expanding,' Emma said.

'Wow…' Pete looked impressed. 'That's way faster than getting a tube in.'

'We'll still need to do that but it's not urgent. When I let the soft tissue fall back over the wound like this, it acts as a flap valve. If he tensions again, you can release the pressure by putting your finger in again. Just make sure you've got a fresh pair of sterile gloves on. Now… what's caused this? Blunt trauma or was he stabbed?'

'He said he was stabbed but I haven't found the entry wound yet.'

'Have you checked his back?'

'We were just about to when he crashed.'

'Let's do it now, then.' Emma stepped back to let Pete take charge again, glancing across to the other bed. 'How're you doing there, Alistair? Need a hand?'

'I think we're good, thanks. I've got a clamp on this artery and I'm about to tie it off.' He looked up at Emma, with a wry smile. 'It must have been quite some fight. Not really in the Christmas spirit, is it?'

She smiled back but then turned her attention to making sure Pete's secondary survey was revealing all the information he would need to treat his patient. A part of her brain had caught on Alistair's comment, however.

Christmas spirit…

Peace…

Why had it never occurred to her before that Jack might have been blaming himself for that terrible accident? His hatred and avoidance of the festive season had been a joke. Sarah had been laughing about it when she'd rung Emma to share the exciting news that they would be bringing their baby up to Glasgow for the celebration.

'There's no way Jack would come to Christmas voluntarily so we're bringing Christmas to him, whether he likes it or not. We're going to show him just how good it can be when you're with your family...'

If Jack had gone to London to be with his brother's brand-new family, they would never have been on the road that night.

They would still be alive...

There was no point in even thinking about those kind of 'what ifs'. Emma had known that at the time.

But now...

Imagine adding that kind of guilt to the overwhelming grief that Jack had been going through and then layering on the responsibility for a tiny person who had no other relatives in the world? On someone who had no experience of a committed relationship, let alone how to care for an infant.

No wonder he'd freaked out and hadn't been able to handle it.

Had she done enough to help? Or had she made it worse, by channelling her own grief into an obsession to keep her promise to Sarah and look after Lily? Had she, in fact, pushed Jack into the combination of events that had culminated in his walking out?

Not that there was any time to explore that train of thought.

'There it is...' Pete had found the small puncture wound

on the man's back, just under his ribs. 'Doesn't look like it could have caused that much trouble, does it?'

'Surface wounds can be very deceptive.' Emma felt like she was talking to herself as much as to a junior colleague. 'It's what's going on underneath that matters. And sometimes you have to look hard to find it. Let's get a scan organised to see what's going on in there.'

Her words seemed to hang in the air and take on a rather different meaning after she'd stopped speaking. She wouldn't be the only one who needed to look a bit harder beneath the surface as far as Jack Reynolds was concerned. People were judging him again already and it wasn't fair. They didn't know the whole story.

Maybe *she* didn't know the whole story, either.

There was something different about Emma when she came back to his bedside but Jack couldn't figure out what it was.

Maybe it was because the light felt so bright when he opened his eyes that he needed to shade them with his hand.

'That sounded full on next door. You must be a bit shattered.'

'I'm okay. Pretty good considering I've been on duty since seven o'clock this morning.'

'What?' Jack was horrified. 'You're doing a *double* shift?'

'It wasn't intentional. Stuart Cameron was taking over from me but he came into work trying to ignore the fact that he was having a massive heart attack.'

'Oh, *no…*'

The look on Emma's face told him that she was remembering the same thing he was—his last encounter with Stuart.

It had been the well-respected head of this emergency department who'd stopped him that day, when he'd come here to confront Emma. He'd smelt the alcohol on his breath and had practically frog-marched him into his office and away from making any more of a spectacle of himself.

Stuart had read him the riot act and told him to sort himself out. That while he could sympathise with what he was going through, the way he was acting wasn't going to help anyone, least of all himself.

Jack had walked out. Just to get his head together, he'd told himself. Stuart was right. He was in no state to talk to Emma. But the mess he was in seemed to get bigger and bigger and so he'd kept on walking. Packed his bag and gone in search of a place where it didn't feel like the world was exploding around him.

It was possible that Stuart Cameron had been left with the impression that he'd pushed Jack too far and maybe he'd felt at least partly responsible for his vanishing act, which meant that Stuart was one of the people well up on his list of those he needed to make peace with.

'Is he…? Did he…?'

'He's fine.' Emma's smile was soft and her eyes looked bright enough to suggest unshed tears. 'We got him straight into the cath lab and they got his artery open in time to prevent any major damage. He's resting up in the coronary care unit at the moment. I'm going to go up and see him as soon as I get a chance. Hopefully soon. I won't say the dreaded Q-word but it's looking a bit calmer out there right now.'

'Please pass on my best wishes when you see him. I owe him a big apology, too, but I'd better do that myself.' Jack's frown deepened. 'It's not right that you're having to work such long hours. Isn't someone else coming in to relieve you?'

'Not for a while. The morning staff are going to try and get in a bit earlier but we were short-staffed anyway. There's a lot of flu going round at the moment.' Emma blinked, clearing away the glimmer in her eyes. 'Hey, I'm fine. I'm not the only one who's stayed on. And the others were planning a Christmas party in the pub after work.'

'Weren't you going to go?'

'Oh, no… I was going home. To…you know, do the usual kind of Christmas Eve stuff you do when you've got children.'

Jack tried to imagine what that kind of stuff was and he could feel himself frowning. Maybe Emma had misinterpreted the frown as disapproval because she dropped her gaze and changed the subject.

'The good news is that you haven't broken any bones, including your skull. We're going to shift you into a side room to clear this resus area and we'll do some RICE treatment while you're under observation. I don't want that haematoma on your leg leading to a complication like compartment syndrome.'

'I don't need to be observed. I can get right out of your way if you discharge me.'

But that would mean he'd have to find somewhere to go.

Somewhere that would put him a long way away from Emma.

He wasn't ready for that. There was too much that still needed to be said.

'I'm not discharging you until I'm sure you haven't got a head injury we might have missed. That light's bothering you, isn't it?'

Jack lowered his hand but he couldn't stop himself squinting against the brightness.

'Have you got a headache?'

'No worse than a hangover.'

A flash of something that looked like anger crossed Emma's face. 'That's not funny, Jack.'

He sighed. 'It was supposed to be. I haven't had a drink in nearly a year, Red. And I hadn't been coming in to do a theatre list that day, no matter what everyone might have said. I'd only been coming in to see you. To find out where Lily was…'

Emma echoed his sigh. 'It's certainly what everyone assumed but…it's good to know that, Jack. I never really believed that you would have put your patients in danger.'

That's what the difference was.

Jack realised that some of the tension he'd seen in Emma's face, from the moment she'd seen him again, had gone. She was ready to hear his side of the story. She wanted to listen and maybe she would be prepared to forgive?

Something had definitely changed and Jack knew this was an opportunity he might have struggled to find otherwise.

Maybe fate had known what it was doing, to have given him the fright of his life and then put him here— under Emma's care. On this particular night, when the memories and emotions were so raw they provided a background where things could be said that might have otherwise been buried forever.

And Emma was in no hurry to get rid of him.

That flicker of hope he'd felt when he'd been holding her hand gave a tiny spurt and became a steady glow.

Was it his imagination that he could see that glow reflected in Emma's eyes?

Or was it because she was smiling?

'Let's get you sorted,' she said, standing on the pedal that released the brake on his bed.

'I can walk.'

'I don't think you'll be weight bearing on that leg any time too soon. And certainly not until it's properly bandaged. Oh…' Emma let go of the bed rails and headed to a corner of the room behind him. 'We'd better take the rest of your gear.'

The scraped helmet was a sad sight. The bag Emma put beside it on the end of his bed was a surprise. He hadn't noticed that the paramedics on the scene had taken it from the pannier of the bike.

The flap of the soft rucksack flopped open as Emma put it down and the bright green Christmas paper with a cheerful snowman print could be clearly seen.

Emma hadn't missed it. She seemed frozen to the spot as she stared at it and when she raised her gaze, she looked almost shocked.

'You've got a *Christmas* present in your bag?'

Had it always been so obvious that he was a complete Scrooge? That he loathed the festive season, and the big day in particular, so much that he wouldn't touch it with a ten-foot bargepole?

'It's just something for Lily,' he muttered. 'A bear that has stuff all over its clothes. Like zips and buttons and buckles. Apparently it's educational. And very popular.'

He couldn't decide whether Emma looked like she was about to laugh or cry.

Her voice sounded equally precarious.

'She'll love it. She's got the busiest little hands ever and she's at her happiest when she's trying to figure something out with them. It's…it's a perfect choice.'

Jack nodded but one of those words seemed to have

gone to his throat via his ears and was sitting there as a lump.

'She's…happy?'

'Always. Here…' Emma reached into the pocket of her scrubs and produced her phone. 'Mum took these tonight after I'd told her I couldn't get home when I'd thought I would.'

There was Lily, in a pink jacket, with silver tinsel in her hair and a big carrot in her hands. And then she'd looked up with the proudest grin on her face and that had been captured in the next photo.

Jack couldn't identify the wash of emotion that flooded his senses. Those dark curls… That joyous grin…

She looked so like Ben had looked as a child.

And Ben had been his own mirror image.

He couldn't begin to articulate how he felt—it was too big.

'What's with the carrot?' he queried, his voice gruff.

'It's for the reindeer. It's one of those things you do on Christmas Eve. You put carrots and water out for the reindeer and some milk and cookies for Santa.'

'Oh…of course… I'd forgotten.' Or he'd tried to. Hadn't he and Ben watched through a window one year when the 'real' kids in that foster family had got to do exactly that?

Focusing on something as trivial as a carrot hadn't made the big feeling get any smaller.

'Can you find my wallet in there? In the side pocket?'

Emma looked puzzled but did as he asked. Jack opened the old, leather flap and then searched for an internal pocket he hadn't touched for a very long time. The scrap of photographic paper he pulled out was creased and had tattered edges but the image was still perfectly clear. Two small boys, in their Sunday best, standing hand-in-hand on a London bridge.

'It was our fifth birthday,' he told Emma as he handed her the photo. 'Mum took us to see the sights in London as our birthday treat. She died not long after that.' It felt painful to swallow. 'It's the only photo I've still got from our childhood.'

'Oh, *Jack*...' There was no doubt that tears were winning any battle for Emma right now. 'Look at you both... Lily's got your smile. Exactly the same hair...'

'She's a Reynolds, all right...'

He could identify that big feeling now. It was recognising a bond of limitless power. The kind of bond he'd had with Ben as a child that had meant he would never be alone in a huge and terrifying world. A bond that had given his life a meaning it would never have otherwise had as an adult.

The bond of family.

Love...

Was it possible that he loved Lily?

He hadn't seen her in so long. She'd been no more than a distressed and miserable baby and the only feeling he'd had coming through the onslaught of grief had been...fear. Fear that he couldn't deal with the overwhelming responsibility that had just been dumped into his life.

Fear that he could never even begin to love her because he'd just been reminded of what it was like to lose the people that you loved...

And yet, here he was, feeling the stirrings of that kind of love without even trying. It was just there...

He had to clear his throat. 'She's beautiful,' he said softly. 'And she does look *so* happy.' His gaze held Emma's. 'How can I ever thank you for what you've done?'

'You don't have to,' Emma said. 'I made a promise to

Sarah that I would never have broken. I didn't realise it at the time, but it was the most amazing gift I could have ever received. I couldn't imagine life without Lily now.'

She caught her lip with her teeth, as if she could hear the echo of her vehement threat of not letting Jack take Lily away from her. There was something very different showing on her face now. Something very vulnerable.

'Actually...there is a way you can thank me.'

'Tell me.'

The deep breath that Emma took advertised that this was something huge but if he could do it, he would.

'You could be part of her life. Maybe even enough to be the father figure she's going to need.'

Oh, man... This was even bigger than he'd imagined. Despite the fear she'd displayed when she'd thought he was coming back to try and take Lily away from her, she was prepared to open a door into her life and invite him in?

She trusted him.

And that felt as big as the concept of taking on a role as a father figure.

Too big?

There was a voice in the back of his head, telling him that this was the time to warn Emma he was only here to visit. To make peace so he could move on with the rest of his life.

But there was another voice. A much softer one. So soft that it was more of a sensation than a sound. And it was asking him how on earth he thought he could move on and...and leave his family behind...

Emma clearly sensed that he needed space to absorb her suggestion.

'You good to go? I'm supposed to have this resus area cleared by now.'

Jack nodded and she folded the flap of the rucksack to cover the brightly wrapped gift.

'I'm sorry I didn't bring a gift for you,' he said as he felt the bed start to move. 'I'm not good at this Christmas stuff yet.'

'Oh, but you did, Jack.' Emma's smile was the loveliest he'd ever seen. 'You brought yourself.'

CHAPTER FOUR

THE DECORATIONS IN the corridor leading to the coronary care unit made Emma smile.

Long strands of green tinsel had been attached to the pale walls in the shape of an ECG trace of a heart rhythm. Whenever a green length ended, red tinsel had been used to make a heart shape.

Very Christmassy, but it wasn't going to offend anyone with over-the-top jolliness if they were on their way to visit a loved one who was critically ill with a heart condition.

The joy of the season was very much with Emma as she slipped quietly into the private room at the end of the unit, where Stuart Cameron lay resting on the bed. The steady, soft beep of the cardiac monitor was as reassuring as the smile coming from this patient.

Emma took hold of his hand as she sat on the chair beside the bed, carefully avoiding the IV port taped into place. It was a long moment before she could trust herself to speak.

'Don't ever give me a fright like that again, Stu.'

'I won't, lass.' He squeezed her fingers before letting go of her hand. 'Sorry about that. What a night to choose, hmm?'

'Mmm. They tell me you're doing very well, though.

Your enzymes are dropping fast and your ECG looks almost normal again. Any chest pain?'

'I thought you came here as a visitor, not a doctor.'

Emma grinned. 'As if you wouldn't be giving me the third degree if it was you visiting me.'

'That's the downside of being a doctor sometimes, isn't it? Often it's more about who we are than what we do.'

'Which is why you never retired when you were supposed to.'

Stuart shrugged. 'It's my life. I don't intend to stop now, either. With the new set of pipes they've given me, I'll probably be good to go for another ten years.'

Emma shook her head. It wasn't the time to suggest that the stress of running an extraordinarily busy emergency department might not be the best way to continue his contribution to medicine.

'How's it going down there? I've been lying here worrying about you.'

'Well, you can stop doing that right now. We're under control, obviously, or I wouldn't have been able to escape up here for a bit. Alistair stayed on, bless him. He's a great right-hand man. He'll page me if anything else big comes in.'

'Anything else? What's come in so far?'

'Ah…' Emma wanted nothing more than to confide in this man who was a real father figure for her, but she wasn't about to give him any unnecessary stress. He needed to rest. 'We got a couple of stabbed Santas a while back. A turf war in the middle of town about who had the right to sell the twinkly earrings and necklaces, apparently. Oh, and those reindeer horns with the flashing stars—you know the ones?'

Stuart snorted. 'I've seen them.'

'Anyway. One had an arterial bleed that Alistair had to control with forceps and then tie off and while he was doing that, the other one crashed with a rather dramatic tension pneumothorax. I got dragged in and ended up demonstrating a finger thoracostomy for my new registrar.'

'Successful?'

'Textbook. He's since put a drain in himself. He's doing well.'

Stuart's glance was shrewd. 'What was it that you had to get dragged away from?'

Emma's glance slid sideways. 'Nothing important. Motorcycle MVA. He's okay. Bit bumped and bruised. I'm just keeping him in to watch for any signs or symptoms of a head injury.'

She was trying to keep her voice light enough to make the report completely impersonal but Stuart knew her too well.

'What's going on, Emma? There's something you're not telling me.'

She summoned a smile. 'I didn't come here to give you something to worry about, you know. It's nothing.'

'If you don't tell me, I'm going to lie here and worry even more. Given everything I've seen in the far too many years I've been doing this job, I can assure you that my imagination will conjure up far worse things than whatever is bothering you probably deserves.'

Emma started to get out of her chair but then sank down again, biting her lip. 'I guess you're going to hear about it soon enough anyway, given how fast gossip goes along the grapevine around here.'

'Everybody tells me everything.' Stuart nodded. His smile was almost mischievous. 'And if they don't tell me what I want to know, I'll go and find out for myself. If you disappear now, I'll give Alistair a call before you've had time to get back downstairs. Or maybe Caroline…' He nodded slowly. 'Yes…she always knows what's going on.'

'It's not that big a deal,' Emma said hurriedly. 'Honestly. It was a bit of a shock that it happened today, that's all.'

'That what happened?'

'Jack Reynolds is back,' Emma said quietly. 'He was the motorbike accident victim.'

The beeping of the monitor beside her didn't change its tempo or rhythm and Emma felt herself relaxing into the silence that followed her words. What took her by surprise was that Stuart's hand covered her own and gave it a pat. Looking up, she could see that he understood exactly how hard that had been for her and that he was ready to give her whatever support she might need.

That was enough to bring tears to her eyes.

'Oh, lass…what a day to have chosen, hmm?'

'He says that's why he came. Because it's Christmas and…and he wants to make peace…'

Stuart closed his eyes, nodding slowly. The hint of a smile touched his lips. 'At last… I'm so pleased about that.'

'Why do you say that?'

The older consultant opened his eyes again. 'He's a good man, at heart. I always knew that. He had his demons—more than most—but I had a feeling he'd be back to do the right thing one of these days.'

'The right thing?' It was Emma's heart that was speeding up after missing a beat. 'He swore he hasn't come to take Lily away from me…'

'I mean making peace. He has to do it for himself if he's not going to be fighting the demons forever but he can't do that without making peace with the most important people in his life.'

'Lily…'

'And you…'

Emma couldn't meet his gaze. 'I'm not important. I was the best friend of his brother's wife, that's all.'

'Oh, lass…don't you go trying to pull any wool over *my* eyes. Do you think I didn't notice that extra sparkle in your eyes back then? The way you and Jack used to look at each other whenever you were in the department together? You didn't actually need to be looking at each other, come to that. The electricity in the air was enough to make my skin tingle.'

'Oh, no…' Emma could feel her cheeks colouring. 'Do you think everybody knew?'

'On the contrary, I know they didn't.' The pat on her hand was reassuring rather than sympathetic this time. 'And I know that because it never hit the grapevine. Not sure how it got past Caroline, mind you…but there you go. Maybe it was because I knew you so well.'

How mortifying was it to think that Stuart had seen so much? Had he guessed that she had been stupid enough to fall in love with the Eastern's heartbreaker when everyone knew that Jack wasn't capable of a long-term commitment?

And, if he had guessed—because he knew her so well—had Sarah guessed too?

No… Emma would probably have to think about it again later to reassure herself properly but Sarah couldn't have known. The spark between herself and Jack might have ignited at Ben and Sarah's wedding but nothing had happened before the newlyweds had gone off to start their new life in London so Sarah hadn't been around to notice anything different about her.

And that last night?

An illicit affair was the last thing any of them had been thinking about and the only sparkle in her eyes that night would have been due to the bright lights of the emergency department being reflected in her tears...

Right now, a change of subject was most definitely called for.

'Jack asked me to pass on his best wishes to you. He said that he owed you a big apology, too, but he'd do that in person.'

'I never really thought he intended seeing patients that day, you know.'

'No. I didn't either. But he shouldn't have come here.'

'I don't think he had anywhere else to go. He was desperate to find a way through all that grief.' Stuart sighed heavily. 'I've always felt I did the wrong thing, coming down so hard on him. I should have been kinder.'

'He was too angry to accept kindness. God knows, I tried and he kept pushing me away.'

'Everybody has to find their own way through grief, I guess. To lose a twin must be dreadful and those boys didn't have the best start in life, did they?'

'I've never heard the whole story—just bits that Sarah told me. That their mother died when they were five and that they ended up being separated into different foster homes. They both misbehaved until they got sent to some home for the kids that nobody wanted and then they turned their lives around. They both got scholarships to go to med school and...and the rest everybody knows about.'

'It's an extraordinary story.'

Emma nodded. But there were too many gaps in that story. Huge gaps that might explain Jack's demons and offer insight into how someone could help.

Someone like herself...

There was only one person who could fill in those gaps, though, and it wasn't something Jack had ever talked about.

Maybe because they'd never done much talking during their stolen time together. Oh, no… Flashes of memory were touching Emma's senses.

That look in Jack's eyes that told her he was about to kiss her senseless…

The way her skin came alive with that first touch of his hands…

That every time always felt like the first time all over again, only better…

Perhaps it was just as well she had closed her eyes as soon as she'd felt the memories ambush her. Stuart didn't seem to have noticed.

'Where's he been for the last year?'

'I don't know. I haven't asked him.'

Stuart's eyes were drifting shut and Emma knew it was time to leave him to rest. His quiet words as she got to her feet sounded like he was talking to himself rather than her.

'I hope he didn't walk away from medicine. We can't afford to lose that kind of young talent and passion.'

And then Stuart opened his eyes and smiled at Emma. 'Talk to him, lass. You're a lot more important to him than you might think you are.'

The morphine had worn off and Jack's aches and pains were making their presence felt.

His arm didn't feel too bad now that the raw skin had been well dressed and the ice and elevation was definitely helping his leg but that bruising on his chest made it painful to take a deep breath and Jack's head was throbbing.

He wasn't about to complain, however.

Jack Reynolds knew exactly how lucky he was. The odds of coming out of a crash like that alive were low enough, let alone with what could only be considered minor injuries.

He couldn't sleep. The light might have been dimmed in this side room he was now occupying but he could still hear the sounds of a busy emergency department and it pushed buttons that were deeply ingrained now. He should be in the thick of it, helping—not lying around taking up valuable space.

A junior doctor called Pete was coming in at regular intervals to run through the standard neurological checks that were required for a patient under observation for a possible head injury but Jack was waiting for someone more senior to pay him a visit.

Emma...

He wanted to see more pictures of Lily on her phone. He wanted to ask so many questions. Was she talking yet? Walking well? Had she had all her vaccinations?

And who took care of Lily while Emma was at work?

Did she have a partner?

She wouldn't have avoided a new relationship because of him, would she?

'I've been hoping—every day—that this *might be the day I'd hear something...'*

For Lily's sake, Jack told himself.

But what if it wasn't just for Lily's sake?

And why did thinking about Emma and the way she'd looked when she'd whispered those words give him that same, overwhelming sensation of a family connection that he'd had in looking at that faded image of his childhood? Of recognising the likeness that Lily had to his twin. To himself.

The confusing swirl of his thoughts was making his headache worse. Jack closed his eyes, only to have to open them again and have them raked with a bright light when Pete bustled back into the room only seconds later.

'Pupils still equal and reactive.'

'Good to know.'

'Do you know what time of day it is?'

'Must be about two a.m. by now.'

'Yeah…' Pete was looking weary. 'Merry Christmas, mate.'

They exchanged a wry smile, acknowledging that there was nothing particularly merry about the day for either of them, so far.

'Things still busy out there?'

'Not too bad. I might even catch forty winks soon if I'm lucky.'

'What's Emma doing?'

'She took a break and went up to see how Stuart Cameron's getting on. She should be back soon.'

'I'm back now.'

The sound of Emma's voice was more welcome than Jack had expected. A tension he hadn't been aware of was loosening its grip on his muscles and he could feel his face softening into a smile.

But Emma's attention was on Pete, who had stepped closer and lowered his voice. Jack shouldn't have been able to overhear the conversation so clearly but the bump on his head had given him more than just a headache. His hearing seemed to be hyperacute as well.

'Can you have a look at the patient in the paediatric corner when you've got a minute? Four-year-old boy. I think we might have to call Social Services in.'

'Oh, no… Why?'

'His aunt brought him in. She said he was running a temperature and thought it might be measles.'

Jack watched the way Emma instantly focused on what was being said to her. He could almost see her brain turning over other possibilities and their implications.

'The houseman decided the multiple facial lesions were due to impetigo but then she found some more on his back and limbs. And they're all the same size...'

'Cigarette burns?' Emma looked as if she was experiencing something physically painful herself and, weirdly, the pain seemed contagious. This ache in Jack's chest had nothing to do with his bruised ribs.

And all he wanted to do was to take Emma in his arms and hug her. Or touch her face, perhaps, and smooth away those lines of distress.

'I reckon. No, actually, I'm positive. I've seen it before.' Pete sighed. 'Poor kid.'

'Where are his parents?'

'Still at some Christmas party, apparently. The aunt's a bit cagey.'

Emma nodded. 'Make sure they don't leave before someone from Child Protection gets here. It might take a while at this time of night.'

'I'll say that we need to run some more tests.'

'Tell the aunt that it's very important that they stay where they are. Say that if it's measles there are very strict quarantine regulations. And come and find me when someone gets here. Things might get a bit nasty.'

Jack might have expected Emma to follow Pete from the room but, instead, Emma came and sat down in the chair beside his bed. For a long moment, she sat there with her eyes shut, as if she was gathering her strength or refocusing. Sure enough, when she looked up, Jack felt as if he was the most important thing on her mind.

'How are you feeling?'

'I'm fine.'

'Pain level? That morphine must have worn off by now.'

'It's nothing a couple of paracetamol tablets couldn't cope with.'

'I'll get you some.'

'No, stay where you are for a minute. You look exhausted.'

'Mmm. I am a bit.'

There was a shadow in her eyes that was more than physical fatigue. Did she need a break before having to handle a case that might involve removing a child from its family?

Having to interact with people from Social Services and Child Protection?

That was going to stir memories from last year that would be difficult because they marked the point where Emma had apparently become his enemy instead of his lover.

The point at which his life had begun a downward spiral he hadn't been able to control.

That scene was one he would never forget. The bodies of both Ben and Sarah had been taken away and Jack had been left standing in the emergency department with no clue of what to do next. Or where to go.

Emma had had Lily in her arms, trying to comfort a baby who'd wanted only her mother.

Someone from Child Protection had arrived.

'We can't simply let anyone take a baby who's just been orphaned. We have to be sure that she's going to be properly cared for.'

'That's me. I promised her mother. I'll take care of her.'

'But you're not a relative. There's a process that has to be followed.'

Something had snapped inside Jack. His brother had been snatched from his life and now some stranger was about to snatch his brother's child. To put her into a foster home? No way was he going to let history repeat itself like that. He'd never been so furious.

'She's my brother's child. Now she's mine.'

It only took a split second for the flash of memory but Jack couldn't let them grow. It was the last place he wanted to drag Emma back to.

He had to find a distraction, for both their sakes.

With an effort, he found something. 'How's Stuart?'

Emma's smile said it all. 'He's as good as new. Better, probably. They put in three stents and he's heading towards normal baselines.'

'He's lucky he was in the right place at the right time.'

Emma nodded. 'He's really pleased to hear that you're back.' Her gaze held his. 'He asked where you'd been for the last year and I had to say I didn't know. Where *have* you been, Jack?'

'Africa.'

Emma's jaw dropped. 'Really?'

'I joined Médecins Sans Frontières. I've been at a base in South Sudan for most of the time.'

He had certainly distracted Emma from the next case she had to deal with. She was still looking astonished.

'That must have been an extraordinary experience.' Now she was frowning. 'And a dangerous one?'

It was written all over her face that she hated the idea that he'd been in real danger. Again, Jack felt the curious warmth of realising that someone genuinely cared about his safety. About *him*.

'Our hospital did get shelled once—in the first week I was there, in fact.'

And he'd kept working right through the attack, ignoring the danger. He was living in a world without Ben, so what did it matter?

It hadn't occurred to him that the news would have got back to Emma. That she would have had to grieve for him on top of everything she was having to cope with herself.

He wanted to apologise. No. He wanted to do more than that. Suddenly, it was important that she understood.

'I needed to be somewhere where everybody's problems were so much bigger than my own.'

The tilt of Emma's head was a subtle nod. Her voice was soft. 'Because it forced you to think about others instead of yourself. To keep putting one foot in front of another and moving forward until, one day, you found you were looking over your shoulder at the dark place instead of having it all around you.'

He held her gaze. Oh, man…she understood perfectly. His own voice cracked a little.

'Is that what looking after Lily did for you?'

Another nod. 'At first I was going through the motions. Just doing what had to be done, and I wouldn't have managed that if I hadn't had my mum to help. I didn't know any more about looking after babies than you did and… and it seemed like we both spent most of the time crying.'

And he hadn't been here to help.

He couldn't have helped even if he had been.

'But then…' Emma's face came alive. 'One day, I went in to pick her up because she was sobbing and she stopped crying and…and smiled at me…'

Emma was smiling now, too. 'That was the moment I realised I'd fallen completely in love with her. That she had brought something magic into my life.'

It was Jack's turn to nod slowly. 'And I fell in love with my job in Africa. With being able to do small things that made such a huge difference to people's lives—like repairing a fistula from a complicated childbirth that meant that a young woman wouldn't be ostracised because she was incontinent. Or vaccinating babies so they wouldn't die from something preventable like meningitis or measles.'

'I'll bet you did a lot of big things, too. I've read about the kinds of challenges doctors face in places like that.'

There was admiration shining in Emma's eyes and Jack found himself sitting up straighter even though he was sure he hadn't actually moved.

Yes, he'd done things he could be very proud of. Some incredibly difficult surgeries on people who had been horrendously injured in nearby conflicts. He'd lost count of the number of lives he'd saved, sometimes working in the most difficult conditions imaginable.

There had been enormous satisfaction to be found in those successes but it was only now that Jack could feel the pride in what he'd done. To realise that the experience had made him a better man. To feel that he wanted to continue that journey so that Emma would always admire him like this.

So that Lily would be proud of her uncle. Her father's brother...

'Will you go back?'

The question was tentative. Jack had the impression that, if he said 'yes', Emma would admire him for that decision.

He had been intending to do exactly that. Not to the same place, mind you, because he didn't do attachment—to places or people.

But now...

'I don't know,' he said, trying to choose his words carefully. 'I don't know what there might be here for me now. Or whether it's what I want for my future. I just know that I…did things I'm not proud of. I need to try and put them right.'

The breath Emma was holding still didn't want to come out.

Partly because it felt trapped by the ring of pride she was feeling for Jack. His own life had been destroyed to a point where he couldn't face being in it anymore and what had he done? He'd taken himself somewhere isolated and dangerous and devoted himself to helping people that were in an even more hopeless situation.

What had Stuart said?

'He's a good man, at heart. I always knew that.'

Everybody knew that Jack Reynolds was a brilliant surgeon but opinions of him as a man were far less flattering. People thought he was shallow. Selfish, even. A playboy who couldn't care less about the damage he might do to the lives of others as he did exactly what *he* wanted to do.

None of it was true.

Okay, he had commitment issues but he'd never been less than honest about not wanting anything long term.

And he did care. Too much, perhaps, which might be why commitment was such a terrifying prospect.

He was more than a good man in Emma's eyes.

Jack Reynolds was a hero.

She had heard the undertone of those carefully chosen words. Jack hadn't intended coming back here for anything more than a visit.

But now he wasn't sure.

Something had changed.

And, judging by the way he was looking at her right now, that something had a lot to do with her.

The breath was still trapped. Because when she released it, what words might come out?

She'd already told him that his coming back was the best Christmas gift he could ever have given her. Saying anything more could be a mistake. Jack was standing at what could be the biggest crossroads his life was ever going to present but the choice of which direction he took next had to be entirely his own.

'Dr Matthews?' The urgency in the voice of the nurse behind her was unmistakable. 'You're needed. Curtain Four.'

Her breath came out in a whoosh.

'Coming…'

CHAPTER FIVE

ONE LOOK AT the young woman lying on the bed behind Curtain Four was enough to tell Emma she had walked into a medical emergency. Pete, the young Australian registrar, was pulling the pillows from beneath her head to lay her flat.

'What's going on?'

'She's not breathing…' Pete tilted the woman's head back to open her airway. 'The crash cart's on its way.'

He was putting his fingers on the woman's neck to check for a pulse but Emma knew there was little point. You only had to look at the skin colour to know that this was a cardiac arrest. She put her foot on the control that lowered the bed and immediately positioned herself at the side, her hands on the middle of the woman's chest to start compressions.

'How long has she been like this?'

'I don't know.' Pete was looking distressed. 'She was asleep. Her boyfriend went home a while ago.' He had a bag mask in his hands now, waiting for Emma to pause her compressions.

'Twenty-eight, twenty-nine, thirty…' Emma stilled her hands to let Pete deliver two breaths.

'How old is she?'

'Twenty-nine.'

Emma could feel the tension around her increasing. Or maybe it was coming from within herself. Twenty-nine? This woman was younger than she was. She wasn't going to die on her watch if there was anything Emma could do about it.

'How did she present?'

'Epigastric pain. It didn't seem too bad but it wasn't going away. I decided to send her for a scan but they've been a bit swamped so it's been a long wait.'

Something like guilt added a new layer to the awful tension.

'You told me about her… You asked me to have a look. Ages ago…' Emma's brain was replaying the brief conversation in her head. 'You were bothered about something…'

'I didn't know what, though. It didn't seem urgent but that's why I didn't send her home.'

'Thank goodness for that.'

If this had happened out of hospital, the chances of survival would have been virtually zero. Even here, the chances probably weren't that great but Emma wasn't about to let that thought surface.

The rattle of wheels advertised the arrival of the trolley with the life pack that was urgently needed. Pete attached electrodes while Emma kept up her steady compressions. She waited until the machine beeped into life and she could see the jagged lines on the screen and then lifted her hands to let the artefact settle so they could determine whether there was a rhythm.

Any rhythm would be better than a straight line because then they could shock this young woman and potentially save her life in an instant.

You couldn't shock a straight line.

And you couldn't shock what looked like a slow but relatively normal rhythm, either. This looked like a rhythm that should be providing a pulse but it wasn't. It was pulse-less electrical activity.

'Looks like PEA,' Emma said. 'Let's get her into Resus.'

'They're full.' The nurse who'd delivered the monitor shook her head. 'Alistair's got a kid with a severe asthma attack in Resus One that's just gone into respiratory arrest and there's a stroke patient in Resus Two. They're both being put on ventilators.'

'Fine.' Emma gritted her teeth. 'We'll have to cope here, then. Pete—take over compressions. I'm going to intubate.'

The noise level was increasing steadily and Jack could sense a new tension in the department's atmosphere.

He couldn't just lie here and listen to it.

He couldn't go out and see what was going on either. Not in a hospital gown that was probably gaping at the back.

But his rucksack was sitting in the corner of the room—beside the pile of now useless leather bike clothes and a badly scratched helmet—and he had a full set of street clothes in there. All he needed were his jeans and a T-shirt.

A moment's dizziness when he got to his feet settled back into the headache he was getting used to. It hurt to put weight on his injured leg but the compression bandage was enough support to be able to move and it was no trouble to use his scraped arm to get dressed.

The dizziness returned when he got to the door of this side room and had to blink against the bright lights and take in the scene in front of him. For a moment, his gaze was caught by the flashing colours of the Christmas decorations on the triage desk but then he saw the stretchers waiting in front of it, the paramedics looking as if the night had already been too long.

It took a longer moment to adjust to the movement going on. People were going in all directions. A consultant he recognised, flanked by junior doctors, was disappearing into the resuscitation area he'd been in when he'd first arrived here. A nurse was hurrying towards a cubicle pushing an IV pole, with a bag of fluids in her free hand. Two security guards were pushing a loudly protesting and obviously very drunk man back towards another cubicle. A cleaner was mopping the floor. A technician rushed past him with a polystyrene bucket full of blood samples and a mother was walking back and forth not far away with a howling toddler in her arms.

Jack didn't need to hear an alarm sounding somewhere to see that this emergency department was on the brink of chaos.

There had to be some way he could help but where would he be the most useful?

In one of the two occupied resus areas for the critically ill patients? No, wait... It looked like something was going on in one of the curtained cubicles on the far side of the department. As a nurse pushed an IV trolley into the space, the curtain was pulled back far enough for Jack to see that CPR was in progress. Ignoring the pain in his leg, Jack headed for Curtain Four.

'You need to get a better seal with the mask. Try that breath again.'

Emma glanced up from her task of checking her gear for intubation as Pete spoke, immediately aware of several different things.

That Pete was delivering excellent compressions. That

he was concerned that the young nurse who had been given the task of delivering breaths via the bag mask was struggling and that someone else had come into the curtained cubicle.

Jack...

He was moving towards the head of the bed.

'I'll do that,' he told the nurse.

Pete was looking shocked. 'What are you doing out of bed?'

'I'm fine.' Jack had the mask firmly held between his thumb and forefinger. 'I could see that some help was needed.' The other fingers of his same hand were under the jaw of their patient, making sure the seal of the mask was perfect. With his other hand, he held the bag attached to the mask, waiting for Pete to pause the compressions so he could deliver a breath.

Emma could feel her own chest fall in a sigh of relief as she watched the rise and fall of her patient's chest.

'You sure you're up to this?' she asked quietly, meeting Jack's gaze for a heartbeat.

'I'm sure.'

The relief kicked up another notch. Jack had many years' more experience than Pete and...and everybody knew what a brilliant doctor he was. If she could have chosen anybody to face this challenge with her, it would have been Jack.

The light on her laryngoscope was working. The stylet was inside the endotracheal tube and the cuff was inflating. She was ready.

'Can you give me some suction, please?'

Jack delivered one more breath, cleared the mouth of any secretions with the suction unit and then moved out of the way. Emma tilted her patient's head back and positioned herself. She gave Pete the nod he was waiting for to interrupt the chest compressions. As she slid the laryngoscope blade into place, she took a breath herself and held it. Holding her own breath while her patient was without oxygen would let her know if her attempt was taking too long. The goal was to secure the airway within ten seconds if she could.

The tube slid into place through the vocal cords. She pulled the laryngoscope blade and then the stylet out before pushing the plunger on the attached syringe to inflate the cuff. Jack attached the bag to the end of the tube and squeezed it and they could both see the rise of the chest.

'Good job,' Jack murmured.

Emma said nothing. She hooked her stethoscope into her ears and placed the disc on one side of the chest and then the other as Jack squeezed the bag again. Finally she nodded, reaching for the plastic device that would stabilise the tube and ensure it didn't get displaced during the chest compressions that Pete was recommencing.

But he had already been doing the compressions for longer than the two minutes protocol demanded for efficacy.

'How's your arm?' she asked Jack. 'Do you think you can take over compressions?'

'Of course.'

'We need IV access, too.'

'You do that. I'll do compressions. Pete—you come and bag her.'

The small team shifted positions. Emma clicked a tourniquet into place, watching the screen during the brief pause.

'Still PEA,' she said.

'What's her name?' Jack asked.

'Melissa,' Pete answered. 'But her boyfriend calls her Mel.'

'She's very young…'

'Twenty-nine.'

Emma caught Jack's gaze again. The briefest of glances but she knew he was as determined as she was to save this young woman.

They both knew how devastating it could be to lose someone so young. Mel had a boyfriend. Probably a whole family who were unaware of this catastrophic development and were probably expecting her to come home within hours to share their Christmas celebrations.

'There has to be a reversible cause,' Emma said. 'There *has* to be…'

'How did she present?'

'Epigastric pain.'

'Poisoning? An anaphylactic reaction to something?'

Emma slid the cannula into place and taped it down. 'I don't think so. We can rule out hypothermia, hypovolaemia and a tension pneumothorax, too.'

The list of potentially reversible causes was getting shorter. As Emma reached up to move the small wheel on the IV line and start fluids running, her gaze caught Jack's.

'Thrombosis,' they both said at the same time.

Emma's gaze flew to Pete. 'Has she been on any long-haul flights recently?'

'Not that she mentioned.'

'Is she on an oral contraceptive?'

'Yes.' Pete's eyes widened. 'It's the only medication she takes.'

Emma looked back at Jack. 'Abdominal pain is an unusual presentation.'

'But not unheard of.'

'No.' For the first time Emma felt a glimmer of hope. They could potentially do something about this. The flash in Jack's eyes told her he was thinking the same thing. More than that, it was all the encouragement she needed to pull out all the stops and tackle this head-on. They could do this…together…

'Pete?' Emma reached to take hold of the bag. 'Go and grab the transoesophageal echo from Resus One.'

'Are you thinking thrombolysis or surgical embolectomy?' Jack asked.

'I'm thinking anything and everything right now,' Emma responded. She squeezed the bag to deliver another breath. 'I just hope we're right…'

Jack focused on his compressions again but he could feel that Emma was still watching his face. He had to resist the urge to look back at her. To see that hope in her eyes. That confidence that they could do this if they did it together.

To feel that connection that made him want to shift heaven and earth to give her exactly what she wanted.

To see that hope morph into joy.

He channelled the edge that these unfamiliar emotions created into doing the best he could with the task he was responsible for. He kept his arms straight with his weight balanced over them so he could keep going for as long as necessary without tiring. He pressed hard enough to make sure the pressure was squeezing enough blood from the heart. Fast enough to ensure there was enough circulating oxygen to keep this young woman's brain alive.

He tried to keep his own breathing steady too and kept his lips pressed together so that nobody would guess how painful it was to keep standing on his injured leg or that his head was throbbing with the physical effort.

'You need a break,' Emma said, a minute later. 'I'll take over compressions.'

But Jack didn't pause. 'Have you used TEE before?'

Emma nodded. 'A few times now. We got trained by Cardiology. They use it to rule out clots before converting atrial arrhythmias.'

'Then I'll keep going. Pete can take over when he gets back.'

Except that Pete was looking worried when he got back. 'Everything's hitting the fan out there right now. Can you cope without me for a few minutes?'

A glance at the nurse who was looking terrified at the prospect of taking over compressions was enough to elicit a terse response from Jack.

'Yes,' he said. 'Go.'

Emma must have seen the look on the nurse's face as well.

'Go to the drug cupboard,' she told her. 'We need drugs to deal with a clot, if that's what's causing this. We'll need TPA. Alteplase or tenecteplase. Get someone to check it with you.'

The ultrasound probe was on the end of a long, flexible tube that Emma could easily slip into their patient's mouth and down into the oesophagus.

'The beauty of this is that you don't need to stop compressions,' she told Jack. 'We can still get a clear picture. Look at that...' She angled the probe. 'You can see the valves opening and closing. And if I put the colour flow on...' For a moment she watched the movement of the red and blue on the screen. 'You're doing fantastic compressions, Jack. The flow looks almost normal.'

For a moment, pride wiped out any physical discomfort Jack was feeling. He was doing a good job. They were doing a good job. And the skill Emma was demonstrating in using this sophisticated equipment shouldn't be a surprise but it was certainly impressive.

He was proud of *her*, too.

'Oh, my God…' Emma breathed. 'Look…'

The rhythm of Jack's compressions didn't alter as he turned his head and focused on the screen.

'Is that what I think it is?'

'It's a massive clot. Moving from the right atrium into the ventricle.'

The nurse was back with the drugs needed to break down the clot that was stopping Mel's heart from working. Emma injected the first dose and then took over compressions from Jack.

Minutes ticked by as they kept up the resuscitation effort. Five minutes and then ten. He could see by the determined lines on Emma's face that her arms were aching more each time she took over the compressions. It was Jack who finally glanced up at the clock. 'How long has she been down?'

'Twenty-five minutes.'

The glance Emma gave him was shocked. Did she think that Jack was going to suggest they give up this resuscitation? That he was going to walk away from this team effort?

Of course he wasn't.

'Swap,' he said, his shoulder pressing against hers as he moved into place to take over. 'Are you going to give a second bolus?'

Emma nodded, reaching for the syringe that was already loaded with the second dose of the clot buster.

It was past the time when Jack would have expected Emma to insist on changing over the task of compressions but she had her hand on the echocardiography probe again, clearly wanting to see whether there had been any change first.

Jack watched the frown on her face deepen as she changed the angle of the probe.

'I can't see it…the clot… I can't see it…'

'Maybe it's gone…'

'Stop compressions for a sec.'

Emma looked like she was holding her breath. She pushed a button that put the colour flow mode on. His hands were nowhere near Mel's chest but there was movement on the screen. Valves opening and closing. Blood flowing…

Emma's lips were parted as she looked up at the ECG monitor. Jack knew exactly how she was feeling.

That she couldn't believe what she was actually seeing. The trace looked like it had before—almost normal—but now it wasn't just electrical activity with no result. There was blood flowing again.

Had they won this fierce battle?

As if to dispel any lingering doubt, Mel's chest heaved as she took her first breath unaided. And then another…

They both looked up at exactly the same moment.

At each other.

Emma's lips were trembling, hovering on the brink of a joyous smile, but it was the expression in her eyes that caught Jack's heart and made it squeeze so hard it hurt.

We did it, that expression said. *You and me—we've made a miracle happen, haven't we?*

He didn't need to say anything. He simply held that gaze. And smiled.

It was Emma who finally broke that memorable moment, gently removing the echo probe. 'We need to get Mel up to Intensive Care. Keep her sedated and on the

ventilator until we're sure we're out of the woods. And…
and we need to get hold of her family.'

'I'll do that.' The face of the young nurse who'd been
helping was a picture of sheer relief. 'Shall I get the ICU
consultant paged?'

'Yes, please.' Emma had her gaze back on the monitor now, her fingers on their patient's wrist as she felt her
pulse. The joy in her eyes had faded when she looked
away again. 'Do you think she'll have any neurological
damage, Jack? It took such a long time…'

'I don't know,' he had to admit. 'We won't know until
we wake her up. But she's young and we did the best CPR
we could have done. What I do know is that if we hadn't
done what we did, she wouldn't even be alive right now.'

Emma nodded. 'And it's Christmas Day,' she said
softly. 'I don't think it's too much of an ask for a bit more
of a miracle. That would be the best gift ever for her family, wouldn't it? And her boyfriend.'

Jack could only nod. That pain in his chest that was
purely emotional was sharp now.

To snatch life back from the jaws of death would indeed be the most amazing Christmas gift.

If only it could have been given to him last year.

And to Emma…

But it hadn't and that was just how it was. How life
was. Emma had moved forward and found something
positive in her love for Lily but that was just the type of
person she was. She gave and gave. She would do anything humanly possible to save the life of a complete
stranger, as she had just demonstrated, and she could
give all her love to a baby, even when every moment with
Lily must remind her of the pain of what she had lost.

She was a better person than he was.

Emma Matthews was…well, she was amazing.

Jack found himself stepping back and simply watching as Emma continued her efforts to make sure Mel got through this unexpected crisis as unscathed as possible. He watched her take an arterial blood sample to check the oxygen level and listened to her handover to the ICU team that arrived a short time later.

'Jack did most of the compressions,' she told them, 'and I could see the blood flow on the echo and it looked virtually normal.'

The ICU consultant glanced in his direction. And then took a second look.

'Jack Reynolds. I remember you...'

Jack cringed inwardly. Of course he did. Everybody remembered him and he would prefer that they didn't. How long had the gossip continued after he'd left?

But the consultant's next words surprised him. 'Your skills have been sadly missed around here,' was all he said. 'Your name still gets mentioned when some of our trauma patients need surgery. I hope you've come back to work.'

Emma didn't look at him but he knew she was listening for his answer. He could sense how still she had suddenly become.

He was feeling a bit of that stillness himself. He'd missed this, he realised. He'd thought that the satisfaction of making a difference to lives by doing small things under such difficult circumstances had been more important somehow but a life was a life, wasn't it? You could do so much more for people when you had all the resources of a major hospital around you. And...and maybe he'd had enough of the adrenaline rush of knowing that his own life could be in danger at any moment. Maybe, for the first time since he'd lost Ben, it felt like his own life mattered, too.

Because of Lily?

Because of Emma?

His head was aching again. Things he had thought were going to be the parameters of the rest of his life were shifting. Becoming confused…

Perhaps it was just as well that the arrival of Pete with the result of the blood gas level shifted the attention back to their patient before he had a chance to say anything. And then there was a flurry of activity as the transfer was begun and Mel started her journey up to the intensive care unit.

'I'll be up to check on her as soon as things quieten down around here,' Emma said.

Unexpectedly, things actually looked well under control when they finally left the cubicle that had been their only focus for so long. The resuscitation areas were empty and the doctors looked as if they were all busy doing the kind of things they had to do on top of face-to-face patient encounters. They would be reviewing past notes or lab results, examining X-rays or writing discharge summaries, perhaps. The only real activity was coming from the other side of the department—the paediatric corner— where Pete was standing beside a woman who was crying loudly. Wailing, in fact.

'*No-o-o*…you can't do this. You can't take him away…'

Emma's head turned sharply. Alistair rose swiftly from where he'd been sitting in front of a computer screen.

'I've got this,' he told Emma. 'I've already reviewed this case and been over it with the Child Protection people.'

'But I need—'

'This is the last case you need to get involved in right now,' Alistair told her. 'Take a break.'

Emma's eyes were wide. She looked…haunted?

Of course she was. She had been exactly where that woman was right now. Having a child she desperately wanted to keep in her arms taken away from her. And he hadn't helped, had he? In the short term, he'd made things worse for everybody involved.

Jack could see the tension in Alistair's body language. He hadn't been there that night but clearly he'd heard about it and he was trying to protect Emma.

And she was nodding slowly. 'I guess I do need a minute to myself,' she said quietly. 'I'll be in the office.'

She turned away without even looking at Jack.

He had to follow her but, as soon as he moved, he felt Alistair catch his arm.

'She needs a minute to herself, mate.'

Jack pulled his arm free of the touch. 'No.'

The muscles in his jaw felt almost too tight to let any words out. Alistair might think he knew the truth but he didn't know all of it and this was none of his business. This was about himself. And Emma. And everything that had happened between them. And it was time to try and put something right.

He was moving again. 'Actually, I think she needs a minute with *me*…'

CHAPTER SIX

HISTORY SEEMED BENT on repeating itself tonight.

The solitude of the office was initially a relief but a few seconds later Emma wondered if it had been a mistake to shut herself away like this.

There was nothing to distract her mind from slipping back in time.

To what had felt like the worst moment of her life.

Her best friend was gone forever, lying only a few feet away, and Emma was holding a baby who must have sensed that her life had just undergone a catastrophic change. Lily had been inconsolable. Words of comfort from someone who'd only seen her a couple of times before weren't going to help and, even if they could have, Emma couldn't get them past the wall of grief that was making her chest so tight it was hard to breathe. If she made any sound at all, it might not have been words. She might have started crying as desperately as Lily was.

It had taken an even deeper level of desperation to force her to speak. When she'd tried to explain that Sarah had begged her to care for her precious child and that she would do whatever it took to honour the promise she'd made.

'I promised her mother. I'll take care of her.'

But they'd taken Lily from her arms.

And Jack had been there. So furious.

'She's my brother's child. Now she's mine.'

Without realising it, Emma had wrapped her arms tightly around herself in the flash of time that was all it took for the memories to coalesce into fear again.

Just how much of history was repeating itself? The date. The accident. And now Child Protection officers were here…

Had Jack been telling the truth when he'd promised that he wasn't here to take Lily away from her?

'Emma…?'

The door had opened so quietly behind her that Emma hadn't heard it. Her name was no more than a whisper but she knew who'd slipped into this private space with her.

She didn't turn around but she could feel Jack step closer. He was right behind her. And then he did something she would never have expected, folding his arms around her body and holding her as tightly as she'd been holding herself. His body was a solid wall to lean on and then he dipped his head to touch it against hers.

Neither of them said anything but Emma could feel the fear begin to ebb.

She trusted this man.

More than trusted him. Okay, she'd known that it had been a mistake to fall in love with him but doing so hadn't been a conscious choice. The connection she'd felt had been so powerful it would have been easier to try and stop the sun rising than not to fall in love. And yes, in the long months of Jack's absence, she'd tried to convince herself that she was over him. That one day she would find someone else. Seeing him again had been enough to tell her she'd been kidding herself. Feeling his arms around her like this took things to a whole new level.

This was nothing like the memories she had of their passionate physical relationship—the way any touch could inflame an irresistible desire.

This was about comfort.

About caring.

It felt like…love.

Releasing a breath she hadn't realised she'd been holding, Emma felt her body loosening. Or maybe the hold of Jack's arms was loosening. Whatever it was, it made it easy to turn around. To put her head in the hollow where she could feel his heart beating. To wrap her own arms around him.

'I should never have done it,' Jack said quietly. 'I'm sorry, Red. I should never have taken Lily away from you that night. I could have stopped them trying to take her and told them you were the person I chose to care for my brother's child.'

'Why did you do it?' Emma whispered. 'Why were you so angry about me having her?'

'It wasn't you.'

Emma pulled back, so that she could see Jack's face. He looked as shattered as she was feeling. The memories were too raw for both of them, weren't they? But he also looked as if he was trying to find the words to explain something. Standing here in a small office wasn't exactly conducive to talking, though. Emma turned her head even though she knew there was nowhere to sit down other than the single chair pushed under the desk attached to the wall beneath a window.

Jack seemed to read her mind. Taking hold of her hand, he sank down to sit on the floor, with his back against a tall bookshelf crammed with textbooks and medical journals, and Emma followed his lead. She leaned her head back against the bookshelf, closing her eyes as she let her breath out in a sigh.

'What was it, Jack? What made you so angry? Were you blaming yourself for the accident?'

'I don't think so. Not then. If anything, I think I was blaming Lily.'

Emma's intake of breath was a shocked gasp as she opened her eyes.

'Why?'

'If they hadn't had a baby, they wouldn't have been coming here. They wouldn't have been so determined to show me how wrong I was.'

'I don't understand.' Still shocked at the notion of blaming an innocent baby, Emma could feel herself trying to pull away from Jack. To remove her hand from beneath his. But he tightened his grip, just enough to hold her.

'They had everything. Ben and Sarah. They were so much in love and now they had a family. Everything I'd convinced myself was the last thing I would ever want.'

A peculiar sensation in Emma's chest felt heavy but sharp at the same time. A dream that was finally dying?

'And it was Christmas and that made it worse because it's the time when everybody celebrates having a family.'

'But isn't that what everyone wants? Family…and love?'

'Of course it is. Unless they've been there before and they know the pain of losing it. That feeling that the world has ended and that you will never be truly happy ever again. That black hole that has sides so tall you know you're never going to find a way to climb out.'

The discomfort in Emma's chest was different now. It felt like her heart was breaking.

'You'd lost Ben,' she said softly. 'Your only family.'

'It was more than that. When I saw those people from

the social services there, I felt like I was five years old again. It was my mother who'd gone and now they were going to take us away. And I could see the pain of what I knew had happened in the years ahead. Being taken away from Ben because nobody wanted to take twins. Being forced to live with strangers. People who pretended to care but they never did. Not really...' It sounded like it was painful for Jack to swallow.

'Is that why you hate Christmas so much?'

'It was always the worst time. It was the real children that got to do the special things like hang the decorations on the tree or put cookies out for Father Christmas. They got the special presents, too, like a new phone or a bike. I'd get the things that had to be provided anyway. Pencils and schoolbooks. A school uniform, one year. Everyone would tell me how lucky I was to have a family that would put up with me but I knew that my only real family was Ben and that he would be as miserable as I was.'

Emma could feel tears gather. She could see that little boy so clearly. Amongst people but so terribly alone. She wanted to reach back through time and cuddle him. To tell him that he would find people that would love him and cherish him. That he would experience the kind of happiness that only love could bring. But he had shut himself away from that, hadn't he? He'd convinced himself that it was the last thing he ever wanted.

As if he could read her thoughts, Jack released his breath in a long sigh.

'Even though there was part of me that was totally irrational and blaming Lily for what had happened, I wasn't going to let Ben's child suffer the same fate we had. I wasn't going to let them take her away.'

There was relief to be savoured now in the wake of understanding better. Jack had been trying to protect Lily that night. He was being honest in saying it wasn't about Emma. He'd been distraught and not thinking clearly but his automatic reaction had been to try and protect his niece.

'It was such a stupid thing to do,' Jack said. 'As if I knew anything about looking after a baby. Even with all the supplies and advice I got, there was no way I could have coped. You could see that when you came to visit after the funeral and that made it even worse. I felt like I'd done something dreadful. It wasn't just me at the bottom of that black hole—I'd dragged Lily into it as well.'

'I didn't help,' Emma said. 'I hate to say it but maybe at some level I *wanted* you to fail. So that I could take Lily and keep my promise to Sarah. I could have tried to make things easier for you, instead of being so horrified at the mess. Accusing you of drinking too much. Of putting Lily in danger…' Her breath hitched. 'I had no idea of how cruel I was being, threatening to report you if you didn't let me take her. I didn't have any idea how awful your childhood was. I'm sorry, Jack…'

'I don't blame you.' Jack's fingers closed around her hand. 'Thank goodness you were there. It was the right thing to do. I'm just sorry I made it so hard for you. Especially after you'd taken Lily and I was alone. I *was* drinking too much, then. I was sad and angry and I couldn't see a way past the mess that my life had suddenly become.'

'I was so scared you were going to come and take her back again. You had the right to do that.' Emma sucked in a deep breath, knowing how hard it was to say what had to be said. 'You're still the only real family that Lily's got. The only blood relative.'

'No.' Jack shook his head. '*You're* Lily's family. You're her mother and I know how much you love her. She's a very lucky little girl.'

'She needs you, too.'

'I don't think so.' But there was an edge of doubt in his words. 'She's managed better without me in her life so far, hasn't she?'

'That doesn't mean you wouldn't add something that no one else could give her. And *you* need her,' Emma persisted. 'You can't shut yourself away from caring about anybody, Jack. That's not living. Everybody needs someone special in their lives. Someone to care about.'

Maybe he did have someone, she thought, searching his face. Someone other than the patients he'd devoted his life to over the last year. She didn't really want to know but she needed to.

His gaze held hers. Could he see the unasked question? Was that almost imperceptible shake of his head an answer to that question?

'I care about you,' Jack said. 'I didn't realise how much I'd missed you until I saw you again. You're special, Red.'

Perhaps the dream hadn't really died. Or it was being resuscitated by the breeze of hope.

'I missed you, too, Jack,' she whispered. 'Every day.'

They could have been a world away from the emergency department they'd escaped from temporarily.

It felt like they were a world away from the grief and anger and pain of a year ago.

There had been forgiveness needed on both sides and it felt like it had been given and received already. That nothing more needed to be said.

Maybe it was because they had revisited such an emotional time for them both or that Jack had revealed more than he ever had about his past. Or maybe they had been holding each other's gaze for too long. Or perhaps it was because this small, dim space behind a closed door had given them a privacy they hadn't had since before any of the bad things had happened.

Whatever contributed to the alchemy didn't matter. They both moved at the same time, leaning towards each other so that their faces touched. Emma could feel Jack's nose pressed against her own, his forehead against hers, his lips soft against her cheek. Like a well-remembered slow dance, they both moved again. Their lips brushed gently—once, twice and then again—but this time they settled together and a whole new dance began.

Emma had never fully appreciated that such intense communication could be as subtle as the variations in pressure of lips against lips. Of the briefest touch of a tongue.

This was history repeating itself, too, because she would never forget the first time Jack had kissed her. It had been the first time they'd met properly—at Ben and Sarah's wedding, where she'd been the bridesmaid and Jack had been the best man. Sarah had warned her not to go near Jack and end up being one of his legendary list of broken hearts. Apparently Ben had issued a stern warning to Jack to stay away from her as well but the attraction had been instant and probably all the more attractive for being illicit. Emma had gone into the garden of the old house where the reception was being held for some fresh air. If she was honest, she'd gone looking for a private space, hoping that Jack would follow her. He had. And there, under the moonlight, with the scent of old-fashioned roses around them, he'd kissed her.

And it had been this delicious. That first time and every time after that.

But this was different.

They had a shared history now that went far beyond a physical connection neither of them had been able to resist. It was a history of heartbreak and grief and for-giveness. So this kiss felt both familiar and old but it also felt completely new.

They were different people.

But that physical connection hadn't changed a bit.

He had to stop this kiss.

It was making him remember things that were prob-ably best not remembered. The sweetness of being with Emma.

How hard it would have been to move on even though he'd known it had to happen. At least the accident and its terrible aftermath had ended things in a way that hadn't left her feeling that she was merely being brushed aside so that he could move on to something new. Someone else—the way he always did.

He'd known it wouldn't be that easy that time.

And there hadn't been anyone else. Not since Emma.

He hadn't even kissed another woman, but if he had, Jack knew it wouldn't have been anything like this.

It was so much more than just a kiss. It felt like her whole body was talking to him. Saying sweet things about how special he was. About how much she cared.

And this was the closest he had ever been able to get to saying things like that to her. A physical conversa-tion that was over as soon as the touching stopped and didn't need to be mentioned again.

Except he'd said it out loud, hadn't he? That he had missed her. That he cared...

With a sound a little too close to a groan, Jack broke the contact of his mouth with Emma's and pulled away.

His head was spinning. With memories of what it had always been like to be with Emma. With a fierce desire to go further and take them both into that space where nothing mattered but the intense pleasure of a physical conversation that would leave them both completely sated.

But there was confusion in the whirling thoughts as well. He'd said too much and even though it was true, it might make Emma hope for something that was totally impossible—like a declaration of love or a promise of commitment.

An echo of Emma's voice appeared through the fog being created in his brain. *'But isn't that what everyone wants? Family...and love?'*

Had he agreed with that? He couldn't remember a lot of what he'd said only minutes ago but he had the feeling he'd told her things about his childhood that he never told anybody. Things he did his best to not even remember himself.

It must be his head injury. Concussion could do strange things.

Jack tilted his head back against the bookshelf and closed his eyes. Screwed them tightly shut, in fact, making a determined effort to clear his head. Emma was sitting very quietly beside him but he couldn't look at her. He didn't want to make eye contact and see the effect that kiss might have had. He didn't want to look at her lips because that would only make him want to kiss her again.

'Are you all right?' Emma's question was quiet. Concerned. 'What's hurting?'

'Bit of a headache,' Jack admitted.

'I'll get you something for that. You're not feeling sick, are you?'

'No.'

'How's your leg? And your ribs?'

'I'll live.' Jack opened his eyes and summoned a smile.

Emma smiled back but there was a shadow in her eyes and, again, he heard an echo of her voice.

'You can't shut yourself away from caring about anybody, Jack. That's not living...'

He did care. He cared about Emma and obviously cared about Lily or he wouldn't be here. He wouldn't have that Christmas gift in his rucksack.

He just didn't care *enough*...that was the problem.

He *couldn't*...

'I'd better go and see what's happening,' Emma said. 'I have no idea how long we've been sitting here.'

Jack had no idea, either. That kiss could have been only seconds but it felt like it could have been forever.

Emma started to get up but then sat down again with a groan. 'I don't remember the last time I was this tired.'

'You've been working for far too long. You have to get some rest.'

'I'll get a couple of hours' sleep when I get home. You must be just as tired. You haven't had any real rest in here and you've got your injuries making things worse. You need sleep even more than I do.'

'I'll find somewhere to go.'

'You already *have* somewhere to go.' This time Emma got to her feet. She was staring down at Jack and she was frowning as if she was puzzled. 'You're coming home with me. You have a gift to deliver, remember? That's why you came back.'

The thought that he had anything like a home to go to was comforting enough to bring a lump to Jack's throat. But it was disturbing, too. Heading towards comfort like that was taking a big step towards something he didn't want. Something that he would miss when it was lost again because he would know it was still there.

Like he had missed Emma.

It would be so much easier to stay away.

'I could give you the present,' he heard himself saying. 'And you could give it to Lily for me.'

Emma shook her head. 'It's your gift, Jack. You have to give it to her yourself. Besides, I have an hour's drive to get home and I need someone to make sure I stay awake. You're getting that job whether you like it or not.'

There was something adorable about someone as kind and gentle as Emma being bossy. A little bit of fire showing, to match that glorious hair of hers.

Maybe it was easier to just go with the flow. Already, Jack could feel some of the spinning in his head beginning to slow down. It was a sensible choice, anyway. Someone with any kind of head injury would be ill-advised to shut themselves away in a hotel room and just go to sleep.

And Emma had made it about herself rather than him. She needed him to keep her safe.

He could do that. He owed her a great deal more than that, in fact.

So he nodded. Slowly, because it made the throbbing in his head instantly worse.

Emma looked at her watch. 'It's nearly five a.m. The day shift is coming in early so they'll be here very soon. Let's go and get something for that headache of yours and I'll catch up on what's been happening. I want to look in on Mel before I go. And Stuart.'

It was an effort to get to his feet and painful to stand once he made it but Jack wasn't about to let his discomfort show. Emma was exhausted enough to make the freckles on her nose stand out against her pale skin and she had dark circles under her eyes but she wasn't about to use that as an excuse not to take the time to care for others. She wasn't even thinking about herself.

She was an extraordinarily good person and Jack had nothing but admiration for her attitude. It shouldn't make him want to kiss her again, but it did.

Instead, he reached out and smoothed a wayward curl back from her face.

Emma pushed the curl under a clip. Then she unsuccessfully tried to smooth the crumples in her scrubs tunic. 'I look wrecked, don't I?'

'You look tired,' Jack agreed. 'But not wrecked.' He smiled at her. 'I think you look like a hardworking professional. A very cute hardworking professional.'

Emma snorted. But she straightened her back and smiled. 'Come on. Let's see what we can do about escaping.'

Closing the door of the office behind them closed the door on everything that had gone on in there but Emma wasn't about to forget a moment of it.

She could put it to one side as she melted back into a work space that was now quiet enough to have staff members dozing in front of computer screens and any remaining patients asleep on their beds. A quick call to the coronary care unit reassured her that Stuart was doing well and sleeping peacefully.

A call to the intensive care unit gave her just as much pleasure.

'They've just woken Mel up,' she told Jack. 'She recognised her family and she's talking. It looks like she might have escaped any brain damage.'

'That's wonderful. You did a good job.'

'*We* did a good job.'

Emma basked in the glow of the shared accomplishment and let her thoughts drift back to that time in the office as she led Jack to the drug cupboard to find what was needed for his headache.

She felt closer to him than ever before but not just because of that bone-melting kiss.

He'd told her things that explained so much about him.

Just a few words but they had said so much.

Not enough, mind you. It was a puzzle why the brothers had been so different. Ben had gone through the same childhood trauma of losing his mother and being separated from his twin but he'd moved forward in the opposite direction. Instead of shying away from the things that had caused such grief, he'd set about re-creating them. Finding someone to love and share his life with. Starting a family. Making a big deal about celebrating Christmas.

Surely that meant that Jack was capable of doing the same thing? Part of him was trapped, wasn't it? There was a small boy inside that man who was still afraid and Emma still felt an overwhelming urge to find that child and cuddle him. To make sure he felt loved so that he could find peace and set the man that Jack now was free to embrace life and find true happiness.

But how could you reach back through time and make contact?

How could anyone repair the kind of damage that made people too afraid to love?

Maybe it wasn't possible but at least she had a place to start from.

Jack cared about her.

He'd missed her.

And he'd come back.

Even better, he'd agreed to come home with her. He

would meet Lily and her mother and be surrounded by family on Christmas Day.

It might be the first time he'd had that since he was that small boy. As Emma put the painkillers into Jack's hand a few minutes later, she glanced up and let her gaze touch his gently. Maybe he would see some of the hope she was feeling suddenly. This could be a kind of time travel, couldn't it?

It was certainly the closest thing possible.

And she had a special kind of magic that might just make the difference. Emma's lips curled into a secret smile as she felt the squeeze in her heart that was an echo of the pure love and joy that she knew would be there for them both.

Because Lily was there.

CHAPTER SEVEN

'WHAT'S SO FUNNY?'

The broad smile on Jack's face was as close to a grin as Emma had seen since...well, since before the night that had changed their lives forever.

That he could still smile like that surrounded her in a bubble of happiness but the fact that his face had lit up like that as she walked out of the locker room was a bit disturbing.

Had he forgotten how wild her hair was when she released it from that tight ponytail and those uncomfortable pins? The halo cloud of bright auburn spiral curls that brushed her shoulders always made people turn for a second glance and often made them smile. Emma had long ago given up letting it bother her.

Clown hair.

Ginger Ninja hair.

Red...

That fancy up-do she'd had at Sarah's wedding had unravelled, thanks to Jack burying his hands in it when he'd kissed her that very first time. And it had made him smile then, too.

'I love your hair. It's so you.'

'It's so red, you mean.'

And the very private nickname had been chosen.

A name that could only be used by one person in the world. A name that gave Emma a very particular tingle when she heard it. She'd never expected to ever hear it again but she'd heard it tonight.

'I'm sorry, Red.'

Apparently it wasn't her hair that had tickled Jack's funny bone this time, however.

'You're wearing a Christmas sweater,' he said. 'It makes you look like a kid.'

'Lily chose it for me.' Emma lifted her chin. 'I like it.'

Jack was trying to straighten his lips. 'Matches your hair.'

It *was* bright red. With a very happy red-nosed reindeer on the front and fluffy white blobs that were supposed to be snowflakes dotted over the rest of the garment.

'You're wearing something a bit odd yourself, you know.'

He still had the jeans and T-shirt that he'd found to replace his hospital gown but he had cut the damaged sleeves from the leather jacket and was now wearing it as a sleeveless kind of vest with ragged armholes.

'Yeah…' Jack shrugged. 'But it seemed like a good idea. I don't imagine it's T-shirt weather out there and… I forgot to buy a Christmas sweater.'

Emma laughed. 'The day I see you wearing a Christmas sweater, Jack Reynolds, is the day I will expect the world, as we know it, to end.'

'Hey…' There was a shadow in his eyes, as if he felt that he'd disappointed her. 'Baby steps, okay?'

Emma's laughter died as she remembered the surprise of seeing a Christmas gift in Jack's rucksack. The smile left behind felt soft. Tender. He was trying to change and even the tiniest steps were actually huge.

'Baby steps are fine. Are you okay to walk out to the car? You don't need crutches or anything?'

'I'm good. Pete did a great job on a new compression bandage for me.'

'And your arm's all right? Is that headache under control?' Emma could feel herself frowning. 'Is anything bothering you too much?'

Jack's mouth twisted into a lopsided smile.

Silly question. Physical pain was probably the least of Jack's worries right now. He was being forced to face one of his demons here, wasn't he?

A family Christmas…

Best they got going, before he had time to come up with an answer to that thoughtless question.

Sunrise was still hours away and it felt like the middle of the night as Emma drove out of the hospital car park and took an onramp to the motorway.

The chill that had settled into Jack's bones on his somewhat slow, limping walk to her vehicle was finally ebbing as the heater in her car gathered strength. The car had been a surprise. The roomy SUV was a far cry from the tiny bright green bubble car she'd been driving before he'd left town. He'd barely managed to fold his legs into the space in front of the passenger's seat back then. Now he had enough room to elevate his injured leg on his rucksack.

'Do you miss the frog?'

Emma shook her head. 'It was a fun car for a single girl. Not an option when you need baby seats. Plus, I like having more safety features, especially for rural driving at night.'

She sounded so grown up. So like a parent.

'Just how rural are we going? Where *do* you live now?'

'Achadunan.'

The name hung in the air around them. It seemed to thicken it so that it was harder to take a breath.

Achadunan was a small village off the top of Loch Lomond.

And it was the place that Ben and Sarah had been buried. Together. Because it had been Sarah's home and he hadn't been able to think of anywhere more appropriate for his brother to rest. Truth be told, he hadn't been able to think about anything coherently during those dreadful days.

He hadn't expected to be heading there now.

Emma must have sensed his shock, and the reason for it.

'I had to move out there,' she said quietly. 'Maybe I'll move closer in again one day. I wouldn't want Lily to have to do the long bus trips to school every day that Sarah and I had to do. But I couldn't ask Mum to come and live in the city with me. She's lived in Achadunan since the day she was born. And I couldn't have taken Lily without her blessing—and her help.'

Jack nodded. 'I remember your speech at the wedding. You said that you and Sarah had grown up in the same village. That you'd been sisters from other mothers since you were born, pretty much.'

'Our mothers were best friends, too. We did everything together, especially after my dad died. It was like we were one family. That's why she was so happy to take Lily in. She was Sarah's baby. Joan's grandbaby. Part of our family already.'

It was Jack who was the outsider, wasn't it? He'd barely got to know Sarah given the whirlwind romance and how determined his brother had been to get down the aisle. He didn't like admitting it, but he'd resented

Sarah sometimes back then, because he'd hardly ever been able to get Ben to himself. And the wedding had been the icing on a cake he was still trying to get accustomed to. He'd been thrilled that Ben was so obviously happy but he hadn't really been the best best man. He had to search his memory for people he'd been introduced to.

'I think I remember your mother being at the wedding. Curly, grey hair and glasses? Always smiling?'

Emma flicked the windscreen wipers on. The whirl of moisture hitting the windscreen looked like sleet. Just like it had looked moments before he'd lost control of his bike. Jack suppressed a shiver but Emma was smiling.

'That sounds like Mum.'

'Muriel.'

'That's her.'

Jack was pleased to come up with the name. Maybe he hadn't been too much of a jerk after all. Other patches of the day were still foggy, though. 'I don't remember Sarah's mother being there.'

'No. She'd died a few years earlier. That was a tough time for all of us. Mum still misses her every day. She often watches Lily doing something and gets teary and says how much Joan would have loved to be here, being a grandma.'

Jack was silent for a few minutes. He had no idea what it was going to be like, meeting this child of his brother. Would he get slammed with knowing how much Ben would have loved being a father? Would the sadness be something he wasn't ready to handle?

It was ridiculous but he was increasingly nervous about meeting Lily.

Again, Emma seemed to sense where his thoughts were heading.

'It'll be okay, you know. There's something about Lily that means you can't be anything but happy when she's close. You'll see… Oh, look…'

'What?'

'That's real snow out there now. I thought that might happen when we got out of the city.'

Thick white flakes were sparkling in the headlights and Emma sounded as excited as a child about it.

'I can't remember the last time we had a white Christmas. We don't usually get real snow until January. Lily will be over the moon if we get to make a Santa snowman. Harry loves snow, too. Even at his age, he has to stand outside with his tongue out to catch the flakes. It's hilarious.'

Jack didn't find the notion amusing in the least. *Harry?* There was a man in Emma's life that she hadn't bothered to mention?

Well, why wouldn't there be? Emma was gorgeous. The man that got chosen to share her life would be the luckiest man on earth. And she'd had a year to get over the dreadful time and put her life back together. It shouldn't feel too soon.

It shouldn't feel so completely *wrong*.

But hang on… Jack could feel his scowl deepening. She'd *kissed* him. And it had felt exactly like when they were both single and free to choose the person they wanted to be with, even if they'd both been warned not to choose each other. No. It had felt even better than that. As though they already knew the best and worst of each other but they were still the chosen one. As if there was some special connection that could never be there with anyone else.

Emma's head turned briefly with a movement that was sharp enough to suggest she was aware of the scrutiny. Her eyebrows shot up as she caught the force of his glare.

'What? What did I say?'

'You didn't tell me about *Harry*,' he growled.

'Why would I?'

The flash of anger was a welcome change to the confusion he was grappling with at the thought of Emma being with another man.

'Oh, I don't know… Maybe you could have warned me that I was going to be meeting the man who's taken my brother's place as a father figure for Lily?'

'What?' The car actually swerved a little and Emma was biting her lip as she focused on the road. Then she let her breath out in a huff of something close to laughter. 'Are you kidding me? Harry's a *dog*. A big, goofy retriever that my mother brought home for me a while after my dad died. He's nearly sixteen but when it snows, he thinks he's a puppy again.'

Jack shrank back into his seat. 'Sorry,' he mumbled.

'You think I have time for men in my life when I've got a full-time job and an energetic toddler? You think the thought's even crossed my mind?'

'I'm sure there are plenty of guys who wish it would.'

Emma shook her head. 'Not interested.'

Jack felt himself nodding in agreement. 'Yeah… I know that feeling.'

There was a moment's silence that stretched into a kind of awkwardness. It was Emma that broke it.

'You mean there's been no one in your life in the last year?'

'No.' It was embarrassing to admit, so Jack tried to

brush it off with a joke. 'Didn't you notice how rusty my kissing was?'

Another silence and then Emma cleared her throat. Her voice still sounded a little rough.

'Actually, no... I didn't notice...'

Phew... Had the heating in this car suddenly gone up a level? Were the fans generating some odd kind of electricity that filled the space around and between them?

He hadn't lightened the atmosphere at all. He had, seemingly, set a match to it.

Just as well Emma was ready to defuse things.

'Well... I promise I won't tell. It would do all sorts of damage to your legendary playboy surgeon status around the Eastern.'

Jack stared straight ahead. The snow was falling more thickly now. He could see the sheen of it settling on the tarmac of the road. He didn't like the reminder of who he'd been. It was no wonder Ben had been so keen to try and make him change his lifestyle.

'I'm not that person anymore,' he said quietly.

'Really?' Emma had slowed the car and had her head tilted forward as she peered into the worsening visibility. She still slid a sideways look in his direction, though. 'Who are you now, Jack?'

He closed his eyes. 'I'm not sure I know.'

The silence felt sympathetic this time. Encouraging. For a heartbeat, Jack was sitting in an African desert again, with those gut-wrenching sobs being torn from his soul. Thinking about Ben. And Christmas. And the chill of such well-remembered British winters.

He'd come back here for a reason. He hadn't realised just how important that reason was until now. His words came out in the wake of a heartfelt sigh as he felt drowsiness overtaking him.

'Maybe I had to come back here to find out.'

CHAPTER EIGHT

IT WAS RIDICULOUS how nervous Emma was becoming at the thought of Jack meeting Lily.

Since he'd fallen asleep, there had been no conversation to distract her and on the final stretch of the drive it was easy to channel that nervousness into making sure they got there safely. The snow was lying thickly enough to obliterate road markings and even footpaths now and the streetlights as they passed through the village were no more than a faint glow behind an almost solid screen of drifting flakes.

Emma's childhood home was on the far side of the village where residential streets gave way to farmland. A whitewashed cottage with square, latticed windows and a slate roof, set amongst old trees, it was blending in so well with the landscape right now that if it wasn't as familiar as a body part, she might have driven right past it.

The windscreen wipers ceased their movement as she turned the engine off and, for a moment, Emma watched the snow trying to settle on the glass. The childish wonderment that something so solid looking could fall so softly and silently had never worn off.

It was just as silent inside the car and Emma assumed that Jack was still asleep, but when she turned her head, she found that he, too, was watching the melting flakes on still warm glass. He mirrored her action almost instantly and when his gaze met hers, Emma realised he was just as nervous as she was.

Somehow, that made her feel a whole lot braver.

If he was nervous about meeting Lily, that meant it was important to him and whatever happened today could well change the direction of his life.

He was lost.

How heartbreaking had it been to hear him admit that he wasn't sure who he was anymore?

He needed something to anchor him. Or someone. Could that someone be his little niece?

Was it too dangerous to hope that it might be herself?

Emma needed some serious magic to happen today and so far, so good.

Her mother knew how important this meeting was. Emma had called her when she'd been getting changed to warn her that she was bringing an unexpected guest and, even though Muriel Matthews didn't know the extent of Emma's feelings for Jack, she knew he would be welcomed into the family because of his connection to Lily and Sarah.

The weather was cooperating, too. The setting of a small Scottish village softened by the first fall of snow was a picture postcard background.

And it was the best day of the year for magic.

So Emma smiled at Jack.

'Merry Christmas,' she whispered. 'Welcome home.'

Jack opened his mouth but seemed lost for words so Emma didn't let the moment linger, reaching for the door handle.

'Let's get inside before we freeze to death.'

The snow was thick enough to crunch and squeak beneath their feet as she led him round to the back door.

Across the porch and then into the kitchen. It would be the warmest place in the house because, at this time of the year, the Aga stove was always well stoked. She hadn't expected her mother to be up already and waiting for them but there she was, rugged up in her dressing gown and slippers, standing beside the scrubbed wooden table, pouring hot milk into mugs of her famous chocolate syrup.

Muriel only glanced up, smiling as if the stranger in her house was such a frequent and welcome visitor he was part of the family.

'Jack,' she said warmly. 'I'm so glad you chose today to come.'

Harry seemed to be on board with the plan to make Jack welcome, too. He climbed a little stiffly out of his basket in the corner and, after nudging Emma's hand in an affectionate welcome, he paused to wag his tail at Jack before trudging back to his bed.

Muriel had a more focused glance for Emma. 'You must be totally exhausted, love. I was really worried about you driving.' She handed her the mug of hot chocolate as Emma sank down onto one of the kitchen chairs. 'As soon as you've had this, go and get your head down for a couple of hours.'

She handed Jack the other mug. 'I'm sure you need some sleep, too. There's not much rest to be had in an emergency department and you've been hurt, haven't you?' Her face creased. 'I was so sorry to hear about that.'

Jack smiled and thanked Muriel as he sat down but he was looking dazed. His glance kept roving. Up at the old beams in the ceiling, across to the antique blue and white china that was Muriel's pride and joy, displayed on a hutch dresser that had belonged to Emma's great-grandmother. Down to the flagged stone floor that had the ability to draw heat from the Aga and across to Harry in his basket, who noticed the glance and thumped his tail once as acknowledgement. He turned his head, to look through the arched wall opening into the living room, where a bare tree was standing by the fireplace, its trunk secured in a bucket of sand. There were boxes of decorations on the hearth of a fire that had been set, ready to light, and there were gifts, as well, in a haphazard pile at the other end of the hearth.

Emma had followed that glance.

'I can't go to bed,' she said. 'I need to get the tree sorted and the presents underneath.'

'That can wait.' Muriel waved her hand dismissively. 'I was going to do it last night with Lily but when I asked if she wanted to do it now or wait for Mummy, she was very definite about waiting.'

Emma tensed. What would Jack think about her being referred to as Lily's mummy? He didn't seem to have noticed. He was sipping his drink and still staring at the undecorated tree. Was he thinking of putting that gift in his rucksack beneath it?

'Lily's still fast asleep,' Muriel said. 'And she's far too young to know that we might be doing things a bit differently this year. I think we should all put our heads down for a bit longer. I don't mind having a wee lie-in for once, myself. It's not even going to get light until nine a.m. and we've got all day to do Christmas things. Jack? I'm sorry we don't have a spare bed, but the couch in the living room there is very comfortable. I've put a pillow and an eiderdown on it. And a hottie. It should be nice and warm.'

'Thank you,' he said. He was giving Emma a glance

that reminded her of the way her mother had been looking at her. 'You really do need to get some sleep,' he said.

The genuine concern in that look and tone almost
undid Emma. Because she was so tired that she could
feel herself swaying on her chair?

'Just an hour or two and then I'll be fine. Do you need
anything? Painkillers?'

Jack shook his head. 'A bit of sleep is all I need, too.'

Muriel took their empty mugs.

'There's a toilet out the back,' she told Jack. 'But the
main bathroom's upstairs. We won't be far away if you
need us for anything. Sleep well.'

The couch was huge and soft.

Jack took off his shoes and the remains of his jacket
but left his jeans and T-shirt on. Folding back the old-
fashioned eiderdown with its shiny, embroidered fabric
revealed the hot water bottle and suddenly Jack had a
lump the size of Africa in his throat.

His mother used to do that. Ben's hottie had been
green and his had been red—like this one. He could remember the lovely warm patch in his bed, and how he
would hold the hottie in his arms on the coldest night
as he fell asleep.

There were other things about that house that had the
quality of a distant dream. The smell of chocolate in the
kitchen. The dog asleep in the corner. The way Muriel
had smiled at him…

Emma's smile, but older and wiser.

Full of love…

It felt like a home, this house, that's what it was.

And he hadn't lived in a real home since he'd been
five years old. He'd lived in *other* people's homes. In an

institution. In medical school digs. In bachelor apartments. In a hut in Africa.

This wasn't his home, he reminded himself. This was Emma's home. And Lily's home.

He was only a visitor.

And he didn't want to get sucked back into even tiny fragments of a past that was so long ago it had no relevance to his life now. He didn't want to be reminded of things that had been lost. The protective wall had taken many years to build but it was thick now and he was safely on the other side. Looking over the top could only make things harder.

Despite the headache that continued to be a dull throb in his skull, Jack knew he would fall asleep the moment his head touched that fat, feather pillow. He eased himself onto the couch, pushing the hottie with his foot so that it flopped to the floor with the sloshing sound of the water moving inside the rubber casing.

That sound was another peep over the wall because he and Ben had always discarded those red and green hotties when they were too cold to be comforting. They had to pick them up in the morning, though, and take them downstairs. Their little fingers were too small to undo the stoppers so Mum would empty them and put them away. And then they would magically appear in their beds again the next night, all warm and toasty.

Jack's last thought before sleep claimed him was that he needed to remember to pick the hottie up in the morning. And empty it before Muriel did.

His sleep was deep and dreamless. Until he began surfacing towards consciousness with the awareness that he wasn't alone. He kept his eyes shut, however, as he tried to decide whether he was, in fact, dreaming.

And then he felt it.

A puff of warm breath on his face.

And something small and soft on his eyelid that was applying pressure to open it.

Very cautiously, Jack allowed his eyelid to be lifted. There was a small face only inches away from his own. Big, dark eyes and a tumble of dark curls around them.

Lily...

He opened his other eyelid.

Lily was standing beside the couch, which put her at eye level with him. She didn't seem at all disconcerted to find a strange man staring at her. She met his gaze solemnly and simply gazed back.

This was a photograph that had come to life. A living, breathing image that was so familiar because it was so like him. And so like Ben.

The photograph on Emma's phone had been enough to stir up those feelings of the bond of family. Of a love that was already there, like a part of his DNA.

Did Lily feel that connection as well? Surely children weren't this trusting of people they didn't know?

Jack felt he should say something but had no idea what. Was a child this small even capable of conversation?

Apparently. Sort of.

''Lo,' Lily said.

'Hello,' Jack replied. 'Does Mummy know where you are?'

This question didn't appear to be of any interest. The room was still dark, Jack noted. And Lily seemed to be wearing pyjamas—a fluffy red suit, patterned with white hearts, that had built-in socks and buttons down the front. A warning flashed in his head. What if the others were still asleep and Lily needed something?

He'd already proved how incompetent he was looking after babies.

As if the warning signal had been transmitted, he saw the silhouette of that big, shaggy dog appear in the doorway, with the soft light that had been left on in the kitchen behind him. Harry was standing there, watching. Guarding Lily?

But Lily didn't seem to be in need of anything like a bottle or a change of nappies. And she wasn't in need of Harry's protection. She was, in fact, climbing up onto the couch with Jack. Or trying to. She hung on to Jack's leg and hoisted one small leg of her own up and then tried to roll her body upwards. It was a manoeuvre doomed to fail and she would have fallen onto the floor if Jack hadn't moved his arm to catch her. Given that extra support, Lily could complete her mission. She climbed right over him and snuggled down to put her head under his arm.

Harry moved closer. This time it was dog breath in Jack's face and the look in the dog's eyes told him he had better not break the trust that was being put in him. And then Harry lay down with a sigh and put his nose on his paws.

Jack was hemmed in on both sides. He strained his ears, trying to hear any sound of movement upstairs, but the house was completely silent.

Lily was silent too.

Jack tucked his chin into his neck so that he could see the small body in the crook of his arm. He could feel the warmth of Lily's body and the way her chest was moving as she breathed in and out. Tilting his head further, he could see her face, but if he'd been expecting another moment of that extraordinary eye contact, he was disappointed. Lily's eyes were closed.

Good grief…had she fallen asleep again?

At least that meant he didn't need to demonstrate any incompetency just yet. He could just stay here, Jack decided, until Lily woke up again, which could be at any moment. He pulled the eiderdown up a bit further, though, to keep her warm.

But the moments ticked past and Jack found himself relaxing again, little by little. He was in a cosy nest on this comfortable, old couch and Lily's warmth was like the hottie he remembered as a child, only on a completely new level. This small person was Ben's daughter. His niece. And it seemed that she was accepting his presence with the same kind of ease and welcome that everybody in this extraordinary little family had.

As his eyelids drifted shut, Jack remembered how gentle Lily had been in opening them. He fell asleep again with a smile on his face.

Emma woke with a start, sensing the presence of someone in her room.

'Sorry, love… I didn't mean to wake you. I thought Lily must be in here with you.'

The sound of her mother's voice brought Emma wide awake. 'She's not in her cot?'

'You know how good she's got at climbing out.'

Emma nodded. But Lily always headed for snuggly morning cuddles in bed with her mother or grandmother when she escaped. She'd never gone downstairs by herself. Emma was out of bed in a flash, reaching for the big woollen cardigan she preferred to a dressing gown. 'You have the bathroom, first,' she told her mother. 'I'll go and make sure she hasn't got into mischief.'

Not that she ever had. Harry would have woken them with his warning bark if she'd gone too close to the Aga or something. Emma rushed downstairs anyway. How long had Lily been out of her bed? And where was she?

Not in the kitchen. And Harry wasn't in his basket, either.

It was only a few steps to the entrance to the living room. The first thing Emma saw was Harry lying by the couch and her beloved old dog lifted his head and thumped his tail on the carpet. She could see Jack's face and he was clearly deeply asleep. And...*ohh*...

Emma put her fingers over her mouth to stifle her gasp. So *that* was where Lily had got to. Somehow, she had climbed up onto the couch and there she was, snuggled under Jack's arm, also sound asleep.

How extraordinary...

Lily had chosen Jack for morning cuddles?

How had she even known he was in the house, let alone that he was someone that could be trusted to that degree?

Emma had to blink away the sudden moisture gathering in her eyes. She could feel the Christmas magic gaining power and the day was only just beginning.

Misty-eyed, she let her gaze take in the soft tumble of Lily's curls and the sweep of those dark lashes on the perfect, soft skin of her cheeks. It only took a tiny shift of her eye muscles to make a comparison to Jack's shaggy locks, the same enviable lashes and skin that looked as if it would feel deliciously rough beneath her fingers.

Oh, man... Emma's fingers actually twitched with the longing to touch Jack's face.

She didn't want to wake either of them. She didn't want to move herself, for that matter, but standing here staring was beginning to feel uncomfortable. Fantasies about touching the man she loved were fine in the privacy of her own bed but it was bordering on creepy to be doing it when he was unconscious in front of her.

Unconscious…

A beat of alarm kicked in. How long had he been asleep now? At least a couple of hours. If he had still been in hospital, being observed for a potential injury, someone would have woken him to check that he was still responsive.

Indecision like this was an unusual experience for Emma. Maybe Harry sensed her discomfort because the old dog got to his feet and came towards her, his feathery tail sweeping Jack's face as he walked past.

And that solved the problem, because Jack woke up. He was probably horribly stiff after sleeping on that couch with his injuries because the first sound he made was a stifled groan. The sound was enough to wake Lily as well.

'Mumma…'

Lily's face split into a joyous grin but Emma knew how painful that small elbow in Jack's ribs for leverage would have been.

'*Oof*,' he said. 'Hang on, Lily.' He tried to grab the wriggly toddler who was now standing up and threatening to walk over his chest to get to her mother.

'Kisses,' Lily demanded. 'Kissmas.'

Emma dived towards the couch and scooped Lily into her arms.

'Cheers,' Jack murmured.

'Sorry,' Emma said. 'I had no idea she'd come downstairs by herself. She's very good at going down the stairs backwards but she's just learned to climb out of her cot. We have to keep the side down so she doesn't injure herself. It really is time she moved into a bed, I guess…'

She was talking too much. Too fast. She was nervous, Emma realised. She had expected to be there the first time Jack set eyes on Lily and now she had no idea what had happened. Or how either of them had reacted.

There were small fists buried in her hair now and Lily was trying to turn Emma's head so that she could see her face.

'Kiss,' she commanded.

Automatically, Emma turned and planted a soft kiss on the small face. But then her gaze swivelled back to Jack.

'It's okay,' he told her. 'It was a unique experience, having my eyelid prised open to wake me up.'

'Oh, no…' Emma bit her lip. 'She didn't…'

'More,' Lily said. 'More kisses…'

Jack was smiling and Emma couldn't look away. She'd never seen him smile like that before. He was looking at Lily and smiling as if…as if they already had a secret bond.

Last night, it had been the last thing she would have expected to say to Jack but it came out easily this time.

'Merry Christmas, Jack.'

'Merry Christmas, Red.'

The shared glance felt like something new as well. Maybe it was the soft light and that it still felt like night-time. Or that Jack was only just awake and still had the sleep-rumpled softness that she hadn't seen since she'd woken up next to him so long ago. He would smile at her then, too, and it had felt intimate and special but, this time, there was something much deeper than a shared connection of fabulous sex the night before. This glance had more to do with the kind of friendship that lasted a lifetime. Of a connection that was more about this small child Emma held in her arms than themselves.

Was it like the kind of glance parents might share?

And maybe Lily had some level of awareness of the connection the three of them shared?

'Merry Kissmas,' she echoed, in her adorable toddler-speak. She was wriggling now so Emma set her down on the floor and Lily wrapped her arms around Harry's neck and squeezed the dog who sat like the world's most patient canine statue.

Jack and Emma were still smiling. Still holding that glance.

Lily let go of Harry and trotted back to the couch. Emma held her breath as Lily put her face close to Jack's.

'Up,' she commanded.

'No,' Emma corrected quickly. 'You don't have to get up yet. Come on, Lilypad. We're going to get washed and dressed.' She picked Lily up again. 'Do you need any painkillers, Jack?'

'I've got some here. I'll get myself up.'

'Mum will be down in a minute. It'll be bacon and eggs for breakfast in no time.' Emma threw him a smile over her shoulder. 'And that's only the start. I hope you're hungry.'

He *was* hungry, Jack decided, as he towelled himself dry carefully. In combination with the pills he'd taken before pushing himself to climb the stairs, the long, hot shower had done wonders for the stiffness and all the surprisingly painful parts of his body. It hadn't helped his headache so much but he could live with that.

The rumble of his stomach as he caught the first whiff of frying bacon made him realise that he hadn't eaten for a very long time and that meal had only been a rather tired sandwich and some bad coffee at a truck stop on the road from London to Glasgow.

The house seemed to have come alive in the time he'd

been in the bathroom. Lights were on everywhere and a fire crackled in the grate in the living room. There was Christmas music playing and Lily was sitting in a high chair at the kitchen table banging a wooden spoon on her tray as Emma set plates and cutlery around her. She was wearing her Christmas reindeer sweater again and she had a headband keeping her curls away from her face. A headband that had small red and white candy canes attached to it. Jack could feel his mouth curving into a grin.

Emma looked up and saw him smiling and her face lit up.

'Hey…'

She looked so happy to see him that Jack's breath caught. Not that he was about to try and identify that wash of emotion. It was part of that hugeness that he wasn't ready to explore. That vast ocean of feelings that went with things like home and family and…and love…

Things that weren't part of his world.

Things that he didn't want to make part of his world.

Because that would be breaking the rules…

Muriel turned from where she was busy at the Aga, breaking eggs into a pan. She saw Jack and then glanced at Emma and back again. Jack couldn't read her expression but it felt like she knew more than he'd expected about how well he knew her daughter.

She was smiling, though. 'Merry Christmas, Jack. I've put something on the chair for you, there. You might need it.'

It was a jersey, Jack realised, as he lifted what was draped over the back of the chair. An intricately knitted Arran jersey in soft, black wool.

'It was one of Dad's,' Emma told him. 'So it should

fit you. Mum knitted it so she couldn't bring herself to give it away.'

'I wear it sometimes,' Muriel added. She put a bowl of what looked like mashed egg and bread on Lily's tray. 'It's the warmest thing ever in the middle of winter. I've still got my Ian's old parka, too. That should fit you as well, if you feel the need for some fresh air later.'

'Very fresh air,' Emma said. She was helping Lily get a grip on a bright yellow plastic spoon. 'It's stopped snowing but there's a good layer out there.' She smiled at Lily and her voice became more animated. 'You'll be able to make your first snowman today.'

'No,' Lily said. 'No man.'

Emma laughed. '*Snow*,' she repeated. 'Can you say "snow", darling?'

Lily's grin stretched from ear to ear. 'No,' she said obligingly. 'No man.'

Emma shook her head, helping a spoonful of mashed egg go in the right direction. 'Looks like we'll be making a "no man" today, then.' The spoon went into Lily's mouth, leaving only a streak of yolk on her chin. 'Mmm… egg…'

Jack pulled the well-worn jersey over his head and pushed his arms into the sleeves. Emma's father had been a tall man and just as broad in the shoulders as he was himself. It fitted perfectly.

And it felt weird.

He was wearing an item of clothing that had belonged to the man of this household. Was he sitting in the same chair? Would Muriel have set a plate of perfectly cooked bacon and eggs in front of him with that same warm smile?

'Get that into you,' she said. 'You must be starving. And help yourself to some tea. That pot's freshly made.'

Emma was watching him. Did she realise how weird this was making him feel?

'Dad wasn't into Christmas sweaters, either,' she said. Her lips twitched. 'You've got off lightly.'

Her smile—and that twinkle in her eyes—chased the weirdness away. She understood at least part of how he was feeling and she was going to help him get past any obstacles.

He could cope with this, Jack decided. It was only for one day, anyway.

Maybe he could even enjoy it.

CHAPTER NINE

CHRISTMAS HAD NEVER felt quite like this.

Topsy-turvy.

Poignant.

Christmas wasn't just about being with the people you loved, it was about remembering those who couldn't be there and Emma was missing her father badly right now.

It was the first time in thirty years since there'd been a child as young as Lily in this house to share it and how amazing would it have been if Lily was actually his first grandchild? That the man who was stringing the lights on the Christmas tree was Lily's father and his son-in-law?

Would he have been keeping Lily out of mischief?

'Look…' Emma tipped out a box full of decorations onto the rug to distract Lily from the pile of gifts. Especially the one that was at the front of the pile.

Jack's gift for Lily.

Emma had to blink away sudden moisture in her eyes. He had remembered to put it there—probably before he'd gone to sleep. She was reminded of how astonishing it had been to see it in the rucksack of the man who never did anything Christmassy.

It gave her another glimmer of hope. That things were changing. For Jack. For all of them.

They should have all been sitting around opening the

gifts by now, with the breakfast dishes cleared away, but it was part of the topsy-turvyness.

'You two get the tree sorted,' Muriel had ordered. 'I'm going to get the turkey stuffed and into the oven or it'll be bedtime before we eat our Christmas lunch.'

She could hear her mother singing along to one of her favourite seasonal songs, 'We Wish You a Merry Christmas', and Lily was staring wide-eyed at the pile of treasure that had appeared magically right in front of her. She was also making some odd cooing noises that Emma had never heard before.

'No way...' she murmured, a moment later.

'What?' Jack was reaching for the switch on the wall behind the tree. Tiny lights began twinkling behind him as he looked towards Emma.

'I think...' Emma had to press her lips together for a moment to disguise a wobble. 'I think Lily's trying to sing...'

It was a joy to turn back and watch Lily for a minute. She was dressed in her little denim dungarees, with a bright red jersey underneath. Emma had put a clip with a sparkly red bow in her hair and she could have been a model for a Christmas advertisement for television, sitting there surrounded by decorations and...yes, she *was* singing.

'Oooh...mmm...oooh... Merry Kissmas...'

Becoming aware that she was being watched, Lily tilted her head and grinned. Then she picked up one of the decorations and held it up. Her arm was stretched out towards Jack rather than Emma.

He accepted the offering.

'Thank you,' he said.

''Ank oo,' Lily echoed.

Jack looked at the brightly coloured object in his

hand. 'It's an owl,' he declared. 'Do you know what noise owls make, Lily?' He supplied a hooting sound when Lily simply stared up at him.

'Oooh…oooh…' Without breaking eye contact, Lily mimicked the sound perfectly.

'Wow…' Jack sounded genuinely impressed. 'Clever girl. And what's this?' He accepted another offering. 'It's a gingerbread man.'

He now had a decoration in each hand and he looked at them more closely. 'I've never seen decorations like this. What are they made of?'

'Felt.'

'Are they hand-made?'

'Mmm.' This was embarrassing, Emma decided. Jack had known her as a young, single woman who liked nothing better than going out for dinner and a night on the town dancing when she wasn't working. Now she was a young, working mother whose life was the picture of domesticity. By the time her days ended now, the idea of dancing was a lifetime ago and she liked nothing better than being curled up on the couch, with her dog at her feet and something relaxing to do with her hands—like embroidering tiny felt ornaments.

She could feel Jack staring at her.

'Did you make them?'

'Mum started them,' Emma said. 'I was too tired to read a journal one night so I decided to help and…' Her chin lifted. Jack was smiling. He was going to laugh at her, wasn't he? Like he had over the Christmas sweater.

'Hey,' she growled. 'I discovered a splinter skill, okay? Think of it as a kind of suturing.'

Jack was still smiling. He stretched out so that he was lying on his stomach, his head close to Lily and the pile of decorations.

'I think they're amazing,' he said. 'Look at this. You've got reindeers and robins and plum puddings and snowmen. And what's wrapped up in the tissue paper?'

Oh, no… Emma bit her lip. She had never thought Jack was going to see those but he was unwrapping the little parcel.

'They're for the top of the tree,' she said quietly. 'Just for us…'

'They're like the figures people put on the top of wedding cakes.' Jack seemed transfixed by the ornaments. 'Except they're angels.'

'Mmm…' Emma couldn't say anything else for a moment. Would Jack see the significance of the blonde hair and blue eyes on the mummy angel and the shaggy dark hair and brown eyes on the daddy one?

His voice was no more than a whisper—as if he was talking to himself. 'They're Ben and Sarah, aren't they?'

Lily had stopped playing with the other ornaments. She wriggled closer to Jack and reached out to touch one of the angels.

'That's mummy angel, isn't it?' Emma said softly. 'Lily's mummy.'

'Mumma,' Lily said. But she was looking at Emma as she smiled.

'And there's a daddy angel, too. Lily's daddy.'

'Dadda,' Lily said happily. But she wasn't looking at Emma now. She was looking at Jack.

And he was looking back at her.

There was a moment's silence. A long moment that suddenly felt way too significant. Emma could almost feel Jack's shock—as if he'd been whisked into some alternative universe.

She had to break it. Leaning down, she grabbed a handful of the ornaments.

'Let's get these onto the tree.'

Looping the gold cords over the ends of branches gave them both something to do that meant they didn't have to look at each other and Lily crawled back and forth, fetching more ornaments from the pile. By tacit consent, the very top of the tree was left until last and that was when Emma finally risked a direct glance at Jack. She had the Sarah angel in her hand and he was holding the Ben angel. They were standing side by side, their hands almost touching as they found a place to attach the ornaments.

'You don't mind, do you?' Emma asked softly. 'You don't think it's a bit over the top?'

'I think it's very, very special,' he said. 'And I also think that you're the only person in the world who would have thought of it.'

He leaned closer. Maybe he'd intended to kiss her cheek, but Emma turned her head and his lips touched hers. And lingered long enough for it to feel like something significant.

'Well, that's the turkey in the oven and the bread sauce done...'

The sound of her mother's voice ended the kiss as unexpectedly as it had started and Emma felt her cheeks really burning as she concentrated on fastening her angel to the branch. How much had Muriel seen?

'I thought you might both need a nice cup of tea and some shortbread by now.'

If she had witnessed that moment of closeness, Muriel wasn't letting on. She had a tray in her hands. 'Mind out, Lily. This is hot... And, Jack?'

'Yes?'

'If you're up to it, I could do with some help peeling potatoes soon. After presents, of course.'

'I'm good at potatoes.' Emma received a ghost of a wink. 'It's one of my splinter skills.' Jack stepped away from the tree. 'Let me help you with that tray.'

Lily absolutely *loved* her gift from Jack.

Up till now, she'd been more interested in the wrapping paper as Emma had helped her unwrap other presents. There were crayons and colouring-in books, pink fairy wings that she was now wearing, lots of picture books and even a little red trolley that she could fill with toys and push along. There'd been gifts that Emma and her mother had given each other as well and it had been a time-consuming process but Jack had been happy enough to sit and watch, almost half-asleep, until his own gift had been the last to be presented.

'This is from Uncle Jack,' Emma told Lily. 'See if you can open it by yourself this time. Look, I'll start you off.' She lifted a piece of sticky tape and pulled back a corner of the parcel to reveal a fluffy, yellow ear.

Lily did the rest, her eyes widening as she saw all the bright colours. Instead of being instantly distracted by something else, as she had been with her earlier gifts, she seemed entranced by this one and had to touch every part of it.

Who knew how proud it could make you feel having clearly provided the gift of the day?

Muriel and Emma had been just as impressed by the 'learn to dress' teddy bear.

'Look, Lilypad…it's wearing dungarees, just like you.' Emma tickled the bib of Lily's dungarees. 'Only yours don't have a zip.'

''Ip!' Lily grinned. She pulled the shoelace undone on one of the bear's feet. The shoe on the other foot had a plastic buckle. Tiny fingers pulled at the buckle but

Jack could see that you needed to unthread the soft strap to open it so he showed Lily how it worked.

'Looks like you've got yourself a job.' Muriel smiled. 'You stay here and Emma and I will sort the rest of our Christmas lunch.'

Lily seemed more than happy with the arrangement. 'More,' she commanded. ''Ip now.'

So Jack undid the zip and Lily crowed with laughter.

It was the first time he'd heard Lily laugh and the sound did something odd. It was such a happy sound and yet Jack could feel the prickle of distant tears.

Good grief…what was going on here?

There'd been a moment earlier when he'd almost panicked and wondered if he could find an excuse to escape.

When Lily had looked straight at him and called him Dadda.

It had pierced him like an arrow straight to his heart.

Because of the angels. Because he was thinking about Ben and what a proud daddy his brother would have been.

Except it hadn't felt like that in that first instant. Hearing that word with that little face so close to his own had almost made him feel like a daddy himself. For one, blinding moment, he could understand what it would be like to love and be loved by a tiny human. How it could become the centre of your universe.

As it had for Emma?

That had been another startling revelation. A year ago, he would have laughed at the idea of Emma Matthews sitting at home like a nana, making tiny, felt toys to hang on a Christmas tree. It summed up just how much her life had changed and that change had happened because she had chosen to devote her life to a tiny, orphaned child. Her goddaughter. His *niece*…

Lily had finally worked out how to do the zip up. And then she pulled it down and laughed again.

And again, the sound undid something inside Jack's chest. As if his heart had a matching zipper and something had opened.

He could choose to devote his life to this delightful child.

He could love her with all his heart.

And then Jack remembered the kiss as he and Emma had been hanging those extraordinary memorial angels on the tree. How it had felt to be sharing that moment.

He could love Emma too.

No...

Shaking his head made him realise he needed to take some more painkillers but the sharp escalation of his headache was a good thing, in a way. It reminded Jack that he wasn't himself right now. That this confusing jumble of emotions that keep ambushing him were a by-product of a unique set of circumstances. It was the anniversary of a tragedy that had almost destroyed his life. It was Christmas, with all the emotions that this particular day could stir up. And not only was he injured enough to feel, to some extent, physically as well as emotionally vulnerable, he'd been transported into a place that felt more like a home than anything he could remember.

This was only one day. He could cope and then things would start to seem normal again.

He wouldn't be feeling like he was being torn in half.

He didn't belong here. This whole jumble of home and family and love were the things that were on the other side of the barrier he could still reach out and touch. A wall of solid bricks that had been crafted from a mix of grief and fear and loneliness. A mix that was stronger than any baked clay or concrete.

But the longing had never been this strong. It had never made him feel like he was hitting his head against that wall, again and again.

Maybe that was what was making his headache worse.

'Did I see what I thought I saw?'

'I don't know what you're talking about, Mum.' Emma could hear Lily's laughter coming from the living room and it was making her smile. Never mind that peeling potatoes was one of Jack's splinter skills. She was more than happy to be doing this task and leaving him to play with Lily. She just wanted to get it done as fast as possible, so she could go back and join in the fun.

For a moment her mother's low-voiced query had her puzzled.

'You and Jack. When you were hanging the angels on the tree. Was he…kissing you when I came in?'

'Um…' Emma turned on the tap to rinse the potato. 'You did know I used to go out with him?'

'Yes. But I thought that was all over.'

'It was. But then everything seemed to be all over for a while, didn't it? Life was pretty crazy.'

'I know.' Muriel's gaze was soft. 'It was a terrible time—especially for you and Jack.' She was putting the finishing touches to one of her famous trifles. 'But he's back now…' Opening the door of the fridge, she tried to find room for the dessert to chill. And then she glanced at Emma again. 'That's good, isn't it?'

'Mmm…' Emma had to look away. She didn't want her mother to know just how good it was as far as she was concerned.

Hope was a fragile thing and a hope this big had the potential to be crushing if it was broken. Things were changing and the hope was growing, despite warning herself that it might not be a good idea. How could it not grow, when Lily had all but called him Daddy? When Jack said things like she was the only person in the world who could have thought of something as special as the memorial angel decorations?

When he had kissed her. *Again*...

The touch of her mother's hand on her arm was unexpected.

'It'll be all right,' Muriel said softly. 'You'll see... Here, I'll finish those. I've just got the parsnips and brussels sprouts to do now. Isn't it time for Lily's nap?'

Emma glanced at her watch. The day was speeding past, thanks to their late start. Lily did need a nap, if she was going to be awake to share their Christmas lunch.

Heading back to the living room, she found Jack still lying on the floor with Lily. The expression on his face brought a lump to her throat. Had she not realised how sad it might be making him, being with a child who looked so like his beloved lost brother?

Would it be too much to take him even closer to those memories?

It might be. But then again, it could be important. For both of them. It could be the step that had to be taken in order to move forward.

'You look like you need a break.' She scooped Lily into her arms. 'It's time for your nap, sweetheart.'

Her heart beating a little faster, she looked back at Jack as she left the room.

'Harry needs a walk and there's something I need to do once Lily's asleep. I thought you might like to come with me. Get a bit of fresh air?'

'Sounds like a plan.' Jack was getting up from the

floor and it was clearly painful. 'I need to keep moving this leg, otherwise it might seize up completely.'

'You'll find Dad's old parka hanging in the porch out the back door. I don't guarantee the gumboots are still weatherproof but they're out there, too. Mum reckons it's a security thing, making it look like someone with big feet lives in the house.'

That earned her a smile and Emma smiled back.

Okay, she was taking a risk here. Maybe a massive risk.

But it felt like the right thing to do.

CHAPTER TEN

THE ONLY SOUNDS to be heard were the squeak and crunch of footsteps in a deep layer of fluffy, fresh snow and the huff of a panting dog as Harry circled back to see what was taking his people so long.

It was no wonder that he was a little puzzled. Emma was deliberately keeping her pace a lot slower than she would normally walk. The visible puffs of Jack's breath beside her were rapid and short enough to suggest that he was in a lot more discomfort than he was about to admit to.

It was just as well they didn't have too far to go. Emma's house was close to the outskirts of the village so they were already well on the way to her destination. Her gloved fingers closed more tightly around the scrunched top of the bag she was carrying as a niggle of doubt made her wonder again if she was really doing the right thing.

She had planned this as a private mission. When Lily was old enough to understand, they would do it together as another, very private, Christmas tradition but this was the first time and Emma couldn't know how it was going to affect herself, let alone Jack.

He certainly wasn't expecting anything confronting.

'This is like being inside a Christmas card,' he said.

'Look at that blanket of snow on everything—it's picture perfect.'

It was. Pale sunshine was peeping through spaces between cotton wool clouds and the snow on every roof glistened as if embedded with microscopic diamonds. Tree branches bowed under the weight of the snow they had captured and garden shrubs were shrouded into soft shapes that disguised the stark barrenness of winter.

A group of children were building a snowman on the sports field at the end of her street, red cheeks and bright eyes between warm woollen hats and thick scarves. An older boy hurled a snowball at the group and there was a shriek of outrage as snow found a gap to trickle down a small neck. As they turned the corner, they could hear a burst of laughter and shouts that indicated a good-natured declaration of war.

'We used to do that.' Emma smiled. 'Sarah and me. It's a village thing. There's always that time to fill, waiting for Christmas lunch, and all the kids would get shooed outside to give the adults a break.'

'So you'd build snowmen?'

'Do you know, I can't remember a real white Christmas? There were always things to do, though. Someone would have a new bike or scooter and we'd get to watch them learn how to ride it. One year, Sarah and I both got rollerskates and everybody watched us…' Emma's sigh was a happy one. 'Good times…'

'I'll bet.' Jack's breath came out in a longer puff of icy mist. 'The first time I remember having a Christmas with Ben, we were teenagers. The best gift we got was an old record player one year, with a box of albums.'

'Vinyl?' Emma grinned. 'That was pretty retro.'

'I wish I'd kept them,' Jack said. 'Everybody wants them now.' He shrugged. 'Back then, they were junk.

The sort of thing you could donate to a kids' home and not miss.'

Emma was silent for a minute. Harry came trotting back and circled around her legs before taking off again with an excited bark. He'd made this trip many times and knew exactly where they were going.

Jack shook his head. 'How old did you say he was?'

'Nearly sixteen.'

'He's acting like a puppy.'

'Mmm. It's always there, inside. For people as well as dogs, I reckon.'

'What is?'

'How it feels to be young. To see the magic in things. To feel that joy.' Emma glanced up at Jack but he was still watching Harry, who had stopped to dig in the snow. 'We forget. Or we realise that we have to start acting like grown-ups. It's one of the best things about being with Lily. It makes you remember. You can see things through her eyes and remember the magic.'

Jack didn't respond so Emma touched his arm. 'I'm sorry you and Ben had such a rough time when you were little. It really sucks.'

'Yeah…' Jack's bare hand came out of the pocket of the parka and took hold of Emma's. Even through the wool of her gloves, she could feel his warmth. 'But there were good times, too. You should have seen us playing air guitar to the Rolling Stones' "Satisfaction".'

Emma laughed. Any doubts that it hadn't been a good idea to bring Jack with her on this mission evaporated. The sun was still shining on them and Harry was coming back, his plume of a tail waving proudly, a large stick clamped between his jaws. And this was a new closeness with Jack that she'd never had before. How good was it that you could find something so happy to remember beneath layers of sadness? Poignant, but wonderful.

And then she recognised the matching clipped yew trees that met in an archway over the ancient iron gate.

And Jack realised where they were too.

He dropped Emma's hand abruptly. 'Oh, my God...' he breathed.

Emma didn't give him the opportunity to pause long enough to decide to turn back. She had to push hard to get the gate open against the weight of the snow and then she kept going. She didn't look back. Maybe Jack would choose to follow her. Maybe he wouldn't.

There were gravestones here that dated back to the fifteenth century, so worn it was almost impossible to read the inscriptions. Even the more recent stones had deep drifts of snow on top and in front of them but Emma didn't need to read any of the words. She knew exactly where she was going.

To Sarah and Ben's final resting place—off to one side at the far end of this peaceful site—beside one of the massive oak trees that closed them off from the rest of the world.

Snow marked by nothing except the patterns of birds' feet advertised that nobody else had been here yet today. Maybe most people preferred to simply raise a glass to family and friends that couldn't share their celebration. Very few people were unlucky enough to have Christmas as an anniversary like this but, having been forced to become a member of such an exclusive club, it was a comfort to have someone to share it with.

It was a bond that she and Jack would always have. Would always remember on this particular day.

And she could hear the crunch of Jack's footsteps behind her.

He had chosen to follow her. A bloom of something like pure pride filled her chest. How brave was he, to be fronting up to what must be his biggest demon of losing his twin? It would have to feel as though he'd lost the other half of himself.

Emma cleared the snow from in front of Sarah and Ben's stone. The inscription that went around the dates was very simple.

Ben Reynolds and Sarah Reynolds
Dearly loved parents of Lily
Together forever

Jack was standing as still as any of the marble angels dotted around this old cemetery but Emma was still crouching. She opened the bag she had brought with her and took out the small items.

A wreath of plastic mistletoe with its bunches of tiny, white berries.

A photograph of Lily in a heart-shaped silver frame.

A piece of star-shaped shortbread that was decorated with tiny silver balls.

She looked up at Jack as she placed the last item on the ground. The glance apologised for what probably seemed such an unusual choice.

'Sarah loved Mum's shortbread so much. Mum would post a box of it to us when we were away at medical school and she'd always be so excited when it arrived.'

'I seem to remember it got a mention at the wedding.' Jack's voice sounded strained. 'Wasn't it part of the cake?'

'There was a pile of it around the bottom of the cake. Tiny, heart-shaped ones.'

Emma had to put her fingers against her mouth to

stifle a sob. Then she touched the names on the stone, as if she was transferring a kiss. Her legs were starting to ache from crouching so she stood up. In summer she had often sat on the grass right here, talking to Sarah, but when it was wet, or cold, she would go and sit on the bench under the oak tree. So that was where she headed now. There wasn't much snow to brush off the wooden slats of the bench. It would be cold and probably a bit damp, but that didn't matter.

It was this time that mattered. The memories.

It felt weird doing it in company other than Harry's. How could she talk to Sarah if there was anyone to hear her? But when Jack came to sit beside her and took hold of her hand again, that didn't matter, either.

Conversation didn't have to be in words, did it? It could simply be thoughts. And feelings.

Like the conversation she and Jack were having as they sat here silently.

It was a long time before the silence got broken. It was Jack who broke it.

'I get the shortbread. And the photo of Lily, of course. But why the fake mistletoe? Just because it's Christmas?'

'It was a joke.' Emma's smile felt misty. 'You know Sarah and I shared an apartment and from the moment she met Ben they were inseparable. And they couldn't keep their hands off each other. It felt like every time I went into a room, there they were, kissing...'

Jack snorted. 'Yeah...in our place, too.'

'So one time I said, *For heaven's sake, guys, it's not Christmas—there's no mistletoe around here.* And...' Emma had to clear her throat. 'It was so like Sarah. I don't know how she managed it in the middle of summer, but she went out the next day and bought this huge, horrible sprig of plastic mistletoe and hung it from the lampshade in our living room. It was always there.' Emma's voice wobbled. 'It was always kissing time for those two…'

The grip on her hand tightened.

'They were so happy, weren't they?'

'I've never seen two people so much in love. Their wedding day was so special.'

'It was…'

Jack's gaze met Emma's and she knew he was thinking the same thing she was. That the day hadn't just been so special because two people who loved each other so much were making a public commitment to share their lives forever.

It was the day that she and Jack had connected. Oh, they knew who the other was well before that, of course. She'd seen him around the hospital often enough but she'd kept a careful distance. Everybody knew Jack Reynolds's reputation and Emma had no interest in becoming another chalk mark on a bedpost.

Yep. Jack was definitely following her train of thought.

'Do you think they knew?' he asked quietly. 'About us? Did you tell Sarah?'

'Of course not. She would have been horrified.'

'Yeah… Ben would have been horrified, too. He told me right from the start that you were out of bounds. That I'd be in big trouble if I even thought about messing with his girlfriend's bestie.'

Jack's face creased into lines of deep discomfort. Shame, even? He let go of Emma's hand and she saw his fingers clench into a fist. He seemed to be watching his own hand as well.

'Was I really that awful?'

'Quite the opposite.' Emma had to smile. 'You were too charming. Sarah knew I'd be in danger of falling for you. That I'd end up with my heart broken like half the women at the Eastern.'

She wanted him to look up. To see her smile. To see that she'd understood what she had been letting herself in for and that she didn't blame him for leaving a hole in her life that couldn't be filled by anyone else, any more than the Sarah-shaped hole could be filled.

But Jack was still staring down at his hand. His breath came out slowly enough to make a cloud of mist that hung in front of his mouth. What if he asked her if that had been what had really happened in the end? Would she confess that she *had* fallen in love with him? That she still felt the same way?

'I never set out to hurt people, you know.'

Emma put her hand over his fist. 'I know that, Jack.'

When he looked up, his eyes were so dark they looked haunted.

'I wanted what Ben had found, even though I pretended I didn't.' A tiny shake of his head sent a lock of that shaggy hair across his forehead. It was long enough to be hanging over one eye and Emma badly wanted to reach up and smooth it away.

Jack didn't appear to notice it.

'No...that's not really accurate. I wasn't pretending. I really believed that it wasn't something I'd ever want.'

Emma felt a shiver slide down her spine. Was it due to sitting so still in this chilly air? Or was it a premonition that she was about to hear something she really didn't want to hear?

'You mean...marriage? Having a family?'

'All of it. The thing that makes it happen. Makes it work...'

Emma swallowed hard. 'Love,' she whispered.

'I've learned something in the last year,' Jack said.

'You can't not learn things when you see the kind of stuff I saw. When you get time to sit under a scrubby apology for a tree in the starkness of a desert and there's nothing to do but think about things.'

His fist finally opened beneath her hand and his fingers laced themselves through Emma's.

'I learned that I'd been lying to myself for most of my life. Of course I wanted those things. I just… I just can't have them…'

Words were extraordinary things, weren't they? Sometimes they could be so heavy, it felt like they were crushing you. Making it almost impossible to breathe. Making it just as hard to find your own words and make them into sounds.

'You *can*, Jack… You can have all those things.'

They were right here, waiting for him. All he had to do was open his arms and embrace them.

But he was shaking his head.

'I can't get past the wall,' he murmured.

'What wall?'

'The one I started building after Mum died and then Ben got taken away from me. The wall I could hide behind so that I couldn't see the bad stuff.'

'But you and Ben were together again. You went through med school together. You were working in the same hospital. Living together… You looked like you were the best friends anybody could ever have.'

'And then Ben died…' There was anger in Jack's voice. Or was it desperation? 'So I had to make the wall even bigger. Stronger.'

Emma could feel tears gathering. 'I don't understand,' she said into the silence. 'You're not just shutting yourself away from bad stuff. You're shutting yourself away from the *good* stuff, too. The things that make life worth living. You know what's on the other side of that wall, don't you? Love…'

Jack's voice sounded raw now. 'Oh, yeah…the kind of love that's there when you're little and your mum is alive and there's someone to hold you when you get hurt and tell you everything's going to be okay…'

Emma's heart was breaking for that little boy who'd lost his mother.

'And the kind that's there when you've got a twin brother and it doesn't matter how bad things are anymore because you're never, ever going to be completely alone…'

'But that's a good place,' Emma whispered. 'There's still love there for you. From Lily… From *me*…'

There. She'd said it. It was out in the open.

'It's the hole,' Jack said.

'Sorry?'

'Just behind that wall, before you get to any place that's good, there's a hole. The one you fall into when you lose that love. The one that doesn't have a bottom. Or sides that you can climb up.'

Finally, Emma could understand.

'The wall is there to stop you ever falling into the hole again?'

Jack didn't say anything. He just looked at Emma and the sadness in his eyes said it all.

'Oh, Jack…' Emma wrapped her arms around him and hugged him as hard as she could. For her own sake as well as his. Her heart was still breaking for that little boy he'd been. It was breaking for the man who'd lost his brother. It was breaking for the man who believed he couldn't ever open his heart enough to love again.

And it was breaking for herself and Lily, because they were on the other side of that damned wall. On the other side of that hole that Jack was too afraid to fall into again.

Was it time to accept that her dream was never going to come true?

Emma gave that thought a mental shove. She wasn't ready to do that. She'd held on to it for so long now, despite evidence that it was already impossible, and it was even harder to contemplate now, when she had Jack right beside her. When she had his arms around her.

It was, however, time they went home.

Time they sat down to the Christmas lunch that would be ready by now. Around that old kitchen table.

As if they were a real family…

Letting go of Jack, Emma looked around for her beloved shaggy dog, who was rolling in a snowdrift away from the trees.

'Come on,' she called. 'Time to go home, Harry.'

Jack paused for a long moment before he followed them but Emma just waited at the gate until he was ready to leave.

He was standing so still beside the graveside, his head bent.

As if he was having a quiet word with Ben.

The walk home had become a marathon.

Jack had never felt this exhausted in his life. He couldn't hide a limp as he put weight on his sore leg. His ribs hurt every time he sucked in another breath of that icy air and his head was aching unbearably but he knew that the real exhaustion was emotional.

To feel Ben's presence like that, as he stood up to leave, had been a bombshell.

This had just been a place. A place he had never

wanted to be in and he hadn't even thought of coming back since the day Ben and Sarah had been laid to rest here. He had avoided ever thinking about that horrible day and it hadn't been that difficult because he had been so grief-stricken during those hours of the ceremony that the memory was barely more than a blur.

It had taken all his courage to walk through that gate and he couldn't have done it alone.

But Emma had been with him and she'd made it possible. Maybe because she'd teased a happy memory out of him before they'd even arrived at that gate.

Even now, the image of him and Ben playing air guitar on that long-ago Christmas Day made him want to smile.

And that plastic mistletoe…

He'd never been that inventive when he'd found Ben and Sarah kissing in his apartment. *Get a room*, he'd tell them, but he'd be smiling then, too. He'd been happy that his brother had found exactly what he wanted for his future. He'd found the love of his life.

Ben Reynolds and Sarah Reynolds
Together forever

And then it had hit him.

This was the last place he had ever physically been in his brother's presence. And it felt as if that presence was still here.

Words had come from a place that had been so well hidden he wouldn't have been able to find it even if he'd felt like looking.

I miss you, bro. Like you wouldn't believe…

His whole body had hurt as the words had taken form—but not as much as he might have feared.

And it felt like something locked up had been re-leased. The relief that came in the wake of the pain made him realise that unlocking that space was the right thing to have happened. That it should have happened a long time ago?

There had been relief to be found in confessing his greatest flaw today, too. That he simply wasn't capable of loving someone again. Emma didn't seem to hate him for that. The way she'd held him had told him that she understood. That she loved him even if he couldn't re-turn it. That meant he could be himself, didn't it? That maybe he didn't have to avoid giving what he *was* ca-pable of, because he wasn't going to be blamed for what he couldn't give?

But Emma thought he could...

She and Lily were on the other side of that wall...

Waiting for him?

Maybe...just maybe...he was wrong...

Had he shut Emma and Lily away in the same space that Ben had been trapped in? The space that had just been unlocked?

He had to bow his head as remorse flooded him.

I'm sorry, mate. I should have been here for your daughter. For Emma... She looks like you, man. She's a mini-me except that she's a girl. A gorgeous, won-derful little girl. You would have been so proud. I'm proud for you...

It wasn't just the exhaustion and the pain that was making this walk home so hard. The fragments of mem-ories and the kaleidoscope of emotions still swirling in his head were too much. Coherent thoughts were be-coming too difficult and confusion came in like a fog that made his head spin so much that he felt like he was actually falling as he tried to put one foot in front of the other.

'Whoa…' He could feel the grip of Emma's arm coming around his waist. Keeping him upright? 'Thank goodness we're almost home. You need to sit down for a while. It was too much, too soon, this walk. I'm sorry I made you come with me.'

'Don't be.' Jack screwed his eyes tightly shut as he stopped for a moment, trying to push the dizziness away. 'It was the right thing to do and…and thank you for taking me.'

He opened his eyes to find Emma smiling up at him. For a moment, his head felt clear again. It wasn't even hurting. And his heart? It felt full enough to burst.

'You're the best thing that's ever happened to me, you know,' he said. 'You're…well, *you're* just the best, Red.'

He had to kiss her. Judging by the way Emma stood on tiptoe and held her face up to his, she felt exactly the same way.

It was like the kiss beside the Christmas tree. A kiss that was heartbreakingly tender. But it was also like the kiss in her office last night. The one that had been less than a hair's breadth from spiralling into the kind of desire he'd never expected to feel again.

Heat that started in his body but seemed to explode into his head with enough force to make him groan softly. He didn't want this. It was just another burst of emotion that he simply didn't have the strength to handle.

'Come on.' Emma had taken his hand again. 'Let's get you inside. Some good food and a long rest and you won't know yourself.'

He didn't feel as if he knew himself now. Was it the combination of physical and emotional exhaustion that was making things feel so weird?

The warmth of the house was too much after being outside in the cold. He stripped off the parka and the old woollen jersey but it still felt too warm as they gathered around the kitchen table.

The feast arranged in front of him was everything a Christmas lunch should be. Muriel was carving succulent-looking slices from the roast turkey. There was a steaming bowl of brussels sprouts sprinkled with what looked like crumbs of pancetta and a platter of crispy, roasted potatoes and parsnips. There were jugs of gravy and bread sauce and a bright bowl of cranberry sauce. It should have all looked and smelt delicious but Jack had to fight a horrible wave of nausea and he could feel beads of perspiration break out on his forehead.

Lily was sitting in her high chair. She was laughing. Banging a spoon on the tray, and the sound was getting louder and louder until it felt like every bang was cracking his skull.

Muriel was asking him something. He could see her mouth moving and hear the sound coming out but he couldn't understand the words.

And Emma...

Emma was staring at him and she looked...terrified? He had to tell her everything was all right.

That he'd make it all right, because he loved her.

He needed to touch her hand so he leaned sideways to reach her. But then he couldn't stop.

He was falling into space...

Black space...

It sounded as though Emma was calling him from the other side of the world.

Or maybe it was just the other side of the wall...

'Jack... Oh, my God... *Jack*...'

CHAPTER ELEVEN

SHE COULDN'T STOP it happening.

The best that Emma could manage was to hold on to Jack and protect his head from directly hitting the stone flags of the kitchen floor.

Lily was crying. A frightened wail, the likes of which Emma had never heard before.

Or maybe she had. A tiny corner of her mind registered notes that reminded her of this time a year ago, when a small baby had become an orphan. When all Lily had wanted was to be held in her mother's arms and she couldn't understand why it couldn't happen.

Her mother's voice sounded odd, too, because her mother never got frightened—Muriel Matthews could cope with anything. Even now, she was crouching beside Emma, with a folded dish towel to provide a pillow.

'What's happened?'

'I don't know for sure…' Emma gently put Jack's head onto the towel. She lifted his eyelids and another fragment of memory tried to sabotage her focus. A much more recent memory, this one—of Jack telling her that Lily had prised his eyelid open to wake him up.

This wasn't about to wake him up. There was enough light in the kitchen for Emma to see that the response of one of his pupils was too sluggish. Even worse, the other pupil didn't move at all in response to the light. It was fixed and dilated.

'I think…' Emma had to take a deep breath. 'I think Jack's bleeding. Under his skull. It's putting pressure on his brain.'

'Oh…dear Lord…' Muriel was on her feet again. 'We need help, don't we? Shall I call for an ambulance?'

Emma shook her head. 'Bring me my phone. I'll have to call for a helicopter. An ambulance would take too long. We need to get him into hospital as quickly as possible or…'

Or there would be little chance of saving him.

Emma couldn't bring herself to say the words. Couldn't bear to think them, even. Part of her wanted to cry—the kind of cry Lily was still making—but a much bigger part wasn't about to crumple.

'You're not going to die, Jack.' Her voice was low and fierce. 'I won't let you… Not today. Not ever, if I have anything to do with it.'

Muriel rushed back with Emma's phone and she knew she sounded far calmer than she was feeling as she requested urgent assistance.

'A thirty-six-year-old male,' she told them. 'He was involved in a motorbike accident yesterday. He appeared to have concussion but no skull fracture. He's now collapsed and showing signs of raised intracranial pressure. I'm suspecting an epidural or subdural haemorrhage. GCS is currently three and he's bradycardic, with a heart rate of fifty-six.'

Glancing up, Emma saw that her mother had lifted Lily from the high chair and was doing her best to calm the little girl. Lily had her head buried against her grandmother's shoulder and she'd stopped crying. Muriel was looking shocked, however, as she listened to Emma's side of the call.

'Yes…' she said then. 'Church Street, Achadunan. There's a sports field a short distance from the house. We'll get someone out there to signal the crew… Please hurry…'

Muriel was dispatched to warn the neighbours and gather help. They would need to make sure that there were no children on the sports field and have enough people to signal that the rescue helicopter had reached its destination. She bundled Lily into her pink coat and rushed out, leaving Emma alone with Jack.

Time seemed to stop after that. There was little Emma could do except monitor Jack and watch for any deterioration in his heart rate or breathing. She had no oxygen in the house. No IV fluids or kit that contained intubation gear. No way of paging a neurosurgeon or getting fast-tracked for a CT scan.

Why hadn't they done a CT scan last night as well as all those X-rays? Jack had admitted to a headache but there'd been no fracture visible on X-ray and she'd assumed he'd been under observation long enough for something serious to have become obvious.

He'd been in pain today, too. She'd seen that when they had been walking to the cemetery. He must have had a terrible headache but he hadn't said anything.

'Oh, Jack…' Emma smoothed the hair back from his forehead and checked his pupils again. She watched his chest rise and fall. Was his rate of breathing getting more rapid—showing signs of distress? She kept her fingers on his wrist for a minute. Was his heart rate getting slower?

Harry was lying beside her, his nose touching her knee, and he was watching every move she made.

This shouldn't be happening, Emma thought, blink-

ing back tears as she saw how anxious Harry looked.
They should all be eating their Christmas lunch. Harry
should be in his usual position, thinking that he was hidden under the kitchen table. Waiting for a scrap of delicious turkey or a crunchy edge of a roast potato to fall
from the tray of Lily's high chair so he could do his duty
and keep the kitchen floor clean. Lily would giggle, as
she always did, and another piece of food would 'accidentally' fall within seconds.

Emma could almost hear an echo of that adorable giggle. She could hear something, anyway. Harry could hear
it, too. He lifted his head and pricked his ears up.

'Oh…' Emma let out a breath with no idea of how long
she'd been holding it. 'It's the helicopter coming, Harry.
Coming for Jack.'

The sound got louder and louder. She could imagine
the big rescue chopper hovering over the sports field and
stirring up a cloud of snow as it came down to land.

'They're here,' she told Jack. 'Hold on, love. You're
going to make it. You're going to be okay. You have to
be…' She didn't want to be sitting here with tears pouring down her face when the paramedics arrived but there
was no stopping the flow just yet.

'I can't lose you,' she whispered brokenly. 'And Lily
can't lose you. We need you.' Jack's face was a blur as
she leaned closer. 'And you can't hear me and you might
not believe me, even if you could hear me, but *you* need
us, too. We *love* you…'

If time had slowed while waiting for the rescue team
to arrive, it sped up to an astonishing degree the moment
they burst through the door.

This was a new experience for Emma. These people
were highly skilled in dealing with this kind of trauma
and the team included a doctor. For the first time, she was

in the realm of being a scared relative. It was worse for her knowing how serious this was but, on the positive side, she knew that the team were doing all the right things.

'Blood pressure's one hundred and five on seventy.'

'Let's get IV access and some fluids running, but keep an eye on the BP. We don't want it any higher than one-twenty. We don't want that ICP going up any further. Draw up some mannitol, too.' The doctor caught Emma's gaze.

'How many hours did you say it is since the original injury?'

'About fifteen,' Emma told them. 'It's more likely to be subdural with that time frame, isn't it?'

'Could be a venous rather than an arterial bleed. Okay… we're going to intubate and then get moving. Keep that oxygen on…'

Emma kept watching. Would they remember to elevate Jack's head by thirty degrees and make sure his head and neck were maintained in a midline position as they got him onto the stretcher?

'Is someone coming with us? We've got room for one.'

'Me,' Emma said instantly. 'Are you okay with Lily, Mum?'

Things had been moving so fast she hadn't even looked in her mother's direction for some time. Muriel was standing at the other end of the table, Lily still in her arms. Harry was behind her, in his basket.

'Of course. You go.'

Emma's head turned to see the stretcher already moving towards the door, the portable units to monitor heart rhythm and respiratory function clipped onto a frame over Jack's feet.

Turning back, she noticed the tabletop that she'd forgotten about as she'd crouched on the floor close to Jack.

Their uneaten Christmas lunch. The unpulled crackers. The bright paper hats that had never been worn.

'I'm so sorry, Mum…'

'Go.' Muriel's voice cracked. 'And call me—the moment you know anything.'

Emma made her first call a little over half an hour later.

'They've taken Jack to Theatre, Mum.'

'What did the neurosurgeon say?'

'That he was young and fit and…and that the odds are in his favour. He was stable by the time we arrived at the emergency department.'

'Did he regain consciousness?'

'No…' Emma pushed back the wave of helplessness and fear she had been swamped with as she'd watched another team that didn't include her working to save Jack.

'Oh, love… I'm sorry. But he's in the best place. They'll be doing everything they can.'

'I know.' Emma had to clear her throat. 'How's Lily?'

'She's fine. Still playing with that toy that Jack gave her. And Harry won't let her out of his sight. It's like he thinks she's in some kind of danger…'

Emma was nodding but couldn't say the words aloud. Lily was in danger—of losing her uncle and one of the strongest links to the people she had already tragically lost. Emma felt like she was in danger herself. It would have been a comfort to have Harry here in this waiting room with her, his head heavy on her knee, and those kind brown eyes telling her how much she was loved.

'I'd better let you go, Mum. I'll call again when I know more.'

Christmas Day was drawing to a close by the time she called again.

'He's in Intensive Care now, Mum. I've had to come out to make this call but I've been sitting with him for a bit. They say the surgery went very well. He's breathing for himself and everything that's being monitored looks fine but…'

She could hear her mother's sharp intake of breath. 'But…?'

'He's not showing any signs of waking up yet.'

'Give it time, love…'

'I know…'

'Lily's asleep. With Jack's bear clutched in her arms.'

Emma couldn't say anything. Her heart was hurting too much.

'Have you had anything to eat?'

'I couldn't. Have you?'

'No…' The huff of sound was almost a chuckle. 'I think we'll be eating turkey sandwiches until New Year.'

'I'm sorry, Mum. It hasn't been the best Christmas, has it?'

There was a moment's silence. Emma knew they were both thinking of how bad last Christmas had been. Fielding a shock wave that history could be trying to repeat itself with another tragedy? And then the feeling of the silence changed, as if they were both finding and clinging to the ways in which this Christmas Day had brought them joy—like the surprise of Jack coming home and the sheer delight that their precious little girl generated for all those around her.

'I'll come in tomorrow, shall I? When the roads have been cleared? I could bring Lily in.'

'That's a good idea, Mum.' Maybe the sound of Lily's voice would be enough to bring Jack back from wherever he was resting at the moment.

A peaceful place, hopefully. A very different place

from that dark hole he was so afraid of. That she was desperately afraid of too, right now. The need to get back to Jack was so intense she could feel it in every cell of her body. She needed to be beside him. Close enough to touch him. So that he would know she was there…

'I have to get back,' she said aloud. 'I need to be there when he wakes up.'

'Of course you do, darling. I'll see you tomorrow. Love you.'

'Love you, too. And, Mum?'

'Yes?'

'Bring me a turkey sandwich tomorrow, okay?'

The night ticked on, with every second marked by the beeping of the monitors around Jack's bed.

Emma sat on a chair, close enough to be able to hold Jack's hand. The need for sleep had evaporated along with any need for food. There was only one thing she needed right now and that was for Jack to wake up. And be all right.

Between the visits of the doctors and nurses caring for Jack, Emma talked to him quietly. She told him what had happened. What was happening now. What the monitors were revealing about how well he was doing. She reassured him, over and over again, that he was going to be okay. That they would get through this.

In the quietest hours, just before dawn, when exhaustion was threatening to overcome her, Emma's spirits sank a little.

'This is my fault,' she whispered. 'I should have noticed. I shouldn't have pushed you into going for that walk but… I wanted you to…' Emma stopped on a sigh. Whatever she had thought she wanted, like breaking through to a point of real connection, had backfired, hadn't it?

That glimpse at the impenetrable barrier Jack believed he had put in place to protect himself from ever losing someone he loved again had been so heartbreaking.

But…

'You were wrong, Jack.' Taking hold of his hand, being very careful not to disturb the IV line, Emma picked it up and held it against her heart. 'You think you're behind your wall and you're not capable of really loving anybody again but it's not true. I think you already love Lily. I saw your face when you looked at that photograph of her and…and you said, "She's a Reynolds, all right…" You felt the pull of family, didn't you? The love…'

Emma swallowed hard. 'And I think you love me, too. You said I'm the best thing that's ever happened to you but I see more than that when you look at me sometimes. I *feel* more than that when you kiss me…'

The beeping around her seemed to miss a beat and then speed up. Alarmed, Emma gently put Jack's hand down again while she scanned the figures on all the screens until everything settled again.

Her elbows on the edge of the bed, she buried her face in her hands as it all became too overwhelming. Tears were forming and she knew she couldn't stop them falling. Perhaps she didn't want to try.

'Loving people isn't what destroys you,' she whispered, brokenly. 'Sometimes it's the only thing that can save you. You can be in that black hole, but when there's someone who loves you on the same side of that wall, they can reach down and take hold of your hand. That's how you climb out, Jack… Every time…'

She couldn't say anything more. She couldn't even think straight anymore. Her eyes tightly shut, Emma didn't even open them when she heard the beeping change pace again. If something was wrong, an alarm would sound and others would come running. There was nothing she would be able to do, anyway.

She had done everything she possibly could.

And maybe it wasn't enough.

The touch on her arm was so soft Emma barely registered it at first. But then the pressure increased and she took her hands away from her face and scraped away the tears that were blinding her.

Yes... Jack's hand was moving.

Touching her arm.

Her gaze flew to his face. His eyes were still shut but his lips were moving, too.

'I… I need…'

'What, Jack?' Emma's heart was in her mouth. Whatever he needed, she would give it to him if she possibly could. How could you do anything else, when you loved someone with all your heart and soul?

'I…' It was clearly an enormous effort for Jack to form any words. But, at the same time, the corners of his mouth were curving into the beginnings of a smile. 'I need…to hold your hand…'

EPILOGUE

'How long has it been since we had a real, white Christmas?' Emma paused in her task of peeling potatoes to peer through the window over her mother's kitchen sink.

'Five years.' Muriel didn't look up from the pot of bread sauce she was stirring, but Emma could hear the smile in her voice. 'And I'm sure you remember the last one as well as I do.'

'Mmm…' Of course she did. Every minute of it. But Emma could find joy in those memories now. There had been sad moments, of course, because it had been so soon after losing Sarah and Ben. There had been terrifying moments, too, like when Jack had collapsed at the table and she'd been so afraid of losing him forever.

But there were joyous moments that always took precedence when she thought about that particular Christmas.

Finding Lily asleep in the crook of Jack's arm.

Being kissed in front of the Christmas tree.

Sharing happy memories of two people they had both loved so much.

What she could see through the kitchen window right now was giving her even more joy. Emma could feel a bubble of happiness expanding inside her that would break free in laughter at any moment now.

The potatoes were forgotten.

'We're going to have eight very wet paws coming through that door any minute now.'

The sibling golden retrievers, Bert and Ernie, were romping in the snow, playing chase around the old oak tree that still had her childhood swing hanging from its lowest branch.

They'd only intended to get one puppy when Harry had peacefully passed away a couple of years ago but Muriel had come with them to make their choice from the litter and she had fallen in love herself. She'd told them her house was too lonely without Harry. She'd never complained that the house was too empty without Emma and Lily but losing Harry had hit her hard.

'There's a good pile of old towels on the back porch,' Muriel said calmly. 'It's those eight gumboots *I'm* worried about.'

Emma dried her hands on a tea towel. 'I'll sort them. Have you got a carrot?'

'No… Why?'

'I reckon that snowman is about finished out there. He needs a nose.'

'I gave you my last ones yesterday, so you could put them out for the reindeer, remember? You'll have to make do with a parsnip. Here…' Muriel chose the largest of the vegetables waiting their turn to be peeled. 'And I'll be shooing any bairns out my kitchen when they come in. If I don't get these veggies in the oven along with that turkey, it'll be bedtime before we get to eat our lunch.'

Emma laughed. 'You always say that, Mum.' But she paused as she turned. 'It's a bit much, us coming out here for Christmas Day now, isn't it? We're bursting at the seams. We could do Christmas at our place next year, if you like.'

Their place. The huge, rambling, two-storeyed stone

house in Dumbarton, with its big, high-ceilinged rooms and a huge garden, that had been home for nearly four years now. Halfway between Achadunan and the Eastern Infirmary. Not too far to drive to work. Not too far for Muriel to drive in to help with childcare.

But Muriel shook her head. 'We have Christmas here,' she said. 'It's what we do and you know why as well as I do. I *like* it that we're bursting at the seams.' Her glance slid down from Emma's face and her smile became tender. 'You're just about bursting at *your* seams. Don't you go having that baby today, will you?'

'No chance. We don't do hospitals at Christmastime anymore. It's a rule.'

Emma's smile was just as tender as her mother's as she headed for the back door, parsnip in hand. It wasn't a rule, exactly, but it had definitely been a promise. One of the many promises she and Jack had made in those quiet hours, so long ago, as he'd slowly but completely recovered from his injuries and his surgery.

Like the promise to always be there to hold each other's hands that they'd written into their wedding vows. Nobody else present had known the private significance of those words. That had been exchanged silently, as they'd held each other's gaze and uttered the promise that no hole would ever be too deep to reach into. That they could survive anything by being brave enough to love...

Misty-eyed, Emma stepped into sunshine and noise. The dogs were barking and the children shouting and laughing.

Gorgeous Lily, six and a half years old now, with her big, brown eyes and long, dark braids—threaded with tinsel today—and her gentle nature. The perfect big sister for her twin brothers, Andrew and Jamie, who would be turning four in a couple of months.

Fate had given their lives a very unexpected twist in giving them twin boys. Initially such a poignant surprise, it had been a complete joy ever since. A chance to rewrite a little bit of history, even, and give these twin brothers the kind of life that their father and uncle had been denied.

Not that these two looked anything like Jack and Ben. Or Lily, for that matter. No... The Matthews genes had declared their dominance on that occasion and these happy, boisterous little boys had curly red hair and freckles. But they were Reynolds through and through as well. You only had to look at those amazing, dark brown eyes to see that.

An exact match of the pair that had spotted her arrival into the chaos of the small garden and were telling her that life had just become that much better thanks to her presence. For a moment, just before any of the children saw her, Emma could bask in that gaze and send her own message back.

Life's good, isn't it? Love you so much...

'Mumma!' Two small bodies hurtled towards her. Four small arms wrapped themselves around her legs. 'Kisses,' they chorused. 'Kisses for Kissmas.'

It was getting increasingly hard to bend over so Emma just ruffled curly heads and blew kisses.

'Look, Mumma...we made a snowman.'

'You did. He's a fantastic snowman.' She could feel cold little ears beneath her fingers. 'Where are your hats?'

'I've got them.' Lily had a woollen hat in each hand. 'They won't keep them on. Andy... Jamie... Come *here*...'

But the twins had other ideas. They were taking off their parkas now.

'A *snowman*,' Jamie shouted, gleefully. 'Just like ours.'

While Lily had chosen a Christmas sweater with an

angel on the front this year, the twins had chosen identical versions that had cheerful-looking snowmen with carrot noses on a blue background.

'Just the same,' their father agreed, but he flashed a wink at Emma. Their rather short creation only had one ball for its body, the head was at a distinctly odd angle and the stones that had been found for its eyes were on very different levels.

'It's a wonderful snowman,' Emma said. 'Here's a carrot for the nose.'

The boys stared at her offering.

'It's a funny colour,' Andrew said. 'I don't like it.'

'Maybe the snowman has caught a cold,' Emma suggested. 'That can make your nose a funny colour. Who wants to put it on?'

'Me!' the boys shouted in unison.

'I'll do it,' Lily announced. 'Because I'm the oldest. And you did the eyes.'

Jamie scowled up at his sister. 'Not fair. You got to do the angels on the top of the Christmas tree.'

'That's because they're *my* angels. My angel Mummy and Daddy.'

The parsnip nose had been forgotten. 'I want an angel Mummy and Daddy too,' Andrew said.

'You've got a *real* Mummy and Daddy.' Lily took the parsnip from Emma's hand.

'So do you.' Muriel had come outside, too. 'And you boys have got an angel uncle and auntie.'

'And a nana,' Jamie said. 'Because we've got *you*…'

It was Muriel's turn to have her legs encased by small arms and she was smiling. She stooped to kiss each boy in turn.

'Kisses,' she said.

'For *Kissmas*,' they chorused.

The adults shared a fond glance that included Lily. She was the one who had invented this tradition and it was one they would always happily maintain.

'You're going to come inside with Nana now,' Muriel told the twins, 'because I'm going to read you a story. Mummy and Daddy and Lily have somewhere to go before lunch. Before it starts snowing again.' She handed two leads to Jack. 'Take the dogs with you. Sarah would love that.' She took a small, tissue-wrapped item from the pocket of her apron. 'And here's the shortbread. I didn't forget.'

'I'll get the bag from the car,' Jack said. 'You ready, Lily?'

The parsnip was in place and Lily's nod was solemn. 'I'm ready.'

They had to walk more slowly this year so Lily was well ahead of them, a dog trotting on either side, as they reached the quiet cemetery.

'I'm waddling, aren't I?' Emma sighed. 'I might not even fit through that gate.'

'As if...' Jack's hold on her hand tightened and Emma had to stop. Not that she ever minded being pulled into her husband's arms like this.

Being kissed like this...

'I love you,' Jack whispered against her lips. 'Even when you waddle. *Especially* when you waddle.'

Emma tilted her head back so that she could see Jack's eyes.

'I love you, too. Always have. Always will...' She smiled. 'And I love kisses for Kissmas, too.'

The kiss was even more tender this time. It acknowledged the unbreakable bond that was the foundation of this growing family. Maybe it was because this bond had been forged by the fires of shared agony that it was strong and fierce enough now to produce such incredible tenderness.

Jack's arms tightened around Emma but it was harder to get close enough at the moment. The baby between them moved as it was pressed into the hug and they could both feel it. They drew apart far enough to share another glance—one that shone with the wonder that came from creating a new life together, in more ways than one.

'Mummy? Daddy?' Lily's call was faint. 'Are you coming?'

'Coming, sweetheart.' Jack took Emma's hand again and held it firmly as he made sure she didn't stumble on any hidden dips in the snow-covered path.

The ritual stayed the same every year but there were always changes, too, because that was life. Some things stayed the same but some things always changed. And some of those changes were so good it was always worth getting through the rest.

The plastic mistletoe would last forever, but there was no need of a photograph of Lily anymore because she was here in person. She had made a special Christmas card at school and Emma had had it laminated so it wouldn't be ruined by any rain. The shortbread was still star-shaped but the decorations were different because the children had helped their nana with the baking. This one had a wobbly smiley face.

And it seemed that there was another change this year. With an expression that Emma couldn't read, Jack opened the fastenings on his parka.

It was Emma who had a wobbly smiley face now.

'What's funny?'

'Nothing. I just love it that you're wearing a Christmas sweater.'

It was green and it had a huge plum pudding as its motif, with a sprig of holly on top.

'Hey… I love Christmas now…'

Emma blinked back sudden tears. 'I know…'

'Thanks to you. Which was why I went looking for this. I was thinking about that first time we came here.'

He was reaching inside his parka. Lily was staring at the small, black circle he produced.

'What is it?'

'It's a record. A vinyl record like they had in the old days. This one's small, because it's a single.'

'A single what?'

'A single song. Well, it has one on the other side, too, but only one that's special.'

Lily was trying to read the paper disc around the hole. 'What is it? A Christmas carol?'

'No.' Emma's voice felt thick, as if it was having trouble getting around the lump in her throat. 'It's a song by a very famous group called the Rolling Stones.'

'It's called "Satisfaction",' Jack added.

Lily's nose wrinkled. 'That's a really weird name for a song. What's satisfaction?'

'It means that you have something that makes you very happy,' Emma explained. 'Something that means you don't want anything else.'

She was talking to their daughter, but her gaze locked with Jack's as he straightened from placing his contribution to the memories. Her heart was being squeezed, so hard it was almost painful, by an image of two teenage boys playing air guitar on a long-ago Christmas Day.

'I have *so* much satisfaction,' she said softly. 'Thanks to you, my love. I will never, ever want anything else.'

Jack's gaze was suspiciously bright. And then she

couldn't see it anymore because she was once again in the arms of the man she loved so much.

'Same,' he murmured against her ear. 'Let's go home…'

* * * * *

Look out for the next great story in the
CHRISTMAS EVE MAGIC *duet*

THE NIGHTSHIFT BEFORE CHRISTMAS
by Annie O'Neil

And if you enjoyed this story, check out
these other great reads from

Alison Roberts

THE FLING THAT CHANGED EVERYTHING
THE NURSE WHO STOLE HIS HEART
DAREDEVIL, DOCTOR…HUSBAND?
ALWAYS THE MIDWIFE

All available now!

THE NIGHTSHIFT
BEFORE CHRISTMAS

BY
ANNIE O'NEIL

MILLS & BOON

Published in Great Britain 2016
By Mills & Boon, an imprint of HarperCollins*Publishers*
1 London Bridge Street, London, SE1 9GF

© 2016 Annie O'Neil

ISBN: 978-0-263-91522-8

Our policy is to use papers that are natural, renewable and recyclable products and made from wood grown in sustainable forests. The logging and manufacturing processes conform to the legal environmental regulations of the country of origin.

Printed and bound in Spain
by CPI, Barcelona

Dear Reader,

Thank you so much for coming along to *The Nightshift Before Christmas*. I realise I have said this before—but this book really, *really* ate my heart alive when I was writing it. Josh and Katie were so real to me that my friends began to wonder if I actually knew them!

I don't want to give anything away at this point, but the loss they have each suffered is something I can imagine might too easily define a person. Grief is a strange beast, and it can shape-shift even the strongest of people into someone even they don't recognise themselves. Coming out of the fog of initial grief and back into 'the world of the living' is often overwhelming—especially if you don't have the one you love most by your side.

This is such a journey. One in which the gorgeous Josh and the heartbreakingly wonderful Katie are just trying so hard to *live* again—despite all that has happened to them. I hope you are as swept away as I was as they quest for their HEA in a busy mountainside hospital in Copper Canyon. And at *Christmas*! I do love a good holiday story, don't you? Just perfect for a little miracle of the L.O.V.E. variety.

Happy (Ever After) Holidays to you! And don't be shy about getting in touch. I can be reached at annie@annieoneilbooks.com or on Twitter @AnnieONeilBooks.

Annie O' Xx

This one's for my guy.
You're my Christmas, birthday and HEA all
wrapped up into one handsome, blue-eyed Scottish package.
Wifey xx

Annie O'Neil spent most of her childhood with her leg
draped over the family rocking chair and a book in her hand.
Novels, baking and writing too much teenage angst poetry
ate up most of her youth. Now Annie splits her time between
corralling her husband into helping her with their cows,
baking, reading, barrel racing (not really!) and spending
some very happy hours at her computer, writing.

Books by Annie O'Neil

Mills & Boon Medical Romance

The Monticello Baby Miracles

One Night, Twin Consequences

The Surgeon's Christmas Wish
The Firefighter to Heal Her Heart
Doctor...to Duchess?
One Night...with Her Boss
London's Most Eligible Doctor

Visit the Author Profile page at
millsandboon.co.uk for more titles.

Praise for
Annie O'Neil

'This is a beautifully written story that will pull you in from
page one and keep you up late and turning the pages.'
—*Goodreads* on
Doctor...to Duchess?

Annie O'Neil won the 2016 RoNA Rose Award
for her book *Doctor...to Duchess?*

CHAPTER ONE

"OKAY, PEOPLE! LISTEN UP, it's the start of silly season!"

"I thought that was Halloween?"

"Or every full moon!"

"First snowfall?"

"Hey, Doc? Is that where your locum tenens is? Stuck in one of the drifts?"

"He won't last long in Copper Canyon if that's the case. A man needs snow tires."

"A *woman* just needs common sense! I follow the snowplows! Got them tracked on my phone!"

Copper Canyon's Emergency Department filled with laughter. Impressive, considering they were down to a quality but skeleton staff. Never mind the fact it was almost always one of the busiest weeks of the year. The town was full of holiday visitors and the ski resort up the hill always had an emergency or six their small clinic couldn't handle.

Katie scanned the motley crew who would see her through Christmas Eve and, for some double-shifters, into the Big Day itself. Valley Hospital was no Boston General, and that was just the way Katie liked it. The facility was big enough to have all the fancy equipment, small enough to be able to give the personal touch to just about everyone who walked through those doors. And if they needed an extra hand, there were always the emergency services guys up on the mountain, willing to lend a hand. It wasn't home yet…but she'd get there.

"Thank you, peanut gallery. Time to focus." Katie tried her best to smile at the small but vital crew, all visibly buzzing with Christmas cheer. It wasn't their fault she wanted to rip every bauble, snowman and glittery snowflake from the walls. Someone else took that prize. "Thanks for wearing your red and green scrubs, by the way—you all look very…festive."

"Who doesn't love Christmas, Doc?" a tinsel-bedecked RN quipped.

Me.

"Right!" Katie soldiered on. They were used to her grumpy face—no need for Christmas to morph her into a jolly, stethoscope-wearing elf. "Just in time for the lunchtime rush, I've got our first Christmas mystery X-ray!"

A smattering of applause and cheers went up as she worked her way through the dozen or so staff and slapped the X-ray up on the glowing board with a flourish.

"Any guesses?"

"Why would anyone stick one of those up their—?"

"I know! Especially at Christmas."

"At least it's not a turkey thermometer. We had one of those last year. Perforated the intestine!"

The group collectively sucked in a breath. *Ouch.*

"C'mon, Dr. McGann, that's too easy. Give us a hard one!"

"All right, then." She turned to face the cocky resident. "If it's so easy, what's your guess?"

"Cookie cutter?"

Katie winced and shook her head.

"Nope. Good guess, though. Try again."

She joined the staff in tipping their heads first in one direction then the other. It wasn't that tough…

"Tree decoration. Six-pointed snowflake. My Gramma Jam-Jam used to have one. It was my wife's favorite."

Katie's body went rigid with shock as the rest of the staff turned to see who the newcomer to the group was. She didn't need to turn around. She didn't need to imagine who or what Gramma Jam-Jam's tree was like. She'd helped decorate a freshly cut fir in her old-fashioned living room as many times as she had fingers on a hand.

As her thumb moved to check that the most important finger was still bare, waves of emotion began to strike her entire body in near-physical blows. She willed her racing heart to still itself, but every sensory particle within her was responding to the one voice in the world that could morph her by turns into a wreck, a googly-eyed teen, a blushing bride…

Dr. Joshua West. Her ex-husband.

Well. He would be her ex if he would ever sign the blinking divorce papers!

She couldn't even manage to turn around and look at him, and yet her body was already on high alert to his presence. He was close. Too close.

She heard a shifting of feet. Maybe it was one of the nurses… Maybe it was… Her eyes closed for a moment. *Yup. There it was.* That perfectly singular Josh scent. The man smelled of *sunshine.* What was *up* with that? It was the dead of winter. Freezing-cold, snowing-right-now *winter.* And yet she could smell warm sunny days and the rural lifestyle only her husband—her *ex-husband*!—could turn into something delicious. Talk about evocative! One whiff of that man had never failed to bring out her inner jungle cat. From all the excitement swing-dancing around her chest cavity in preparation for a high dive down to her…*nethergarden*…it was clear the cat had been in hibernation for some time.

Her spine did a little shimmy, as if she already didn't get the point.

She did a laser-fast mental scan of her medical books. Maybe her body was trying to tell her something different!

Frisson or *fear*?

Her tongue sneaked out and gave her lower lip a surreptitious lick.

Guess that answers that, then.

How could that rich voice of his still have a physical effect on her? Hadn't two years apart been enough to make her immune to the sweet thrill twirling along her insides every time she heard him whisper sweet—?

"Nice to see you, Katiebird."

Don't even start *to go there!* She took a decidedly large step away from Josh. *Sweet or not, they'd been* nothings *in the end.*

"Right, everybody! Let's get these patients better."

Katie clapped her hands together—more to prove to herself that she had her back-to-work hat on than anything else. That, and she didn't want anybody around to witness the showdown she was certain was coming.

The group dispersed back to their posts, with a couple of interns still marveling over the human body's ability to deal with the unnatural. Precisely what Katie was experiencing at this exact moment. Fighting a natural instinct. Every time she laid eyes on Josh it was like receiving a healing salve. Her eyes were still glued to the X-ray, but she knew if she only turned her head she was just a blink away from perfection.

She sucked in a breath. Not anymore! No one and

nothing was picture-perfect. Life had a cruel way of teaching that lesson.

"Are you ever going to turn around?"

His words tickled her ear again. The man clearly didn't believe in personal space when his wife was trying to divorce him.

"Are you going to tell me what you're doing here?" Katie wheeled round as she spoke. Her breath was all but sucked straight out of her as she met those slate-blue eyes she'd fallen so deeply in love with. It had been a long time since she'd last seen them up close and personal. A really long time.

She fought the sharp sting of tears as she gave a quick shake of her head and readjusted her pose. She could do nonchalant while her world was being rocked to its very core. She was a McGann, for goodness' sake! McGanns were cool, analytical, exacting. At least that was what she'd told herself when her parents had swanned off to another party in lieu of spending time with their only daughter. McGanns were the polar opposite of the West family. The Wests were unruly, wayward, irresponsible! Invigoratingly original, passionate, loyal…

Her teeth caught her lower lip and bit down hard as her brain began to realign the Josh in her head with the one standing in front of her. Thick, sandy-blond hair, still a bit wild on top and curling round his ears, softening the edges of his shirt collar. No tie. *Typical Josh.* He rarely did formal, but when he did…

She swallowed and flicked her eyes back up to his hair to miss out on the little V of chest she knew would be visible. No hat. *Natch.* Why follow the same advice you'd give your patients? There were a few flakes of snow begging to be ruffled out of the soft waves. Her fingers twitched. The number of times she had tucked a wayward strand back behind one of his ears and given in to the urge to drop completely out-of-character sultry kisses along his neck…

No! And double, triple, infinity no! No Josh West. Not anymore!

"Didn't the agency tell you?"

The expression on his face told her he knew damn well it hadn't told her. The twinkle in his eye told her he was enjoying watching the steam beginning to blow out of her ears. Typical. He always had been spectacular at winding her up and then bringing her to a whole other plane of happy—

Stop it, Katie McGann. You are not falling under his spell again.

"Tell me what?"

"No need to grind your teeth, darlin'." He tsked gently. "It'll give you a headache."

"Headache?" Maddening and headache-inducing didn't even *begin* to cover the effect he was having on her. "Try migraine."

"Good thing I'm around, then."

He gave her one of those slow-motion winks that had a naughty tendency to bring out the…the *naughty* in her.

"Those things can knock you out flat."

An image of a shirtless Josh slowly lowering himself onto her…into her…blinded Katie for an instant. The muscled arms, the tanned chest, slate eyes gone almost gray with desire and lips shifting into that lazy smile of his—the one that always brought her nerves down a notch when she needed a bit of reassurance.

She scrunched her eyes tight and when she opened them again there it was in full-blown 3-D. The smile that could light up an entire room.

"Josh, I can't do this right now. Our locum hasn't

bothered to show, and as you can see—" her arms curled protectively around herself as the sliding doors opened to admit a young man with a child "—I'm busy. Working," she added, as if he didn't quite get the picture.

Never mind the fact he'd come top in the class above hers at med school, so clearly had brains to spare. Or the little part about how she was standing there in a lab coat in the middle of an ER. A bit of a dead giveaway. *Urgh!* If she used coarse language, a veritable stream of the colorful stuff would be pouring forth! Why was he just standing there? *Grinning?*

"What's the game here, Josh? Yuletide Torture? Our last Christmas together wasn't horrific enough for you?"

His expression sobered in an instant. She'd overstepped the mark. There was no need to be cruel. They'd both borne their fair share of grief. Grinding it in deep wasn't necessary. They would feel the weight of their mutual loss in the very core of their hearts until they each stopped beating. Longer if such a thing was possible. Forgetting was impossible. Surviving was. But only just. Which was exactly why she needed him to leave. *Now.*

"Sorry, Kitty-Kat. You're stuck with me. I'm your locum tenens."

To explain why he was late for his first shift, Josh could have told Katie how his car had spun out on some black ice on the way in, despite it being a 4x4 he drove, and the all-weather tires he'd had put on especially, but from her widened eyes and set expression he could see she had enough information to deal with. The latest "Josh incident," as she liked to call his brushes with disaster, could be kept for another time.

"No. No, I'm sorry, Josh—that's not possible. We can't…"

He heard the catch in her voice and had to force himself to stay put. In his arms was where his wife belonged when she was hurting, but it was easy enough to see it was the last place she wanted to be.

He flexed his hands a few times to try and shake the urge. With Katie right there, so close he could smell her perfume… It would be futile, of course, but one thing people could always say about Josh West—he was a man who never had a problem with attempting the impossible. How else could he have won Katie McGann's heart? Cool East Coast ice princess falling in love with the son of a Tennessee ranch manager, scraping his way through med school with every scholarship and part-time job he could get his callused hands on? It was when he'd finally got his hands on her—man, they'd shaken the first time—he'd known the word "soulmates" wasn't a fiction.

"Dr. McGann?"

Both their heads turned at the nurse's call, and the strength it took to keep his expression neutral would have put a circus strongman out of work.

So. Katie had gone back to her maiden name.

Another nail in the coffin for his big plan, or just another one of Katie's ways of ignoring the fact they belonged together? That everything that had happened to them had been awful—but survivable. Even more so if they were together.

"Can you take this one? Arterial bleed to an index finger. He says it's been pumping for a while. Shannon's in with him now." The nurse held out a chart for her to read.

"Absolutely, Jorja. How long's a while?" Katie asked, taking the three strides to the central ER counter while scanning the chart, nodding at the extra information the charge nurse supplied her.

Josh took the chance to give his wife a handful of

once-overs—and one more for good measure. It had been some time since his eyes had run up those long legs of hers. Too long. He'd been an idiot to leave it so long, but she had been good at playing hide-and-seek and he'd had his own dragons to slay. A small flash of inspiration had finally led him to Copper Canyon—the one place he'd left unexplored.

He stuffed his hands into the downy pockets of his old snowboarding coat, fingers curling in and out against the length of his palms. Laying his eyes on her for the first time in two years was hitting him hard. She'd changed. Not unrecognizably—but the young woman he'd fallen in love with had well and truly grown up. Still beautiful, but—he couldn't deny it—with a bit of an edge. Was this true Katie surfacing after the years they'd spent together? Or just another mask to deal with the disappointments and sorrows life had thrown at them in the early days of their marriage?

Gone was the preppy New England look. And in its stead… He didn't even know where to begin. Was this Idaho chic? Since when did *his* Katie wear knee-high biker boots, formfitting tartan skirts in dark purple and black with dark-as-the-night turtlenecks? Yeah, they would be practical in this wintry weather, but it was a far cry from the pastels and conservative clothes she'd favored back in Boston. The new look was *sexy*.

A hit of jealousy socked him in the solar plexus. She hadn't… He suddenly felt like a class-A *idiot* for not even considering the possibility. She hadn't moved on. Not his Katie. Had she…?

His eyes shot up the length of her legs to the plaid skirt and then up to her trim waistline, irritatingly hidden by the lab coat. His eyes jagged along her hands, seeking out her ring finger. Still bare. He would never forget the moment she'd ripped off her rings and slapped them onto the kitchen counter. Throwing had been far too melodramatic for his self-controlled wife. The word "Enough!" had rung in his ears for weeks afterward. Months.

He exhaled. Okay. The bare finger wasn't proof positive she wasn't seeing someone else, but it was something. He scraped a hand through his mess of a hairdo, wishing he'd taken a moment to pop into a barber's. But he hadn't worried a jot about what he'd looked like over the past two years, let alone worried about impressing another woman. From the moment he'd laid eyes on Katie to the moment she'd hightailed it out of his life— *their* life—he'd known there was only one woman in the world for him. And here she was—doing her pea-pickin' best to ignore him.

His eyes traveled up to her face as she scanned the chart, listening to the nurse. He knew that expression like the back of his hand. Intent, focused. Her brain would be spinning away behind those dark brown eyes of hers to come to the best solution—for both the patient and the hospital, but mostly the patient. One of the many traits he loved about her. Patients first. Politics later. Because there were *always* politics in a hospital. He knew that more than most. It was why staying at Boston General hadn't worked out so well. Why a new job in Paris just might be the ticket he needed to wade out of that sorry old pit of misery he'd been wallowing in.

But he wasn't going anywhere until he knew Katie was well and truly over him. He checked his watch. Seven days to find out if she was cold- or warm-blooded. It ended at the stroke of midnight on New Year's Eve. He'd either hand her a plane ticket or the divorce papers.

He sucked in a fortifying breath of Katie's perfume. *Mmm...* Still sweeter than a barn full of new summer hay.

Well, then. He gave his chin a scrub and grinned. *Best get started.*

CHAPTER TWO

"WHAT YOU GOT THERE?" Josh stepped up to the desk, shrugging off his jacket as he approached. Out of the corner of her eye Katie could see Jorja's lips reshape into an O. Josh—or rather his body—had that effect on women. It was why she'd never thought she'd stood a chance. People always mistook her shyness for being stuck-up. But Josh had seen straight through the veneer and gone directly to her heart.

He turned his Southern drawl up a notch. He could do that, too. Pick and choose when to play the Southern gent or drop it if he saw it detracted from his incredibly sharp mind.

"Dr. McGann, may I help keep you out of the fray while you sort out the big picture?"

Katie eyed him warily for a second, then made a decision. By the hint of a smile that bloomed on his lips she could see it was the one he had been hoping for.

He would stay.

Never mind the fact that showing up on Christmas Eve when they were a doctor down wasn't giving her much of a choice. She had it in her to kick him the hell outta Dodge, if that was where he needed booting. But right now there were patients to see, and pragmatism always trumped personal.

"Twenty-five-year-old male presented with an arterial cut to the bone on his index finger." She tapped the chart with her own.

"Turkey?"

"Ham. Too easy for the likes of you."

She pressed the chart to her chest, claiming it as her own. Katie let her eyes travel along all six feet three inches of her ex. Josh had always been a trauma hotshot. And he'd always looked good. She'd steered clear of the Boston General gossip train, so didn't really know what path he'd chosen professionally after she'd left, but personally nothing had changed in the looks department. He still looked good. She looked away.

Too good.

"You're the next one down." She pulled the X-ray down from the lightboard and passed it to him with a smirk. "Make your Gramma Jam-Jam proud. You can put your stuff in my office for now—the staff lockers are further down the corridor and this patient's been waiting too long as it is."

She tipped her head toward a glassed-in cubicle a few yards away. Josh took advantage of the broken eye contact to soak in some more of the "New Katie" look. Her super-short, über-chic new haircut suited her. It sure made her look different. *Good* different, though. No longer the shy twenty-one-year-old he'd first spied devouring a stack of anatomy books in the university library, a thick chestnut braid shifting from shoulder to shoulder as she studied.

He cleared his throat. Whimsical trips down memory lane weren't helping.

"Green or red scrubs," she added, pointing to a room just beyond her office.

"You always liked me in blue."

The set of her jaw told him to button it.

"Green or red," she repeated firmly. "The patients like it. It's *Christmas*." She handed him the single-page chart with a leaden glare and turned to the nurse. "Jorja MacLeay, this is Dr. West, our locum tenens over the next few days. See that he's made welcome. His security pass should expire on the first of January."

"At the end of the day?" Jorja asked hopefully.

"The beginning. The very beginning," Katie replied decisively, before turning and calling out her patient's name.

He flashed a smile in the nurse's direction, lifted up his worn duffel bag to show her he was just going to unload it before getting to work. The smile he received in return showed him he had an ally. She shot a mischievous glance at his retreating wife and beckoned him toward the central desk.

"Don't mind her," Jorja stage-whispered. "A kitten, really. Just a grumpy kitten at Christmas." She shrugged off her boss's mysterious moodiness with a grin. "As long as she knows you've got your eye on the ball, she's cool."

Josh nodded and gave the counter an affirmative rap. "Got it. Cool. Calm. Collected. And Christmassy!" he finished with a cheesy grin.

"Says here you're double-shifting."

"You bet. Where else would a fellow want to see in Christmas morning?"

Jorja laughed. "Cookies are in the staff room down the hall if you need a sugar push to get you through the night. Canteen's shut and the vending company forgot to fill up the machines, so there might be a brawl over the final bag of chips come midnight!"

"Count me in! I love a good arm-wrestling session. Especially if the chips are the crinkly kind. I love those."

"I can guarantee you'll have a fun night…at least with most of us." She shot a furtive look down the corridor to ensure Katie was out of earshot and scrunched her face and shoulders up into a silent "oops" shrug when Josh raised his eyebrows in surprise.

"You two don't know each other or anything, do you?"

"We've met." It was all Josh would allow.

It was up to Katie if she wanted to flesh things out. He'd been the only crossover she'd allowed between personal and professional and he doubted she had changed in that department. She was one of the most private people he had ever met, and when news of what had happened to them had been all but Tannoyed across Boston General, it had been tough. Coal-pit-digging tough.

Jorja giggled nervously and flushed. "Sorry! Dr. McGann is great. We all love her. The ER always runs the smoothest when she's on shift."

Josh just smiled. His girl always strove to achieve the best and ended up ahead of the game at all turns. Except *that* night. She'd been blindsided. They both had.

He shook off the thought and waved his thanks to Jorja. First impressions? Young to be a charge nurse. Twenty-something, maybe. She struck him as a nurse who would stay the course. Not everyone who worked in Emergency did. She was young, enthusiastic. A nice girl if first impressions were anything to go by.

He'd gone with his gut when he'd met Katie. Made a silent vow she would be his wife one day. It had taken him a while, but he'd got there in the end. And today the vow still hit him as powerfully as the day they'd made good on a whim to elope. Five years, two months and fourteen days of wedded… He sighed. Even he couldn't stretch to "bliss." Not with the dice they'd been handed.

He thought of the divorce papers stuffed inside his duffel bag. There was only one way Katie could ever convince him to sign them. Prove beyond a shadow of a doubt that she felt absolutely nothing for him anymore. He gave a little victory air punch. So far he'd seen nothing to indicate she would be able to get him to scrawl his signature on those cursed papers tonight.

Just the shift of her shoulders when she'd heard his voice had told him everything he needed to know. She could change her name, her hair and even her dress sense if she wanted to—but he knew in his soul that time hadn't changed how his wife felt about him. No matter how bad things had become. She couldn't hate without love. And when she'd finally turned round to face him there had been sparks in her eyes.

Katie stuffed her head into the stack of blankets and screamed. For all she was worth she screamed. And then she screamed some more. Silent, aching, wishing-you-could-hollow-yourself-out-it-hurt-so-bad screams. There was no point in painting a pretty picture in these precious moments alone.

Seeing Josh again was dredging up everything she had only just managed to squeeze a lid on. *Just.* In fact, that lid had probably still been a little bit open because, judging by the hot tears she discovered pouring down her face when she finally came up for air, she was going to have to face the fact there was never going to be a day when the loss of their baby didn't threaten to rip her in half.

What was he thinking? That he could saunter into her ER as if it were just any old hospital on any old day? With that slow, sweet smile of his melting hearts in its wake?

She'd not missed the nurses trying to catch his eye. Jorja's giggles had trilled down the hallway after she'd stomped off. Josh did that to people. Brought out the laughter, the smiles, the flirtation. The Josh Effect, she'd always laughingly called it. Back when she'd laughed freely. Heaven knew, *she'd* fallen under his spell. Hook, line and sunk. If only she'd known how far into the depths of sorrow she'd fall when she lost her heart to him, she would have steered clear.

She swatted away her tears and sank to the floor of the supplies cupboard, using her thumbs to try and massage away the emotion. Her patient was going to be wondering where she was, so she was going to have to pull herself together. Shock didn't even begin to cover what she'd felt when Josh had walked into her ER. Love, pain, desire, hurt…those could kick things off pretty nicely.

"Of all the ERs in all the world, he had to walk into this one."

Talking to herself. That was a new one to add to her list of growing eccentricities. Maybe she should have fostered some of those friendships she'd left behind in Boston.

"Sounds like the start of a pretty good movie." Josh's legs moved into her peripheral vision as his voice filled her ears.

"More like the end of one."

"No, that's the start of a beautiful friendship."

"Well—well…" She trailed off. Playing movie quotation combat with Josh was always a bad idea.

She huffed out a frustrated sigh. Couldn't she just get *a minute* alone? She should have gone to the roof. No one went there in the winter, and she relished the moments of quiet, the twinkle of Copper Canyon's Main Street. She swiped her hands across her cheeks again, wishing the motion could remove the crimson heat she felt burning in them. Against her better judgment she whirled on him and tried another retort.

"Should I have said 'of all the *stalkers* in all the world'?"

"Oh, so going to the supplies cupboard to track down some mandated holiday scrubs has turned me into a stalker, has it?" he asked good-naturedly.

The five-year-old in her wanted to say yes and throw a good old-fashioned tantrum. The jumping-up-and-down kind. The pounding-of-the-fists kind. The *Why me? Why you?* kind. The Katie who'd shored up enough strength to finally call their marriage to a halt knew better. Knew it would only give Josh the fuel he wanted to add to a fire she could never put out.

She wasn't going to give him the satisfaction of knowing how much she still cared. That had been his problem all along. Too trusting that everything would be all right when time and time again the world had shown him the opposite was true. Who else had become an adrenaline junkie after their daughter had been stillborn? Hadn't he known how dangerous everything he'd been doing was? And she'd always been the one who'd had to pick up the pieces, apply the bandages, ice the black eyes, realign the broken nose... Trying her best to laugh it off like he did when all she'd wanted to do was curl up in a corner and weep.

Couldn't he see she had to play it safe? That losing their daughter had scared her to her very marrow? If she were *ever* to feel brave enough to move forward—let alone try and conceive again—he needed to call off his game of tug-of-war with mortality.

She scratched her nails along the undersides of her

legs before standing up, using the pain to distract herself from doing what she really wanted.

"Large or extra-large?" she bit out.

"Guess that depends on if you need me to play Santa later." He grabbed a pillow from a shelf and stuck it up his shirt.

Without bothering to examine the results, Katie yanked a pair of extra-large scrubs from a nearby shelf. Not because she needed a Santa but because she didn't need to see how well he filled out the scrubs. The first time they'd met—*woof!* And she was no dog owner.

The first time they'd met... He said it had been in the library, but she was convinced to this day that he'd made it up. The day she'd first seen him—easily standing out in a crowd of junior residents, all kitted out in a set of form-fitting scrubs—his eyes had alighted on her as if he'd just gained one-on-one access to the Mona Lisa herself... Mmm... That moment would be imprinted on her mind forever... She'd never let anyone get under her skin—but she'd been powerless to resist when it had come to Josh.

"Green! Good to see you remember red always makes my complexion look a bit blotchy."

Katie blew a raspberry at him. She wasn't playing.

"Or is it that you remember green always brings out the blue in my eyes?" He winked and took hold of the scrubs, trapping her hand beneath his.

Just feeling his touch reawakened things in Katie she had hoped she'd long-ago laid to rest. Her eyes lifted to meet his. Stormy sea-gray right now. Later... He was right. Later they'd be blue, and later still the color of flint. She had loved looking into his eyes, never knowing what to expect, trying to figure out how to describe the kaleidoscope of blues and grays, ever-shifting...ever true.

As the energy between them grew taut, the butterflies

that had long lain dormant in her belly took flight, leaving heated tendrils in their wake. She tugged her hand free of his and gave him a curt smile. Physical contact with Josh was going to have to be verboten if she was going to keep it together for the next eight days. It was bad enough he'd seen her red-rimmed eyes.

She glanced at her watch.

T-minus...oh, about one hundred and ninety-two hours and counting!

"Twenty-four hours."

"Beg pardon?" Josh shook his head.

Hadn't he been riding the same train of thought she had? If she'd gone off on a magical journey down memory lane, the chances were relatively high he'd done the same thing. Different tracks—different destinations.

She cleared her throat. There was about half an ounce of resolve left within her and she needed to use it. "I'm giving you twenty-four hours."

He raised his eyebrows and gave her his *What gives?* face.

"Oh, don't play the fool, Josh. You've ambushed me. Pure and simple. And on—" She stopped, only just missing having her voice break. "It's the minimum notice I have to give the agency if I want a replacement."

"What are you on about, Kitty-Kat?" He pulled himself up to his full height. Josh always played fair and he could see straight through her. This was a below-the-belt move.

She jigged a nothing-to-do-with-me shrug out of her shoulders, her eyes anywhere but on his. "If it's quiet enough we might be able to let you go earlier without telling the agency."

She might not want him here, but she didn't want to tarnish his record. He was a good doctor. Just a lousy husband. She squirmed under his intent gaze, pretty sure he was reading her mind. A sort of, kind of lousy husband.

"Don't be ridiculous. Christmas is always busy! You're going to need me. What kind of man would I be, leaving you to deal with a busy ER all on your own?"

"That's terribly chivalrous of you, Josh. I'm going to need a doctor—yes. But I don't need *you*." She looked at her watch again, not wanting to see how deep her words had hit. Laceration by language was *way* out of her comfort zone—but tough. Josh had pushed her there—and she had an ER to run.

"Sorry, I've got to get to this patient."

"Yup! I'm certainly looking forward to mine!" He mimed snapping on a pair of gloves with a guess-it's-time-to-suck-it-up smile.

If she was feeling generous, she had to give it to him for keeping his cool. Assigning him a rectal examination as a "welcome gift" was not, she suspected, the reunion he had been hoping for. Then again, finding out her estranged husband would be her locum for the next week wasn't much of a Christmas present for her, so tough again! Hadn't two years' worth of sending him divorce papers given him enough of a clue?

"Uh… Kate?"

"Yes?"

"Are you going to move so I can get my patient's Christmas ornament back on the tree?"

"Yes!" she blurted, embarrassed to realize she'd been staring. "Yes, of course. I was just…" She stopped. She wasn't "just" anything. She stepped back and let him pass.

"I'm happy to see you, too, Katiebird," he said at the

doorway, complete with one of those looks she knew could see straight through to her soul.

She rubbed her arms to force the accompanying goose bumps away.

"Me, too," she whispered into the empty room. "Me, too."

"Hello, there… Mr. Kingston? I understand you've got a bleeding—" Katie swiftly moved her eyes from the chart to the patient, instantly regretting that she'd wasted valuable time away from her patient.

Unable to resist the gore factor, the young man had lowered his hand below his heart and tugged off the temporary tourniquet the nurse had put in place. Blood was spurting everywhere. If he hadn't looked so pale she would have told him off, but Ben Kingston looked like he was about to—

Oops!

Without a moment to spare Katie lurched forward, just managing to catch him in a hug before he slithered to the floor.

"Can I get a hand in here? We've got a fainter!"

Katie was only just managing to hold him on the exam table and smiled in thanks at the quick arrival of— Oh. It was Josh. *Natch.*

He quickly assessed the situation, wordlessly helping Katie shift the patient back onto the exam table, checking his airways were clear, loosening the young man's buttoned-at-the-top shirt collar and loosening his snug belt buckle by a much-needed notch or two as she focused on stanching the flow of blood with a thick stack of sterile gauze.

"Got a couple extra pillows for foot elevation?"

"Yup." Katie pointed to the locker where they stored

extra blankets and pillows. "Would you mind handing me a digital tourniquet first? I'll see if I can stem the bleeding properly while he's still out."

"Sure thing." Josh stood for a moment, gloved hands held out from his body as they would be in surgery, and ran his eyes around the room to hunt down supplies.

"Sorry, they're in the third drawer down— Wait!" Her eyes widened and dropped to Josh's gloved hands. "Weren't you in the middle of…?"

She felt a sharp jag of anger well up in her. *Typical, Josh!* Running to the rescue without thinking for a single moment about protocol! Was simple adherence to safe hygiene practices too much to ask?

"Done and dusted." He nodded at the adjacent exam area. "He's going through the paperwork with Jorja." He took in her tightened lips and furrowed eyebrows and began to laugh. Waving his hands in the air, still laughing, he continued, "You didn't think…? Katie West—"

"It's McGann," she corrected quietly.

"Yeah, whatever." The smile and laughter instantly fell away. "I always double-glove during internal exams. These are perfectly clean. You should know me better than that." His eyes shifted away from hers to the patient, the disappointment in his voice easy to detect. "You good here?"

She nodded, ashamed of the conclusion she'd leaped to. Josh was a good doctor. Through and through. It was the one thing she'd never doubted about him. He had a natural bedside manner. An ability to read a situation in an instant. Instinctual. All the things she wasn't.

She slipped the ringed tourniquet onto the young man's finger and checked his pulse again. It wasn't strong, but he'd be all right with a bit of a rest and a finger no longer squirting an unhealthy portion of his ten pints of blood everywhere. He'd need a shot of lidocaine with epinephrine before she could properly sort it out, so she would need to wait for him to come to. Being halfway through an injection wasn't the time when a patient should regain consciousness. Especially when Josh was leaping through curtained cubicles, coming to her rescue. She jiggled her shoulders up and down. It wouldn't happen again.

"Are you nervous, Doc?"

"Ah! You're back with us!" Katie turned around in time to stop the young man from pushing himself up to a seated position. "Why don't you just lie back for a while, okay? I have a feeling your finger didn't start bleeding half an hour ago, like it says in your chart, Ben."

He looked at her curiously.

"Is it okay if I call you Ben?"

"You can call me what you like as long as you stitch me up and get me outta here, Doc! It's Christmas Eve. I've got places to go…things to do—"

"Someone to drive you home?" Katie interrupted. "After your fainting spell, I don't think it's a good idea for you to get behind a wheel."

"And I don't think it's a good idea for *you* to boss someone around on Christmas Eve!"

Katie backed away from Ben as his voice rose and busied herself with getting the prep tray ready. Emotions ran high on days like this. Especially if the patient had had one too many cups of "cheer." Unusual to encounter one on the day shift, but it took all kinds.

"Cheer" morphed into cantankerous pretty quickly, and Ben definitely had a case of that going on. She stared at the curtain separating her from her colleagues, knowing she'd be better off if there was someone else in the room when she put in the stitches.

She sucked in a breath and pulled the curtain away.

"Can I get a hand in here?" She dived back into the cubicle before she could see who was coming. Josh or no Josh, she needed to keep her head down and get the work done.

"Everything all right, Dr. McGann?"

At the sound of Jorja's voice, Katie felt an unexpected twist of disappointment. It wasn't like she'd been hoping it would be Josh. Her throat tightened. *Oh, no...* Of all the baked beans in Boston Harbor... Had she? *Clear your throat. Paste on a smile.*

"Yes, great. Thank you, Jorja. Nothing serious, just thought we could do with an extra pair of hands now that Mr. Kingston here has rejoined us."

Josh tried his best to focus on the intern's voice as he talked him through how he saw things panning out on Christmas Eve based on absolutely zero experience, but he couldn't. All he could hear was Katie, talking her patient and the nurse through the procedure in that clear voice she had. The patient had definitely enjoyed a bit of Christmas punch before he'd arrived, and Josh didn't trust him not to start throwing a few if he was too far gone.

"Hey." He interrupted the intern. "What did you say your name was again?"

"Michael," the young doctor replied, unable to keep the dismay from his face. He'd been on a roll.

Tough. Fictional projections weren't going to help what was actually happening.

"Michael, what's your policy on patients who've had a few too many?" He mimed tossing back some shots.

"Oh—each ER head is different, but Katie usually calls the police." He looked around the ER as if expecting to see someone stagger by. "Why?"

"Just curious." He gave Michael's shoulder a friendly clap with his hand, hoping it would bring an end to the conversation. "Thanks for all the tips," he added, which did the trick.

He tuned his hearing back into the voices behind the curtain where Katie was working. The patient was young and obviously a gym buff. As strong and feisty as she was, Katie was no match for a drunk twenty-something hell-bent on getting more eggnog down his throat. Drunk drivers on icy roads were the last thing the people of Copper Canyon needed on Christmas Eve. Or any night, for that matter.

"Okay, Ben, you ready? I'm just going to inject a bit of numbing agent into your finger."

"What *is* that?"

Josh inched a bit closer to the curtain at the sound of the raised voice.

"It's a small dose of lidocaine with epinephrine," Katie explained. "It will numb—"

"Oh, no, you don't!" The patient—Ben, that was it—raised his voice up a notch. "I've been on the internet and that stuff makes your fingers fall off. No *way* are you putting that poison in me!"

Josh only just managed to stop an eye roll. Self-diagnosis was a growing epidemic in the ER…one that was sometimes harder to control than any actual injury.

"I think if you read all of the article you'd find that's more myth than reality."

Always sensible. That was his girl!

Ben's voice shot up another decibel. "Are you telling me I'm a *liar*?"

"No, I'm saying digital gangrene is about the last thing that's going to happen if I—"

"You—are—not—putting—that—sh—"

"Hello, ladies." Josh yanked the curtain aside, unable to stay quiet. "Need an extra pair of hands?"

"No," Katie muttered.

"Yes," Jorja replied loudly over her boss.

"They're trying to give me gangrene!"

"Really? Fantastic." Josh rocked back on his heels and grinned, rubbing his hands together in anticipation. "I haven't seen a good case of gangrene in ages." He flashed his smile directly at Katie. "Are you trying to turn Mr. Kingston here into *The Gangrene who stole Christmas*?"

Everyone in the cubicle stared at him for a moment in silence.

"The Grinch!" Josh filled in the silence. "Get it? Gangrene? Grinch?"

There was a collective headshake, which Josh waved off. "You guys are hopeless. They're both green!"

Jorja groaned as the bad joke finally clicked.

"Well," he conceded, "one's a bit more black and smelly, and isn't around for the big Christmassy finish, but, Ben, my friend…" Josh took another step into the cubicle, clapping a hand on the young man's shoulder from behind and lowering himself so that he spoke slowly and directly into the young man's ear. "I've known this doctor for a very long time, and if she needs to stabilize the neuronal membrane in your finger by inhibiting the ionic fluxes required for the instigation and conduction of nerve impulses in order to stem the geyser of blood shooting from that finger of yours, she knows what she's talking about, hear?"

Ben nodded dumbly.

"Right!" Josh raised a hand to reveal a set of car keys dangling from his fingers.

He saw Katie's eyebrow quirk upward. He would have laid a fiver on the fact she was thinking he'd taken up pickpocketing to add a bit more adrenaline to his life. He'd win the bet and she'd be wrong. He'd just seen enough drunks in his Big City ER Tour. The one where he had done everything but successfully forget the brown-eyed beauty standing right in front of him.

He cleared his throat and stepped away from Ben. "You owe Dr. We—Dr. McGann an apology. And while you do that—" he jangled the keys from his finger "—I'll just be popping these babies over to Security until we get someone to pick you up."

Ben opened his mouth to object, his eyes moving from physician to nurse and back to Josh before he muttered something about being out of order, his mother's stupid car, and then, with a sag of the shoulders, he finally started digging a cell phone out of his pocket.

"Excellent!" Josh tossed the keys up in the air, caught them with a flourish, gave Jorja a wink and tugged the curtain shut behind him before anyone could say *boo*.

"Well…" Josh heard Jorja say before he headed off. "He's certainly a breath of fresh air!"

Katie muttered something he couldn't quite make out. Probably just as well.

Josh grinned, his shoes glued to the floor until he was sure peace reigned behind Curtain Three. He heard Katie clear her throat and put on her bright voice—the one she used when she was irritated with him.

"Now, then, Ben, if you can just show me that finger of yours, we can get you stitched up and home before you know it. Jorja? Could you hand me some of the hemostatic dressing, please? We need to get the wound to clot."

Josh began to whistle "Silent Night" as he cheerily worked his way back toward the main desk. Job. Done.

"How long do you intend to continue this White Knight thing?"

Josh's instinct was to smile and tell her he would wield

his lance and shield as long as it took for her to see sense and come back to him. Longer. Until the day he died, he would protect Katie. He'd taken a vow and had meant it. He had broken part of it, and he was going to spend the rest of his life making good on it. Even if that meant walking away, no matter how hard it hurt.

But this was work. Personal would have to wait.

"Where I come from, people stick around to help one another when the going gets tough." He laid the Tennessee drawl on as thick as molasses. It always got to her and this time was no different.

He watched as her hands flew to her hips in indignation, then shifted fluidly into a protective, faux-nonchalant crossing of the arms. Her eyes widened, the lids quickly dropping into a recovery position. One of her eyebrows arched just a fraction before her face became neutral again. But she couldn't keep the flush of emotions from pinking up her cheeks.

He shifted his stance, ratcheted his satisfaction down a couple of notches. He wasn't playing fair. He knew more than anyone that teamwork in an emergency department was something Katie valued above all else. Unless, it seemed, it came from him.

He stood solidly as she gave him the Katie once-over. He wouldn't have minded taking his own slow-motion scan over the woman he'd dreamed about holding each and every night since she'd told him in no uncertain terms she'd had enough of his daredevil ways. He'd have to play it careful. Divorce rules shifted from state to state, and he hadn't checked out Idaho. If she'd moved to Texas he would have shown up a lot earlier. No need to wait for a signature there. As it was, he thought two years had given them each more than enough time to know they were meant for each other. Given *him* enough lessons to know she'd been right. He'd suffered enough loss to know it was time to change. Move forward—whatever shape that took.

"Where are you staying?"

Unexpected.

"Here." He pointed at the hospital floor.

There went that eyebrow again.

"Locum tenens wages aren't enough to get you a condo?"

He shook his head. "I didn't know how long I'd be staying."

She refused to take the bait.

"Usually housing comes with the contract."

What *was* she? The contract police? Or… A lightbulb went off… Was she trying to figure out where he'd be laying his sleepy head? Was she missing being held in his arms as much as he had longed to hold her? Truth was, he never bothered with separate housing on these gigs. Hospital bunks suited him fine… Friends' sofas sufficed when he was back in Boston. Home was Katie, and it had been two long years…

He heard the impatient tap of her foot. Fine…he'd play along.

"Not this time of year. And it was too short a contract for me to put up a fight."

Katie's jaw tightened before she shifted her chin upward in acknowledgment of the obvious. She knew what he meant. The locals had dibs on all the affordable properties. Everything went to the top one hundred highest-paid, most famous, with the biggest bank account, et cetera, et cetera. Life in Copper Canyon was a heady mix of the haves and those who *worked* for the haves.

Mountain views, private access to the slopes, sunset, sunrise, heated pools, wet bars, ten thousand square feet minimum of whatever a person could desire—you name it, they had it. Copper Canyon saw most of America's glitterati at some point, on the slopes or at one of the resorts…if, that was, they didn't have a private pad.

"You staying at your parents'? I remember them having a pretty plush pad out here and not using it all that much."

Risky question, but he couldn't imagine why else she would have moved here. She walked over to the board and began erasing patient names and rearranging a few others.

"They're usually at the Boston brownstone or in the Cayman Islands, right?"

"Jorja? Could you make sure the tablets are all updated to reflect what's on the board? We've got quite a few changes to note," Katie called over her shoulder to the main desk.

"Sure thing, Dr. McGann. On it!"

Josh leaned against the wall, one foot crossed over the other, hands stuffed in his pockets, happy to just watch her play out her ignoring game. He threw in an off-key "Rudolph the Red-Nosed Reindeer" whistle for good measure.

"And let's pop something different on the music front, Jorja. Some *nice* carols."

Josh grinned at Jorja, dropped her a wink and dropped his whistle simultaneously.

"They just don't stop, do they? Your parents?"

Only the squeak of the whiteboard pen could be heard over the usual hospital murmur.

Wow. Having a conversation with a brick wall would have yielded more return.

"The indefatigable McGanns! That's how I always thought of them."

Katie's lips tightened. She didn't do chitchat. Especially when it came to her parents. They were the source of any well-packed baggage Katie had hauled around through the years. Parents who'd discovered they hadn't really been up to parenting so had handed it over to nannies and boarding schools to do the work for them. They were harmless enough folk at a cocktail party, but he knew their lack of interest as parents hurt Katie deeply.

"I'm not staying there this week."

Interesting.

"I always stay at the hospital over Christmas," she volunteered hastily, with a quick pursing of her lips. "My parents have come in to ski for the week—"

Josh snorted and was relieved to see Katie join in with an involuntary snigger.

"Well…at least they'll look fabulous in their ski gear before they hit the cocktail circuit."

Her eyes flicked away with a shake of her head. She must have remembered she'd told herself not to enjoy being with him.

"It's easier not to get stuck in a storm if I'm here."

Wow! Two whole sentences! They were on a roll. He kept his ground. Nodded. Tried not to look too interested. He'd learned long ago that it took a lot to get Katie talking, but once you opened the floodgates…

"So…where are you really staying?"

Bang goes that theory.

"Honestly, Kit-Kat. My plan was to just stay here."

Her brown eyes were briefly cloaked by a studied blink. Then another. Her lips twitched forward for a microsecond in a moue. Was that a response to his being there? Had an image of the two of them wrapped together as they'd always been in bed flashed across her mind's eye as it had his?

He cleared his throat and shifted his stance. "Casual"

was getting tough to pull off. What he wouldn't give to take the two steps separating them and start to kiss those ruby lips of hers as if each of their lives depended on it. It felt as though his did, and standing still was beginning to test his fortitude.

"I see." She abruptly turned to face the main desk, where Jorja was checking in a new patient. "We'd best get you to work, then."

Fair enough. *She wasn't saying no.*

And... A smile began to tug at the corners of his mouth. Depending on how you looked at it, Katie was saying *yes.* Yes to his staying. Yes to his being in the hospital. Yes to their being together.

Okay, it was a bit of a leap, but he was willing to take the risk. In for a penny and all that...

He pushed away from the wall and took a step behind her when she turned back to face the board, unsurprised to see her shoulders stiffen...then relax when he kept just enough space between them for her to know he wouldn't do what he'd always done before their lives had been ripped in two.

He closed his eyes and pictured the scene. She'd be studying something—anything—an X-ray, a chart, the wall—it didn't matter. He'd step right up behind her, arms slipping round her waist, hands clasped against her belly, his chin coming to a rest on her pillow of chestnut hair or slipping down alongside her cheek for a little illicit nuzzle or to drop a kiss on her neck...

He heard her sigh at the exact same time he was blowing out a long, slow breath between his lips. *Oh, yeah.* They were on the same page all right. It just hadn't been turned for a while.

"Hey, you two—you're in for the Secret Santa, right?"

Josh and Katie both whirled round to see a grinning

Jorja holding out a Santa hat with folded pieces of paper being rapidly jiggled around.

"Count me in." Josh reached into the hat and grabbed a bit of paper. If he was going to show Katie he knew how to settle down, enjoy small-town life… "Who doesn't love a bit of Secret Santa action?" He turned to Katie. "That is if it's all right with the boss lady?"

"Who am I to curtail your holiday cheer and our small-town ways?"

And they were back in the ring! Three years ago the idea of going back to his small-town roots would have made him run for the hills…or the bright lights of Manhattan, more like it. But after he'd quit Boston for Manhattan, Chicago, Miami, none of them had stuck. Not one had sung to him. Nothing worked without Katie.

"I'm just a small-town boy, and nothing says home like…" His eyes sought hers and in that instant he was sure each of them knew what he might say.

"Like what, Dr. West?" Jorja pressed.

Katie. It had always and only been Katie.

"Like having an opportunity to put down roots! In the form of a Secret Santa. I just love a good old-fashioned round of Secret Santa."

Too emphatic?

He felt Katie giving him a curious glance. *Good.* He wanted her to see the changes. Maybe not all of them. The pins in his leg could wait. And the scars along his hip and spine. It wasn't looking like she'd be ripping off his clothes for a moment of unchecked ardor anytime soon, so he was good with that. But he'd been careful that she didn't see him walk too much. She'd know. She'd definitely know. And she'd never come back to him then.

"Dr. McGann? Are you taking part in the draw?"

Jorja waggled the hat in front of his wife's face. She

might be a good nurse, but that girl sure didn't read body language all that well.

He watched Katie put on her bright face and return her focus to Jorja. "Of course. In for a penny…"

Josh felt Katie's eyes land on him as the words came out of her mouth, her hand plunging into the hat blindly to grab a bit of crumpled paper.

She remembered. They'd both said it. A lot. Especially in the early days of their marriage, when they'd needed every penny to repay their medical-school bills, making their own way after just about the best elopement a couple could ever have had when Katie had decided her parents didn't deserve to put on a society wedding. A church full of her parents' business associates and bridge pals mixing with his ruckus of a family, who would show up to a black-tie event wearing their funeral clothes? No, thanks.

His lips twitched as her eyes stayed locked on his. They'd spent just a few hundred dollars on rings, the honeymoon, and a huge chocolate cream pie that they'd set between them at a roadside diner and eaten in one go… Then, not too long after, they had been putting down deposits on cribs and—

Josh raked a hand through his hair and looked away first. It was still hard to go there. Still impossible to believe they'd really lost their little girl. That sweet little baby who'd never even had one chance to look into her parents' eyes…

"Right! You said you wanted me to get to work." He craned his neck to look around at the waiting room and stuffed the bit of paper into his lab coat pocket. "Who's next?"

Katie had to shake her head for a minute before she could think clearly. Having Josh here was like receiving a physical assault of emotions she hadn't wanted to feel again.

Pain...

She unnecessarily scrubbed her hands through her super-short hair, having forgotten, just as her eyes connected with Josh's, that she didn't have a ponytail to curl her fingers through anymore. *Yup.* The pain she could certainly do without.

Fear.

That Josh would be safe. That he'd come home from his latest escapade unscathed. That he would come home at all. Bearing another loss in the wake of their stillborn baby girl...wondering if he'd well and truly be there for her if they decided to try and conceive again... No. She just hadn't been able to do it.

Desire.

The desire felt good. *Too* good. And it was too much of a link to the pain and the fear. A trilogy of Josh, all wrapped up in a gorgeous sandy-haired, blue-eyed package she had never been able to resist. But she had to. For her sanity, first and foremost. For her heart.

"What do you think? You happy to let me go with the photocopy girl?"

"Beg your pardon?" Katie forced herself to focus on the words coming out of Josh's mouth about a patient newly arrived from an office party gone wrong. Photocopies. Bottoms. Broken glass.

His front tooth was still crooked. She'd always liked that. The imperfection made him more...perfect. Hmm... Maybe she shouldn't focus on his mouth. His eyes— definitely blue-gray in this light. Flinty? Steel-blue. Was there such a thing? And with little crinkles round the edges. Those were new. Sun, maybe? Or just the passage of the two years they'd put between them?

It might have felt like an eternity, but two years wasn't really that long. Then again, they'd been through a lot. But Josh had always seemed impervious to it all. Definitely a glass half-full— That was it! *Glasses.* He probably just needed glasses. Typical Josh to put practical needs like getting his eyes checked on hold. She tilted her head to the side. They *were* kind of sexy. The crinkles…

Nope. *Nope.* Still not hearing words. Still not focusing. What about the little bridge between his eyes? That was just like anyone else's. Just part of someone's face. A plain old face just like any other doctor in any other hospital. With a nose and high cheekbones and two perfectly formed… *Argh, no!* And she was back to his lips.

"Apologies, Dr. West." She put on her best interested face. "I didn't quite catch that."

A low laugh rumbled from his chest. Josh knew damn well she'd been ogling him and he was loving it. From the first day he'd draped a stethoscope round her neck, he'd known he had the power to cut straight through her prim-and-proper exterior and bring out the hidden tigress in her. The one she hadn't known existed. Bookish only children who preferred the company of their elderly nannies weren't obvious contenders for being horny minxes aching to see how it felt to be scooped up in a single swoop, her legs wrapped round his waist, his hands cupped on her—

"…derriere."

"Beg pardon! What was that again?"

This time Josh didn't even bother going for subtle.

"Katie, do you just wanna sneak off and make out for old times' sake while the anesthetic gets to work?"

"What? *No!*" She shook her head, sending a horrified look over her shoulder to see if anyone had overheard him. "No!" she added, with a look. She didn't *make out* with people. Let alone with the one man on the planet she needed statewide clearance from if her brain was ever going to work properly again.

She forced herself to play a quick game of catch-up.

"You say she broke her office's copy machine by sitting on it? Why on earth was she doing *that*?"

"You never butt-copied—?" Josh stopped himself, his smile shifting from astounded to tender. "It's something that happens when an office party gets out of hand. This gal clearly likes to get her cray-cray on."

"I have *no* idea what crayfish have to do with it."

"Crazy!" Josh laughed. "Cray-cray is crazy, if you're down with the kids—know what I mean?" He struck a pose for added emphasis.

Katie sniffed. She could do zany. If she put her mind to it. But photocopying her butt? That was just ridiculous. The germs on one of those things should be off-putting enough!

"Well, you two sound perfect for each other."

Katie saw the sting of hurt her words caused and wished she could yank them straight back. Josh might do wild but he also did wonderful. If only he hadn't kept pushing the boundaries after their loss. If only he'd convinced her he could play things safe—even for a while—they might…

"I best get on, then."

Katie watched as Josh turned and made his way toward the curtained cubicle where his patient was waiting. There was something…different about his gait. Something different about *him*. He'd changed. Really changed. Her teeth caught hold of her lip and gave it a contemplative scrape.

Changed enough to hear what she had to say?

A series of loud guffaws burst from the curtained area where Josh was de-sharding his patient's booty.

No. Same ol' Josh! Some stray Christmas spirit must have sneaked into her coffee that morning. No one changed *that* much. She would just see through the time they had to work together as professionally as she could. No point in reopening old wounds. She'd borne enough hurt for a lifetime.

She scanned the board and picked a good old-fashioned broken arm. Some enthusiastic decorative touches to a snowy rooftop, no doubt. Fixing. Setting. Repairing. That was what she did. It was how she survived.

Once again she shook on her bright smile and pulled open the curtain.

"Right! Mr. Dawsen, I understand you've broken your arm?"

CHAPTER THREE

"I'LL JUST BE in the residents' room—cool?" Josh popped a finished chart onto the RNs' central desk, flashing a smile to the two nurses trying to untangle a set of twinkling lights. A patient's or some late decorating? They paid him no attention, so he hightailed it down the corridor, hoping for a few moments to regroup. It was time to pull up his socks and tell Katie the truth. The real reason he was there.

She'd yanked six of his safety-net days out from under him, unwittingly putting all his partridges in the one pear tree. It was do-or-die day *now*. For a man who didn't plan much, he had definitely planned this out. A whole week to gauge her mood…time to maybe inject a bit of romance into snatched moments alone. But with this stupid twenty-four-hour thing she showed no sign of shifting from, he had to get a move on. They were just a few hours away from midnight, and once that clock pinged upon the Christmas star, his time would be well and truly running out. Josherella was going to have to get a move on.

He looked at his backpack, slung on the back of the lone chair parked across from the bunk he'd thrown himself on for a catnap. He wouldn't have been surprised if the sheaf of official papers lurking in the side pocket had taken on a life of their own, unzipped the bag and come out and danced at him like an evil sugarplum fairy…or whoever the evil one was in *The Nutcracker*.

He cursed silently. He'd once loved Christmas and all the schmaltzy, cheesy, sentimental stuff that went along with it. When they'd lost their daughter just a few days before the holiday, it had sucked the season dry of any good feeling. He wanted that back—and the only way to get it was to woo his wife back into his arms. And if this was the season for miracles he was a first-rate candidate.

Otherwise…? Otherwise he would have taken the job in Paris when he'd got the offer. Moved to France to study with the most elite team of minimally invasive fetoscopic surgeons? Hell, yeah! It would have been a gargantuan leap forward for his career. He'd spent the past two years doing locum residencies in every single obstetrics unit he could. He would never know why his little girl had been stillborn—but if he could help other women he'd be there.

But his heart wouldn't be. And to end up in the City of Love without the woman he adored by his side would have been pointless. Not to mention the fact that Dr. Cheval insisted on total focus. No distractions and no demons. Right now Josh was hauling those things around big-time.

When the job offer had come, he'd seen it as life's way of grabbing him by the scruff of the neck, giving him a right old shake and demanding, for once, that he take responsibility for everything he had done. Own up to how his behavior had driven his wife away. And after she'd gone he'd pushed at life a bit more. A *lot* more. Life had pushed back, and now he had the metal infrastructure to prove he hadn't come out the winner.

He gave his head a good old scratch, shooting a look up to the heavens to see if there were any clues there.

Mistletoe.

Of course. *Love.* The high-voltage current he'd felt the first, second and every other time he'd laid eyes on his wife was electric. But going to the city where hand-holding and kisses on bridges and feeding each other delectable morsels of…

Hey! Now, *there* was an idea. He and Katie had always enjoyed a good picnic. Out on the common—or on a bench if it was pouring down—regardless of the sideways glances they'd received from passersby. It was what supersized umbrellas were made for, right?

A smile lit up his face. He'd do a Christmas dinner picnic! The smile faded just as fast. The canteen was closed. The way the snow was coming down meant leaving the hospital would be a challenge. Or just plain stupid. He'd already done stupid…

"Hey, Dr. West." Jorja poked her head round the corner with an apologetic expression. "Sorry to ruin your break, but we've got mass casualties coming in!"

Adrenaline shot through him and he was up and out of the bunk before Jorja had even removed herself from the door frame.

"What happened? How many? Do we have enough on staff? Is there any chance of diverting any of the patients to another hospital?"

Jorja's eyes widened, along with her mouth. Streaks of red began to color her cheeks.

"Uh…" She pushed at the floor with the stub of her toe.

"Sorry, too much television! I forget Copper Canyon is totally different from what you get out east."

"There are two. Patients, that is. With gastro. Dr. Mc-Gann is already down there."

Josh's heartbeat decelerated and he tried not to laugh. Much. The poor girl looked mortified. He slung an arm around her shoulders and tugged her in for a half hug as they made their way out into the main corridor. "Hey, Jorja, don't you worry. I can adjust my big-city ways…"

The words stopped coming. What the heck was he doing, bragging about his big-city machismo when he'd grown up in a town with two unlit junctions? Junctions where he'd been guaranteed to see his math teacher or his father heading off to the cattle markets. There was no hiding anywhere in that place if you stuck around—which was why he'd loved losing himself in the big city. And then he'd met Katie…like an angel he hadn't known he'd needed to meet. Found him. That was what she'd done. She had found him. Shown him how important it was to be grounded.

He looked straight up, silently cursing the invisible heavens. She was his lighthouse, his beacon, his…whatever analogy best fit the scene. She was his heart. His soul. And if he didn't get a move on he was going to lose her for good.

"Uh… Dr. West? Are you trying to…?" Jorja was shifting underneath his arm, turning toward him, shifting her gaze upward as well.

Damn. Mistletoe.

Katie heard them, then saw them. A twist of nausea squirled around her stomach as she took in the nervous laughter, the awkward shuffle of feet and the chins tipping up toward the ceiling. Jorja had practically covered the hospital in mistletoe, so it was hardly surprising that the one person who would find a way to put it to use

was Josh. He had always been a flirt. It was his nature.
To charm, to delight, to dazzle.

She turned away quickly, not wanting either of them
to see the hurt in her eyes, the sheen of tears she'd only
just managed to check when she'd spotted them. The
last thing she was going to do was stick around and
watch her husband kiss someone he'd only just met!

At least she knew Josh showing up out of the blue
wasn't some clever plot to see *her*. It was a fluke. A
needle-in-a-haystack chance of Yuletide torture. *Just
terrific.* She'd spent two entire years patching the shred-
ded remains of her heart together, and just when she'd
come to terms with her play-it-safe, hiding-out-in-Idaho
lifestyle, Josh had parachuted in and undone years of
exacting damage control.

Adrenaline began to surge through her. She tugged
at the high ribbing on the neck of her sweater, suddenly
wishing she had scrubs on. Why hadn't one of her patients thrown up on her? Then she could have missed
this nauseating scene of mistletoe magic. She checked
herself. Wishing patients ill wasn't her style, and thankfully the two gastro cases had turned out to be overin-
dulgence rather than food poisoning.

Who ate massive portions of something called Chocolate Decadence and *didn't* expect a sore stomach? People
who weren't careful. People who were reckless. People
who made decisions on a whim—like Josh.

She made a beeline for the doctors' locker room and
grabbed her winter coat before pushing through the
heavy door into the stairwell and pounding up step after
step toward the roof, letting out an involuntary wail of
relief when she found it was empty.

Silent screams into blankets while trying to retain her
control were one thing—but seeing Josh with another

woman… Words couldn't even describe how much it had hurt. Throat-scraping wail after howl poured out of her throat as the snow bit at her cheeks and the wind swirled through her hair and into her tear-blinded eyes. Why had Josh—of all the people in the world—had to show up? Hadn't he done enough harm? It was worse than shock. It was Shock and Awful.

Chest heaving from the effort of purging her sorrow, Katie forced herself to take more level, steadier breaths. Knowing a chill could turn into pneumonia in the blink of an eye at this time of year, she excavated a woolly hat from the depths of her pocket. She hadn't let those Girl Scout sessions go to waste.

Prepared at all times. Self-contained at all times. She tugged on her hat and scowled. Which one had she left out?

"And a smile in the face of adversity."

Katie's frown deepened. She turned this way and that, taking in the roof as though she were a child stuffed into an over-thick snow outfit. The urge to throw a tantrum was welling within her again. Twice in one day? Must be a record! Maybe she should have gone the bad-girl route as a kid. It might have garnered her a bit more attention from her parents.

She harrumphed. Unlikely.

She pulled out her phone and trawled a finger along the not-very-long list of names to see if there was anyone on there she could talk to. Colleague. Colleague. Colleague. Mentor. Nanny.

Alice Worthing! Her shoulders softened. She had absolutely *loved* her Irish nanny. Alice was the only person she'd told in advance of her elopement, and the second she'd seen the twinkle in the dear woman's eyes, she'd known she was doing the right thing.

Wow—had they both been wrong!

She pushed at the phone symbol anyhow. It would be nice to hear a friendly voice on Christmas Eve.

After a couple of rings she heard laughter and then the lilted *hello* she knew so well. Fifteen years in the US, married to an American for ten of them, and her accent hadn't changed a jot.

"Hello? Is anyone there?"

Katie started. "Sorry, Alice. It's me, Katie Wes— Katie McGann."

"Katie! My sweet Katie. Darlin', how the devil are you? It's been so long. *Too* long! What is it? Over a year now since you went out west. Are you all right, love? Is everything okay?"

"Yes. Fine." She kicked her boot into the thick roof-top snow.

"Well, that's a lie and we both know it."

Katie smiled at the phone, double-checking that she hadn't video-dialed her friend by accident.

"It's just—I—um—wanted to wish you a merry Christmas."

"Well, that's a lovely sentiment, Katie, but why not tell me the real reason you called?"

"I'd forgotten how quickly you see through me." Katie grinned, now wishing she *had* video-called Alice.

"Well, you and I both know how precious life is, so come on—spit it out."

"Josh."

"Oh, Katie, no—nothing's happened to Josh, has it?"

"No! God, no!" Katie felt surprised at how glad she was that was true. She might not want to be married to him, but she couldn't bear the thought if… "He's shown up at the hospital as my locum."

Another round of laughter followed as Alice called

out to her husband, saying Josh had found Katie. She heard the click of the receiver as Alice's husband got on the line.

"So he finally tracked you down, did he?" James's deep voice rumbled down the line. "He tried to plumb us for info but we didn't breathe a word. We knew you wouldn't want us getting involved. Want me to come out and beat him up for you?"

Katie knew he was joking, but James had always been very protective of her. Her relationship with her own father had never been a close one, so she liked James's concern.

"What sort of nonsense are you talking, man?" Alice hushed him. "Josh's dead romantic. Always was. A bit wild, but showing up on Christmas Eve and all…"

"It wasn't exactly as if they left things on a good note," James riposted.

"Yeah…well…" Katie's mind whirred, trying to catch up with everything as Alice and James bantered. "He came and asked you where I was?"

"Course he did. The boy's mad for you. Always was."

Then why was he trying to kiss Jorja?

Katie and Alice talked for what felt like hours. They had a lot to catch up on. But as the roar of doorbells and barking dogs started to drown out their voices, Katie knew she had to let Alice get back to her own life. She tipped her head to see if she could differentiate between clouds and the falling snow.

"Sorry, Katie. Our little girls' choir has just shown up to sing carols. Please forgive me but I need to go. You'll sort it out for the best. You always do. Lots of love."

"Oh! How is Catherine?"

"She's grand, darlin'. Must dash, but call again soon!" And the line went dead.

Katie didn't know if she felt better or worse for having made the call. A thousand questions and no answers added to her frustration. She kicked a satisfying lump of snow up into the glowering sky and watched it float back down to the rooftop.

The helicopter hadn't been used in a while, and from the looks of things, the crew hadn't been up yet with the blower. The snow was a good foot deep where she was standing. The drifts were deeper over by the edges. A good three feet by now. Maybe deeper. Winter had started early in Copper Canyon, and no matter how hard they tried to stay on top of the accumulating snow, they couldn't. Which, in this case, was all right. Because it was…beautiful.

She felt the fight go out of her. Maybe that had been her problem all along. Trying too hard to control things. Josh. Herself. She'd even broken down the seven stages of grief, giving herself a month to go through each stage, fastidiously identifying and eradicating anything that would hold back her progress to—to what, exactly?

Josh's angry words came back to her in echoing anvils of self-recognition. *Micromanager. Risk-averse. Exacting perfectionist! Control freak.*

The last one wilted her shoulders into a hunch against the buffeting wind. She looked around the roofscape again, as if it would conjure Josh up from the lower reaches of the hospital so he could call her out himself. Except the only voice she heard those words in was her own. *She* was the one who had shaken off the rest of the words he'd said and turned those remaining into insults. The words she wouldn't let herself remember?

Gorgeous. My love. Sweetheart. Angel. Darlin'.

She blinked away the sting of tears. When things had been good between them, they had been, oh, *so* good.

Josh had given her reserves of strength she hadn't known she had. Lit her up like a…oh, the irony…lit her up like a Christmas tree!

She blinked again, feeling a tear drop this time. She swiped it away and tried to shake off the memories. She was in a new place now, and up until the start of this double shift on Christmas Eve, things had been pretty good. Well… She tugged a foot through the snow and stomped toward the roof edge.

Neutral.

How pathetic was that? Even *she* had to snicker at herself. To aspire to have a *neutral* day? Wow! That elite education she'd aced had *really* prepared her for life. She scrunched her eyes tight and forced herself to open them with the promise of seeing something that made her smile.

Not too far away the twinkling lights of Copper Canyon's main street were glittering away like a perfectly decorated window display. The town council always did well. Never too opulent, never mistaking the decor for any holiday other than Christmas. At the far end of Main Street, where the two-lane road split and circled round the town's green, an enormous evergreen twinkled and shone like a bejeweled Fabergé egg through the fat snowflakes swirling around it. At the base of the tree, Katie could make out the lit outline of the bandstand, its columns rising in twisted swirls of red and white lights.

She reached the edge of the roof and eyed the drift. Higher than she'd thought. Enough snow to cloak the thick safety barriers she knew ran around the edges. She should make a note to hospital admin that they really must be raised—

She checked herself. As far as she knew, she was the

only one who was mad enough to come up to the roof in the middle of a snowstorm.

See, universe? Katie McGann can be just as much of a nut burger as the rest of them!

She gave the elements a satisfied grin as she pulled her emergency pair of waterproof mittens from the inner pocket of her down jacket.

Well...pragmatism *was* useful. And it was hardly a storm. A bit of wind. Thick latticed snowflakes big enough to catch on her tongue. She eyed the split-level roof just below her. The empty administrative offices...

She pushed her lips in and out as she considered. Without snow...? Maybe a six-foot drop. With snow...? Hmm...two feet of emptiness before she hit several feet of fluffy virgin snow. Her mind shot back to the rare trips up to her late grandparents' cabin in Vermont, where she, Alice and her grandmother had made endless snow angels.

"Always room for more angels to look out for us." That was how her grandmother had put it. So when she was upset and there was some snow to hand...snow angel. Magic recipe for a better mood.

Would it be fluffy enough to...? *Yeah...why not?* She could throw caution to the wind as easily as the next person...right?

She opened her arms wide, eyed the tilt of the snow-drift, turned around and began to press her weight into her heels. She wobbled for a moment...regained her footing...then reasoned with herself that this was precisely the sort of litmus test she needed to pass in order to prove she could well and truly survive without Josh... beyond *neutral*.

She sucked in a breath and smiled—at the world for just being there and being all snowy and twinkly so that she could make a snow angel when she sure as hell needed one.

As she shifted her heels along the edge again and raised her arms, the door to the stairwell burst open. Josh was calling out her name at ten decibels. His face was a mix of horror and fear when his eyes lit upon her. He called her name again, the vowels bending and elongating in the wind.

"Kaaa-tieee!"

Their eyes connected in a way they never had before. For the first time she saw he had been through it, too. The harrowing, mind-numbing pain of loss. And in that moment she wished back the two years they had spent apart.

Josh watched in horror as Katie's arms windmilled for balance. His eyes raced down her legs as she shifted her heels to regain traction on the icy ledge. Each micro-move she made became overexaggerated with her fruitless efforts to stay upright. Their eyes stayed locked as she completely lost her footing and fell helplessly back into the void.

Never in his life had he felt such searing pain. He had thought the grief at losing his daughter was the worst thing he could have lived through, but losing Katie as well would kill him.

An infinity of darkness spread out before him as he shouted and stumbled toward the edge, not even sure he was making a single sound above the howling in his skull.

Katie's comprehension of the world shifted as her body lost its fight with gravity. Apart from the terror she'd seen in her husband's eyes, she suddenly understood what he meant about the freedom in letting go. Just the release of falling backward was exhilarating.

She opened her throat and screamed as sensations hit her in surreal hits of slow-motion recognition. The breeze swept past her cheeks. She blinked away a snow-flake. With the surprise of the fall she'd lost her sense of where she was actually falling. It might have gone on forever.

The sky was astonishingly textured with clouds and the odd hit of stars… When was the last time she'd just looked up and enjoyed the sky?

Before she could take it all in, she hit the powdery snow with a fluffy *ploof!* and lay utterly still as her breath came back to her.

A dim awareness of sound came to her. A male voice. *Josh!* It had to be Josh. Her mind whirled into catch-up mode, her eyes widening as she realized what she was hearing.

"Katie! No!"

Ragged. Rough. Grief-stricken. Why was Josh so upset? She was just making a snow angel, for heaven's sake.

His face appeared over the edge, his features etched with anxiety.

"I fell."

"Yes!" The air came out of his mouth in thick, bil-lowed huffs of breath. "Yes, you did."

"It's nice down here." She saw the sheen of tears rise in his eyes before he had a chance to disguise it as some-thing else. Josh had never been a weeper. He swiped at his eyes with his sleeve. Maybe she'd been mistaken.

"Are you all right?"

Katie could tell Josh was trying to keep his voice under control. Behave as if he saw his estranged wife fall off the edge of a building every day. It suddenly struck her that his reaction was utterly different from what she would have expected. The old Josh would have just leaped over the edge and joined her. Pulled her into his arms and then, after a deep, life-affirming kiss, would have made snow angels with her. Right?

"Katie?" Josh knelt on the ledge and began to scan her acutely for injury. "Are you okay?"

"Pretty good." She moved her arms and legs just a little bit, suppressing a surprise hit of the giggles as she did so. Nothing hurt. She'd landed on an enormous pillow of snow, for heaven's sake! "Actually…" She met his eyes properly this time. "It was pretty fun."

"Fun, huh? Is that what you think? Near enough giving me a heart at—?"

He stopped himself and she watched silently as Josh rearranged his features into a long, studied look before visibly deciding to swallow whatever lecture he'd been about to give. She knew the expression well…and it gave her a hit of understanding she hadn't known she needed. It was the look Josh must have seen on *her* face time and again after they'd lost their baby girl and he'd come back from yet another high-octane experience.

Josh looked away from Katie and gave the vista a scan. The early-evening gloaming left hints of light on the tips of the mountains…gave the glittering Main Street more of a festive punch. His lips thinned as he slowly inhaled and exhaled, trying to get his racing heart under control.

His relief at finding Katie alive and well was morphing into anger. How *dare* she do this? Take such a huge risk? Didn't she know how precious she was to him? His anger welled up further into his chest, searing him from the inside out. *How dare she?*

"A thank-you for stopping you killing yourself might be nice."

"Killing myself?" She pushed herself up to sit and squinted at him through the falling snow. "You think if I—Katie West—Katie McGann," she corrected herself, annoyed, "was going to do something so stupid as to kill myself I'd do it by jumping two feet into a snowdrift?"

"That was difficult to see from the doorway." Josh cleared his throat again and swore under his breath. "So you weren't—?"

"Of course I wasn't. I was just…" She let herself plop back into the lightly compacted drift. "I was just trying to make a snow angel."

She spoke softly. More truculent than apologetic, but, hell, he'd take it. She was alive. That was good enough for now.

He tipped his head to the side and eyed her. "You only make snow angels when you're upset."

"No, I don't!" she shot back, her eyes anywhere but meeting his.

Yup! She was upset. He knew his arrival had upset her, but he hadn't thought launching herself into a snowdrift four floors off the ground would be her response. Maybe he should have called. Scheduled lunch. Done something normal, like she'd been begging him to do all along.

He knelt on the ledge and hitched up his bad leg before slipping over into the snow mattress Katie was pillowed in. He winced. The old-timers were right about feeling the cold differently once your body had proved itself fallible.

He gave her a grumpy glare and flopped down onto the snow beside her, where they lay in silence for a few moments. He'd thought he'd lost her just now. Lost the love of his life.

Okay, firebrand...cool your jets. You've both had a shock.

He shot a sidelong glance at Katie and saw her all wide-eyed and... *Seriously?* Was she *grinning*? That grin near enough sucker punched the rest of the breath out of his chest and he only just managed to reel in the angry words.

His emotions were running so wild it was impossible to tell if he should just whip out those stupid divorce papers and give her his signature right now. Then maybe they could both get on with their lives.

He swiped at the snowflakes clustering on his lashes. There was no way he could move on. Not like this. Not yet. And if Katie didn't give a monkey's about him she wouldn't be flinging herself off the sides of buildings on Christmas Eve. So...it was a silver-linings moment. A weird one. But a moment to count himself lucky. Blessed.

It didn't stop him from needing to expunge a bit of "grumpy," though.

Eyes rigidly glued to the heavens, he leveled his voice before starting. "Well, isn't *this* cozy?"

"That's one way of putting it," Katie grumbled.

"This a new Idaho thing? Hurling yourself off the side of buildings without an audience?"

"Something like that."

"Any reason in particular, or did whimsy just overtake you?"

"Yeah," she bit back drily. "That's how I roll. Got it in one, Josh. Crazy Katie West, hitting the fast lane again!"

"West?" He tried not to sound hopeful.

"Whoever."

He let the words settle for a moment. It took one to know one, and she was calling him out. She always read life's instruction book. He barely looked at the book's cover before flinging it away and just going for it. Especially once he'd met his wife. With Katie by his side he had felt invincible.

"It was pretty reckless." He couldn't stop the words choking him as they came out. He sounded like his dad.

"Yeah? Well, the fact you couldn't see the four-foot-deep drift of snow I was aiming for probably gave you the wrong idea. I calculated the risk in advance and determined there was little to no damage that could come to a girl trying her best to have a little *alone time* and make herself a blinking snow angel! And if you want to talk about reckless, you'd better be careful with Jorja. She's got a reputation."

Josh pushed himself up on his elbows and gave her his best *what are you talking about?* look. "Jorja?"

"Yes. Jorja." Her voice went singsong as her hands started to make the beginnings of angel wings in the snow. "Josh and Jorja, sitting in a tree…"

"What are you talking about?"

"The mistletoe?" Her arm movements widened and her legs joined in, occasionally giving his own hand or leg a bash as she worked out her frustration on her snow angel.

"You think I made out with Jorja under some mistletoe?" His voice rang with pure incredulity.

"I *saw* you!" Katie all but snarled.

"No, you did *not*!" Josh retorted, dredging up his best five-year-old's retorts. "You might've seen me standing there—but dodging mistletoe in that hospital of yours is as easy as avoiding patients!"

"Which—by the looks of things—you're doing a

pretty good job of. You were hired to work—not to gallop round like an errant King Arthur, swooping up damsels in distress at every hint of a berry! You're a doctor, if my memory serves me correctly! Shouldn't you be behaving responsibly for once? *Doctoring?*"

Katie's words hit him with rapid-fire precision—her body was moving as quickly as she could speak. Josh had never seen her like this—in full flow. Her arms and legs swinging hither and yon. It was going to be one hell of a snow angel.

He couldn't let her words go. Wouldn't stay silent. He was hurting, too. Always had. Putting on a brave face had been the hardest thing he'd done, but he'd thought that was what she'd needed from him.

"You're the one in charge, Katie. Shouldn't you be down there, bossing people around? Making sure everything's in order? Everything in its right place?"

Again and again he'd bitten back words like these in the depths of their grief. But this was Last Chance Saloon time. Despite the widening shock in her dark eyes, the words continued to fly, unchecked, past his lips.

"C'mon, Katie—you always seemed to know what was best for me. What would you advise? What would you suggest I do now?"

"What—what do you mean?" She pushed herself up to stand, distractedly brushing the snow off her clothes, discomfort taking the place of fury.

"You're really good at laying down guidelines. Heaven knows how they're getting on down there without little Miss Perfect dotting the 'I's and crossing the 'T's. How would you *recommend* I comfort myself after seeing my wife take a swan dive off of a building?"

He was all but shouting, rising to his full height before they both awkwardly swung themselves over onto the roof, then stood for who knew how long like two cowboys frozen in a standoff.

"I wasn't—" Katie finally broke the silence then stopped herself, unable to resist glaring at him while she tried to regain her composure. Her common sense.

They'd had a variation on this fight a thousand times and she didn't have it in her to have it again. Didn't want to. She'd seen the fear in his eyes and she'd never meant to be cruel to him. Not then. Not now. But this very moment was proof positive that they couldn't be together. Not when they couldn't even bring a bit of good out of the other as they had once done. They needed to wrap this up. It was the only way to go forward.

"Why are you here, Josh? What exactly is it that you want?"

"You," he answered. "I came here because I want *you*."

The air between them grew electric. With unspoken words. Unspent desire.

His blue eyes told her a thousand things at once. Gone was the recrimination. The anger. In their place was the heady, crackling energy that had never failed to draw them together. Katie hadn't realized how much she missed Josh on a physical level.

He didn't wait for an invitation.

Two of his long-striding steps and he'd pulled her up and into his arms. All thought was gone. She was reduced to sensation only, such was the power of his touch. She felt his lips against hers, both urgent and tender. Her every pore ached with the immediacy of her body's response to his touch. Winter jackets, woolen hats, leather gloves—none of the clunky gear of the season detracted from the pure, undiluted hunger Katie was experiencing.

Somewhere out there in the far reaches of her mind

she knew she should be pushing him away. Knew she shouldn't be returning hungry kiss after kiss, each one filled with two years' worth of need. His hands cupped her jaw as the kisses grew deeper still. A low moan met one of his as they pressed tightly against the other. Everything felt familiar and new—as it always had—but their connection was... It felt unbreakable. Timeless.

Had she been wrong to send him away?

A vibration jostled at her waistline. Her pager.

Another one sounded. Josh's.

She pulled back, wondering if her mouth looked as bruised with kisses as Josh's did. Her fingers fumbled with the pager, her eyes still glued to her husband's face.

He was part of her. She knew that now. Making him leave had been ridiculous. No amount of time or distance could sever the ties between them. But what they had wasn't healthy. Wasn't meant for long-term—especially if she were ever, one day, to hold a baby of her own in her arms.

"Multiple injuries. We'd better get down there."

"What?" Katie shook her head clear of the "Josh and baby" fog.

"Read your pager. Ambulances are due in a few minutes."

"Right. Yes." She grabbed her phone from her pocket, relieved it hadn't been lost to the snowdrift in her snow-angel frenzy, and punched out the numbers of the ER desk. "It's Dr. McGann. Are the teams setting up the trauma units?"

Josh watched as Katie listened, responded, thumbed away the stray wisps of lipstick from around her mouth and tugged her clothes back into place. Moment by moment she became Dr. McGann again. This reinvention of herself who was all business. The Katie he'd first met.

Not the one who came alive each time they touched or when their eyes lit upon the other. *This* Katie's eyes were near enough devoid of life. His heart ached to put back each and every spark he knew lay dormant within them. Now wasn't the time.

He shifted his hips. His body was trying to fight down the force of desire kissing Katie had elicited in him. She felt good. Ridiculously good in his arms. It made the idea of Paris even more insane if she weren't by his side.

The peal of ambulance sirens became faintly audible.

If he'd had a spare half hour he would have made a snowman up here and then kung fu'd its head off. It would have been satisfying. For about a second.

He shook his head and took up the pace Katie was setting to the roof door. At least he knew work would keep him distracted for the next hour or five, depending upon how bad the traumas were. Snow and automobiles? The onset of darkness on Christmas Eve, when everyone's expectations were just a little bit higher than any other time of year…? Yeah. It wasn't going to be pretty. Not in the slightest.

CHAPTER FOUR

KATIE STOPPED IN her tracks. Now, *this* she certainly hadn't expected. The first ambulance had pulled into the covered bay with a horse trailer attached to it, and the crew, along with the help of a teary girl dressed up as the Virgin Mary, were unloading a donkey.

"Can you help Eustace, please?" the girl wailed when her eyes lit on Katie.

Eustace the donkey?

"Ooh! A nativity donkey!" Jorja appeared alongside Katie, rubbing her hands together and blowing on them as her feet sashayed her from side to side.

"I think we'd better take a look at *you* first." Katie's eyes were on the girl who, through the folds of her costume, was clutching her side. "What's your name, hon?"

"Maddie."

"What a lovely name! Is there anyone you can leave in charge of the—Eustace—while we bring you inside?"

"No!" The girl's eyes widened in fear, and as she and the donkey stepped into the bright light of the ambulance bay outside the ER, Katie could see she also had a cut on her forehead over what appeared to be a growing lump. "I am not leaving Eustace. He is my best friend and we have to get to Bethlehem tonight!"

"Maybe we can find a hitching post for Eustace."

"But he's bleeding!"

"What have we got here?"

Josh's voice shot along Katie's nervous system as she approached Maddie. Her fingers flew automatically to her lips, and she wished the remembered pulse of their kisses weren't so vivid. She pushed down the thoughts and forced herself to focus. A Mary intent on getting to Bethlehem and a donkey with quite a serious cut to his haunch. Hospital protocol to adhere to...

A lightbulb went off. Josh's passion for medicine had come about by fixing the local wildlife and working under the wing of the country vet on the ranch his father had managed. It wasn't really playing by the rulebook, but... Were there different rules at Christmas? Or at least a bit of Yuletide flexibility? The emergency vets were on the other side of town, and using ambulances to tow livestock trailers had already been done—

"What do you say we pop you on a gurney, Maddie? Out here? That way Dr. McGann can take a look at you and I can stitch up... What did you say your pal's name was?"

Mind reader.

"Eustace!" Maddie replied with a broad smile, then another wince.

"Eustace! I had an Uncle Eustace, and he was as stubborn as a mule. Did you say your Eustace was a mule or a donkey?"

"A donkey! Can't you tell the difference?" Maddie giggled through her pain.

Katie couldn't fight the smile his words brought. Josh's way with patients—especially children—had always been second to none. He still had the magic touch. Something she'd worked hard at and never fully achieved. Especially after the baby.

The thought instantly sobered her. They had two or even three more ambulances due in from the same crash, so they needed to get down to business, bedside manner or no. Maddie's parents, or whoever had been driving the truck pulling the trailer, must be incoming. Otherwise they surely would have shown up with Maddie and Eustace.

"Jorja, can you—?"

"Already on it!" the nurse called, halfway through the electric doors.

"Hey, fellas!" Josh was signaling to the ambulance drivers to move the livestock trailer outside of the bay so the other ambulances would have room to pull in when they arrived.

Katie's two interns had appeared, with a gurney each, and Jorja had shouldered an emergency medical kit.

"Where would you like this one, Dr. McGann?" asked Michael. She smiled gratefully at the curly-haired intern and pointed over to a well-lit spot by the sliding doors. He was quiet—very committed and ultraserious. Birds of a feather. They got on well.

"Make sure those brakes are on." She pointed at the gurney wheels. If they needed to whisk Maddie inside for any reason, they could—but out here they needed to be as safe as possible.

"Where are your parents, honey?"

"Be careful with his halter." Maddie's eyes were glued on Josh as he expertly knotted Eustace to a pillar, petting and soothing the donkey, who seemed also to have fallen under Josh's spell. *Dr. Doolittle strikes again!*

Maddie threw tips at Josh for keeping Eustace happy, her fears about his welfare quelled by his verbal updates. Katie gave an internal sigh of relief. If Maddie had been in that livestock trailer when the crash happened, she was bound to have had a heck of a knock, and inspections for broken ribs were less than fun. If she was properly distracted that would help.

"We're going to put a little numbing agent on Eustace's rump, here. Is that all right, Maddie? Do we need your parents' permission to go ahead and give him stitches?"

Katie shot him a look. She received a nod of response. One that said he knew what was going on and was playing the Distraction Whilst Gathering Information Game.

"Michael," she whispered, "can you get me some scissors, please? We need to cut these off." Katie needed to get the layers of robes off Maddie without moving her ribs. If she lifted the robes off over the girl's head and there had been any acute breaks or internal injuries, the movement might make things worse. Broken ribs were one thing... Punctured lungs were a whole new kettle of fish.

"Dr. McGann." Shannon, her other intern, tapped her on the shoulder, magically appearing with a pair of scissors in hand. "A second ambulance is five minutes out. They've got a male patient presenting with suspected fractured wrist and extensive leg injuries and another young adult male presenting with a broken nose and other minor injuries from an air bag."

Katie nodded whilst deftly dividing the robes of Maddie's costume. The girl's face was growing paler, and the sooner she could get her lying down for an examination the better. "Want to give me a hand here, Shannon?"

"Sure, but don't you want me to do the incoming—?"

Shannon was always keen to be first on scene for whatever "A-list" injuries came through the emergency room doors, but Katie had been very careful to divvy them out between her gore-hungry intern and Michael, whose "ladies first" attitude Katie hadn't quite figured out. Nervous or just genuinely polite?

Tonight wasn't about politics, though. It was about priority.

"If you could help me get Maddie out of these robes and then make sure there are two triage areas prepped, nurses on standby with gurneys and a couple of wheel-chairs, that would be great. There doesn't sound like much the EMTs won't be able to handle in terms of stabi-lizing. Let X-Ray know someone will be on the way up."

Shannon's lips pursed in disappointment, and Katie knew better than to think the evening would run smoothly. If you relaxed, things went south. That was how it worked in an ER. That was how it worked in life.

"Ouch!" Maddie gasped and wobbled.

Katie and Shannon each reached for an elbow as the last of the biblical robes dropped away. Maddie's hands flew to her side, where blood was seeping through her shirt, and Eustace brayed softly, as if he knew his owner was in pain.

"You cut my robes?" Maddie was properly tearful now.

"Easy there, boy. I just need you to stay steady," Josh was saying.

"It's all right, honey. We can get those stitched back up for you—no problem."

Katie's eyes flicked back to Josh as he made a general callout for an electric shaver. The donkey's winter coat was making the topical numbing agent less effective, and she could tell he was trying to play by the rules as much as possible. They could use xylocaine without too many questions. But proper injectable painkillers…? Less easy to explain where vials of lidocaine were—much less to write up a chart for Eustace. Off the books was best—even if it bent the rules.

Katie thought for a second of stopping him. This was

how doctors got fired. Risks. She never took risks. Josh never needed to think twice about it.

"Nurse!" he called, without looking up from what he was doing.

Katie flinched infinitesimally as Jorja appeared by Josh's side in an instant. He had said it was all a mistake. The mistletoe mishap…

She pulled her gaze back to Maddie, whose eyes were widening at the sight of the blood on her white shirt.

"It's all right, Maddie. Let's get you up on the gurney, honey." She looked at Michael, who had arrived back at Maddie's other side. "On three." They eased Maddie up and onto the gurney on her count. "Right! Let's check you out. I'm going to have to lift up your shirt, and it's pretty cold out here. Are you sure you don't want to go inside?"

"No!" There was no mistaking the determination in the girl's voice. "Where Eustace goes, I go." She twisted suddenly, trying to get a better look at her pricked-eared pal. Her eyes tightened with pain. "It hurts to breathe."

Fear suddenly entered the little girl's eyes. She couldn't be more than eleven…but Katie was sure an old soul was fueling her.

"Lie down again, hon. I think you might've bruised a couple of ribs. Michael, could you get me a couple of blank—?"

"Already on it, Doc."

Katie rucked up Maddie's shirt, relieved to see the bleeding was from a gash and nothing more. But in a dirty livestock trailer? They'd have to put a booster tetanus shot on the girl's tick-list as well.

She tried to go for Josh-casual. "Say, it looks like you and Eustace are both going to be getting stitches tonight."

A grin lit up the girl's face. "Really?"

Hmm... Josh-casual obviously works.

A sting of guilt shot through her at the words she had flung at him when things had seemed too dark to continue. *Reckless. Unthinking. Careless.* Maybe his laissez-faire attitude had been to soothe her. To comfort her in a time of great sorrow.

She swallowed hard and continued her examination of Maddie.

"That hurts!" Maddie yelped.

"That's your rib cage acting up. Where exactly were you when the accident happened?"

"With Eustace."

Katie's eyes widened, her suspicions confirmed. *Well, that was just about as health and safety unconscious as things got.*

"And your parents let you ride in there?"

Maddie's eyes began to dart around the covered area. "Not exactly..."

"Who was driving the tow vehicle?"

"My bro—" She reconsidered giving the information, swallowing the rest of the word. Tears sprang into her eyes. "Am I going to get in trouble?"

"No, honey. Of course not. But riding in trailers with live—with Eustace—isn't really legal."

"Are my brothers going to jail?"

Katie's eyes shot across to meet Josh's, but he was one hundred percent focused as stitch after stitch brought the sides of the cut on Eustace's rump neatly together. She had always loved watching Josh's hands at work. They were large, capable hands. The intricate work they completed with skillful dexterity always surprised her.

Just as easy to picture him whipping a lasso into action as he had when he was a boy as it was to see him deftly tying a miniature knot at the end of a row of immaculate stitches as he was now.

"Probably best if you keep pneumonia out of the symptoms…"

Josh didn't look up as he spoke, but he had always had a second sense for when Katie's eyes were trained on him. She stiffened. It wasn't often he had to remind her to keep her eye on the ball. The role reversal didn't sit well.

"Maddie?" Josh raised his voice a bit. "Eustace is doing pretty good, here. Mind if I snaffle him some carrots from somewhere, then let him have a bit of a lie-down in the trailer?"

"That would be nice." Maddie sniffled, her fear and pain visibly kicking up a notch. "There are carrots already in the trailer."

"Michael." Katie snapped into action. "Let's tuck these blankets round Maddie and get her a tetanus shot before bringing her up to X-Ray, please, to check on her ribs. Maddie, honey, Michael's going to need your parents' phone number so we can get in touch—just to okay any treatment you're going to need, all right?"

"You're not going to let them arrest my brothers, are you? We just wanted to get to the nativity early!"

Tears began to pour out of Maddie's blue eyes and Katie's heart all but leaped to her throat. There was such love and protectiveness in her words. "Why don't we take things one at a time? We'll call your parents, sort you out, and then deal with everything else as and when it happens."

"Do you think there will be an angel looking after my brothers?"

"Dr. McGann?" Jorja stuck her head through the sliding doors. "That second ambulance is incoming."

"I sure do, Maddie," said Katie. And she meant it. "This is Michael—Dr. Rainer. He's going to take you up to X-Ray. We'll see you in a little bit, all right?"

"Okay…" The young girl snuffled. Her head turned to find Josh within sight. "Thanks for looking after Eustace."

"You bet, kiddo. It was my pleasure." Josh flashed her one of his warm smiles and gave her arm a quick squeeze before Michael and a nurse wheeled her off to the ER.

The wail of the sirens grew louder and Katie ripped off her protective gloves, quickly wiggling her fingers into the fresh pair one of the nurses handed her. If she'd thought things had been busy earlier, they were going into full-time Christmas Eve Crazy now the sun had set.

"Teenage male, presenting with multiple leg injuries and compound fracture to the wrist."

"Got it." Josh helped unload the gurney along with the EMT. This was Chris, Maddie's older brother.

Josh took in the EMT's rattle of information as he scanned the teen's face again. Chris couldn't have had his first whiskers for long, let alone gained much experience behind the wheel in a snowstorm.

A nurse met him at the doors and took over as the EMT finished reeling off the treatments Chris had already received. His injuries were severe. Compound fracture to the femur. Possible compression to the ankle. Severe dislocation of the knee. And who knew what muscles and ligaments might have been torn or burst? He'd be off that leg for months. Minimum. From the looks of the blood loss and extensive damage, the boy would need to be in surgery sooner rather than later. No time to wait for parental consent.

"Right, we'd better take a look at the mess you've made of yourself."

"Where's Maddie?" The boy's eyes were wide with panic.

"It's all right, buddy. Maddie is up in X-Ray. Looks like you messed your leg up pretty well."

"Where's my brother? Have you seen Nick? Where's Maddie? Is Eustace all right?"

A gurney went past with one of the interns at the helm. The keen one. Shannon...? Didn't matter.

"Hey, bro!"

Another teenage boy called from a gurney as he was wheeled past. Blood was smeared all over his face and winter coat. This was obviously the one with the broken nose.

"You haven't given them Mom and Dad's number, have you?" he shouted, before his gurney turned the corner to one of the triage areas.

"No way—what do you think I am? An idio—? *Ow!*" The scream Chris emitted filled the corridor, and just as quickly as the howl of acute pain had taken over the soundscape, it disappeared as Chris lapsed into unconsciousness.

"Anyone think to check on the femoral artery?"

Josh didn't know why he was asking. There was blood everywhere, the EMTs were long gone, and the nurse had been with him for no more than a few seconds.

"Let's skip triage and get straight up to surgery—"

"Only for a handover." Katie's voice broke in.

"This guy's going to bleed out if we don't get him on a table fast. And who knows what sort of filth is in that leg? Time's against us, Katie."

"Yes, it is. And that's why we're going to let one of

the orthopedic surgeons cover this one. They're already prepping the room."

Josh nodded curtly. He thrived on make-or-break surgery, and if there was one person in the world who knew that was true of him, she was standing right there looking the picture of officiousness.

"We need you in Trauma, Josh. There are more patients incoming. The rescue crews only just opened up the car that got hit by the snowplow."

"Understood."

And he did. Katie did prioritizing. He did gut instinct. It was why they had always worked together so well. The yin to the other's yang. Sure, there were fiery moments—but balance always won out in the end.

Well… He watched as she flew past him into one of the cubicles, where a patient could be heard arguing with one of the nurses. He scrubbed his jaw hard. Balance hadn't *always* won out in the end.

He gave the nurse on the other side of the gurney a tight smile.

"Let's get this whippersnapper up to surgery so we can get back for the incomings."

"You bet, Dr. West."

"Mrs. Wilson goes into Three and Mr. Wilson into Four." Katie was issuing directions faster than a New York traffic cop in rush hour. She was in a fury. The Wilsons had been the hardest hit but had been the last to be brought in.

"It took the fire crew a while to dislodge their car from the snowplow."

"One more patient incoming!"

Michael was hurtling down the corridor with a gurney. Gone was his quiet, serene demeanor. He looked near wild with panic. For an instant Katie thought the gurney was empty and that her reliable intern had all but lost the plot entirely—until she saw the tiny figure lying on the gurney. A little girl. She looked about three.

The same age her daughter would have been if she had lived. The hollow ache of grief began to creep into Katie's heart. Josh appeared on the other side of the gurney. *Great. Just what she needed.* The one person in the world who could make these feelings multiply into Infinityville.

"What have we got here?"

"Three-year-old girl presenting with abdominal bruising and pain, blood in the urine, internal bleeding— suspected trauma to the left kidney."

Michael rattled out a few more details as they raced the gurney toward the trauma unit.

"Can we get her into OR Two with Dr. Hastings?" Katie kept her eyes trained on Michael. This was a nightmare blossoming out of control.

"Nope. He's busy with an emergency appendectomy."

This little girl couldn't wait. If her kidney was bleeding out, she needed surgery immediately or she would die. Her eyes flicked from Michael to Josh.

"What about Dr. Hutchins?"

"They're all busy, Dr. McGann." Michael churned out the information, oblivious to the emotional storm brewing between Katie and Josh. "We've prepped OR Four for you. Do you need me to assist?"

Katie's eyes widened. She blinked, doing her utmost to wear her best poker face. All the other surgeons were busy. She'd have to do it—keep this child alive. She felt her hands go clammy as they clutched the side rails of the gurney. Her heart rate quickened and she knew if she looked into a mirror right now she would see her pupils were dilating.

"Are you up to doing a nephrectomy?" Josh's voice was low. Not accusatory—the tone *she* would have used for someone out of their depth. Safety was paramount, particularly with lawsuits swinging like an evil pendulum above their every move these days.

"Of course!" she bit back.

Josh accompanied her, uninvited, into the lift on the way to the surgical ward, dismissing Michael from gurney duty with a smile.

"It's a routine surgery. I did one last week."

But not on a child...a little girl. And not with you here.

Katie didn't dare meet his eyes. If she was going to keep it together to save this little girl's life, a shot of Josh's deep blue eyes was exactly what would have calmed her three years ago. That time had long passed. Even so, she could almost see her heart pumping beneath the scrubs she'd tugged on after Snow-Angel-Gate.

She couldn't help herself. As the doors slid closed and the pair of them were left alone with their tiny patient, she lifted her eyes to meet his. They said everything she had wanted to see in them when they'd lost their little girl.

I'm here for you. You can trust in me. Let me help you.

"Don't worry. I've got this." Katie ripped her eyes away from his. "You should go back down. If anything major happens in the ER—"

"If anything major happens in the ER," he interrupted, "they will page us. I'm staying with you."

"What are you saying, Josh?" Katie couldn't keep the disbelief out of her voice. "Are you saying I'm not up to this?"

"No," he began carefully. "I'm saying you've had a long day, a couple of shocks, and whether you like it or

not, you need me by your side. I'll just stay for a minute
or so—until you get going."

The elevator doors opened before Katie could reply.
Which was just as well. Because what could she say
other than *You're right*?

She had struggled over the past three years, doing
operations that reminded her of her little girl and the
life she might have had. Earlier on she'd deftly handed
over any critical surgeries on young children to her colleagues. Just being responsible for the delicate life of a
child had been too overwhelming—her own body had
proved she didn't have what it took to care for one. But
in the past year she'd taught herself to close down—to
behave like the clinician she was.

But with Josh here…? Game-changer. She had to prove
to him she was over it. Over *him*. That she had moved on
from the loss of their child.

Elizabeth.

Elizabeth Rose West.

A beautiful name for their darling little girl, who was
nothing more than a statistic now. One out of seventy
mothers give birth to a stillborn baby in America every
day. The volume of that annual loss was almost too much
to bear. She'd never even bothered to check the statistics
on failed marriages in the wake of such a loss. Just shut
it all out and moved away.

Katie gritted her teeth and gave her head a quick
shake. Cobwebs and history didn't belong in there now.
This child's life depended upon clear, swift thinking.

The anesthetist met her at the OR door for a quick
handover. "A necrotomy?" He tipped his head toward
the little girl.

"'Fraid so." Katie tried to keep her tone bright.

"Well, you did a great job with the last one—no reason this should be any different."

"Thanks, Miles. I appreciate it."

"Well, if you'll both excuse me, I'll go in with the patient and get the anesthetics in order."

"Sure thing. Oh! This is Josh. He's—" *Er...my husband, and I still love him, and...*

"Dr. West." Josh jumped in to rescue her. Again. "Locum over the holiday period. I would shake hands, but—" He gestured at the gurney he was trying to navigate into the OR.

"Miles Brand. Good to meet you." He took over moving the gurney, along with a nurse who had materialized from the OR. "Let's get this girl inside and on the table, shall we?"

"I'm going to scrub in while she's prepped," Katie said needlessly after he'd left.

"I'll join you," Josh offered with a soft smile.

An encouraging one. One she should graciously accept. Because what was happening right now was ticking all the I'm-Not-Ready-For-This boxes she'd systematically arranged in her brain's no-go area.

"Thanks."

They pushed into the scrub room together, shoulders shifting against each other's as they had back in the day.

Josh allowed himself a millisecond of pleasure before he realigned his focus. Covert calming. It was his specialty.

"What's the layout here?"

"Near enough the same as Boston," Katie answered, pointing out the shelves that held surgical caps and masks.

Their eyes met as she tugged on a standard blue surgical cap.

"Where's the one I got you?" It had been covered in

wildflowers. What she smelled of, he'd told her when she'd unwrapped it.

"In the wash."

Her eyes flicked away and he knew she was lying.

He tried not to notice her tying on her face mask in an effort to hide the painful thickets of emotion she was stumbling through.

Never mind, sweetheart. I feel it, too.

Stepping up to the sink, they both let muscle memory take over. The warm, steady flow of water was the predominant sound in the room as he and Katie took a good five minutes to systematically wash and scrub, first their nails, then their hands, which they held above the level of their elbows to prevent dirty water from dripping onto them.

Josh hit the taps with his elbows when they'd both finished. Katie nodded at the stack of sterile hand towels—one for each arm.

"You sure you're good?" He handed her a towel.

"Medicine is the only thing I *am* sure of these days."

Two nurses pushed into the scrub room with gowns before he could reply. There was room for hope in her response. Room to believe he was right to have sought her out. His lips parted into a smile for which he received a quick, grim nod.

Fine. He felt he'd been thrown a buoy. He could work with a nod.

She could do this, Katie silently assured herself. She'd done it before, and she would do it again.

"Arm," instructed the surgical nurse.

Katie stuck her arm into the sterilized blue sleeve and made a one-eighty twist to fully secure the surgical gown around her, finding herself standing face-to-face with

Josh while his gown was tied. He arched an inquisitive eyebrow.

Are you ready? it said.

She arched one back. Hadn't they been through this?

"Left hand, please, Dr. McGann."

She lifted it up and widened her eyes to a glare. Why didn't he stop *smiling*?

"And the right."

Katie raised her hand, holding her arm taut as the nurse tugged on the glove. The other nurse was clearly pleased she had won Josh in the surgeon crapshoot.

"Thank you, Marilyn. Merry Christmas to you."

"Merry Christmas to you, too, Dr. West." The nurse giggled.

Katie frowned. How on earth did he know *Marilyn*?

She had half a mind to step across the small room and lick Josh's gloved hands, rendering him unclean for the surgery.

Childish? Yes. Something the head of the ER should do right before surgery? Probably not.

There was a life to save—and she was going to be the doctor who saved it.

CHAPTER FIVE

"ARE YOU DOING it open or laparoscopically?" Josh kept his voice low and steady. Curious.

"Open."

Katie's eyes flicked to his as he skirted the periphery of the surgical team gathering in the OR.

"Unusual."

Not for his girl, but he knew she was always at her calmest when she talked systematically through her surgery.

Katie nodded. Blinked. His heart skipped a beat before she responded in a clear voice.

"Not in a trauma like this. Laparoscopically is better for routine."

She wasn't saying anything he didn't know, but with a team of people in the room, communicating with a nod or a look wasn't good enough. Everyone had to be on the same page or mistakes would be made.

"There is potentially a lot of other damage in here, and we're better off with a clear view of what we're dealing with."

"Rib removal?" one of the surgical nurses asked, indicating that she wanted to have the correct instruments to hand.

"Hopefully not, but one could've been broken on impact. We'll have to check."

Katie was grateful other members of the OR team were chiming in. She knew Josh's steady, careful breakdown of the steps in the guise of "reminding himself" was to keep her mind off the tiny body lying on the operating table. Josh could have done this surgery in his sleep. So could she. And he was just reminding her of what was true.

"A partial nephrectomy with so much damage could lead to the need for another surgery," Katie continued. "I don't want that for her. I won't know until I see the damage, but radical is the best option to keep things minimal for—"

"Casey," volunteered one of the nurses as the little girl's body was stabilized for Katie to make the first incision. "Casey Wilson's her name. The parents sent up her information when you were scrubbing in."

Perfect. A name. Just the way to keep it clinical.

Her grip tightened on the scalpel. "I'm preparing to make the incision."

"The bruising certainly indicates massive trauma."

"The EMTs said the snowplow hit her side of the car. She's lucky to have survived at all."

Katie shook away this new piece of information as she made an eight-inch cut from the front of the girl's soft belly to just below her small rib cage. Her mind began to take over, and her heart beat with a steadier cadence. A clock could have marked time with her breaths.

Massive trauma to one kidney. The other, thankfully, was untouched.

She switched instruments and began to cut and move muscle, tiny pieces of fat and the collection of tissue that held the kidney in place. It was steady, systematic work.

A glance at the stats here. A minute cut and stitch there. Updates from the nurses. Eyes fastidiously avoiding the tiny little girl's head, just beyond the surgical drape. A vague awareness of Josh moving opposite her at the surgical table.

As she guided her hands through the surgery, it hit her how quickly she'd lapsed into deriving comfort from Josh's rock-solid presence across the table from her. From the moment before she'd stepped into the OR, when fear had threatened to compromise all that she worked so hard for, even the tiniest of tremors she had felt in her hands had left her. And something deep within her heart told her it was having the man she'd once believed to be the love of her life with her.

She flicked her eyes up to meet his. Blue, pure, unwavering. He nodded before returning his eyes to the operation. There was severe bruising along Casey's rib cage—no doubt from the seat belt—but the kidney seemed to have taken the bulk of the trauma. Katie worked her way around the tiny organ, taking particular care to properly clamp and seal the blood vessels before ultimately and successfully removing the kidney.

Textbook.

"You want me to close?" It was an offering, not a doubt about her ability.

Katie shook her head. "I'm good." She'd made it this far. She was going to see it through.

Again, muscle memory took over as she pulled the surgical area back together, minus the small kidney, with a series of immaculately executed stitches. She ran the nurses through the aftercare before allowing herself another glance across the operating table.

"See?"

Josh's blue eyes twinkled at her. Katie could tell from the crinkles round them he was smiling.

"You did it."

"You ready for Secret Santa?" Jorja, despite nearing the end of a sixteen-hour shift, seemed just as sprightly as she had when Josh had first met her.

Was she rechargeable?

"Sure thing."

"We're all meeting down at the central desk at midnight." Jorja's hand shot up to cover her mouth as she stifled a yawn.

Ah! She was human.

Josh kept a good arm's length between them as they walked down the corridor toward the ER. He didn't want any more misunderstandings under the mistletoe. He'd tried dating a couple of times after he'd decided the only way forward was moving on, but had never got past ordering a drink before faking a pager call. Cheap trick, but faking affection would have been worse.

But that didn't mean he couldn't be chatty.

"This was a long shift for you. A double?"

"No longer than yours."

She nodded her head in acknowledgment. "I do it every year." She continued when Josh raised his eyebrows. "So I can be with my family on Christmas Day."

"Oh, right! So you're a local?"

"Yup." She nodded, her voice swelling with pride. "Born and bred Copper Creeker. All six of my brothers and sisters, too."

"Six!" Josh couldn't keep the surprise out of his voice.

"Yup!" Jorja chirped again. "It means the turkey has to be absolutely ginormous—so my brothers have started deep-frying it outside to keep the oven clear for Mom."

"Sounds good."

Jorja brightened. "Want to come? You're welcome. Everyone brings a boyfriend or a girlfriend."

Josh widened the gap between them. "Oh, no. No, thanks. Not for me. I'm on shift. Thanks, though."

Jorja's smile faltered a bit. Josh scrubbed a hand through his hair. She was a nice enough girl, but... But he already had a girl. The girl of his dreams. And he was a little busy proving to her how indispensable he was.

"It was a lovely invitation—it's just…"

"Don't worry." She stopped to pick a piece of errant tinsel off the floor and wove it round and round her finger, turning it pale, then pink again…pale, then pink.

"I'm sorry, Jorja." Josh checked an instinct to reach out and give her shoulder a comforting squeeze.

"I saw how you looked at Dr. McGann when we were under the mistletoe."

This time Josh really *was* surprised. He didn't know he'd been that obvious.

"You two know each other from before, don't you?"

That was one way to put it.

"We met in medical school."

Jorja discarded the tinsel in a bin and gave a wistful sigh. "It's always the good ones who are taken!"

Responding to that might be awkward.

"Hey!" The young woman's features brightened again as she tugged her errant ponytail back into place. "Who'd you get for your Secret Santa?"

"Isn't that supposed to be secret?"

"Yeah—but wouldn't it be fun if you got Dr. McGann?"

Josh considered for a moment and then lifted an eyebrow to indicate that, yes, there just *might* be some fun there…

"Here!" She dug into her nurse's smock and pulled out a crisply folded bit of paper. "I got Dr. McGann. Who'd *you* get?"

"Didn't you get her a present already?" Josh fought the urge to seem too keen.

"Oh, I just snagged a plateful of my grandma's Christmas cookies. She makes an amazing selection. Snickerdoodles, gingerbread men, buckeyes, peppermint crunch—you name it, she makes it."

"She sounds like my Gramma Jam-Jam! Never met a Christmas cookie she didn't like."

Her passing had been like losing a limb. Another loss he'd had to deal with without Katie by his side. It struck him that this mission was about more than trust. He'd known the second Katie had laid eyes on him that she still loved him. What they had was chemical. No amount of spreadsheets or flowcharts or "stages of grief" steps were going to take the connection they had away.

But this little reunion had brought more questions than answers so far. He knew in his heart that she could trust him. But when he'd needed her most she'd upped and left. Could he trust her to stick by him if things got tough again?

"Dr. West?"

Josh could see Jorja was talking to him, but did he have a clue about what? Not one.

Jorja threw her hands up in the air. "Typical man! Concentration factor…nil! No wonder I can't get a boyfriend. I can't even get a male to *listen* to me, let alone like me."

She swatted his arm, bringing his focus back to her. Again. *Oops.*

"Sorry, Jorja—I didn't quite catch what you said."

"Yeah," she deadpanned. "I got *that*. I was asking who your Secret Santa was so we can trade. If you still want to."

"Well…it sounds like—" he dug his scrap of paper out of his lab coat pocket and read "—Dr. Michael Rainer is going to be one lucky guy…having a plate of your grandmother's cookies all to himself."

"Michael…" She said the intern's name as if she were tasting it and wasn't entirely sure what she thought of it. Then clearly a decision was made. "Michael." She said it again, this time looking as though she'd just enjoyed a delicious bite of peppermint candy.

Josh grinned. Michael might have to watch himself around the mistletoe. He threw an arm round the nurse's shoulders and gave her a quick squeeze. This Secret Santa swap could be just what he needed.

Katie nodded at the cleared ER board with a satisfied smile. It probably wouldn't last long—but even a few moments of clean board always lifted her heart.

"Someone looks happy. Did the surgery go well?"

Michael appeared at her side, giving her a little jump.

"Yes." Katie nodded, feeling the weight of the success lighten her heart. "Yes, it really did."

And it meant more than anyone will know.

Well. One person would know.

She heard Josh's laugh before she saw him—and the hit of response in her belly shifted the charge of success into something more electric. It didn't take a doctor to know it was pure unadulterated attraction. It was adrenaline from the surgery, she reasoned. It would pass.

"Right!" Katie went into efficiency mode. "We've got both shift groups together. Quick reminder: Secret

Santa gifts go into lockers, please—not here in the reception area."

A nurse guiltily tucked the foil package she'd been edging onto the counter back into her pocket.

Katie gave her lower lip a guilty scrape with her teeth. She hated being a Scrooge, but this *was* a place of work.

"Good work on clearing the board after a pretty hectic run. A couple of patients are in Recovery after surgery, but there's no one unexpected in Intensive, thanks to you all."

A smattering of applause filled the area around the central desk. The staff looked tired, but triumphant. Shannon—her keenest intern—for once looked as if she'd had enough. Michael still looked doggedly studious, but she could see the fatigue in his eyes when he pulled off his glasses and gave them a rub. A few of the nurses were hiding yawns. Most of them, actually.

They'd all been through the wringer and Katie didn't feel any different.

Despite her best intentions, Katie locked her eyes with Josh's. She might not have made it through surgery without him by her side and he knew it. It made her feel vulnerable and protected at the same time. The look in his eyes made her breath catch in her throat. Pure, undiluted love.

Saying goodbye at the end of this shift was going to be harder than she'd thought.

Her eyes widened, still holding the pure blue magic of Josh's gaze. *She hadn't called the agency for a replacement!* And, realistically, was there going to be a locum tenens out there in the mountainscape of Copper Canyon—or anywhere in Idaho—willing to tear themselves away from whatever they'd planned to do with their family over the holidays?

When she and Josh had had the holidays off they'd been inseparable. In more ways than one.

She hunched her shoulders up and down. She was just going to have to suck it up. Getting a replacement for Josh at this juncture was about as likely as Santa Claus walking through the sliding doors.

"Where *is* he?"

A huge gust of wind and winter storm burst into the waiting room, along with a bearded man dressed in full Santa regalia with a rosy-cheeked Mrs. Claus following in his wake.

"Where's my son?" the bearded man roared again.

Temperatures often ran high in the ER, and it looked like Santa's temper was soaring.

"What's your son's name, sir?" Josh was by his side in an instant—with a mix of concerned doctor and *Watch yourself, Santa* in his tone and body language. Josh was tall, and he had the confident carriage of a rodeo cowboy. Santa, however, seemed immune to what had all but buckled her knees.

"Klausen. Check your list, Doc. Check it twice if you have to!"

If Katie hadn't been so taken aback by Mr. Klausen's arrival, she would have tittered at this similarity to a certain red-suited fellow who, by all accounts, should be pretty busy shooting down chimneys about now.

"Chris Klausen," the man bit out.

His tone was so sharp Katie choked on her giggles.

"I've seen the trailer in the parking lot. It's the busiest night of the year and I *know* they've got Eustace in there. The nativity was a shambles!"

"Dad?" Maddie appeared round the corner, a bandage on her head, her arms wrapped protectively round her ribs and a slightly fearful look on her face. "Mom?"

Katie stepped toward Maddie—ready to intervene if things grew more heated.

"Maddie!" Mrs. Klausen rushed to her daughter's side. "What happened? We just got the call that there was an accident."

The tension eased from Katie's face as the anger obviously born of fear for their children turned into protective hugs and kisses.

"Where are your brothers?" Her father pushed her back to arm's length. "I'm going to wring their necks!"

Then again...

"Dr. McGann, I was the one who brought him up to—"

Katie waved Michael to silence. They didn't need to hear the gory details out here with a crowd gathering.

"Sir, perhaps you'd like to follow me?" The last thing the couple's son needed, still in Recovery from surgery, was his father dressed as Santa shouting at him.

"You all right?"

Josh's voice trickled along her spine as she felt him approach. He was doing it again. White Knighting it in the face of adversity. She was glad he couldn't see her face as she pressed her lips together. Hadn't she just proved she could hurdle her demons in the OR?

Not without Josh by her side.

"Would you like to come with me, Mr. and Mrs. Klausen?" Katie put her hand up in an *I got it* gesture to Josh and snapped a glare back at Jorja, who was busy choking down her own case of the giggles. Most likely born of nerves, but inappropriate all the same.

"What for? Show us where the boys are, Maddie, and we'll get on our way."

"I think it would be best if we had a chat before you

saw your boys." Katie was solid now—shifting her gaze from one rosy-cheeked face to the other.

"Maddie…" Josh put a protective arm around the young girl's shoulders. "Why don't we see if we can track down some gingerbread?"

"All right," Mr. Klausen grumbled, his attention fully focused on Katie. "Let's hear how naughty they've been."

Katie led the way into one of the comfortably furnished family rooms the hospital had created for delivering tough news. She and Josh had been led to one like it after the postmortem on their little girl.

No discernible evidence to indicate a problem. Just one of those things.

The words had sat in her heart like an anvil. If there had been a reason, she could have *done* something. Fixed it. Not felt the living, breathing, growing terror that she had no control over what might happen if they tried again.

"So what've they done? How's Eustace?"

"Your donkey is fine, sir." Katie's eyebrows lifted in surprise at the parent's priorities—but you never knew a person's history. Never knew how someone would respond in times of extreme stress.

"One of our surgeons had to give him a few stitches—"

"He was *hurt*?" Mrs. Klausen's hands flew to her mouth in horror. "Eustace!" She exhaled into her cupped hands. "Eustace… We've had him longer than the boys! Our first baby."

Okay. Well, that explained that.

"Your son Chris has some pretty serious injuries. Maybe we should sit down so we can talk through them before I take you through to Recovery."

"Recovery?" Mr. Klausen's face was twisted in incomprehension. "What do you mean?"

"He's really been hurt?" Tears sprang to Mrs. Klausen's eyes.

"Yes." Katie shifted her tone. The Klausens would need a gentle touch now that the fog of displacement was beginning to clear. Rage, anger, even disbelief were common when the worst thing that could happen to someone actually happened. Particularly when it came out of the blue.

"Why don't we all take a seat and I'll talk you through the surgery Chris has had? Then we'll get you up to see him and Nick, who is with him, as soon as possible. No doubt seeing you both will be the perfect medicine."

She hoped no one could see the fingers she crossed in the depths of her lab coat.

Josh eased the locker open with yet another surreptitious over-the-shoulder check that he was alone. Subterfuge hadn't been his initial plan of attack, but it seemed alone time with Katie was going to be hard to come by, so he was going to have to find just the right pocket to tuck his wrapped present into.

He was hit by Katie's scent in an instant. She'd always smelled like fresh linen with a teasing of vanilla. He gave himself a moment to close his eyes and take a scented trip down memory lane.

A noise further down the corridor jarred him back into action. Winter coat or…? What was that? In the very back of her fastidiously tidy locker, behind the hanging lab coats and winter wear, was a grainy black-and-white printout. The image of their little girl hit him straight in the solar plexus. If kissing Katie on the roof had brought back everything good about their marriage, seeing the last fetal scan they'd had of their baby girl brought back the blackest.

"What are you doing?"

Josh whirled around at the sound of Katie's voice, the sheen of emotion blinding him for just an instant. His hand shot protectively to his hip. He'd turned too sharply. Abrupt turns always gave him a stabbing reminder of how far he'd pushed the envelope. Why Katie had asked him to leave. Why he was here.

To make a smart move. For once.

Katie's eyes flicked from his hip to his eyes. He saw the questions piling up in her deep brown eyes and the flicker of her decision not to ask.

"What are you doing in my locker, Josh?"

He heard the tiniest of wavers in her voice—but her body language told another story. Hands curled into fists on her hips. Mistrust laced through those dark eyes of hers. Her chin tilted slightly, as if daring him to confirm all her worst fears.

He'd gone too far. Just as she'd predicted.

"Even angry, you are the most beautiful woman I've ever seen."

She stepped back, shocked at his words. He was a bit, too, but he meant them. Her face still carried the broad features youth afforded. Full lips. A cute little gap between the two front teeth that had rebelled against the years of expensive orthodontics she'd once confessed to enduring. It made for a slightly crooked smile that lit the world up when she unleashed it. Something she wasn't even *close* to doing now, from the looks of things.

"Josh…" Her smooth forehead crinkled. "Are you all right?"

"I—uh…" He swung his gaze back to her locker, still

holding the wrapped package in his hand. The pendulum of Tell or Don't Tell bashed the sides of his brain.

You were right. I should never have taken up motorcycle racing.

You were wrong—you always needed me.

He thrust the tiny package forward so it sat between them like a buffer against all that was going unsaid. "I know it was supposed to be secret, but… Merry Christmas…"

A rush of emotion crossed her face, darkening her eyes so that they were near black.

"I didn't… I don't have anything for you."

"Well, it was the luck of the draw that I got your name in Secret Santa." He hoped the white lie wouldn't come back to haunt him. "It's not exactly as if you were expecting me to turn up in Copper Canyon, now, is it?" He laughed softly, hiding a swipe at his eyes with a scrub along his forehead and a finger-whoosh through his hair.

Her expression softened.

"Are you going to unclench that thing or do you just want me to guess?"

He released his grip and let the small box rest on his palm. His eyes narrowed a bit as he watched her reach out to take it. The paper was crumpled. Worn, even. He'd wrapped that thing up the day after she'd thrown it at him and told him she'd had enough. Waiting…waiting for the perfect moment.

He cleared his throat when her fingers gained purchase on the box, her skin lightly skimming across his. He couldn't even remember how many times he'd imagined this moment. Her response would trigger a chain of events that would either make or break him.

She withdrew the box from his hand. He felt the absence of its weight and her touch instantly. Maybe ignorance *was* bliss. As long as he didn't really know how Katie felt about him, he could believe there was hope. Believe he'd never have to put his signature to that ragged pile of papers he'd been dragging around in the same backpack as the little box she was now slowly unwrapping.

The dawning of recognition wasn't far off. He'd used the same box the rings had come in. Placed them—engagement and wedding—side by side. The rings they had bought with downright giddy smiles wreathing their faces and the last handful of notes and coins they had between them.

There were only two other times when he'd seen her smile as much. Their wedding day and the day they'd found out she was pregnant.

Katie's expression became unreadable. That hurt as much as no reaction. There had once been a time when he could have told anyone her mood before she'd walked into a room. They had been *that* connected. Genuine soulmates.

"Oh…" It came out as a sigh. "Josh…" Beads of tears weighted her lashes as she held the box open, her eyes fastened to what lay inside. "I can't do this. Not right now. I just can't do this."

She turned on her heel, all but knocking Michael off his feet as he entered the locker room.

"Everything all right?" Michael pulled off his glasses and gave his eyes a rub.

"Yeah, sure." *No.* "She probably just got paged or something."

"Mmm…"

Michael seemed to take his response at face value, which came as a relief. Fatigue hit him like a truck. Heavy and unforgiving.

"Say, Dr. West… Would you like to have a coffee or something later?"

"What? Tonight?"

"No, no. Just before you hit the road again."

"Like a debrief?"

Michael's forehead scrunched. "I guess…"

"Sure thing. Just grab me next time you're free."

He gave him a gentle back-slap as he pushed the door back into the corridor open, smarting at Michael's words. The icing on the cake! So much for his fairy-tale moment when Katie slipped her rings back on her finger and his life became whole again.

He fought the urge to punch the wall. *It* hadn't done anything wrong. *He* had. He'd made a complete hash of giving Katie the rings and now Michael wanted an exit interview. Fan-freakin'-tastic.

His eyes shot up. *More mistletoe.* Merry Christmas, everyone!

CHAPTER SIX

"DR. MCGANN, WOULD you mind signing these...? Hey, are you all right?"

Jorja skidded to a halt, openly gawking at Katie. Her go-to neutral face obviously wasn't cooperating tonight.

"Of course," Katie answered briskly. "What can I do for you?"

"Before I go I just need your signature on these release forms for Mr. and Mrs. Wilson."

"The parents of the little girl? The one who had the nephrectomy?"

"Yes, that's the one. Luckily they just had a few cuts and bruises. Nothing serious. So they want to head up to the Pediatric recovery ward. Hey!" Jorja's face split into an impressed grin. "I heard you aced that baby!"

Katie's heart tightened at the choice of words, but she couldn't stop a shy smile in return. She *had* done well. And Josh had been right. She didn't need to be pinned down by her grief. Just needed to learn from it and move on. Eyes forward was a lot healthier than always looking over your shoulder at the past.

She scribbled her signature on the forms and told Jorja where the Wilsons would be able to find their little girl. They must be frantic to be with her. Hold her small little hands. Kiss those soft cheeks of hers.

Katie's fingers tightened round the ring box in her pocket.

"I'm just going for a quick power nap. Are you off for the night?"

"Yup—me and my five thousand relatives are meeting up at Midnight Mass. Spouses, girlfriends, boyfriends, uncles, aunts—you name it. And little ol' me. Late, as usual, and all on my lonesome!"

"There's plenty of time for that." Katie smiled and gave the nurse's arm a squeeze. She was pretty, vivacious, and would be a great catch for the right man. One with lots of energy. Heaven knew, her brothers were busier than an online dating agency trying to find her a beau, if all the staff-room gossip she'd caught was anything to go by. "You have a good time with your family, Jorja."

"You too, Dr. McGann." Jorja's eyes widened as her lips opened into a horrified O. "I mean—keep manning the ship like you always do! It's what you always do, isn't it? Meticulous Dr. McGann!"

Jorja's face contorted into an apologetic wince as she thudded her forehead with the heel of her hand.

"Stop while you're ahead?" Katie suggested.

"I think that's best." Jorja pulled Katie in for an unexpected hug with a whispered "Merry Christmas" before skip-running back down the hall to the main desk, her tinsel scarf trailing behind her like a glittery red boa.

Katie stood and watched her for a moment, slightly envious. Not of her youth—she was only a few years older—but of all that was yet to come for her.

She eased open the door to the residents' room, grateful to see the two beds were empty, and dropped onto one of them with a sigh of relief. Double shifts were never fun—but today had been particularly taxing. Physically and emotionally she'd been through the wringer. Seeing Josh…? That alone was enough to send her into a tailspin. But on Christmas Eve… The night they'd lost their baby girl…

She twisted the small box round and round in her fingers until finally daring to open it again. The night she'd hurled her rings at him… Well…sensibly placed them on the counter—hurling things had never been her style… That night had been like ripping her own heart out.

She fumbled in her other pocket and pulled out her phone. Yes, it was super-late—but if she knew Alice, there would be no begrudging an after-hours call.

The phone rang a couple of times and Katie grinned, remembering the silly ringtones Alice had kept putting on her phone when she hadn't been looking.

"Hello, angel…" a sleepy Alice answered.

"Hi—sorry. I know it's late, but—"

"It's all right, darlin'. I'm just watching the dying embers of the fire. What's that little scamp done now?" Alice cut to the chase.

"He gave me back my rings."

Katie heard Alice rearrange her position on the sofa, or wherever she was. "What? For good?"

"Well, I presume so." She hadn't got that far yet.

"On bended knee? Or with a scowl in a *Here, let's have done with it* kind of way?"

"Well…" She'd been so annoyed at seeing him in her locker it hadn't even occurred to her that there might have been a plan. "There wasn't a bended knee—but there wasn't a scowl either."

"So," Alice said in her perfunctory Irish way. That meant any number of things, and in this case Katie was guessing it meant *What the hell are you going to do now?*

"I don't want to give them back." The words rushed out before she'd had a chance to edit them.

"In a good way? Or in a *Fine, you've done your business now let me get on with mine* kind of way?"

Katie laughed. She loved this woman. There were incredibly few people she'd let into her heart…well, okay, Alice and Josh were really it…and she'd missed speaking with her.

"I was sorry to cut you off earlier."

Alice didn't wait for Katie to explain herself.

"I know it's a hard day for you, and there was me prattling on about my daughter and all. It was thoughtless. What you both went through, losing Elizabeth like you did… I can't begin to imagine."

"It wasn't thoughtless." And Katie meant it. "It's… it's life. And other people have it."

"What? Are you saying to me you *don't* have your own life?"

Um…a little bit?

"No."

"My goodness. Is that Katie McGann all grown up now? Are you telling me you're done hiding away in your idyllic mountain village, pretending you're the only one to have ever gone through something awful?"

"Say it like it is, why don't you?" Katie muttered.

Alice let her stew for a moment.

She looked down at her hands and realized she'd been fiddling with her rings during the call and had unconsciously slipped them back into their rightful place. On her left hand's ring finger.

"Well?" Alice had never been known for her patience.

"I've not been hiding. I've been…thinking."

"Thinking about getting on with your life or thinking about hiding away there forever?"

"Thinking about letting go."

"Of what, exactly?"

Katie lifted her hand and eyed the rings in the half dark.

"Fear?"

"That's a good way to start the New Year, love." Alice's voice was soft, but then it took an abrupt turn. "But don't go hurtling yourself off of a mountainside with a couple of fairy wings for support."

Katie laughed again.

"I will be sure to have on full reflective gear and the entire mountain rescue crew on standby if I ever do such a thing."

"That's my girl. Now, let me get some sleep and I'll speak to you soon, all right? I love you."

"I love you, too. Merry Christmas, Alice."

"And to you, angel. And pass on my love to the rascal, won't you?"

Katie nodded and said goodbye. She rolled onto her side, putting her left hand in front of her face, flicking the backs of the rings with her thumb again and again, even though she could see they were right there.

All the emotion she'd been choking back throughout the day abruptly came pouring out of her in barely contained wails of grief. If she was going to let go of fear, she was also going to have to let go of the sorrow that the fear had been protecting. Sorrow over the family she would never have. The child she had only held once. The husband she loved so dearly that the thought of losing him all but crippled her.

She was so consumed with heartache she barely registered the door opening and the arrival of a pair of male legs appearing by her side. She rocked and cried as a pair of familiar arms slipped around her, holding her, soothing her.

Josh.

Of course it was. He knew her better than anyone. Knew she would need him.

After all this time apart, he was finally there for her in the way she had longed for. Present. Still.

He slipped behind her on the bed and gently pulled her into his embrace so that she could curl up in a tight little ball, chin to knees, arms tangled through his, fingers pressing into his shoulder as if her life depended upon it.

There were no whispered placations. No *There, there* or *It'll be all right.* They might love one another, but how could he assure her about a future they would never have? Neither of them knew if anything would be all right…if they'd have the big family they both longed for. If they'd be together at all.

When at long last she was all cried out, Josh eased them down into a seamless spooned embrace. For a moment she thought to fight him. *How could she trust this? This deep, organic comfort she had longed for during those cavernously dark days?* The weight of her fatigue decided for her. She was so tired, and lying there in his arms…the one place she'd always found comfort…she began to feel the release of dreamless sleep overtake her.

It would be all right. Just this once.

It was Christmas.

Her body instinctively snuggled into his. She heard his breath catch as her own steadied. With his arm as a pillow, she became tuned in to his heartbeat, to that warm, spicy scent she would know until the end of time, to his strength. Her own body hummed with a growing heat. A sense of familiarity and comfort.

One night.

There'd be no harm in that. Right? Just one night before they said goodbye forever.

She felt his fingers stroke along her cheek, then slip down along her arm so that their fingers were intertwined. It was what she needed. To simply…*be*. Without hope or expectation. Just some peace. Some sleep. Some long-awaited comfort in her husband's arms.

Josh moved his hand along an upward curve. What the—? He waited another moment until his brain caught up with his hand. It wasn't a pillow he was caressing. It was his wife. And that sweet scent wasn't hospital antiseptic… It was the ever-mesmerizing Essence de Katie.

He nuzzled into her neck, instinctively tipping his chin to drop a kiss onto her shoulder. He stopped himself, then decided just to go for it. It was Christmas Day and Katie was asleep.

His lips sought and found a bit of exposed shoulder in the wide V-neck of her scrubs. Mmm…just as he'd remembered. Silk and honey.

Katie rolled over to face him, eyes still closed, an arm slipping round his waist. He couldn't tell if she was still asleep or not. When they had been together, the night had always found them tangled into one pretzel shape or another. Just so long as they were connected, everything had been all right.

A little sigh escaped her lips and he couldn't resist pressing his own lips to that beautiful mouth of hers.

She responded. Slowly, sleepily at first, but with growing intent as their legs began to tangle together in an organic need to meld into one.

He felt Katie's hand slip onto his hip and under his scrubs. Their kisses deepened. He couldn't believe how good it felt to feel her hands on his bare skin. Especially, he realized with a smile, when the cool silver of her wedding rings intermingled with the warmth of her fingertips.

Her fingers slid along his hip and up his spine, causing him to jerk back sharply when her fingers hit his scars. She didn't need to know about the accident. Not yet.

"Josh?"

Katie remained where she was but he could feel her heart rate escalating.

"Are those—?"

"It's nothing." *It had been huge.*

"It didn't feel like nothing." Katie's eyes blinked a couple of times before refocusing more acutely on him. He could almost see the wheels whirring in her mind to make sense of what she'd felt.

"Merry Christ— Oh, my gosh, I'm so sorry!"

Josh felt Katie shoot out of bed at the sound of Michael's voice and a blast of light. For a moment he couldn't understand why the intern looked so embarrassed. He was too busy trying to figure out how to explain to Katie what she'd discovered.

"I'll just—leave you to it, then… Uh…" Michael wasn't moving, so why on earth was he—?

Wow. Did twenty-eight-year-old men still blush?

"Merry Christmas, Michael. You're up with the lark."

Katie was tugging her scrubs top down along her hipline. Ah…the slow dawn of recognition began to hit him. No one knew they were married. No one knew Dr. McGann was Katie West. *His* Katie.

"Not really, Dr. McGann. It's nine o'clock."

"What?" Katie shot Josh a horrified look.

He just grinned. He hadn't slept until nine o'clock since... That wasn't a tricky one to figure out.

"My shift started at *seven*. Why didn't you page me?"

"Oh..." Michael began awkwardly. "Jorja said you looked really tired last night, so I left a note with the morning shift to let you sleep in."

Michael nervously shuffled his feet, still unable to connect his gaze to Katie or to Josh, who thought he might as well stand up and be counted.

"Right. I see..."

Katie didn't really seem to know what to do with the information. Or how to explain being discovered in the arms of a man she wasn't meant to know.

"Well, let's get going, shall we?"

"Merry Christmas, Michael," Josh contributed merrily. If he was going to fake it about having been critically injured, he might as well go the whole hog and rustle up some fake Yuletide jolliness.

"Uh... Merry Christmas..."

Katie steered Michael away from the room without a backward glance.

Josh huffed out a mirthless "Ho-ho-ho..." and plunked back down on the bed. *Merry Christmas, indeed.* It shouldn't have come as a surprise. Shouldn't hurt so much. A psychiatrist would have a field day with them. No fluid Seven Stages of Grief for the Wests! No, sir. Just a tangled mess of How-the-Hell-Did-We-End-Up-Like-This?

He scrubbed at his thickly stubbled jaw. It had been a long time since he'd thought of himself as a plural. They had both been bulldozed by shock. At least they'd done *that* by the book. He'd skipped the next few stages and gone straight to testing. Testing limits. Pushing boundaries. Trying his best to show Katie there was still so much life to be lived and all along only succeeding in pushing her away. Making her more fearful than he had ever thought she could be.

From everything he'd seen, she was still sitting pretty in the snowcapped Village of Denial. As long as she didn't see him, everything that had happened could be her own little secret, locked away wherever it was she locked things up.

His heart ached for her, and at the same time he wanted to roar with fury at how fruitless blocking out the past was.

Hmm...good one. Anger.

Okay. He'd probably hit that one a few times, too. Depression? Didn't really compute. He simply wasn't that kind of guy. There were too many good things in life to counterweight the sorrows. Otherwise—what was the point?

Bargaining?

Maybe that was what being here was. If he won Katie back then his life would feel complete again. Just like in these last few precious hours. The first time he'd held his wife in his arms for two years. The first solid sleep he was guessing either of them had had since the split. The first time he'd let himself really believe they might be together again.

If he didn't believe...?

Nah. He wasn't there yet. No point in accepting things you didn't know the answer to.

"Dr. West! Good of you to finally join us."

Katie was back to her crisp efficient self. Surprise, surprise.

"Granny dump in Four."

She handed him a file without a second look. *Wow.*

Talk about terse! Even at her most efficient Katie was never rude. Her heart normally bled for the elderly people families dropped off in the ER on Christmas Day so they wouldn't have to look after them on the holiday. It happened a lot in the city. Had to be pretty rare out in these parts.

He watched her reorder a few files, the crease between his eyebrows deepening. Katie knew exactly how Josh felt about caring for the elderly, given he had been near enough raised by his grandmother, with his parents so busy on the farm. He clamped his teeth together to bite back a snarky comeback. He'd expected more from her. Maybe she *had* changed and he was the last one to see it. The last one to accept the truth. They were different people now.

He shook his head. This sat wrong. At the very least she should have opted to tell him the condition the so-called "dump" was for.

He glanced at the chart.

"Peripheral edema." The notes went on to say the patient was complaining of swollen ankles and feet. Could be anything. Ankle sprain, obesity, osteoarthritis—and so the list went on, all the way up to congestive heart failure. That would have to be one cold family to drop their grandmother off at the ER, without so much as grandchild in tow.

"And what have *you* got this fine Christmas morn?" Josh asked Katie, thinking he'd make a stab at civility. It wasn't like they'd spent the night wrapped in each other's arms or anything.

"New bride having a panic attack." Her eyes flicked to his. "Trying to live up to unrealistic expectations."

He turned and went to Exam Four. She was obviously in a mood. He'd already opened up about his expectations. She'd felt his scars. Thought the worst. Maybe this was her way of saying all bets were off.

He stopped just before entering his cubicle and turned, catching a glimpse of Katie's hand as she went into the cubicle beside him.

Ha! He just resisted throwing a punch up into the air. She still wore the rings. Hadn't sent him to the scrap heap just yet.

A grin lit up his face. Maybe it *was* going to be a merry Christmas after all.

"Now, Mrs. Hitchins, is it? I'm Dr. West. I understand you're not feeling at your best?"

"I don't think this is working."

The young woman sitting on the exam table lowered the paper bag she'd been breathing into when Katie entered.

"Is she going to be all right? Is she having a heart attack?" asked the young man beside her, presumably her husband. His face was laced with anxiety.

Katie pulled her stethoscope from around her neck and gave the couple as reassuring a smile as she could muster.

"I understand you've got your in-laws visiting for the first time, Mrs. Davis?"

"My family. Yes." Her husband answered for her. "Emily had just put the roast in the oven and then my mother, who has *always* made our Christmas dinners in the past, started asking about what Emily's family ate for Christmas. The next thing I knew, she was hyperventilating, saying she could hardly see… My mother kept offering to take over in the kitchen, and that's when Emily really took a turn. Is she going to be all right?"

Katie took Emily's vitals while he spoke, gently encouraging the twenty-something newlywed to return the paper bag to her mouth, assuring her husband they would do everything they could to help his wife.

She could hear Josh merrily chatting away with the woman next door. He was obviously bringing out the best in her from the sounds of their joined laughter. She would have expected nothing less. He had a wonderful way with grandmothers. Everyone, really. *Why had she been so sharp with him?* He didn't deserve to be sniped at when all he'd done was show her kindness.

What were those scars all about?

She forced herself to tune back in to her patient's husband.

"I'm happy to call my mother and tell her to take over. My mother does a *perfect* Christmas dinner. Doesn't she, Ems?"

Emily's breathing suddenly accelerated, and her eyes dilated as they darted from her husband to Katie.

"Deep breaths, Emily. Keep the bag up. *Deep* breaths. Mr. Davis—do you mind if I have a moment with your wife alone?"

"Are you sure there's nothing—?"

"Absolutely. If you could just take a seat in the waiting room, I'll be with you in a few moments."

After her husband had dropped a nervous kiss on his wife's head and left the cubicle, Emily's breathing changed. Lost its harsh edge. Katie rubbed her hand along Emily's back as she might a small child and kept repeating her mantra.

"Breathe slowly. Deeply. Count to three…count to five…deep and slowly…"

It was what had got her through her first few attacks after she'd left Josh. Part of her had actually been shocked that she'd done it. It had been so out of character! She'd checked into a hotel when her car had all but run out of gas and had just sat at the end of the bed and shaken for who knew how long?

She gave her head a little shake. This wasn't about her. It was about Emily and a mother-in-law whose son seemed to have problems letting go of the apron strings.

"First holiday meal for the in-laws?" Katie asked gently, lowering herself into the seat beside the exam table and making a Christmas-tree doodle on the corner of the chart.

Emily just nodded. Tears springing to her eyes.

Katie tugged a tissue out of the packet she always had in her lab coat and handed it to her.

"Would it be safe to say this is the first time you've ever experienced these symptoms?"

Another nod and a sniffle. A tear skidding down her cheek.

Katie stood and patted the empty space on the examination table. "Mind if I join you?"

Emily shook her head and Katie scooched up onto the table, her feet crossed at the ankles.

"I remember making my first—my *only*—Christmas dinner for my in-laws. I was a wreck!" She laughed softly at the memory. "My husband's family loved their food and they were happy slaves to their long-established Christmas traditions. And, of course, there was Gramma Jam-Jam's unbelievably perfect cooking to contend with. What I *didn't* realize was that most families *don't* buy the entire meal in from a fancy grocery store and heat it up."

She laughed again before going on, pleased to see Emily's breathing was becoming more regular as she spoke.

"I mean, I obviously knew people made Christmas dinner—it was just that my family never had. And when I volunteered to cook for my husband's family, I didn't realize what I'd gotten into until they started sending me emails about how they liked three-peak dinner rolls, whatever they were, homemade cranberry sauce—but only if there was orange zest and no orange pulp— mashed potatoes— but made with a ricer, which made no sense at all. And lots of butter—salted."

She held up her fingers and added another memory. "A big enough turkey so that there'd be enough leftovers for sandwiches to see them through at least the next week. There I was, a grown woman, and I'd never so much as *peeled* a potato, let alone mashed one."

"At least they ate the same thing!" Emily cut in. "David's family don't eat a single thing my family does. Beef instead of turkey, because they feel the one at Thanksgiving is enough. Roasted potatoes instead of mashed. Which is just *wrong*." She reeled off a list of her family's specialties before giving Katie a wide-eyed look. "What's Christmas without turkey and stuffing?" She spread her hands out wide in a *what gives?* gesture. "I mean—I've never, *ever* had Christmas without turkey and stuffing! It's like a sign that this whole marriage was never meant to happen!"

"Hey," Katie soothed. "Marriage involves a whole lot of things we don't think about when we say our vows. But you can *do* this! Think about your guy. Maybe he's been pining for beef each Christmas he's spent with your family? Embrace the changes as learning opportunities. Doesn't mean they have to be *your* things."

She took both of her patient's hands in her own and gave a decisive nod. "How 'bout this? When your in-laws leave, why don't you make a turkey for New Year's? Just the two of you. Stuffing. Mashed potatoes. The whole nine yards."

Emily sniffled, swiping at her tears to reveal a hint of a smile, giving Katie a nod to continue. Not that she would have been able to stop her. She was on a roll now.

Her own marriage might be in tatters, but she damn well wasn't going to let *this* pair of young lovers fall to bits over a piece of roast beef!

"Have your *own* traditions! My husband and I made ours. Pancakes on Tuesdays after a double shift. Grilled cheese sandwiches with pickles and tomato soup on Valentine's…"

Katie felt a flush of pleasure begin to color her cheeks at the memory of the goofy traditions they'd made up through the years, then sobered. She was at work here—not on a magical trip down memory lane.

"You know what, Emily? If your mother-in-law is so desperate to cook…let her! Have your husband drive you home via a restaurant and get a to-go bag filled to the brim with turkey sandwiches—then put your feet up and enjoy letting someone else cook dinner. I bet you've spent days making the house and everything just perfect?"

Emily nodded, the light shadows under her eyes offering the proof that Katie wasn't just making a stab in the dark. "I do feel pretty tired."

"Okay! Why not go home, play the sick card? Put your feet up and enjoy the day with your husband. Play a board game and enjoy the aromas wafting from the kitchen. And in a few days…when they're gone…pull out your apron and make exactly what you want—just for the two of you. It sounds to me like you know how to cook! That's more than *I* could ever do!"

"The grilled cheese sandwiches?" Emily grinned at her.

"Burned at the corners, gooey in the middle. My specialty." Katie smiled back, giving her patient's knee a knowing pat. Family life could be tough. And the holidays could make it tougher.

"Don't give yourself such a hard time, Dr. McGann."

Katie started when Josh poked his head into the exam area, with his own patient grinning up at him adoringly from her wheelchair.

"I have it on good authority that your husband thinks your cooking is fantastic."

He dropped her a wink and pushed Mrs. Hitchins away, leaving Katie at a loss for words.

"He's cute. If your husband is anything like *him*…" Emily gave a low whistle of appreciation.

Katie briskly jumped off the exam table. Her husband was *nothing* like the Josh who'd just strolled past as if they hadn't just spent the past two years apart. This guy seemed reliable, steady…*present*. Someone she could trust *not* to scale sheer cliff faces or zip wire across the Grand Canyon. *That* was the Josh she knew. This guy…? He might have some scars she didn't know anything about…but he was here for her exactly when she needed him and she hadn't even known it.

"So!" Katie picked up Emily's forms. "I'm going to make a note that you were suffering from mild hyperventilation. Effectively you had an in-laws-induced panic attack—but we won't put that down," she added conspiratorially. "It is not uncommon this time of year. If you like, you can tell your family it was exhaustion. But you know how to fix it now…right?"

"Step back, take a look at the big picture and remember I married the guy I love?"

Her words bull's-eyed Katie right in the heart.

She'd never done that. Taken a step back from it all. The grief. The sorrow. She'd never remembered to take in the big picture. She'd just pushed Josh away as hard as she could. Even put a mountain range between them!

Images of her heart soaring over the Rocky Mountains with a goofy pair of fairy wings pinged into her head.

For a smart woman, she was feeling like a first-class ding-a-ling.

How could you hide from what was alive in your heart? Especially if it was love? Had time finally given her the perspective to see the situation for what it had been? Awful, *awful* luck.

"Exactly." Katie forced a smile. "You married the guy you love. Now, get out there and go hunt down some turkey sandwiches!"

Emily gave her a tight hug and all but bounded out of the cubicle, tugging on her jacket as she went to find her husband.

The unexpected flush of emotion at their encounter made Katie pause. *Whoo!* She needed a few extra seconds for private regrouping.

So…if Emily was The Patient of Christmas Past…

Had she been so blinkered about Josh's adrenaline-junkie ways that she'd forgotten to look at the big picture? To look at *him*? He had been grieving, too. Maybe his relentless drive to cheer her had been the same desperation *she'd* been feeling for him to weep with her. Sob his heart out as she'd done, hidden away in the back of her closet so no one could hear her mourn.

There just wasn't any way to prepare for a loss like that, let alone know how to react. Had *she* been the one to react poorly? To lose sight of what was important?

The weight of the realization nearly buckled her knees.

What had she done?

The iron taste of blood in her mouth brought her back to the present. *Hey! Let's just add a self-inflicted bloody lip to the mix.* Precisely the Christmas look she'd been hoping to present to her patients. To Josh.

She needed a Christmas cookie.

Stat.

If she got to the staff room fast enough, there just might be a few left after Jorja's grandmother's annual Christmas bake-fest.

CHAPTER SEVEN

"SOMEONE'S GOT THE MUNCHIES!"

"Hi, Michael." Katie guiltily swiped some crumbs away from her lips as she swallowed down an unsuspecting gingerbread man's leg. His head and arms had already been snapped off and munched. "Sorry, I was just…"

Just trying to drown my sorrows by massacring a gingerbread cookie?

Not strictly what you wanted your boss to say.

"Don't worry. I've already eaten a dozen. Maybe more."

The unexpected hint of a wicked smile crossed his face and brought out one on her own. She had a soft spot for Michael. Hair always a tousled mess. Ink marks regularly dabbing his cheeks. He'd joined the internship later than most medical graduates, having taken a year out to work with a charity in South America. Methodical. Steady. He was a serious guy. Not to the point of being humorless, but it was nice to see a smile on his face.

"Lucky you—getting Jorja as your Secret Santa."

"Yes! Yes, it was most excellent. A real surprise. Incredibly generous."

And a really effusive thanks for a plate of cookies Jorja hadn't even baked herself.

Katie looked up from her cookie to give Michael a closer look and was surprised to see a hint of color pop onto his cheeks. Did he…? Could he really…? Bouncy, gregarious Jorja? Who wore costumes on any given holiday? Well… Katie had been all but surgically attached to her books at university and Josh-the-Gregarious had certainly brought *her* out of her shell. Maybe Jorja brought out the hidden Romeo in Michael.

Katie felt her beeper buzz and tugged it off her scrubs waistline.

911—suspected cardiac arrest.

Katie didn't bother to wait for Michael's response.

The patient was her father.

"Who does a woman need to call to get a cappuccino in this hospital?"

Josh knew that voice. He knew it very well. And he knew the bottle blonde coiffure that went along with it.

"Mrs. McGann?"

"Josheeee!"

Katie's immaculately turned out mother twirled around on her heels with the style and panache of a nineteen-fifties screen legend, holding her hands out in a wiggly fingered show of delight before planting a big lipsticky kiss on his cheek. Nothing had changed there, then.

"What are you doing here, Mrs. McGann?"

And…why don't you find it strange that I'm here?

"Oh, Josh…"

Sheree McGann placed a perfectly manicured hand on Josh's forearm. She was as touchy-feely as her daughter was reserved. No apples had fallen near *her* tree.

"It's Randall. He's gone and had a blasted angina attack and he didn't have any of his squirty stuff left so we could finish—you know—*business*."

She raised her eyebrows and smiled when he made the connection.

"Josheeee..." She gave his arm a squeeze. "I would just *murder* for a cappuccino. Any top tips from an insider?"

She dropped him a knowing wink, but before he had a chance to answer, Katie skidded to a halt alongside them. Perfect timing? Or damage control?

"Mom! Is everything all right? Where's Dad?" Katie shot him a wary glance while she waited for a response.

"Katie, darling! You didn't tell us Josh was back in town. *Naughty* girl. It does explain why you've turned down our invitation to stay at the condo whilst we're here. Now, what does a girl have to do to find a barista on Christmas morning?"

"I bet we can rustle something up for you, Sheree."

Katie's blood ran cold, then hot, then cold again.

This isn't happening! This isn't happening. No, no, no, no, no, no. No!

She squeezed her eyes tight shut. Then opened them.

For the love of all the Christmases past and present... please be gone!

She eased one eye open. Nope. They were both still there. Josh and her mother, nattering away like a day hadn't passed since they'd seen each other last. At Elizabeth's funeral. That was the last time they'd all been together. At least her parents had managed to make good on *that* promise.

"Oh, Josh!" Sheree gushed. "It is *so* good to see you again. I kept telling Katie to stop hiding you away in all of those specialist hospitals and to join us up here in the Canyon. What did she do to finally lure you to our little mountain retreat?"

"Mom!"

Katie blanked Josh's wide-eyed expression. So she hadn't strictly told her parents she and Josh were no longer together? So what? They'd never been close. On top of which, shouldn't her mother be behaving a bit more as if her husband was having a heart attack?

"Where's Dad?" She wheeled on Josh. "Are you— is *someone*—looking after my father? I just got a 911."

"That was me, dear. I wanted to get back home as soon as…"

Her mother's voice trailed off and she pulled back to view her daughter at arm's length.

"Oh, honey. Couldn't you have made a bit more of an effort?" Sheree tsked as she top-to-toe eyeballed Katie with obvious disdain at her choice of scrubs and trainers. "It's *Christmas*."

Katie crinkled her nose and shook off her mother's comment. Typical McGann reaction. Ignore the real problem and focus on something superficial.

Fine.

She obviously wasn't going to get any sense out of her mother, whose breath smelled as though she'd already hit the wet bar. Mimosas or martinis? She leaned in for a sniff. Mimosa. Her eyes flicked to the clock. Eleven-thirty.

Well. It *was* Christmas.

"Where's Dad? Is he okay?"

"Oh, honey. He didn't have a heart attack. He was just behaving like his usual greedy guts self—eating too much foie gras last night—and he's out of his whatchamacallit… Nitro-something-or-other."

"Nitroglycerin?" Katie crinkled her nose. "You didn't tell me Dad was on medication."

Katie's mother gave a tiny shrug and continued speaking as if Katie hadn't said a word. "Remember what a little piggy he is, Josheee? You know, we were both just talking about you, and I said to him—"

"Why don't we all go see him together? I think I overheard Dr. Vessey saying *she* was doing a preliminary check on an angina case in Two."

Josh smoothed over his mother-in-law's ruffled feathers with the promise of a shot of espresso somewhere in the near future in exchange for a few moments with her husband and daughter.

"Oh, your father won't like that. That's why we had the girl at the desk send out the 911. You know him— refused the wheelchair, staggered in like a drunken pirate, insisting on seeing his little girl. He won't be treated by anyone but you, Katie."

"But—" Katie's face was wreathed in confusion.

"You know your father, dear. You always were his favorite."

"I should think so, Mother. I *am* his only child," Katie ground out, looking a little less like a glowering twelve-year-old.

Josh's grin widened. He was enjoying every single second of this. Not the part about his father-in-law staggering into the ER bellowing to see his daughter before his heart gave out…but all of this complicated, messy family stuff? This was a side of the McGann family he'd never known existed. And on top of everything, Katie hadn't told them they weren't together anymore. It was like fifteen Christmases all rolled up into one!

Out of this world. Heart-thumpingly out of this world.

"Shall we?" Katie bit out, clearly displeased with the notion of the proposed family activity.

Josh tucked his mother-in-law's hand into the crook of his arm as Katie stomped off in the lead.

"Temper, temper!" Sheree stage-whispered.

Katie's shoulders stiffened, but they weren't rewarded with the glare Josh was fairly certain would be playing across Katie's face. She could have whipped round and stuck her tongue out at them for all he cared.

Deck the halls with Katie's white lies, tra-la-la-la-la, la-la-la-la!
She's not told her parents she left me, fa-la-la-la-la!
Merry Christmas to me!

Maybe that dream of running off into the sunset hand in hand with his wife hadn't been so silly after all. And…seeing as it was winter…sunset came early this time of year!

Katie unceremoniously yanked back the curtain to her father's cubicle, shooting Josh a *back off, pal* look as she did.

Then again…

"Hi, honey! Will you tell this kid to stop it with her tests, already? I told her my daughter and son-in-law would sort me out. I want Copper Canyon's best."

"I'm a fully qualified intern—" Shannon began, before her reluctant patient gave her a dismissive pat on the hand.

"They're here now, honey. Thanks for being so attentive. I'm sure you've got a great career ahead of you." He dropped her one of his aging soap star winks in lieu of a wave farewell.

Katie shot an apologetic look at Shannon, indicating that she could leave. She had this one. Josh received a similar look, but it was a bit more of a bug-eyed *Scram, pal!*

"Oh, don't go, son!" Her father held up a hand in protest. "Josh, Katie's mother and I have been asking ourselves why you and Katie haven't come up to the house yet. Heaven knows we've had no luck getting Katie up this season—as per normal. Where's she been hiding you anyway? It's been—has it been *years* since we've laid eyes on you? Sheree, honey—when was the last time we saw Josheee here?"

"Dad! Can you stop jabbering for a minute, please? I just want to listen to your heart."

Katie fastidiously avoided Josh's twinkling blue eyes, blowing a breath or two onto her stethoscope before positioning it over her father's heart.

Randall McGann's words were like music to Josh's ears.

They really don't know. Katie hasn't told them.

He ran the words over and over in his mind like a healing mantra.

A few seconds of silence reigned before Katie's mother jumped in.

"Darling, I think your father just needs a refill of his medicine. This little incident started when we were in the middle of a...a *bedroom workout*." Mrs. McGann's voice slipped into a slinky-dinky tone appropriate for a perfume commercial and her husband gave a knowing chortle. "If you know what I mean."

"Gross." Katie shook away the mental image building in her head. "Mom. Just... Can we stick with the facts, please?"

"What, honey? Your father and I were having sex.

You and Josheee still have sex, right? It's what loving couples do?"

"Mom!" Katie's eyes darted to Josh and then assumed a full glower on her mother. "Can we *please* just…?" Katie huffed out a sigh. "Dad. Can you tell me what sensations you experienced?"

"Well, your mother was in the middle of a new trick she read about in a magazine, and I was just on the brink of having a wonderful—"

"Whoa! Whoa! Still too much detail. Let's just stick with your heart. The pains in and around your heart."

"Well, I didn't have the shooting pain down the arm that says you're having a heart attack, if that's what you're after, honey."

"Dad!" Katie's exasperation was growing. "I need details. Did you experience shortness of breath? Sweating? Did you lose consciousness—?"

"Uh… Katie, would you like *me* to do the examination?" Josh only just managed to keep the corners of his mouth from twitching into a broad smile. "I think you might be a bit too close to the patient. Your questions are coming out a bit more Guantánamo than—"

"This is *hardly* an interrogation, Josh!" Katie bit back, fastidiously keeping her eyes glued to her stethoscope. "And I am *perfectly* capable of assessing an angina attack, thank you very much!"

"*Honey!* Is that *any* way to speak to your husband on Christmas?"

"Mom, he's not—" Katie froze.

This could be interesting.

Josh quirked an eyebrow. Her parents, for once, were silent. What to do? Break some pretty painful news to Mr. and Mrs. McGann on Christmas Day or come to his wife's rescue? The wife he really wanted back in his arms.

He held up his hands in mock surrender.

"Confession time! I'm not really supposed to be here."

"Ooh, you old rascal." Randall threw a high five at him from his hospital bed. "Did you fly in special, just to make sure our Katie's Christmas was a bit more naughty than nice?"

"Dad!"

Katie could not have looked more horrified than she did now. Josh couldn't help but laugh. He might be having the best Christmas of his life, but he would put money on the fact this was very likely Katie's worst.

The smile dropped from his lips.

Second worst.

There would never be a Christmas more devastating than the one they'd had three years ago.

"Nope. Sorry. Nothing quite so thrilling. I just meant I'm on shift, and my boss here—" he nodded at Katie "—would probably like me to see some of the patients I hear building up in the waiting room. Lovely to see you both."

Katie exhaled a sigh of relief when Josh left the cubicle.

"Okay, Dad. Will you hush for a moment and let me get through this exam?"

"As long as you promise to bring Josh over for dinner. Tonight."

"I can't tonight—I'm on duty."

"On *Christmas*?"

"Mom! People don't have health problems just during office hours."

"Tone, Katie! Your mother's had a rough morning." Her father gently chastised her. "Tomorrow, then. Or how 'bout New Year's Eve? That'd be fun. See in the New Year together as a family."

Katie looked at him dubiously. Since when did her parents give a monkey's if they did *anything* as a family?

"Surely the hospital doesn't have you working round the clock?" Her mother added to the appeal.

If only she could!

Her father crossed his arms across his chest. "Sheree—get a yes out of our daughter and promise not to cook."

"Honey—we'll get delivery. I know an excellent Korean barbecue here in town. They do the most delicious ginseng pork—"

"New Year's Eve—fine! Okay? I will bring Josh and we will have dinner with you. Now, can you just *hush* for a minute so I can see how clogged up your arteries are?"

Her father, duly chastened, nodded his assent whilst making a *zip it* gesture on his lips.

Case. Closed.

"You can clear the mistletoe poisoning and the burned fingers from the board."

"Both of them?" Katie's eyes widened in surprise but she whooshed the eraser over the names on the whiteboard.

Josh couldn't tell if he'd startled her or if she was amazed he'd seen two patients to her one—albeit particular—patient.

"Yup. The mistletoe-berry-swallower had to revisit the berries, if you know what I mean."

"Induced vomiting with charcoal?" She gave a shiver at his grossed-out face.

"Not quite the lump of coal Santa had in mind—but, yes. We ran an EKG, did some blood and urine tests and apart from discovering that the hallucinatory effects of mistletoe aren't just a myth, and seeing the magic of receiving fluids through an IV, I think he'll be okay. Michael's just signing him out."

"The little girl with the burned fingers?"

"Minor. But each and every finger. Her teenage cousins were having a contest to see how many votive candles they could put out in three seconds. She came first."

"Nothing like the holidays to bring out the best in a family!" Katie intoned, her eyes still solidly on the board.

"Speaking of which—is everything all right with your father?"

Josh thought he'd better test the waters before going in for the proverbial kill. Telling Katie how much he loved her. Inviting her to Paris. Asking her to renew their vows.

"If being blackmailed into having dinner at my parents' on New Year's Eve is your idea of 'all right,' then yes."

"That should be fun for you!"

"Well, you're coming too, so you can wipe that smug look off your face."

"Ah!" His heart gave a satisfying thump. She hadn't called a replacement.

"Is that a good 'Ah!' or a bad one?" She frowned.

His eyes did a quick dart down to her hand. Yup! The rings were still there. His eyes flicked back up to Katie's.

"Your mother's not cooking, is she?"

"No way!" Katie looked horrified at the thought. "I don't think Dad even lets her heat things up for him anymore. He had food poisoning three months ago, from something she insisted she'd had in the oven all day. Turned out she'd only had the lightbulb on, and had put on the grill at the last minute to sear it and cover up the mistake."

"Maisie's on Main?"

Josh had stopped at the local diner on his way to the hospital when he'd arrived in town. Damn good toasted cheese sandwiches. They'd even put in the dill pickles when asked.

"Nope. Korean. Mom's into 'Asian trilogy ingredients,' whatever those are."

"Aphrodisiacs, I'm guessing."

"Joshua..." Katie's voice was loaded with warning.

"Uh-oh!" He put on a mock dismayed face. "You only ever call me Joshua when I'm in trouble. What did I do?"

Katie maintained a neutral expression on her face, but the tone of her voice spoke volumes. "Don't. Even. Go. There."

"Which 'there'?" He tried to joke. "The embarrassing fact your parents are still heavily sexed up and you act more like a parent than they ever did? Or the very interesting news that you haven't told them you've been asking me for a divorce for the past two years?"

"Holy cow!"

Michael popped up from underneath the central reception desk, much to Katie's obvious horror.

"You two are *married*?"

"No!"

"Yes."

Katie's negative response was drowned out by Josh's emphatic affirmation.

"Not that we're telling anyone—are we, Katie?"

"Uh..." Michael's eyes shifted from one to the other, as if he were expecting one or both of them to sprout wings. Or horns. "I'll just leave you two to it, then..." And he promptly bolted from the desk toward the staff room.

"Now look what you've done!" Katie's expression was one of pure dismay.

"What *I've* done? Are you *kidding* me? All I've done is everything you've asked of me for the past three years, Katie."

Whoops. Not quite the love-heals-all-wounds tack he was hoping to take.

"Everything but one!" She furiously obliterated her father's name from the whiteboard.

Josh's heart plummeted to his guts, then rebounded with a fiery need to lay his cards on the table. Katie didn't need to know he'd almost died. Didn't need to know he was being offered the chance of a lifetime in Paris. Didn't need to know a single one of those things to know if she loved him. But she *did* need to know them if they were to go forward truthfully. With trust.

He steadied his breathing before he began speaking, but the moment the words came out, he knew he should have walked away. Thrown a snowball. Pulled her into his arms under some mistletoe and showed her the other side of his love. Something—*anything*—to temper the volcanic strength of rage and sorrow he felt at what had happened to them.

"Is that really what you want? You honestly want me to sign those papers? Or do you just like holding it over me so we can both pretend *I* was the one who pushed *you* away after Elizabeth died?"

Josh could have punched himself in the face when he saw the look on her face.

There had been no need to be cruel. It was just that it hurt so *bad*. A physical pain compounded tenfold when he saw the tears spring into Katie's eyes before she turned on her heel and strode away.

It was time. Every pore in his body was rebelling, but the decision he'd needed to make since his arrival had been made.

CHAPTER EIGHT

NOT EVEN A snow angel was going to help dilute the bad mood Katie was in. A good stomp around the corridors of the hospital might do her good. Instill a bit of calm now that... She checked her watch... Nope! Wasn't over yet.

She glanced out the window... A perfectly beautiful white Christmas. If this day would just hurry up and be over, the little gremlins of Christmases Past could just go back to where they came from! She checked her watch again, tapping the surface of the glass as if the hour hand would suddenly leap forward.

Nope! Time didn't really seem to be playing ball today. Not in the slightest.

She kicked her pace up a notch. Including stairwells, she could get in a good three-mile walk. All she needed was to keep her pager from...

Zzzzt! Zzzzzt!

...going off.

She turned her race-walk into a run toward the surgical recovery ward. Was it the little girl she'd operated on yesterday? Casey Wilson? She offered up silent prayers as she kicked up her pace. Of all the surgeries in her entire career that needed to come out golden...

Please, please, please...

If she could just block out the fact that she might not have made it through Casey's surgery without the sandy-haired, blue-eyed boy she'd lost her heart to way back in the innocent days of her junior residency...

She swiped at the tears cascading down her cheeks. Try harder. Block harder. *Shut him down.*

She was going to have to. Lives depended upon her ability to focus and to block out the pain that would drive her wild if she let it surface. Block out the need to be held in her husband's arms and have him tell her everything would be okay when she knew it wouldn't be. Couldn't be.

Where had those scars come from?

Run. Work.

Run faster. Work harder.

She reached the recovery ward breathless, more from fear than exertion. Was Casey all right?

"Hey, Dr. McGann." One of the nurses looked up when Katie approached the desk. "Sorry to set off your pager like that. It's just the Wilsons. They wanted to thank you for everything you did for Casey, and no one down in Trauma knew where you were."

"Oh! Good. That's all right." Katie's heart was still thumping away as she registered the nurse's words. "Fine. Good. Um..."

She saw Casey's parents through the glass door of the recovery room their daughter was in. Faces soft with pride and affection. She felt a swell of pride and a stab of loss squeeze all the breath out of her.

She and Josh could have been those parents. That family. Would most likely have been home with their little girl right now instead of haunting the corridors of the hospital, sniping at each other.

She could see it so easily. The three of them gathered round their Christmas tree, decorated with a mix of preschool decorations and generations of hand-me-down ornaments. A fire crackling away and all three of them sitting together in a sea of wrapping paper, gifts and laughter...

"Can you just let them know I stopped by, got their message, but had to dash? Apologies."

"They're just right—" The nurse looked at her strangely as she angled her pencil in the Wilsons' direction.

"Sorry." Katie faked getting another page. "Gotta dash! Give them my best." She threw the words over her shoulder but kept moving. Away from the memories. Away from the pain.

T-minus I don't think I can do this much longer.

Katie rattled through the days and hours on her fingers and clenched them into fists. Didn't matter.

Too many. That was how many more hours she had with Josh.

She swept past the patients' rooms, hoping to find somewhere else to burn off her excess energy before returning to the ER.

"Merry Christmas, Dr. McGann! Can we offer you some eggnog?" A familiar rosy-cheeked woman caught her by the elbow before she flew past another recovery room.

"Mrs. Klausen?" Her eyes widened at the scene playing out before her. "What's going on here?"

A small card table had been set up next to her son Chris's bed, and the other children—Maddie and Nick—were busy hanging up stockings along the curtain rail. Mr. Klausen was poised to start carving an enormous roast turkey.

"Well, we couldn't let Chris be here all alone on the big day, could we?" Mrs. Klausen asked.

Katie scanned the family, each sporting an atrociously jolly Christmas sweater, faces wreathed in smiles. The delicious scent of turkey floated toward her as Mr. Klausen began slicing the large bird. Gone were the recriminations. The threats to wring necks, revenge plans for Eustace's injuries. There were just faces glowing with happiness. An overall sense of contentment that only being together as a family could bring.

"Join us!"

"You shouldn't be all alone on Christmas Day!"

"Eustace sends his love!"

"Can we at least give you a sandwich?"

A sting of guilt at her brisk treatment of her own parents hit her. It deepened as she wove Josh into the equation. She'd all but built a physical wall around herself to distance her from the things—the people—she thought had hurt her most in the wake of Elizabeth's death. But if she came at it from a different angle...?

Her parents and Josh were warriors. Relentless, driven, undeterred warriors. Carrying wave after wave of love with them.

Flawed? Hell, yeah! But who wasn't? She doubted Santa would have a long enough scroll if she were to start cataloging the ways she might have dealt with her grief in better ways. Been a better daughter to parents who clearly weren't the picket-fence type of mom and dad.

A more loving wife.

"Dr. McGann?" Maddie broke into Katie's reverie. "Are you all right?"

"Yes," Katie responded after a moment. "You know... would you mind if I took that turkey sandwich to go?"

* * *

"Truce?"

Katie approached Josh, who was doing his best sit-like-a-Buddha on a gurney he'd wheeled into a quiet corner.

"Truce?"

She tried again, her voice sounding more uncertain the second time.

Josh only just stopped himself from making a snarky comment about not knowing they were at war. But if he stopped and counted just how many scars he'd taken on in the past three years—both figurative and literal—maybe they had been. Heaven knew Katie had been nursing her own wounds, and these past two days had done nothing but reopen them.

He shifted across when she turned and pressed her hands against the gurney to hop up alongside him.

"Want some?" Katie offered when she'd settled.

Josh warily eyed the sandwich she waggled within his eyeline. He wouldn't have blamed Katie if she had laced the thing with strychnine, the way he'd spoken to her last.

"A peace offering." Katie held out a triangle of sandwich on the flat of her palm. "C'mon." She nudged him with her knee. "Go halvesies with me. I'll take a bite first, to prove I didn't load it with mistletoe berry sauce!"

He grinned. *Mind reader.*

He angled his head to take a surreptitious look at her through narrowed eyes. When she'd plunked herself down beside him on the gurney, he'd figured minimal eye contact would be the best way to go, but now that she was here...sandwich in hand... She took a smile-sized chomp of the thick sandwich and made a satisfied *"Mmm..."* noise.

He exhaled slowly. No doubt about it. No matter the time, date, place…no matter how angry he was or wasn't… she still took his breath away. If this were the olden days, there would be a kiss on her cheek, a hand slipped round her shoulder or her waist, a cheeky tickle somewhere or other and laughter. By God. He missed the sound of her laugh.

"Truce."

He put out a hand and received half of the turkey sandwich in his palm.

"It's from Santa."

"Really?"

"Sort of," Katie continued, almost shyly. "Remember the Klausens?"

"The 'I'm going to wring their necks when I get my hands on them' Klausens?" Josh held back from taking his first bite.

"The very ones. They're feasting it up on the recovery ward. Mashed potatoes, sweet potatoes, turkey bigger than an emu, stuffing—the whole kit and caboodle!" Katie took another chomp and grinned before her tongue slipped out to swoop up an escaped bit of cranberry sauce.

If this were the olden days, he would have licked that off, then hung around for a bit more lip-lock. He shifted again. For another reason this time.

Sweet dancing reindeer, who made this girl so sexy?

He thought back to this morning's escapade with her parents and felt the corners of his lips twitch before giving in to a full-blown grin. They might be the most surreal parents he'd ever met—but they were a good-looking couple. A good-looking couple who'd created one spectacularly beautiful daughter. A daughter who clearly didn't keep her parents up to date with everything in her life.

"Any chance you want to talk me through why you haven't told your parents we're not—?"

"Nope," she cut in, as if she were dodging questions about ditching school for the afternoon. "Aren't you going to eat that?" Katie popped the rest of her sandwich into her mouth, her fingers automatically reaching toward his untouched triangle.

He took a huge bite, smiling as he chewed, eyes hooked on hers. This was nice. And in the best possible way nice. He slipped his fingers through hers, eyes glued to the snow falling outside the window they were parked across from, not wanting to break the spell. This was more than he had hoped for. Just a few moments to sit and eat a turkey sandwich on Christmas Day with his wife.

He felt a tiny little squeeze from her fingers to his, and out of the corner of his eye he saw Katie lean her head back against the wall and close her eyes, a soft smile playing across her lips. His thumb shifted along her ring finger. His grin widened. Yup. Still there.

He took another bite. It was a helluva sandwich.

"I'm on my pager if you need me. And you know Maisie's number is just on the—"

"Go!" Jorja insisted, her finger pointed firmly at the exit.

Katie obeyed.

The instant she turned the corner outside the ambulance bay, she felt her step become a little bit lighter. She tilted her head back and let a huge snowflake land and melt on her tongue.

It was the first time she'd stepped outside the hospital for four days, and the crisp air gave her an unexpected shot of energy. She needed a little reflection time in advance of New Year's Eve, and seeing as it had crept up on her all of a sudden, she was stealing an hour or two of alone time.

The truce she and Josh had been observing had given her some much-needed time to regroup. And the steady flow of patients had kept them both busy enough not to have to talk about things. Sometimes you needed that.

She stood still for a moment, not wanting to hear the crunching of her boots on the snow, and listened to the perfect wintry silence Copper Canyon did so well.

Maybe "silence" wasn't the best word to describe it. Perhaps…peaceful winter wonderland soundscape? Her eyes scanned the hillside—the trees and houses still twinkling away with all their holiday lights. The wind wasn't strong, but there was the occasional creak and shiver of the evergreens as they rocked back and forth with the soothing cadence of a cradle.

She resumed her journey toward Main Street. The call of one of Maisie's grilled cheese sandwiches had grown too loud to resist. There was only so much hospital canteen food a girl could take, and she wasn't technically due back on shift for a few hours now.

With everything that had happened over the past few days, Katie found herself looking at the picture-perfect town with fresh eyes. She'd always been a big-city girl. Moving out here two years ago had been less by design and more a matter of the most convenient way to put as much distance as possible between herself and Josh as she could.

Now that he was here, she realized how little of it she had actually *seen*. Her parents' condo. Maisie's. That was about it. It was all she had been able to handle. How her mother—who only came out here once or twice a year—knew about a Korean restaurant that did home delivery was beyond her. Had she lost all curiosity about the world around her? Or just needed things to be as straightforward as possible?

Probably the latter. It was as if grief had physically filled her up and rendered her incapable of living in a big city. Too frenetic. Too much to process when she could barely take on board what was happening in her own life. And now…? Now she was getting better. Able to take on a bit more razzle-dazzle in her day.

Ready for Josh?

She opened her arms wide, as if to ask the small town what it thought. *Was* she ready? *Could* she consider life with her husband again? Or was all of this just life's way of wrapping up their marriage in a gentler style?

Her feet picked up the pace, as if leading her to the answer. Within a few minutes she found herself outside Maisie's big picture window, trying to decide whether to laugh or cry. Sitting in her favorite booth was none other than Josh West. She could only see the back of his head. He looked bent in concentration over something. The menu? She doubted it. He walked into a diner and ordered one thing and one thing only.

Maybe that had changed.

She moved toward the door, then hesitated. Something about seeing Josh sitting there felt big. Momentous, even. Magic Eight Ball spooky.

Maybe just a quick walk round the block would help her. If he was still there when she'd done a lap, she'd go in. If not…?

She'd cross that doorway when she came to it.

Josh couldn't believe he'd actually done it. Put his signature on the divorce papers. He'd wanted to see what it looked like. Having his name there in black and white. Well… Black typeface and blue ink from the pen he'd sweet-talked from the waitress. He wondered if she would have handed the thing over if she'd known what he was going to sign.

Just looking at the Petition for Divorce made him wish he hadn't ordered anything to eat. Hadn't pushed his curiosity so far.

Nausea welled deep within him and he sucked down the rest of his ice water to try and rinse the taste away. His head began to shake back and forth. It looked wrong. Both their names on those papers. It *was* wrong. The best place for these papers was in a shredder or on top of a roaring fire.

The past few days working alongside Katie had been good. Really good. But she had shied away from any heart-to-heart business. Which was fair enough, but he was beginning to feel the strain. Two more days and he needed to call the hospital in Paris with an answer.

"Can I fill you up there, hon?" The waitress reappeared with a jug of water and Josh guiltily stuffed the papers into the inner pocket of his coat. No need to make her complicit in his need to experience everything first-hand.

"Mind if I join you?"

"Katie!" Josh's eyes near enough popped out of his head as his wife appeared behind the comfortably proportioned waitress.

"I see you've found the best grilled cheese in town." She slipped into the booth after making a *may I?* gesture and receiving a mute nod of assent.

"There are other places that serve them?"

"Not with pickles." She smiled, then conceded. "Not really. I can't imagine a Korean grilled cheese sandwich."

"Kimchi and Swiss on rye?"

They laughed, then fell silent. Josh linked his eyes

with his wife's, wishing he could dive into them and find all the answers he needed.

"Are you stalking me?"

Katie screwed up her face in consternation. "No... this just happens to be the only place to get a good sandwich at—" She glanced at her watch. "At seven-thirty at night on the thirtieth of December."

"So you weren't worried I'd left town without signing your papers?" The words came out bitterly. He took another deep swig of ice water, feeling a shot of iceberg zap straight to his temples as he did.

"Oh, Josh." Katie's voice grew heavy with sorrow. "Do we really have to do this?"

He suddenly felt fatigue fill him like cement.

Yeah. We really do.

"What?" He maintained eye contact. She wasn't going to dodge him now. "You mean talk about why you walked out on me two years ago and why the only contact I've had from you is through a lawyer. Hell, yeah, we've got to talk about it, Katie! That's what adults who love each other do."

Her breath caught, as if she were going to contest him, and a moment passed before a sad smile hinged her lips downward. "Not in my family."

"Well, I'm not your parents. I'm your husband. And the second you ran off to marry me in Niagara Falls I became your family. Doesn't that count for anything?"

"Of course it does—*did*—Josh. It's just..." She shook her head at him, her eyes pleading for him to stop pressing.

"Just *what*?" He stopped himself just short of pounding the table with his fist. If he was going to hand over those papers, he had to know why.

"I just thought it would be easier if I went back to

the way things were before I met you." Her shoulders slumped and she looked away.

Josh's body straightened with a lightning bolt of undiluted indignation. "What does *that* mean?"

"It means that before I met you I was used to having no one to rely on. I didn't *need* anyone to get by."

"Is this because your parents weren't around?" he asked, already knowing the answer as dawn began to break in his thick-as-a-coconut husk of a head.

"Weren't. Aren't. Never will be," she droned, her fingers methodically folding a napkin into an ever-diminishing square.

"Why on earth would you have thought that about *me*?"

"Because you weren't there!"

"Of course I was."

"'I'm going up to the slopes with the guys, Katiebird.'" She mimicked him. "'Off to the track for a few rounds of speed cycling.' 'Heading up to Maine for the switch-backs.' 'Want to jump on the back of my motorcy—?'"

"Okay, okay." He held up his hands. "I get it." And did he ever? Especially when she got to the motorcycle part.

"And I guess..." She trailed off, her eyes filling with tears as she began micro-squaring another napkin.

"Hey..." He reached across the booth and stroked her cheek with his fingers. "What did you guess?"

"I guess I was scared that if—"

Her voice faltered and Josh took hold of her hand, rubbing the back of it with his thumb. Seeing her like this was torture.

"What were you scared of?"

"Josh!" She tugged her fingers through her hair in despair. "For a doctor, you really are thick as two planks, sometimes. Didn't you *see* it? I was terrified to get pregnant again because if losing one child had pushed you that far away, what would happen if I lost another? Or lost *you* to one of your crazy escapades? I just couldn't bear the thought of losing you, so I made the decision that I thought was best for both of us."

The words flew out as if they were all attached to the other in a long string.

Josh couldn't even speak. It hadn't occurred to him for a New York second that Katie had let him down. If anything, he'd felt he'd let *her* down. He was the one person who had been able to draw her out of her shell, make her laugh like a hyena, smile so broadly movie stars would have envied her...

"You know what, Katiebird?" He drew his finger along her jawline and kept it there when their eyes met. "If brains were leather I wouldn't have enough to saddle a June bug."

He felt her chin quiver. Tears...or a snigger?

"I have no idea what that means." She lifted her tear-beaded lashes to meet his gaze.

"I'm saying I don't have the sense Mother Nature gave a goose!"

"Cute Southern colloquialisms aren't helping to make what you're trying to say any clearer, Joshua West." But Katie giggled as she spoke.

"So you think I'm cute, do you?" He jostled her knee with his under the table.

"Maybe a little bit," she eventually conceded.

"Oh, really? And just how big is this little bit of cuteness you are affording me?"

"Maybe this much?" She allowed a pinch of air to pass between her fingers before closing them tight.

"That's pretty cute, if you ask me. My mama said I grew up on the far end of the ugly stick. Never said which end was which, though…" He picked up Katie's hand and put her fingers in a slightly wider pose. "Now, I don't want to go tootin' my own horn, but wouldn't you say *this* much is a bit more accurate?"

Katie gave him a sidelong glance, then burst into hysterics. His laughter was soon intermingling with hers, and it was only when their guffaws began to die out that she realized the handful of other patrons in the restaurant had been caught up in their chortle-fest as well.

"What are we doing here, Katiebird?"

"Apart from ordering grilled cheese sandwiches?"

"Yes, Katie," he replied good-naturedly. "Apart from that."

"Tying up loose ends?"

He shook his head at the same moment as she made a face at her own suggestion. It didn't sit right.

"Clearing the air?" he offered.

"Getting our facts straight," she said with a definitive nod, as if the matter were settled.

"Hi, hon—the usual?" The waitress appeared by their table.

"Yes, please, Eileen." Katie smiled up at her.

"You know—we *do* have a Brie and cranberry special on for the holidays."

"No, thank you."

Katie and Josh recoiled and responded as one, much to Eileen's obvious amusement.

"Funny how the only two people I've ever met who like dill pickles in their cheese sandwiches are sitting together." She gave the pair a *go figure* shrug and turned back to the kitchen without waiting for an explanation.

Josh looked over at his wife, saw her cheeks a bit flushed with emotion. It wasn't peculiar at all… They were the only thing she'd known how to cook when they'd met, so they'd eaten them. A lot.

"Have you already eaten?"

He nodded that he had, but didn't move. "Have you ever known me to turn down a chance to steal some of your dinner?"

She grinned and shook her head. He would stick around. Show his wife he was a changed man.

"Well, then. Prepare to defend your pickles!"

"Dr. West—" Michael ran to the door to catch Josh before he went to warm up the pickup. "Are you still good to meet up for that coffee?"

"Absolutely." Josh nodded, yanking up the zip on his snowboarding jacket before he hit the automatic doors. "Is it something we can chat about here at the hospital?"

"Uh, well…" Michael sent an anxious look over his shoulder back to the main reception desk, where Jorja and a couple of the shift nurses were laughing at who knew what. "Maybe not?"

Ding! Girl trouble.

"Got it." Josh put out a hand to fist-bump but Michael just looked confused. He lowered his hand. "I'm out tonight—but maybe sometime tomorrow?"

"Yeah!" Michael's grin widened. "That'd be great. Thanks, Doc." Michael raised his hand, then turned it into a fist, making a sort of weird revolution-style gesture.

"Tomorrow," Josh said with a grin, taking a hit of cold as the double doors parted to let in a blast of icy air.

He'd need a few minutes to get the truck ready in this

weather. Beautiful to look at. A monumental challenge if you weren't where you were supposed to be.

"Are you ready for this?" Katie hauled herself into the truck and slammed the door against the cold wind.

"As I'll ever be."

Katie gave Josh a sidelong glance as he turned down Ol' Bessie's radio.

"It was a whole lot busier today than I thought."

"New Year's Eve!" Josh singsonged. "All the ailments people didn't want to pay heed to on the big day and the day after—and the day after that—building into a mother lode of excess straight up to the point of no return."

"I know," Katie agreed rigorously. "No amount of 'all things in moderation' speeches seem to stop everyone from going overboard on the holidays, and this year was no different!" she finished indignantly. Then she thought a moment.

Except on one front.

It was the first time she'd worked her way through patient after patient, case after case, and come out the other end feeling a sense of being whole again. Complete. She didn't need to visit Neurology to know what was going on. The wounds she'd thought she'd stitched together hadn't been ripped open when her husband had arrived in Copper Canyon. They had never been fixed in the first place—just hidden away and stuffed in a faraway corner that was too hard to reach. Leaving Josh behind was never going to bring Elizabeth back. Or her old life.

Who knew having Josh here would be more healing than she ever could have imagined it to be?

She couldn't help running her hands along the dashboard. "Check out this old jalopy! Still keeping her pristine, I see."

"Yup. I keep waiting for some movie producer to pull me over and offer me a million dollars to put her in a film, but it still hasn't happened."

She gave a barely contained snort. Ol' Bessie was the one thing in Josh's life he took care of, keeping her immaculate. She shook her head. That wasn't fair. He'd always taken care of her. But after Elizabeth…?

Her rigid belief that he'd gone off the deep end had shifted in the past few days. Maybe pushing life to the extreme had been his way of grieving. His way of trying to help her see the light at the end of the tunnel. She swallowed away the sting of tears and ran her finger along the trim of the red leather bench seats.

"Remember what you said to me on our first date?"

"You can sit here, right next to me." His hand patted the bench seat. Josh needed no time to remember.

"We hadn't even shared a soda or anything together."

"A *soda*?" Josh guffawed. "We weren't *twelve*, Katiebird."

She'd felt twelve. All nerves and jittering expectations of the unknown. But when he'd looked at her…

Mmm…things had started pinging inside of her that she'd never known existed. Sparks, tingles, heated shivers—the whole bag of clichéd responses—each and every one of them feeling utterly fresh and new.

So when they'd discovered they both had some time off, and he'd asked her if she wanted a day out in the countryside, she'd pulled together all her courage and said yes.

Josh had been everything she'd admired in a man and in a doctor. He'd been a year into his residency, having just blasted through his junior residency, and she'd been on the first stint of her rotational internship. He'd had confidence, an infectious laugh, a genuine connection with his patients…and a drawl from somewhere down South that had lit her up like a—she smiled—like the big ball in Times Square on New Year's Eve.

Josh barked a laugh into the cab—with a puff of breath that disappeared shortly after.

"What?"

"You barely even acknowledged me when I held open Ol' Bessie's cherry-red passenger door for you. Me being all gallant and gentlemanly, and your big brown eyes were fixed on the dash, the road, the crazy bright scarlet, orange and yellow blur of the leaves we were flashing past as we left Boston. I thought I might've woken up with the chicken pox or something and not noticed."

He glanced over to see Katie smile at the memory and he patted her leg.

"But three days later you didn't stop talking, did you?"

She shook her head no. It was true. And he was the only thing she'd had eyes for.

She looked across at his hands—one loosely resting on top of the steering wheel, the other holding on at three o'clock. He looked relaxed enough, but she could see his thoughts were about as busy as hers were. On her parents? On the rings she still hadn't managed to take off her finger?

She kept her eyes on his hands, wondering how much the past couple of years had truly changed him. She still hadn't worked up the courage to ask him about those scars. What if what he had been through made him someone she could no longer truly access? That was what it had felt like in that awful dark year. Why would he risk his own life again and again when they'd just lost their tiny precious baby?

Josh would argue that no one changed—they just became more of who they had always been, just a bit smarter about things.

She'd changed. She was sure of it.

Her head tipped against the cool of the window. If she was brave enough to ask, Josh would probably say she hadn't changed—she'd just reverted back to the introvert he'd pulled out of her cocoon that magical first year in Boston. Her butterfly year.

"Are you having an entire conversation in your head again?"

Katie couldn't help but give him a congratulatory laugh. "Got it in one!" Then she surprised herself by chasing it up with a wistful sigh. She'd forgotten the comforting side of having someone know her inside and out.

"Something like that. Remember when—" she started, then hesitated. Memory lane could be a rough road to travel. Especially this time of year.

"The apples?" He shot her a quick look, before refocusing on the road.

How did he do *that?*

"Yes…the apples. What was it—three or four bushels we took down to your grandmother's for canning?"

"I think it was more like five. You were on a high-speed race—dodging all of my clumsy attempts to catch you up in a sexy clinch—so I did the only thing I could!"

"Oh, yeah? And what was that?"

"I had to win you over with my apple-picking prowess!" He dropped her a quick wink, his eyes barely leaving the road as he did.

"Ha!" Katie barked out. "Don't be ridiculous. I didn't know you were trying to kiss me."

"Course you did, Katiebird." His voice was soft now. Gentle. "You were just scared of what would happen once I caught you."

She had been terrified. Her whole life she had always been in control. Of everything. It had been easier that way. Easier to understand why her parents had never been around. Easier to zone in on a high-stakes medical career, knowing she could harness her mind and shape her ability to learn into an aptitude to heal. If she let herself fall for Josh, it would be a whole different ball game. Whole different park. She'd known then that she would never be able to control her heart once she gave it to him. And from the increased hammering she was feeling in her chest, it still held true.

She narrowed her eyes and slid them over to the driver's side of the cab to take in Josh's profile. Her tummy did its usual trip to the acrobatics department. Gold medalists had nothing on her!

All of a sudden she hurt inside. Hurt so much she could actually put a name to it. *Regret.* She regretted making Josh decide between adrenaline fixes or her. Regretted packing her bags and hightailing it without even scribbling a note to explain. Leaving him to grieve on his own.

She twisted the rings on her finger. She still hadn't quite managed to put them back in their box. The rings she had accepted with a vow to love Josh until her very last breath.

"I don't think I've ever seen Gramma Jam-Jam look more surprised than when we pulled into the drive." Josh's quiet voice and soft laughter broke into the silence filling the cab.

"What?" Katie exclaimed, tucking a foot under her leg on the bench seat as she turned to face him. "You told me she was expecting us."

"You believed me?"

"Of course I did!" Katie insisted. "People don't just *spontaneously* drive down the Eastern Seaboard to their grandmother's to can and preserve and…"

"Uh-huh?" Josh started nodding, the smile on his face growing. "It's coming to you now, isn't it?"

Little ding-ding-dings of recognition started going off in Katie's head, and her eyes widened as each detail began to slip into a new place. "She set me to peeling and coring all of those apples, saying she needed your signature on something down at the bank in town. It was a Sunday."

"Yes, it was. We couldn't believe you fell for it, what with you being a highfalutin valedictorian and all!"

"*You* were a valedictorian!" Katie protested, fingers digging into the leather seat as Josh took a right turn onto the small lane that brought them up the side of the mountain to her parents' place.

"Doesn't count as much when you're in a class of one hundred in a town that wasn't too much bigger." He reached across and gave her leg a squeeze. "Lucky for me you were too blinded by my good looks to pay any attention."

"Ha! As if!" Katie lied.

"Don't go playing coy with me, Katherine McGann."

He withdrew his hand and Katie immediately slipped her own over the spot on her thigh to keep the warmth in.

"Well…that might've been a little bit true. And when your grandmother assigned someone a task—you did it!"

"That is most definitely the truth! Gramma Jam-Jam was a tough taskmaster!" Josh's laugh ended with a sigh. "I am really sorry to hear she's passed."

"Yeah…well…" Josh drove on for a while before filling the cab with a big laugh. "Lucky for me she had no problem with white lies if the intent behind them was loving."

"What do you mean?"

"Once you were peeling all those bushels of apples, she and I set off like wildcats, scraping the shelves clean of jars, pie tins and whatever else I needed to bribe my grandmother into helping me win your heart."

"She did that, sure enough."

"She did…?" Josh's voice deepened with emotion. "Or I did?"

"Both of you," Katie answered hastily. Then, "You did." It was the more honest answer. "Of course you did."

Her mobile phone jangled, breaking the weighted atmosphere in two.

"It's my mom. Sorry." She winced apologetically as she pressed the button. "Hi, Mom—what's up?"

Josh couldn't make out what Katie's mother was saying, which didn't much matter as everything rattling round his head was making a big enough racket.

Katie still loved him. His wife still loved him.

Was that enough to bring them back together or had time just been too cruel? Maybe knowing she loved him would be salve enough for him to carry on. Go forward. Let each of them get on with lives that could never be the same if they were together.

"You *forgot*?"

Katie's voice had careened up a few octaves.

"Mom, not even five days have passed since you asked us. How could you forget?"

She listened in silence, then gave a brusque "goodbye" before jabbing a finger at her phone to end the call.

"Typical."

"What?"

"My parents are out tonight."

"Better offer?"

"Something like that."

"Are they in town?"

"They're at someone else's condo in the complex. 'Too good an invitation to refuse.'" Katie expertly mimicked her mother's mid-Atlantic accent, then huffed out an exasperated sigh. "I don't know why I let it get to me. Why I didn't *expect* it! You'd think after thirty-one years of being dodged by my own parents I'd be used to it."

"Is that how you see it?"

"That's how it *is*! Whenever I really needed them to just *be* there—nothing else—there was always an excuse. Always something 'too good to miss' for them to go to."

Her words hit home. He wondered if things would have been different between them if he'd let Katie go through a phase of wallowing in dirty pajamas, with a sink full of dishes growing God knew what kind of mold. It had killed him to see her so low, and he'd all but turned into a parody of himself to try and cheer her up.

It was also pretty obvious that Katie had learned some less-than-awesome tricks from her parents. Leaving him on his own when he'd begun to run out of false cheer and had needed her most.

His shoulders sagged. She hadn't known. He'd had just as thick a veneer of protectiveness over his emotions as Katie had over her numbness. Grief had rendered them both loners. She hadn't been avoiding him for the past two years out of malice. It had been out of grief.

"They should've had to apply for a license," Katie grumbled.

"What kind of license?"

"A baby license."

"What do you mean?"

"You have to get a dog license, don't you?"

"Yes…"

"Well, there are countless people out there in the world who actually want children and don't get them—and my parents have a child and don't give a flying pig!"

Josh took his eyes off the road, reaching out to put a hand on Katie's leg.

When he felt the front wheels of the truck start to skid, he instantly regretted not giving the road his full attention. Black ice. He resisted putting his foot on the brake. Drove into the skid. Everything the rulebook said.

"Josh!"

He fought the urge to overcorrect. And still the truck slid. He reached out his arm to brace Katie against the crash. She had on her seat belt but she would always be his responsibility. And in the blink of an eye, that lightning flash loss of control ended in an abrupt thud and a jerk as the truck lodged itself into a roadside snowdrift.

"Are you all right?"

They spoke simultaneously.

"Yes. Are you?"

It happened again.

They both laughed, their breath huffing out into the cold cab of the truck in tiny clouds of confirmation that they had both made it. They were okay.

Before he thought better of it, Josh unbuckled himself and his wife, pulling Katie into his arms, holding her tighter than he ever had. He felt her arms come together round his waist, slipping up along his back and pulling him close. Despite the layers of winter clothes, he could have sworn he felt heat move between the two of them, tightening the bond of connection he had feared was severed.

"That was a bit scary." Katie's muffled voice came from the crook of his neck, where she had nestled.

"It was a bit, wasn't it?" He stroked his hand along her hair, giving in to the desire to weave his fingers through it, enjoying the sensation of silk against skin. "We're all right, Katiebird. We're all right now."

Talk about a loaded statement!

He tugged her in a bit closer, not having a clue *what* they were. Together? Apart? Wrapping things up for good or starting afresh?

Whichever way the wind blew, he would be forever grateful for having her in his arms right now. Feeling her nestle into him a bit more, not pushing him away, hearing their breathing steady a bit. The skid and the jolting snowdrift stop had been a shock. Not a horrible one. But one that needed this sort of quiet recovery time.

He was surprised to discover that his fingers had taken on a will of their own and had shifted beneath the pashmina Katie had tied loosely round her neck. They were slipping up and along her neck, just to the base of her hairline, massaging away any stress or worry. As his awareness of her response to his caresses grew, so did the depth of their breathing. They weren't in their own worlds any longer.

Katie felt Josh spread his fingers wide along her back, fluidly changing the movement into slow circular caresses. Each change of pressure quickened her pulse. The ache of desire overrode her need to intellectualize the moment. She tilted up her chin and after a microscopic hesitation her lips met his.

The explosion of sensation all but overwhelmed her. Heat, scent, taste… Everything was accentuated. Her heartbeat accelerated as the fulfillment from each kiss deepened. Josh's touch felt simultaneously familiar and forbidden. Familiar after the years of shared history. Forbidden because of the deep well of pleasure she felt at his touch. Pleasure she didn't feel she deserved.

As their lips touched and explored, Katie felt as though her body was going through a reawakening. Where she had felt exhausted and dark, she now felt charged and vibrant. Where she had felt deep, weighted sorrow, she now began to feel possibility and renewal. Where she had felt numb...she now felt love.

Her fingers pressed into her husband's shoulders as their breath intermingled in searching kiss after kiss. When it seemed as though time had all but stood still, she felt him pull back. She felt the loss of his embrace instantly and it struck her how time and again over their courtship and marriage Josh had been nothing short of her pillar of strength. Almost shyly, she looked up to meet his blue eyes.

"Look at us, steaming up the windows like a couple of high school kids." Josh's voice was light, but the mood in the truck was laden with meaning. Past, present, future... too much to think about. Too much to consider.

Katie suddenly began to feel claustrophobic in the cab. "We should probably see if we can get the truck out of the drift in case anyone else comes along this road." She pushed open the door, surprised to find it resisting.

"I think we're wedged up against the bank. Come on out my side. We'll have a look."

Josh was reaching across her as he spoke, flicking open the glove compartment, raking around by touch as there had never been a cab light in the old truck. She drew back in the seat, surprised at how Josh's touch suddenly had become something to avoid. Having his warm body all but wrapped around her just moments ago had been like accepting a vital life force, but now that her brain had taken a few moments to play catch-up, she was treating the poor man like he was toxic. It wasn't fair. To either of them.

He tugged a flashlight out of the glove box, clicking the beam off and on as he pulled back into the driver's seat. "Guess that's us in action."

His voice sounded unchanged. Had he not noticed her flinch at his touch, or was he choosing to ignore it—his modus operandi of The Dark Days.

"Can we just get out of here?" Katie knew she sounded impatient, but she didn't have the wherewithal to edit herself. "I feel like a sitting target."

In more ways than one.

"Not a problem." He stepped aside as she clambered out of the truck—a bit less gracefully than she'd intended, but suddenly a deep breath of icy air was paramount. She let the sharpness of the cold hit her lungs hard— hold her static for a moment and then release her with a billow of breath.

"You all right?" Josh's voice was all concern, but his focus was on the front of the truck—the front half of which was soundly encased in the snowdrift, as if it had been put there before the winter had begun.

She mumbled an affirmative, working her hands round herself and giving her arms a rub as she looked around at the quiet lane, surprised at how much she could see without streetlights. It was snowing lightly. And it was peaceful. So incredibly quiet and *peaceful.*

In any other circumstances it would have been romantic. She silently chided herself. Less than a minute ago it had been romantic! Passionate, even. How could five days have changed how she saw the world? As she thought the words, she knew they were ridiculous. Ten minutes could

have an impact. Even less and your life could change forever. For better…or for worse.

She heard Josh crunching through the snow around
the truck. "What's the damage?"

"Doesn't seem to be too much wrong with the truck—
but I doubt we're going to get out of here without a tow
truck. Unless you feel like digging it out of this eight-
foot snowbank?"

"Seriously?" *Okay.* Her voice really couldn't have
gone more high-pitched than it just had. Dogs would
be howling soon.

"Sorry, Katie." Josh shrugged. "This gingerbread
truck has well and truly crumbled."

"I don't know how you do that." Katie shook her head.

"What?"

"Not go mental over Ol' Bessie being near enough
totaled."

"Accidents happen. Life goes on." He shrugged it off.

Cool Hand Josh! One of the many reasons why she
had married him. Her very own cowboy—calm, cool,
and kicking the back tires on his truck.

"Does that make it work faster?"

"Yes," he answered drily, giving the tire another kick
just to prove to her that the total opposite was true.

Katie couldn't stop a burst of giggles from burbling
forth. His eyes met hers—and the familiar deep punch
of connection put her insides through another spin cycle.

*Okay, girl—time to decide if we're playing hot or
cold. Time to stop playing.*

"What are you doing here, Josh?"

"I could ask you just about the same thing, Katiebird."
He leaned against the back of the pickup, one leg crossed
over the other—his body language as stress-free as if
he were talking about a bowling league.

"I *live* here." Her emotional temperature shot up.

"No, you don't." He tilted his chin up in the classic guy move. "You hide out in your parents' chalet—where, I would put money on it, you haven't done a single thing other than unpack your clothes."

Guilty.

She clamped her lips tight. What *was* this? A standing-up psychoanalysis session?

"When anything approaching life comes to your door, you hide out in your work, just like you've always done."

"No, I don't!"

Wow. Good comeback. Someone has playground patter down to a fine art.

She threw in a glare for good measure.

"Look, Katie. I don't want to fight."

"*I* don't want to fight!" she shouted back. Hmm… Maybe she did. And why not? They were stuck out here in the middle of nowhere, with nothing but a truck stuck in a mammoth snowdrift, and…and… Inspiration hit. She scooped up a handful of snow faster than she'd ever done, crunched it into a ball and threw it at him. It landed on his chest with a satisfying thud.

"Feel better?"

"A little."

She sniffed, thought for a moment about using her sleeve, then sniffed again. Usually she was the one who got to play the grown-up. What was up with this role-reversal thing?

Another little marker went up in her Things-That-Are-Different-About-Josh list.

"Should we get a tow truck out here?"

"I'll call. What road are we on again?" She hadn't been paying attention. She'd been too busy making doe eyes at the man she was meant to have hardened her heart to.

"You're going to laugh."

"I doubt it." Being petulant wasn't making much of an impact on her grinning husband.

"Guess."

"No."

"C'mon, Katie. What do you *think* the road's called?" He drew her name out all slow and Southern-style, as if he were skittering the vowels down the back of her sweater with a revitalizing handful of snow. Verbal retaliation for her juvenile attack?

"I don't know. Rudolph Place?"

"Christmas Lane."

"It is *not*!" she retorted, swiping at the air between them.

"Sure is." He looked at his phone screen, where she could see him increasing the size of their location on his map app. "And if my map-reading is still as good as it was in the Scouts...we've got Christmas Farm up ahead, about a mile. Unsurprisingly, they sell Christmas trees."

"You can tell that from a map?"

He turned the screen so she could see it. A little bubble ad had popped up over the satellite image, with "Christmas Tree Farm" on it and their opening hours.

Ah. So he wasn't all-knowing. Just *mostly* all-knowing.

An image of an admissions form pinged into her mind. "That's where the Klausens live! I thought they'd made that up."

"You doubted the rosy-cheeked and extremely jolly Mr. and Mrs. Klausen's good word?" Josh teased.

"Yes." She scrunched up her face. "But you always knew I was a Scrooge."

"I knew nothing of the kind, my little Katiebird."

She didn't say anything in return. Couldn't. He knew more about her than anyone in the world. He'd been the only one she had well and truly let in.

"Look—there's a chapel just a couple of hundred yards down the road. We can hang out there. Safer than here in the pitch-black. Have you called a tow truck?"

Katie shook her head and blew on her fingers. "Let me grab my bag. I've got an automobile emergency services card in there."

"Prepared for everything, aren't you, Katie?"

"What's that supposed to mean?" She wheeled on him, handbag swinging around and banging into her hip as she struck a defensive pose.

It wasn't her fault she had had to behave as a grown-up for most of her childhood, let alone after the death of their daughter, when Josh had rediscovered his inner teenager.

"Nothing," Josh replied, fatigue suddenly evident in his voice. "It didn't mean anything. Should we start walking to the chapel while you call them so we don't get cold?"

Katie rang the company, only just managing to keep the bite out of her voice when she discovered they were short-staffed and the wait would be a while. Everyone had bad days. She and Josh were no different. And compared to what they'd been through in the past, this was a doddle.

They crunched along the side of the road in silence, Josh holding no particular path with the beam of his flashlight. It illuminated an icicle-laden tree here. A slushy puddle there. A thickening of the snow in the air all around them. The silence of the snowy night began to close in on Katie. More accurately, the silence between *them*. Between her and the man she had thanked her lucky stars she'd met all those years ago.

Without warning she suddenly flung herself into a snowdrift and began moving her arms and legs as rapidly as she could. She needed a snow angel—and fast.

Josh had been so wrapped up in his own thoughts he'd walked on a few steps before realizing Katie was no longer by his side. When he turned round, he hooted with unchecked laughter. There was his proper-as-they-come wife, looking like a frenzied wild woman. This was going to be the least peaceful snow angel ever created. Snow Tasmanian devil?

Katie abruptly stopped swinging her arms and legs, her eyes locked on Josh so intently it felt like a make-or-break moment. He opened his mouth, then shut it again.

Katie's hand shot out. "Aren't you going to help me up?"

"Of course."

He reached out his arm and felt himself being yanked into the snowdrift. His boot slipped on a skid of snow Katie had smoothed into angel submission and he fell with a thud onto his bad hip.

Containing the howl of pain was impossible.

"Josh!" Katie pushed herself up, a horrified expression playing across her face. "Are you all right?" She began issuing instructions. "Lie back. Breathe steadily. Follow my finger."

He batted away her hand. "I'm fine." He was still hurting and just needed a minute.

"Josh!" Katie's voice broke as her fingers ran along his cheek. "I'm so sorry. I didn't mean to hurt you."

"You didn't."

Yes, she had. But not in the way she thought.

He could be mean right now. Cruel. Because that was

what it had felt like when she'd left him. Just about the cruelest thing anyone had done. But he'd known Katie hadn't left to hurt him. She'd done it to save herself. Save herself from a man who'd seemed intent on self-destruction. And here was a sign of that self-destruction for her to bear witness to.

Terrific. Everything going according to the Great Win Back Katie Plan? That's one big fat tick.

He smoothed his hand along his hip and gave it a rub, made sure everything was still in place. Ditto for the knee.

"Help me up?"

"Of course." Katie scrambled to her knees, shifting a shoulder under his to help him up from the snow. "What happened there?"

"Just lost my—" He stopped himself. No more lies. "I had an accident."

He felt Katie tense beneath the weight of his arm, but she just mmm-hmm'd him and waited for him to continue as they both pushed upward.

He took his arm off her shoulders when they were standing and gave himself a little wriggle of a once-over. Head, shoulders, knees and toes all in working order. Haphazard as they were.

He tipped his head in the direction of the chapel. "Shall we get in the warm?"

"Do you need a hand?"

He couldn't tell if she was furious or concerned. Probably both.

He shook his head and they walked on in silence. Josh concentrated on working the kinks out of his hip as Katie visibly struggled with the thousands of questions that were no doubt playing through her mind. She'd begged him again and again not to get hurt. Told him that she didn't have the strength for it. And here he was—giving her evidence that her decision to leave because he was too hell-bent on pushing the envelope had been the right one.

"So..." Katie prompted, unable to wait anymore. "This accident. Was it a bad one?"

"Something like that," he admitted, ignoring her exasperated sigh. "I'll tell you everything you want to know. I just need to sit down for a minute, all right?"

The chapel came into view as they turned the corner. It was a pretty little thing. Clapboard, white as the snow, with a green trim, he thought, though it was difficult to tell in the dark. Twists of fairy lights had been spun round the two evergreens flanking the front door to the chapel, and there was enough snow on the steps to tell him no one had been inside for the past few hours. A large and intricate star was shining at the very top of the church. He would have laid money on it being visible near enough everywhere in the valley.

Katie stepped up onto the entryway first and gave a relieved smile when the door opened. "Thank goodness for small-town security systems."

"I don't know if Gramma Jam-Jam even had keys."

"She had neighbors. Same as keys. Were you...?" Katie hesitated.

He shook his head, knowing where the question was heading. "I wasn't with her. One of my biggest regrets."

A huge mistake not worth making again.

"I'm sorry," Katie said with genuine feeling. "I know how much you loved her."

"Yeah, well... I seem to be chalking up valuable lessons left, right and center these days."

They stood face-to-face, there in the quiet of the church, their eyes saying more to each other than they could ever say aloud. Love. Pain. Regret. Josh could have ticked them off one by one and kept going. He hadn't been joking. All he needed to do now was prove he had learned from those mistakes.

"Let's go light a couple of candles."

"What?"

"C'mon. Over here." He tipped his head toward the far corner. "Let's go light candles for Gramma and Elizabeth. We've never done that together."

Katie eyed the end of the church where the candle table stood, her head making the tiniest of shakes back and forth.

He wove his fingers through hers. "C'mon, darlin'. Isn't it time we sent our little girl some light—seeing as we're together? Sent her a blessing at Christmas?"

"I don't *want* to say goodbye!" Katie's words all but echoed through the small church.

Josh pulled her into his arms and held her tight. "It's not goodbye, Katie. I didn't say anything about goodbye." He pressed a soft kiss onto her forehead before holding her back at arm's length so he could look at her. "Think of it as her mother and father saying hello. Letting her know we'll always love her."

Katie began to nod her head. Slowly at first, and then in a pronounced yes. She would never, ever in her heart be able to bid her daughter farewell. But hello? She could say that again and again. And yet without Josh she hadn't been able to say anything to her daughter. It hadn't seemed possible. And now here he was—her big ol' country husband—making the hardest thing in the world one of the simplest and most beautiful.

Hand in hand they approached the small table. Josh lit a candle for his grandmother, and then both of them lit Elizabeth's. As the flame flickered and gained purchase, Katie felt an emotional weight shift from her chest—the light of the flame was offering her a lightness of spirit she wouldn't have believed possible.

The moment lengthened and absorbed them both in its glow. Katie tipped her head onto Josh's shoulder and felt his head lightly meet hers. They'd both lost their little girl. It was right that they were doing this together.

As they watched the candle flicker and flit alongside the one meant for the woman who would have been her great-grandmother, Katie could almost picture Gramma Jam-Jam up there in heaven—wherever *that* was—teaching Elizabeth how to make apple pie. As she swiped away a wash of tears, she was astonished to realize there was a soft smile on her lips.

Was this what it took? Being together with Josh again? Josh, who *still* hadn't told her why he had howled like an injured wolf when he fell into the snow.

"Right!" Katie clapped her hands together a bit too loudly. "Shall we take a pew? Hear all about this big bad accident of yours?"

Josh's heart squeezed tight as he heard her trying to lighten the atmosphere. He was surprised she wasn't a fuming ball of I-Told-You-So.

He wandered a few aisles down and chose a pew, patting the space next to him for Katie.

She sat down next to him, but kept her eyes on the front of the church, where garlands were still strung across the apse. A simply but beautifully decorated Christmas tree twinkled away in the half-light.

"It was a motorcycle accident."

Katie sucked in a sharp breath and tightened her jaw. If the light had been better, he would have seen if those were tears that had sprung to her eyes or if it was just the wintry light.

He reached across to take her hand, and though she

didn't turn to meet his gaze, he was relieved to feel the soft squeeze of her fingers. He had to keep reminding himself…she cared. She loved him. She might not like him very much—especially right now—but she loved him. It was worth fighting for.

The words began to pour out. "It was meant to be a Saturday-morning ride. Just a few guys out for a run— before traffic built up."

"But…?"

"But it got competitive. The roads were tricky. In the mountains up north of Boston."

He saw Katie wince. She knew the ones. They'd used to take breaks up there whenever their hectic hospital schedules would allow. When she'd finally taken those first days of maternity leave.

"We were riding the switchbacks and a logging truck came down the center of both lanes. It was veer or—"

He didn't need to paint the full picture. She was an intelligent woman. Move or get mashed was what it had boiled down to. And he'd moved.

"No one else was hurt, so there was that to be thankful for, and one of the guys was an EMT—he made sure I kept my—"

"Kept your what?" Katie whipped round to face him, tears streaming down her cheeks.

He brushed them away with a thumb. "My left leg. It's good. He knew every trick in the book. I hit some dark moments during recovery, and going through airport security is a bit of a bells and whistles affair these days—but I'm all good, Katie. I'm here."

"How long were you in the hospital?"

Josh sucked in a breath as he did the mental arithmetic. "About seven months. Maybe eight."

"ICU?"

"For a lot of it."

"Internal damage?"

"Some."

Katie's fingers flew to her mouth. *Josh could have died.* He could have died and she would have been none the wiser. She'd left no address, no clue as to where to find her. Strict instructions with Alice never to speak of him again. Nothing. For a moment she thought she was going to be sick.

"What happened when you got out?"

"I roomed with a few guys. Doctors. Long enough to know what an idiot I was to let you walk out the door."

"And your motorcycle?" She registered his words, but needed more facts.

"Hung up my helmet, sold the Jet Ski, my snowboard— you name it. I realized life was a bit more important than what I'd been calling living after you left." He laughed. "You'll love this."

Her eyes widened. What exactly would she love about her husband's traumatic motorcycle accident and harrowing recovery?

"I've taken up yoga."

He watched her take in this new slice of information then reshape her face into something a whole lot happier.

"You're going to *yoga class*?"

All right. It was a tone of pure disbelief. But he'd take that over a telling-off for the motorcycle crash any day of the week.

"Three times a week. Sometimes four!"

"In Boston?"

"No, Katie."

He cleared his throat. Spilling this piece of news was going to be almost as rough as telling her about his accident.

"What?" She poked him in the arm. *"What?"*

She poked him harder when his eyes started taking an unnecessary journey round the small church. It was clapboard. There were pews. And a Christmas tree. *C'mon, already!*

"I can tell when you're holding back information. Where have you been? What happened to our—the house?"

"I rented it out."

"What? Why?" She pulled her hand out of his, clasping her two hands together over her heart.

"Are you kidding me?" Now it was Josh's turn to look astonished. "Live there without you? Sit in those rooms knowing the chances of you walking back through the front door were nil to—?" He sought for a word that meant less than nil and threw his hands up in the air instead. "There was no chance of me staying there once you walked out that door, Katie. Absolutely none."

She suddenly missed her nickname. It had rankled when he'd first used it, but now...why wasn't he? *Wasn't she his Katiebird anymore?*

Her stomach churned and she could feel her hands shake even though she was pressing them tightly together.

Was he finishing things between them?

She blinked and stared, her body and mind not comprehending what exactly it was Josh was saying to her. She felt the backs of his fingers shift away a stray lock of hair, then give her cheek a gentle stroke, and she watched his lips as he continued to speak.

"My life was with you, Katiebird, and then you—you left. What else was I meant to do?"

Katie's eyes shifted back up to Josh's and she just stared at him, hands still clasped as if they were the only things holding her thumping heart inside her chest. *She had left him*. She'd thought of it as saving herself, but in doing so had she destroyed Josh? Her eyes took in his beautiful face, the strong shoulder line, the chest she'd used as a pillow more than once.

The pounding in her heart began to drown out what Josh was saying. She could see him speaking, but the words weren't computing.

Okay. Regroup.

Katie ripped through the index cards in her mind to make sense of things. Reorder what she had believed to be true. Reimagine the last two years.

It hit her—almost physically—that what had enabled her to run away was the knowledge that Josh would always be there. In her mind's eye she had vividly kept Josh on the porch of their sweet little house, with its tiny little porch and tinier backyard, where their daughter would be old enough to ride on a swing about now. How they would have got a swing into the backyard was beyond her, but if anyone in the world would go to any lengths to make his little girl happy, it was Josh.

Leaving had been self-preservation for her—but in saving herself had she destroyed Josh? She swallowed. This was going to be so much harder than she'd imagined.

"If you haven't been in Boston, where have you been?"

CHAPTER NINE

JOSH TOOK KATIE'S hand between both of his and tugged it over into his lap, forcing her to scooch in closer to him. Were they going to do this? They were going to *do* this. There would be a serious amount of beans spilled tonight.

They both felt her pager go off at the same time. Mutual looks of dismay passed between them as Katie pulled back and unearthed her pager from beneath the snow coat, the sweater and finally her tank top.

She took a glance at the small screen, then immediately dialed in to the ER. A few "Yup…yup…" then a rattling of satellite coordinates and a "Got it…" later, she stuffed the phone back into her bag.

"We've got to go." Her expression was pure business now.

"Tow truck should be here any minute."

She shook her head. "No. It will take too long and we have to go by helicopter anyhow. Did you notice an open field near where the truck hit? We're going to have to meet it there in five."

"Helicopter? We?" he repeated, as if he hadn't heard either of the words before.

"We are going on a helicopter to help a woman give birth on a gondola."

"A *gondola*? When did Copper Valley become Venice?"

Katie snapped her fingers before tugging up the zipper on her winter coat. "Earth to Josh! The gondolas that go from the ski resort down to Main Street! Copper Canyon's ingenious way to transport its punters to and from the valley has broken and there is a woman in labor. You've got to help her."

"Me?" Now Josh was fully alert.

"Yes," Katie answered perfunctorily, turning toward the door. "I don't do deliveries. Not since…" She skipped over the explanation. "A tree hit the power lines and took out the power for the gondolas. They're trying to get a generator up there, but that could take hours—"

"Wait a minute," he interrupted. "How are you suggesting I get myself up to this gondola if it's dangling somewhere between Copper Peak and the Valley?"

"You'll get winched down."

"No." Josh shook his head. He wasn't being contrary. He just couldn't do it.

"They're short-staffed at the hospital, Josh. You've done a run in Maternity. You did more winchman training than anyone I can call. Who else do you suggest perform the obstetrics on this?"

"You." There wasn't even a hint of a waver in his voice.

"You're stronger than I am."

"And with the metalwork in my hip and leg, I *don't* get winched into airborne gondolas. I'm not up to the gymnastics. *You* are."

"But—!" Katie didn't even know how to finish her protestation. Every rug she'd believed had been cushioning her feet just a few days ago was being ripped out from under her.

"But what, Katie?"

Josh had her full attention now. Medical emergencies were not something she was wishy-washy about, and something wasn't sitting right.

"I haven't been able to do a delivery since—"

There was no need for her to finish the sentence. They both knew what she was talking about.

"Right." He took her hand in his and headed for the door, already hearing the distant hum of the helicopter on approach. "Today's going to be the day that changes."

Ten minutes later Katie and Josh were watching the ground disappear beneath them as they hustled themselves into flight jumpsuits, secured their helmets and rapidly scanned the small body of the search and rescue helicopter the hospital shared with the emergency services. Bare-bones equipment and no spare staff. It was suck-it-up-and-get-on-with-it o'clock.

Katie had been in the helicopter loads of times over the past year—but tonight everything was blurring. Katie the control freak had…lost control.

"Dr. McGann, we're about four minutes out. How are your headsets working?"

"I can hear you," she confirmed to the young pilot. Jason. His name was Jason. She knew that. She knew *him*. All of this was familiar. Just not the part about going to help a woman give birth in a broken gondola, hanging who knew how many meters in the sky—?

"Dr. West?"

"I'm ready if you are."

Josh's words were meant for the pilot, but Katie could feel his eyes all but lasering through her.

"Jason, what's the word from the crew who are working on the gondola? No chance of getting them down the normal route?"

"'Fraid not, Doc. It's midway between the resort and

the valley—right over the Canyon. So we're looking at maybe…" He paused to calculate. "We're looking at a one-thousand-foot drop."

"Three hundred meters…ish. Not too far." Josh's eyes twinkled, making the number seem less horrifying.

His face told a completely different story from the man who had given up speed thrills for yoga. *This* was the sort of rescue he was made for. During their residency he had all but wrestled his way to the roof every time there'd been a helicopter callout. Adrenaline junkie or not—he was the person she was going to have to put all her trust in today.

Tomorrow? There wasn't time to go there.

She let Josh's steadying voice trickle through her headphones and into her heart as he rattled out statistics and tips. It was obvious what he was doing and she wasn't going to stop him. He was pulling out his "Calm Down Katie" arsenal.

"Want to talk through scenarios?"

"A lot of this is dependent upon that door being open, Doc," Jason piped in.

"Isn't there an emergency release inside?" Katie's heart rate spiked again.

"Yes—but I'm not sure they would've figured it out. From the phone calls, they are sounding pretty stressed."

"How long has the mother been in labor?" Josh's voice cut through to the quick of the matter.

"They reckon she started about three, maybe four hours ago?"

"Dilation?" Katie only just stopped herself from cringing as she waited for the answer.

"Not a clue. We're both going into this dark, Dr. Mc-Gann. Speaking of which—there are night-vision goggles. You both should put them on."

"What about once we lower Dr. McGann down? How will they work in the snow?"

"Not good." Jason didn't mince his words. "There's a couple of head torches. Better bring those down to work in the gondola."

"Hang on!" interjected Katie. "Aren't we going to strap her into the stretcher and bring her straight up?"

"All depends upon what you find, my love."

Josh leaned forward, elbows on knees, bright blue eyes glued to hers, his fingers making a lay-them-on-me gesture. She complied, slipping her hands across his broad palms, but part of her wanted to do nothing more than retreat. Trust a man who had pushed life so far he'd nearly died?

His fingers wrapped round hers, heat shifting from his hands up into her body. And then the lightbulb pinged on with full wattage. She loved Josh. Heart and soul. The last few days had reawakened that knowledge in her beyond any reasonable doubt. But he was the same man who had tested her and tested her when she had been beyond fragile. Did loving him mean putting away her fears from the past and learning to trust again?

"If you look up to your right, you can see the gondola—Wait. I think there are two. That might be the reason for the accident."

Katie and Josh shifted in their seats, craning to see what Jason was describing.

"Is anyone talking to the couple?"

"Someone at the hospital, I think. Want me to patch you in?"

Katie nodded, before remembering she needed to confirm verbally. Josh had shifted across the helicopter floor and started organizing the winch clips.

"What are you doing?"

"Getting you clipped up and ready to go down." Josh dropped her a fortifying wink. "You've got this, my little multitasker. You can listen and clip up at the same time."

And so she did. As her fingers busied themselves with the spring-gated hooks that would secure her rescue kit and the stretcher, she tuned in to the voice of a man describing his wife's labor pains to— Who was that? Jorja? Jorja was on the other end of the line. Good. She was solid.

Katie listened, methodically tugging her straps into place, checking and double-checking the hooks and clips, until she heard the words "I can see something—but I don't think it's the baby's head. Is that all right?"

"It sounds to me as if your baby is in the breech position, Mr. Penton." Jorja confirmed Katie's suspicion.

"We're just about there, Dr. McGann. You ready to go?"

Her eyes met Josh's. Heaven knew what he saw in there. Eight years of shared history? Three years of pain? Whatever it was, it spoke to him deeply. A sheen of emotion misted his eyes for a millisecond, and then just as quickly he was back to business.

"I've got enough fuel to hold here for ten to fifteen. If you think you're going to be any longer, let me know ASAP—so I can get back and refuel."

"Right." Katie put on her medical tunnel vision. Fifteen minutes. Breech birth. In a gondola stuck over a canyon in the dead of winter. Piece of cake.

She looked down at the gondola they were hovering over—high enough not to rock it, low enough to see the door was being jacked open, inch by painstaking inch. She needed to get down there—and fast. If the wind hit and the gondola started to tip—

No. It wasn't worth thinking about.

"Let's do this." Katie nodded to Josh, who set the winch in motion.

Being lowered to the gondola was half-surreal, half-ultra-real. The cold bit at her cheeks, and when she would have expected her heart rate to career into the stratosphere…it slowed. Everything became a detail—as if she were in a film and watching her own life frame by frame. The silhouette of the mountain. The snowflakes. Her breath condensing on the lip of her winter jacket.

She could hear Jorja offering Mr. Penton reassurances while his wife roared at the hit of another contraction in the background.

It streamlined her focus. If ever there had been a time she needed to give herself a pep talk—this was it. This was what she knew. Medicine. She had this one. Never mind the fact she hadn't assisted in a birth in three years. She'd gone to medical school for over a quarter of her life. This was the stuff legendary dinner party stories were made of! The day Katie West delivered a baby in a gondola!

Josh's voice crackled through the headphones to say Katie was nearly there. A sudden urge overtook her to climb right back up that winching cable and crawl into his arms. Seek the comfort she'd so longed for. She didn't want to do this. Couldn't. *He* was going to have to. She'd just stretcher the poor woman up, they'd winch her quickly into the helicopter and Josh could deliver the baby. He'd always been brilliant with obstetrics. He could be brilliant tonight.

Another female bellow of strength and pain and the sound of impending motherhood filled her headphones.

She couldn't go back up. And yet…

She looked down.

Hmm...vast chasm courtesy of Mother Nature, or get into that gondola and conquer three years' worth of fears?

The winch cable continued lowering her, oblivious to the high-stakes tug-of-war occurring between her heart and her mind, bringing her to a smooth halt opposite the gondola door.

All she had to do was unclip herself and...

Katie lodged a booted foot in the small opening Mr. Penton had managed to cleave with his hands. Three years of fears it was.

"Everything all right in here?"

Nothing like starting off with a bit of small talk when you're hanging outside a gondola!

"Not exactly!" howled his wife from the floor, her hand on her husband's ankle. "Mike, honey, we need to get this baby out of me before I rip your leg off!"

The thirty-something husband threw Katie the pained expression she'd seen on many a father-to-be. Times ten.

He was still straining to hold the doors open the handful of inches he'd managed. Katie braced her knee against the opposite door and took hold of the exterior handle. She wasn't there yet.

"Mrs. Penton? My name is Dr. McGann. You can call me Katie if you like. Or anything else that suits. But I need to borrow your husband for a few more seconds. We need the door open wide to get me and my gear in. If you could scooch yourself as far away from the door as possible..."

Adrenaline took over. That and eight years of education and a residency that had made her one of the best.

She locked eyes with Mike. "Fast and strong. Let's get these doors open and your baby out. On three—I'm going to push with my foot and you push the opposite door. Okay?"

She counted. They pushed. And with an awkward swing of her kit and the stretcher, Katie got the equipment in—only to have the doors snap shut behind her with her cable still attached. The roar of blood in her ears threatened to overwhelm her. Spots flickered across her eyes. She had maybe six to ten inches of cable between her and the door. The gondola rocked and Katie felt herself tugged and slammed against the glass-fronted door.

Make that zero. And add a bloody nose to the mix.

"I'm going to guess that wasn't meant to happen." Mike's quiet voice was barely audible above his wife's deep pants.

"It's okay." *No, it's not!*

She flicked on her head torch. *Please, please, please let the winch clip be on this side of the door!*

"Get. It. *Out!*"

"Lisa, babe. It's going to be fine. Just push a little harder," Mike coached.

"No!" Katie wrenched her head around, swiping the blood from her face. "Don't push until we see what's going on—all right?"

"What would be *all right* is to be in a warm hospital bed—like *someone* promised me!"

"Well, how did I know they were going to take so long to make the molten chocolate cake *someone else* insisted upon ordering?"

"Whoa!" Katie interjected. "Time for everybody to take a deep breath."

Including me.

"Everything okay down there?"

Josh's voice gave her a shot of Dutch courage.

"In some ways. Others…not so good."

"But our baby's going to be all right, isn't he?" Mike sent her a pleading look as his wife repositioned herself in between contractions.

"I'm really sorry, Lisa, but this is going to take just a little bit longer than you'd like."

"Katie? What's wrong?" Josh obviously had his mind-reading button on high alert.

"Mike. I'm going to need you to pry the doors open again. They're trapping the cable that has me linked to the helicopter."

"What the—?" She tuned out the expletives coming from the pilot's microphone.

"Katie—you have got to get that door open. The winds are picking up and we can't hold her steady."

"Tell me something I *don't* know," she ground out, taking in the fact that her release hook was inches away—on the other side of the door.

"Get this baby *out of me*!"

Short-circuit and potentially kill everyone on the helicopter and the gondola...or get a grip. Those were the options.

"Katie, my love, you can do this."

Josh's voice, soft and steady, trickled through her headphones.

"I'm right here. I'm not going anywhere."

Her decision was made.

"Mike. Your job is to get these doors open again, and I'm going to unclip myself the second you do." Her eyes hooked his. "It's vital we do this now. When I'm free I'm going to help your wife. If you need to use the stretcher to keep the doors pried apart—do it. If you need to rip one of these chairs out to keep them apart—do it. If I can't get to your wife I cannot help your baby. Do you understand?"

"Katie? Have him tie you to a chair before you do anything," Josh directed.

"Grab that rope. Tie me in and tie for yourself as well— *Ow!*" Her face hit the glass again.

"Katie?"

"Fine. I'm fine. Mike's on the case. Aren't you, Mike?"

"For the love of Pete! *Move*, honey!"

Lisa's voice snapped Mike out of his daze, instantly shifting him into a man of strength and action. Ropes were taken from Katie's kit and turned into lassos round the gondola's chairs.

"We've got maybe ten more minutes of fuel, Katie."

"On it. You should have the cable in less than a minute."

"How long do you think it's going to take to get her stretchered?"

"A few minutes."

"I need to push!"

"Don't push, Lisa. *Whoa!*" A rush of freezing air hit Katie's face as Mike yanked open the door, the movement nearly tugging her out of the gondola but for the rope holding her to a chair. She shot a grateful look up to the helicopter holding her husband.

"Just unclipping now, and then I'm going to have a look."

"You're clear?" The pilot hardly waited for the confirmation to leave her lips before peeling off a few hundred meters.

"Right. Lisa—mind if I take a look?" She received a nod as the poor woman tried to control her pain.

"What's it like, Katie? What are you seeing?"

Josh's voice took away the edge of postcrisis that was beginning to creep in now that life-and-death decisions were off the book.

"We've got about eight more minutes of fuel, Katie."

"Can you see my baby?"

For her anyway.

Now that the focus was rightfully on Lisa, Katie could hear fear taking over the roars of the woman's bravura.

"Let's take a look. I can see his— It is a he, right?"
Katie received a pair of nods from the parents.

Damn. A tiny baby's buttock was just visible at the
birth canal. A breech birth. At the hospital? Not a problem. Whip her into the ER and give her a C-section. In
a freezing-cold gondola, hanging above one of the na-
tion's steepest canyons...

"He's not in the best of positions for a natural birth."
Thank heavens for understatement.

"But everything will be all right, won't it?"

Katie froze. They were the words that had played
through her mind again and again when the doctors had
first told her they were having trouble finding her daughter's heartbeat.

"Will Huckleberry be all right?"
Huckleberry?

"Don't promise them anything, Katie."

Josh's voice appeared in her head. It was hard to tell
if it was real or if she'd summoned up what he might
say if he were there.

"Just tell them you will do everything you can."

That's what the doctors had said to her and Josh.
Huckleberry?

Apprehension was replaced by a need to fight the giggles. Inappropriate! *You're a doctor—act like a doctor!*

"What position is she in, Katie?"

Josh was in her headset for real this time.

"We're going to do our best to turn this little guy
round."

"That's my girl," Josh encouraged softly. "Are you
all right getting the mother into the basket?"

"I need to push!"

Katie began raking through her medical supplies kit.
"Fight it, Lisa. Fight it as hard as you can."

"Katie?" The pilot's voice came through as she was tugging on a pair of gloves. "I'm sorry—we're going to have to refuel. I don't think we're going to have enough time."

"I don't think I can hold off much longer…" came Lisa's strained voice.

"Are you kidding me?" Katie demanded.

"I thought you said you could help." Lisa's voice was little more than a whimper now.

"Sorry. I was talking to the pilot." Katie forced herself to speak calmly. "The helicopter needs to go back to Copper Canyon. It means we'll most likely be delivering your baby here and then getting everyone back to the hospital. Mike, can you grab those heat blankets and lay them out on the floor here? We need to get a clean area for Lisa. Keep everyone warm."

"Back as soon as we can. We'll switch to your cell phone if we lose contact," Josh assured Katie. "I love you, Katiebird. You can do this."

She let Josh's words swirl around her heart as the rest of her body prepared for action. The amount of complications that could stack up against them weren't worth considering. There was only one good outcome here, and the growing fire in Katie's belly told her to start fighting for it.

"I'm going to massage your belly…see if we can shift the baby round."

"Huckleberry," prompted Lisa.

Katie managed a nod. Naming a baby before it came out was dangerous. Naming a baby something that gave your doctor the giggles…? *Awkward!*

"I'm not feeling much of a shift here." She racked her brain to try and remember as many variations as she could.

"I need something for the pain!" Lisa panted. "I had it all planned out. An epidural, some lovely music, soft cozy blankets."

"I've got the music right here, honey. On my phone."

"Why don't you put your playlist on and I'll get you something to see if we can relax the uterus."

Katie's mind went blank as she stared at her medical kit.

"Josh?" She felt like she was speaking to the universe.

"Yeah, babe. I'm here."

Her shoulders dropped an inch in relief. Josh still had her back.

"Talk me through."

"You don't know how to *do* this? I thought you said you were a doctor!"

Mike could not have looked more horrified. Lisa was too busy fighting the onset of another contraction to care.

"You *are* a doctor, and you *can* do this."

Josh's voice came through loud and clear. Katie repeated the words in her head as if she were on automatic pilot.

And Josh continued to speak—a blond-haired, blue-eyed angel in her ear—enabling her to respond, to act, to react. First they worked their way through the basics—blood pressure, heart rate of the baby and the mother, checks for bleeding.

"Do you have an IV of fentanyl in your kit?"

"Yes." Katie reached for the bag, then chose the vial instead. "I think we're going to have to get her on her hands and knees. The massage isn't shifting the baby's position."

"Good thinking."

Josh fell silent while Katie explained to Lisa about

the injection of painkiller. It would decrease the likelihood of having to treat her newborn with naloxone for respiratory depression after delivery—but it would need to be given again if the pain increased.

"Right, Lisa, can we have you on your hands and knees, please?"

Mike helped his wife roll to her side and press herself up.

"Good. Now, can you drop down onto your forearms?"

"Why?"

"It's going to elevate your hips above your heart. That's a great way to encourage your baby to shift position on his own."

"Huckleberry, you mean," Lisa pressed as she dropped to her forearms with a huff.

"Yes." It was all Katie could manage. Naming a baby before it was born was too much for her to take on board right now.

"Have a feel and check the heart rate again," Josh instructed after a few moments had passed.

"I think it's working!" Katie couldn't keep the joy from her voice.

"Great. Katie—I think we're going to land in a second. We'll be out of contact for a minute. But I will call you, and you can put me on speaker if you like."

"No, don't worry," Katie answered as the infant inside Lisa's womb turned into a little acrobat. "I think I've got this one."

She tugged off her helmet and poured her entire store of concentration into Lisa and her child. They were going to *do* this. And when they did she was going to turn her life around. Just because the helicopter needed to refuel it didn't mean Josh was leaving her. He'd made it more than clear over the past few days that he had come here for *her*. To see if what they had once shared was worth salvaging. A year ago she might not have been ready. Wouldn't have been able to see the possibility. Now...? Now she wanted that man back in her life, and she was hard-pressed to keep the smile of realization off her lips.

As the medicine began to take effect and the baby shifted position, Lisa called out that another contraction was on the way.

"Great. Good!" Katie responded confidently. "Mike, do you want to rub your wife's back? Because I think it's time to push."

"Really?"

"Really."

There was a head full of red hair at the entrance to the delivery canal, and in just a few...

"C'mon—you can do it. *Push!*"

And there he was, landing in her hands as if it were any old day. Huckleberry Penton. He was beautiful. Ten fingers, ten toes, a mouth, two ears...as perfect a baby as a family could hope for.

"You've done it, Lisa," Katie said unnecessarily as she cleared away the mucus from the little boy's mouth and nose, making way for a hearty wail. "Turn around real careful now—he's still attached to your umbilical cord."

Katie swiftly gathered together a sterile drape and a heat blanket to swaddle Huckleberry before double-clamping and cutting the umbilical cord between the two clamps. It was cold in the gondola, and the last thing this little one needed was pneumonia.

She dried off his head, resisting the urge to give him a kiss, and handed him to his mother. She kept the swell of emotion she was experiencing at bay by focusing on the postnatal checklist. She gave Lisa a gentle uterine massage, leaving the rest of the umbilical cord in place and checking that the rest of the placenta did not need to be immediately delivered. It would be safer to do that in the hospital.

"Shall we get an IV into you? It'll help replace all those electrolytes you've been losing and make sure you don't dehydrate."

Tears sprang to her eyes when she lifted her gaze to the couple, saw both sets of eyes wide with wonder, delight. They hadn't heard her. The only thing they could see or hear was their newborn baby boy.

Katie was astonished to realize the tears trickling down her cheeks were happy ones. She was genuinely happy for them. Not that she'd wished anyone ill when she and Josh had lost Elizabeth…but it had been tough to see parents with a newborn. More than tough.

It came to her that this was what she'd been waiting for—the desire to try for another baby. Three years ago she wouldn't have dreamed of getting pregnant again. *Ever.* Two years—she'd become numb to the ache to be a mother. But being with these two—being with her husband…could she really have the strength to try again?

The lights in the gondola suddenly flickered into life and almost instantly a hum could be heard, accompanied by a slight jerk as the gondola slipped into action.

"Hold on for the ride!" Katie grinned, but the smile instantly slipped from her face when she saw the expressions on the Pentons' faces.

"Um… Dr. McGann…?" Mike began, making a little dabbing gesture with his hand around his nose area. "I think you might need a little cleanup."

Katie's hands flew to her face. Her nose! With everything that had happened she'd completely forgotten her blood-smeared face.

She grabbed for a packet of antibacterial wipes and gently swabbed at her lips and cheeks, happy to note that there was a big grin on her face it would be near impossible to wipe away.

CHAPTER TEN

"QUIT PACING."

"I'm not pacing," Josh retorted, feeling about ten to Jorja's twenty-five years as he did so.

He'd been ramped up for going back in the chopper to get Katie down from that blasted gondola, but when the generator had unexpectedly kicked into action they'd been told to stand down. Now he was ready to lay everything on the line. See if it was time to hand over the signed divorce papers and try to find a way to move on or—and here was where it got tricky—see if there were some way—*any* way—he could get the real life he wanted back with his wife.

So sitting down, standing still, anything stationary was not an option. Pacing like a caged beast was a bit more like it. He'd just do it in front of the patient board to make it look a bit more...functional.

"The ambulance should be here any minute," Jorja finally allowed.

"And she's in it?"

Jorja looked at him like he was crazy. "Of *course* the woman who just gave birth in a freakin' gondola on New Year's Eve is in it! What are you? Nuts?"

"I meant Dr. McGann."

"Oh," Jorja replied. Then visibly experienced a hit of understanding. *"Oh!"*

Josh narrowed his eyes. "You've spoken to Michael, haven't you?"

"I work with him—of course I've spoken to him." Her eyes flicked back to the files she had been ignoring.

"About Katie—Dr. McGann…" Josh tried to give her his I'm-Not-Messin' look, failing miserably, from the looks of things.

"Sorry, Dr. West. Nothing's secret for long in a small town. But your business is your business. If you want to spend New Year's Eve trying to convince Copper Canyon's most unavailable doctor to go out with Michael so that *he* can get fired for inappropriate behavior and *you* can get his job—be my guest." She folded her arms defensively across her chest. "And good luck tryin'," she added, quite obviously not meaning the last bit.

Ah. Wrong dog, wrong tree.

If he hadn't been so stressed he would have laughed. He'd have to remember to meet up with Michael for that coffee. He owed him for the red-herring behavior. *Hang on a second!*

"Jorja, are you sweet on Michael?"

"I have no idea what you're talking about," she replied primly, giving a stack of patient files a nice clack on the countertop as she did.

"Jorja and Michael, sitting on a—"

"Dr. West!" Jorja put on her most outraged face. "I'll have you know my brothers are all taller than you." She sized him up quickly, to make sure she'd been correct. "And stronger. I will *not* have my name tarnished in such a way."

"Shame…" Josh leaned against the counter, thoroughly enjoying himself now. "I think you two would make a cute couple."

"You do? I mean…" She quickly dropped her happy face and went for nonchalance. "That's interesting. I've never given it much thought."

"Why don't you ask him out for a coffee? The diner makes a mean cup."

The ambulance crew burst through the double doors, pushing a gurney with Lisa on it, holding her baby tightly in her arms, and her husband by her side, sending a mix of anxious and proud looks at anyone who was looking while the EMT crew hurriedly rattled off handover information to Michael, who had appeared alongside them from the ambulance bay.

Jorja gave her cheeks a quick pinch, even though they didn't need any extra pinking, and flew out from behind her desk with a chart to assist.

They all passed him in a whirlwind of activity, leaving the waiting room entirely empty of people save a weary-looking mother with a pile of knitting well under way as she waited for her skateboarding son to get his leg put in a cast after inventing a whole new style of ice-skating.

No Katie.

Josh looked round the waiting room to see if it would give him an answer.

No dice.

Just the clickety-clack of the mother's knitting needles and the low hum of a television ticking off the New Year's Eve celebrations around the world.

He took a few steps closer to see if… Was that…? *Huh*. Paris. He glanced at his watch. That would have been over hours ago. Ah—there was London. He'd clearly hit the replay... Yes, there was the Statue of Liberty...and cut to Times Square...

New York City was moments away from dropping the gong on the New Year. That gave him a paltry three hours. He'd promised himself he'd have this sorted by midnight. He didn't know if he was Prince Charming or Cinderella in this scenario—but whatever happened, he was going to cross everything he had in the hope that Katie was up for a bit of glass-slipper action.

Katie sank onto the bench in the locker room, relieved to have found the place empty. She'd left the EMTs and Michael to sort out the Pentons and had taken a fast-paced power walk round the hospital, sneaking in at the front door in the hopes of just a few more minutes to regroup before she saw anyone—*c'mon, be honest!*—before she saw Josh again.

If the past few days had been an emotional roller coaster, the last few hours had been... She looked up to the ceiling for some inspiration... *Seismic.* Everything she had held to be true over the past two years had been a fiction. A way of coping with the tremendous loss she and Josh had suffered. But ultimately she had been hiding. And not just from her husband. She'd been hiding from life.

Her right hand sought purchase on her ring finger. It surprised her how much relief she felt at finding the rings still there. Side by side. First one promise and then another. Promises she'd blamed Josh for breaking when maybe all along *she* had been the one who had let him down.

He had changed. She could see that now. But she still wasn't entirely sure what sort of future—if any—he was offering her. He'd said he had come here to Copper

Canyon to find her, but to what end? Another chance? Another child?

She opened up her palms and imagined the weight of the newborn she'd just held in them. Tears welled. Could she do it? Maybe she had changed too much. Become too clinical. Or had her time away been more about healing than hiding? Josh's surprise appearance had definitely taught her one thing—there was always room for another way of seeing things.

She glanced at her watch. Three hours and counting. What would this New Year hold in store for her?

She slowly unwound the scarf Josh had twirled round her neck before she'd descended to the gondola, then pushed herself up and opened his locker. His winter coat was hanging on its hook. She folded the scarf and put it in his pocket—but when it was obvious the wool wrap wasn't going to fit, she tugged it out again. A few pieces of paper fell to the floor with the movement.

She knelt to pick them up, eyes widening, stomach churning as she took in the contents of the paperwork.

She shouldn't have looked.

A sour sensation rose from her belly as she absorbed the writing on the letter, the airplane ticket and—her hand flew to her mouth, hoping to stem the cry of despair—the divorce papers.

Signed.

Unsealed.

About to be delivered?

She felt herself going numb. How could she have been such an idiot? Josh was here to give her the signed divorce papers. Why else would he have a job offer and a ticket to France falling out of his pocket? The whole "making peace" thing had just been a ruse to make himself feel better.

Running away again suddenly seemed too exhausting. She pulled her feet up and curled into a tight ball on the bench, no longer interested if anyone saw her. Two years of holding it all together, pretending she was nothing more than a dedicated physician—no personal life, no history, just medicine. And now everything she'd sought to keep under control was unraveling from the inside out.

She lay on the bench, her cheek taking on the imprint of the wooden slats, and for once she just didn't care. Her body was too weighted with the pain of knowing that her life wasn't going to be about suppressing anymore. It was going to be about letting go. She lay perfectly still for she didn't know how long, just thinking. Because once she started to move it would be the start of an entirely new life.

One without the baby she'd had to say goodbye to sooner than anyone should have to. One without the family she'd always dreamed she'd have. A life without Josh. Her sweet, kind, loving husband who had brought out a spark in her she'd never known she'd had.

A surge of energy charged through her, making a lightning-fast transformation into a burning hot poker in her heart. She felt branded. Marked with the painful searing of anger, sorrow and indignation. She'd been such an *idiot* for thinking Josh had changed. It was all she could do not to ball her hands up and try to knock some actual sense into her normally oh-so-logical head. She'd actually believed that he was here to try again— to start anew. To try to make that family they had both ached for. And…for the most tender of moments…she had believed she could do it.

A primal moaning roar left her throat as she pushed herself up and shook her head. Maybe she could shake out everything that she didn't want to carry into the future. Turn into a whirling dervish and spin everything away. A human centrifuge. It would be hard—and by heavens it would hurt—but she could clear her system of Josh West again. And this time for good.

She glanced at her watch, surprised to see how close to midnight it was.

She needed air. Light. Cold. Anything to remind her that she was vital. Alive. Just one tiny thing to show her that she would survive this.

Josh pushed the plug into the extension cord, not even daring to look for a moment. He knew this was a make-or-break moment. He shifted his chin along his shoulder until he could catch a glimpse of his handiwork. It was cold, but with the wind dying down, the stillness added a strange sensation of otherworldliness to the twinkling lights he'd laced into hearts and trees and stars, to the lengths of decorations he'd stolen from the nurses' lounge.

Perfect. Even if he was a caveman in the home-decor department, he'd done a pretty good job of gussying up Valley Hospital's roof. Now to rustle up something poetic to say about—

He whirled around at the sound of the roof door slamming open.

"Can't a girl get a *single* moment alone?" Katie looked little short of appalled to see him standing there. "What *is* all this?" she snapped.

"Oh, just a little decorating…" Josh started—not altogether certain his words were even being received by his wild-eyed wife.

"All I wanted to do was make a snow angel. One tiny little freakin' snow angel to prove that the world *is* nice, and good things *can* happen, and what do I get instead?"

She didn't wait for him to fill in the answer to what was obviously a rhetorical question.

"*You!* The one person I loved the most in the whole world, leaving me again. And just when I thought we were beginning to repair things."

"Wait! What?" Josh strode up to Katie, hands outstretched in a *What gives?* position. "What are you talking about, Katiebird?"

"Oh, don't Katiebird me." She all but spit at him.

Josh had never seen her so riled, and the force of her anger nearly pushed him back. *Nearly.* He ground his feet in and pressed himself up to his full height.

Tough. It was less than an hour to midnight and he was damned if he was going to hit the New Year without finding out if he had a future with his wife. Her face told him everything he'd feared—but he wasn't going to let go of this one without a fight.

He held his ground. "What exactly are you talking about?"

"I'm talking about the divorce papers."

He raised his eyebrows. "You mean the ones you've been sending me by special delivery for the past two years?"

"I mean the signed ones in your locker."

Her stance was defiant but he could see the hurt in her eyes. He wished he'd never put a pen to those damn things. It was the type of thing a trip to the stationery store could never fix. That type of ink was indelible.

His voice softened. This wasn't going remotely the way he'd hoped, but at least it was as painful for her as it had been for him to see his name on those pages. "I thought it was what you wanted."

"I did too," she said after a moment, her booted foot digging a sizable divot in the snow.

"And now?"

"Now it looks like what I think doesn't matter." A guilty frown tugged her lips downward at his raised eyebrows. "I found the job offer and the ticket to Paris. The one-way ticket."

"Oh, you did, did you?" Josh found himself needing to suppress the grin splitting his face in two.

"Yes. Or should I say *oui*?" Katie couldn't meet Josh's eyes but she kept on talking. "Looks like you've gone and done what I haven't been able to do."

"And what's that, then?"

Josh took a step closer.

Katie put her arm between them.

"You've been able to move on. Get past everything we've been through." She lifted her gaze to finally meet his, her tears only just resting on her lids. They'd spill any second now. She tipped her head back to buy herself a few more moments of dignity, if that was what you could call standing on the roof of your place of work and hollering at your husband—ex-husband—for doing exactly what you'd asked him to do.

"When you were busy rifling through my things—"

"I wasn't rifling. I was—" She stopped to search for a less invidious word than "rifling," accidentally biting the inside of her cheek in the process.

"Uh-huh? What *were* you doing?"

The twinkle in Josh's eyes stirred something within her. She knew what it was, but it was embarrassing to admit it considering the turn of events.

Lust. She just wanted to rip his clothes off and have her wicked way with him.

Would that *ever* go away? She stared at him, her body itching to stomp her feet or jump up and down. Anything to stop the skittering of goose bumps working their way across her body. Wow, did she *ever* need to make a snow angel!

She shifted her eyes up to the heavens. How the heck was she going to carry on with her life when she still fancied the pants off her husband?

"Did you happen to see the ticket beneath the ticket?"

"Um…what was that?"

Best not to appear too keen to have gotten the wrong end of the stick.

"Katie McGann." Josh stepped forward and took both her hands in his. His blue eyes were like sunshine, and a halo of twinkly lights lit him up from behind.

Oh, no, no, no, no… This can't be goodbye. Is this really goodbye?

"I came back here to do one thing and one thing only."

She couldn't speak. The other side of her cheek was being chomped on. Hard enough to draw blood.

"I came back here," he said in his soft, beautiful drawl, "with the sole intent of seeing if you would consider becoming Katie West again."

She blinked a snowflake out of her eyelashes. The rest of her body was frozen in place.

"Katie?"

"Yes?" Her insides had started doing a June-bug dance. Her outsides still weren't up to much more than providing a landing zone for the supersized snowflakes.

"I am presuming you heard what I just said."

A little furrow was beginning to form between the one pair of eyes that could light up a room. What made them so *bright*?

"Yes, I did," she managed to croak out.

"And are you planning on drawing out the torture, or are you going to tell me what you think of the idea?"

"What? About Paris? That job offer sounds pretty

amazing. Groundbreaking surgical techniques? Champagne? I bet it's practically free over there. And the architecture! The Eiffel Tower versus Main Street and grilled cheese sandwiches?" She squawked out a mysterious sound that was meant to say *No-Brainer*, wondering why on earth she was trying to talk him out of staying when all she wanted was to tip back her head and scream *Yes! A thousand times yes!*

Josh rocked back on his heels and gave her comments some thought. Katie's stomach began to lurch as her heart plummeted.

Why had she opened her big mouth?

"A chance to work with the world's best prenatal surgeon? It's a once-in-a-lifetime offer," he admitted, before a near-wistful look added a glint to his eyes. "And I *do* love those baguettes. Especially when they're all crunchy on the outside and that gooey cheese they have is just dripping out over the edges."

"You've already *been* there?" Katie's dog-whistle voice sprang into the stratosphere, her game face all but disappearing as she spoke.

"How else do you think I got the offer?" He thumbed away another snowflake. "But then I got to thinking. Do I sign those damn divorce papers you've been sending me, move on—or do I try to win back my girl?"

Katie swiped at a couple of snowflakes that were tickling her nose, too heartbroken to speak. He'd signed the papers and he had a ticket to Paris. Why did he have to be so *nice* about it all? Where was the adrenaline junkie she'd hardened her heart to?

"All of which is a really long-winded way of saying—" he paused to run the backs of his fingers across her cheeks before tucking her hair behind her ears "—there are *two* tickets to Paris in my locker."

Her heart gave a particularly large thump.

"I'm guessing you didn't see the second one."

"That would be a fair guess." Her voice broke with relief. Josh wanted to be with her. He wanted to start again!

The questions began tumbling out in a torrent. Would this really be a new beginning or would they fall into old patterns? Had he really thought through where he wanted to be, what he wanted to do?

She sucked in a breath, closed her eyes and asked the one that scared her the most. "Do you want to try for another baby?"

She felt his breath upon her lips as he spoke. "More than anything in the world."

Their foreheads tipped together and her breath intertwined with his. "Even if it's the scariest thing in the whole wide world?"

"Even if it's the scariest thing in the universe." He pressed a soft kiss onto her lips. "And I promise to be by your side every step of the way."

"Here in Copper Canyon?"

"Wherever you like." He started pressing kisses onto each of her cheeks, her eyelids, the tip of her nose. "We *do* have two tickets to Paris if you'd like to go check it out."

Her eyes flicked open. A penny dropped. "Joshua West—you aren't chicken to go to Paris all on your lonesome, are you?"

"Ha!" A cloud of breath hid milliseconds of acknowledgment. "As if. But it would be much easier to go into the big new world of surgery with my brave and talented wife by my side. If she's interested in giving up her job here at Valley Hospital, that is, for one in Paris…"

"Oh… I don't know. The boss here is pretty hardcore."

Josh grinned broadly. "I hear she has a heart of gold."

He dipped his head to kiss his wife again. It was a kiss filled with the deep satisfaction of a man who had found his way in the world again. Katie returned each and every one of his kisses with all her love. As they sought and answered each other's caresses, they pulled back for a second to grin when the church bell began to toll midnight.

Katie's heart felt full to bursting. Everything was going to get better now—the healing had begun and the New Year couldn't start at a better time or in a better place… right here in her husband's arms.

EPILOGUE

"DID YOU GET to the bakery?"

"Hello to you, too, my little Katiebird." Josh paused to drop a kiss onto his wife's forehead. "And, *excusezmoi*, but I think what you were trying to say was did I get to *la patisserie*."

Katie couldn't help but laugh at her husband's exaggerated French accent. Tennessee meets Paris was an interesting combo. Not that *her* accent was all that hot. Just mastering the medical vocabulary had been enough of a challenge. But they had both impressed not only themselves but their new colleagues as well. Sure, they both might sound like yahoos from America—but nearly a year in Paris had changed everything.

"I thought I'd go for something different, seeing as it's the holiday season."

"And Emmy's birthday," Katie added, as if either of them needed reminding.

Together they turned to beam at their daughter, her face covered in spaghetti sauce after Katie's unsuccessful attempt to get some of her dinner inside the cheeky nine-month-old. With a head of jet-black curls and a pair of bright blue eyes, she was a reflection of the pair of them.

"So?" Katie prodded. "What'd you get?"

Josh pulled out a box from behind his back. A box that wasn't nearly big enough for the kind of birthday cake she'd had in mind.

"What's that?"

"Not what you had in mind for our cherished daughter's birthday?"

She resisted sticking out her lower lip in a pout. *Just.* "Depends… Is this one of those 'good things come in small packages' deals?"

"In a way…" Josh held up the small box and waggled it in front of his wife's eyes. This was fun.

Who was he kidding? There hadn't been a moment in the past year when the smile had been wiped off his face. The world's longest honeymoon, he had billed it. And a move to Paris. His wife back by his side. A daughter to crow over whenever he wasn't learning about mind-blowing surgical techniques with his new mentor.

"Want to open it?" He held up the package when Katie snatched at it.

"You know I do—I need cake!"

"Need or want?" he teased.

"Both."

He handed the box over, watching with bated breath as Katie ripped it open with the glee of a five-year-old.

The myriad of expressions playing across her face as she took in the contents of the box only broadened his grin.

"This is a napkin from Rooney's…" Her big brown eyes met his.

"Best chocolate cake in Copper Canyon," they recited in unison.

"Um…" Katie looked up at him quizzically. "I hate to point out the obvious, but there isn't any cake *in* here, buster."

"What's below the napkin?"

"Oh, my gosh…" Katie's cheeks pinked as she lifted the tickets out of the box. "Are we *really*?"

"I think the first place our baby girl should make a snow angel is in Copper Canyon. Don't you?"

Katie rose up on her tiptoes and gave Josh an appreciatively lingering kiss.

"I couldn't agree more, my love. Christmas in Paris and New Year in Copper Canyon. Doesn't get much better than that, does it?"

"So long as I have the two of you, Katiebird, I have everything I need." He gave her another kiss and dropped a wink in their daughter's direction. "But some of Rooney's finest chocolate fudge for our daughter will be the icing on the cake."

* * * * *

If you missed the first story in the
CHRISTMAS EVE MAGIC *duet check out*

THEIR FIRST FAMILY CHRISTMAS
by Alison Roberts

And if you enjoyed this story, check out these other
great reads from Annie O'Neil

ONE NIGHT, TWIN CONSEQUENCES
LONDON'S MOST ELIGIBLE DOCTOR
ONE NIGHT...WITH HER BOSS
DOCTOR...TO DUCHESS?

All available now!

MILLS & BOON®

MEDICAL ROMANCE™

THE ULTIMATE IN ROMANTIC MEDICAL DRAMA

A sneak peek at next month's titles...

In stores from 1st December 2016:

White Christmas for the Single Mum –
Susanne Hampton *and*
A Royal Baby for Christmas – Scarlet Wilson

Playboy on Her Christmas List – Carol Marinelli *and*
The Army Doc's Baby Bombshell – Sue MacKay

The Doctor's Sleigh Bell Proposal – Susan Carlisle
and **Christmas with the Single Dad** – Louisa Heaton

Just can't wait?
Buy our books online a month before they hit the shops!
www.millsandboon.co.uk

Also available as eBooks.

MILLS & BOON®

EXCLUSIVE EXTRACT

Paramedic Holly Jacobs knows that her night of scorching
passion with Dr Daniel Chandler meant more than just lust.
Playboy doc Daniel has sworn off love – but he can't
resist Holly! By the time they get snowed in on Christmas
Eve Daniel finds himself asking if Holly is for life,
not just for Christmas!

Read on for a sneak preview of
PLAYBOY ON HER CHRISTMAS LIST
by Carol Marinelli

Holly wanted a kiss, Daniel knew, but he was also rather
certain she wanted a whole lot more than that. Not just sex,
but the part of himself he refused to give.

'What?' he said again, and then his face broke into a smile,
as, very unexpectedly, Holly, sweet Holly, showed another side
of her.

'Are you going to make me invite you in?'

'Yes.'

'You're not even going to try and persuade me with a kiss?'
Holly checked.

'You want me or you don't.' Daniel shrugged. 'There's no
question that I want you. But, Holly, do you get that—?'

She knew what was coming and she didn't need the
warning—he had made his position perfectly clear—so she
interrupted him. 'I don't need the speech.'

She just needed this.

Holly had thought his hand was moving to open the door
but instead it came out of the window and to her head and
pulled her face down to his.

He kissed her hard, even though she was the one standing. The stubble of his unshaven jaw was rough on her face and his tongue was straight in.

He pulled her in tight so that her upper abdomen hurt from the pressure of the open window and it was a warning, she knew, of the passion to come.

Even now she could pull back and straighten, say goodnight and walk off, but Holly was through with being cautious.

Her bag dropped to the pavement and he then released her.

Holly stared back at him, breathless, her lipstick smeared across her face, and all it made him want to do was to kiss her again.

But this was a street.

Holly bent and retrieved her bag and then walked off towards her flat. There was a roaring sound in her ears and her heart seemed to be leaping up near her throat.

Daniel closed up the car and was soon following her to the flats.

She turned the key in the main door to the flats and clipped up the concrete steps.

She could hear his heavy footsteps coming up the steps behind her as she turned and Holly almost broke into a run.

Daniel actually did!

He had thought her cute, sweet and gorgeous these past months and had done all he could not to think of her outright as sexy.

Except she was, and seriously so.

Don't miss
PLAYBOY ON HER CHRISTMAS LIST
by Carol Marinelli

Available December 2016